SUMMER UP!

TOM LEIHBACHER

Edited by: Meg Schutte

ISBN 978-1-68517-701-0 (paperback)
ISBN 978-1-68517-703-4 (hardcover)
ISBN 978-1-68517-702-7 (digital)

Christian Faith Publishing
832 Park Avenue
Meadville, PA 16335
www.christianfaithpublishing.com

Printed in the United States of America

In memoriam—Coach Gene Cadman—teacher, coach, friend, and mentor to all.

January 20, 1951–February 9, 2022.

CONTENTS

Preface....................9
Prologue....................11

Chapter 1: Summer Squad....................15
Chapter 2: Work in Progress....................30
Chapter 3: Band on the Run....................40
Chapter 4: Quartermaster....................47
Chapter 5: Golf Bros....................63
Chapter 6: Rescue Dogs....................72
Chapter 7: Dream Team....................79
Chapter 8: Cape Escape....................89
Chapter 9: Good Giants....................98
Chapter 10: Date Night....................104
Chapter 11: Forgive Us Our Trespasses....................109
Chapter 12: Summer Brothers....................121
Chapter 13: Career Closet....................131
Chapter 14: Turf War....................138
Chapter 15: We Hold These Truths....................143
Chapter 16: Ready or Knot....................148
Chapter 17: The Land Is Our Land....................158
Chapter 18: Swim Team....................164
Chapter 19: Summer Love....................172
Chapter 20: Scout's Honor....................177
Chapter 21: Summer of Shove....................186
Chapter 22: Playland....................192
Chapter 23: Troubled Waters....................201
Chapter 24: Truth or Dare....................206
Chapter 25: Snake, Rattle, and Roll....................214

Chapter 26: Then Came You 220
Chapter 27: Swamp Things...227
Chapter 28: The Harder They Fall...235
Chapter 29: Family Fun Day 243
Chapter 30: Rescue Squad 255
Chapter 31: Hometown Heroes 274
Chapter 32: We Do!..283
Chapter 33: So Long, Summer..289
Chapter 34: I'm a Believer...300

Epilogue...307

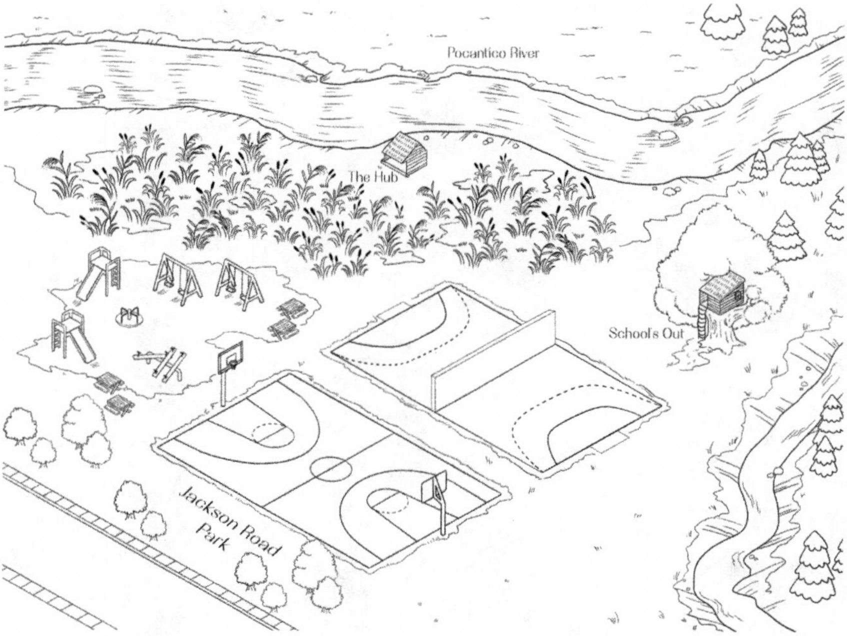
Pocantico River
The Hub
School's Out
Jackson Road Park

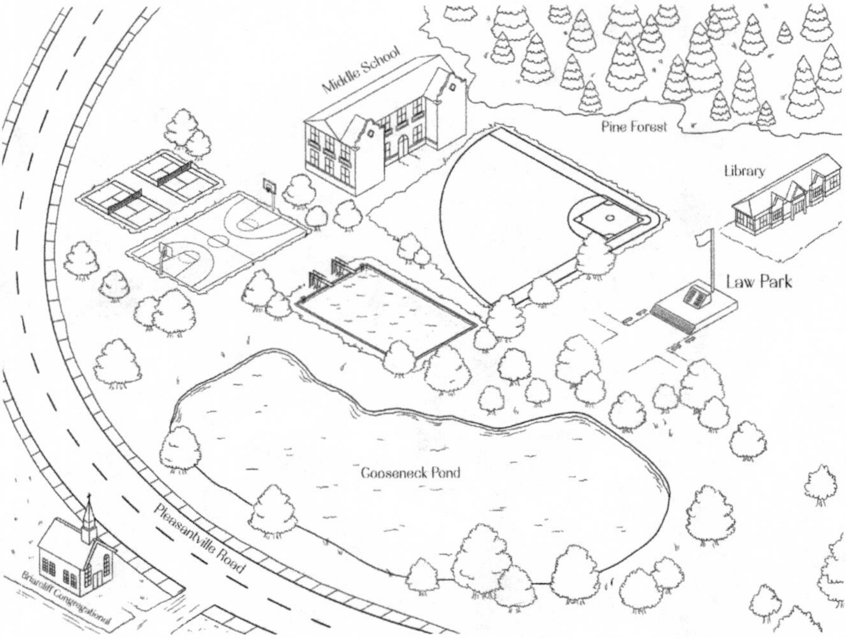
Middle School
Pine Forest
Library
Law Park
Gooseneck Pond
Pleasantville Road
Briarcliff Congregational

PREFACE

Hi there! Thanks very much for purchasing a copy of *Summer Up!*

To those who joined us for *A Gift Most Rare*, I'd like to offer a warm welcome back to the hills and dales of Briarcliff Manor. To those who are first-time visitors, it's nice to be with you.

The primary goal for this book was to write a God-honoring summer tale and period piece set in the early 1970s. Along the way, I tried to capture the unforgettable spirit of school break in the midst of those warm, sunny, fun-filled days.

In this sequel, Charlie Riverton and his group of buddies are back and feeling good about having just graduated from middle school. What awaits them is a wide range of summertime coming-of-age experiences and adventures.

As was the case with *A Gift Most Rare*, most of the characters in this story are fictional. Any resemblances to real-world people are purely coincidental. At the same time, some of the cast, including Coach Cadman, Dr. Cook, and Reverend Higgins are based on actual individuals who made their positive presence felt throughout Briarcliff while they were there.

As the story progresses, you'll also encounter the likes of the great Willie Mays, various members of the New York Giants, and Howard Stern himself (yeah, *that* Howard Stern), all of whom were spending time in and around Briarcliff back then.

There are many people I'd like to thank, starting with my family and friends who encouraged me and provided valuable input as this project evolved.

I also owe a debt of gratitude to my fun and talented friend, Meg Schutte who once again applied her great editing skills to the manuscript for this book.

Major thanks to Stanley Goldstein, a very special friend, for his support and encouragement.

A word of thanks also to Leah Bramson at Yellowbird Communications who is a totally delightful person to work with—and who created my Facebook, Amazon, and Goodreads pages…and to Vance Klein at Crosscheck Designs who created the www.tomleihbacher.com homepage and who adds new meaning to the phrase "rapid responder" whenever there's a need.

One last word of thanks to Darcie Rowan who is a wonderful publicist and a great person to work with.

I hope you enjoy this second installment in the Briarcliff Series—and that it might lead you on a fun trip down the memory lane of your own childhood summers.

The high school sequel is coming soon (working title: *Victory Lap.*) Please look for updates on my website. While there, feel free to leave a message or raise a question if you'd like. I'll do my best to get right back to you.

Thanks—and warm regards to all.

—Tom

PROLOGUE

I tell you, there is joy before the angels of
God over one sinner who repents.

—Luke 15:10

Way back when, nothing stirred excitement and anticipation like the approach of the last day of school.

Summer break came with the promise of two and a half months of fun-filled adventure that would unfold one sun-drenched day after another. There were summer camps, summer trips, summer sports, summer foods, and summer nights to look forward to. Of course, there also was the teenage art of sleeping in.

The promise of new experiences, new discoveries, and new life lessons thrived in the less structured nature of those summer days. Each hour was full to the brim with all kinds of fun pursuits and activities.

Total exhaustion usually set in shortly after dark. But even heading off to bed had its own special appeal as evening soundscapes came alive. The tones and timbres of katydids, brush crickets, and cicadas kept a percussive rhythm beneath the dulcet trills and warbles of meadowlarks, nightingales, and the occasional barn owl. Moreover, the sweet, humid night air passing through always wide-open bedroom windows had its own lulling affect.

On most evenings, kids dozed off with the persistent scent of chlorine from the blue waters of the town pool at Law Park, which was the locus of family and community activity from Memorial Day through Labor Day.

The pool was an Olympic-sized concrete rectangle. The shallow end, perfect for families and young children, was a safe spot to splash around with kickboards and other flotation devices. The deep end held a magnetic appeal to middle school kids and a few upperclassmen. It was home to endless games of Marco Polo, jump or dive, and boys attempting to show off on the diving boards in front of onlooking girls.

Adjacent to the pool on one side was the varsity baseball field which was also used for all-purpose events. On the other side was Gooseneck Pond, which enhanced the bucolic setting. Catty-corner from the shallow end of the pool was the venerable Briarcliff Middle School building. Beyond that was a section of undeveloped land known as the Pine Forest.

Next to the pool and pond complex were four tennis courts, three of which were surfaced with red clay. One court in particular made for a perfect whiffle ball stadium. The fourth had a hard surface and basketball hoops on either end. By midafternoon, the tennis nets came down and it filled up with high schoolers playing round-robin, five-on-five, full-court games.

On days when the weather didn't cooperate, the Briarcliff Public Library on the other side of Law Park offered a welcome change of pace. Although no one wanted to spend time reading on summer break, everyone loved the air-conditioning and the musky scent of books and periodicals. Plus, the Library had all the popular magazines like *Sports Illustrated, MAD, Sport* and *Boys Life*.

In the center of Law Park, surrounded by a thick patch of sturdy rhododendrons, was the war memorial. It bore the names of every person born and raised in Briarcliff who gave their life serving our country in the armed services. A soaring, one-hundred-foot flagpole fortified the sacred spot.

Walking uptown for a roast beef wedge and a Coke at Joe Weldon's Deli was a daily thing. In those days, everyone ambled along barefoot, which always resulted in contests to see who could go the farthest on the hot pavement. Along the way, no one could resist popping any tar bubbles in their path.

Each afternoon around 3:00 p.m., the Good Humor man would arrive, jingling the bells attached to the roof of his refrigerated truck. It took him at least a half hour to serve everyone who came running, opening the freezer door time and again as frosty air blew out. All the kids were fascinated by the change dispenser he wore on his belt.

And so it was on summer days in Briarcliff Manor in the early 1970s…

But not every day was all fun and games for Charlie Riverton and his buddies. They were teenagers now and there were a lot of question marks, new responsibilities, conflicting situations, and tough decisions to be made. After all, a big part of summer break was meant for personal development, especially during the pivotal time between middle school and high school. Sometimes life evolved organically and gradually in a comfortable way. Other times, it came with knotty, unexpected situations that could only be dealt with in the heat of the moment.

During the summer of '75, Charlie, DMarks, George, and BB faced a protracted battle for turf rights in their own backyard. It wasn't easy, and they took their lumps along the way. But with a little help from Skylar Northbridge, Charlie's heavenly friend from two Christmases ago, they stuck together and stood up for themselves. By the end of that memorable summer, their shoulders had grown a little broader and an unforgettable new chapter in their young lives was in the books.

1
CHAPTER

SUMMER SQUAD

Love one another with brotherly affection.

—Romans 12:10

The last day of school had finally arrived. With summer break just a few hours away, students, teachers and staff at the Briarcliff Middle School were fit to burst with excitement and anticipation.

Everyone dressed down for the final half-day of classes. Some wore T-shirts and gym shorts, others wore halter tops and jeans. Some even wore bathing suits underneath their street clothes so that they could go straight to the town pool after the early dismissal. Even the principal showed up in Levi's and penny loafers.

The weather outside was typical for a mid-June day in suburban New York. Golden sunshine and clear blue skies melded with comfortable temperatures in the mid-seventies. Matching conditions prevailed inside the cherished old school building, with cheerful, breezy vibes flowing throughout the student body.

Oversized, heavy-pane classroom windows were opened wide, allowing wholesome summer air to flow freely in. Flowing right back out were waves of happy chatter and joyful noise.

Nicknamed the "Alamo" because of its Spanish-style brick-and-stucco facade, the middle school building was erected in 1909 by Walter Law, the founder of Briarcliff Manor. His son added an entire wing in 1928 to accommodate the growing village. For all its high ceilings and echoing hallways, the rambling structure had a cozy, lived-in ambiance.

To their credit, most of the teachers shifted gears for that day. Rather than trying to fit in one last lesson, they opted to reflect on what had been taught throughout the semester. Some even played fun, competitive quiz games based on the content they had covered. Others took the easy route and just asked the kids to clean out their desks, gum stuck underneath included, and return any unused ditto sheets.

The 1974–1975 school year had been a blast for Charlie Riverton and his buddies. As eighth graders, they'd enjoyed a lot of cool new experiences like independent study, free periods, and playing organized sports against other schools. They were big men on campus, and they made the most of their status.

Still, summer recess was close enough to taste and they were happy to have turned in their textbooks. As the minutes ticked toward the noon dismissal, time itself seemed to slow down to a point where it was almost touchable.

As they took it all in, Charlie, DMarks, George, and BB daydreamed about sleeping late, swimming at the town pool, playing sports, going out at night, and working on their secret tree house and network of pathways throughout the swampy woodlands behind Jackson Road Park.

Everyone kept an eye on the large Seth Thomas clocks which hung above the chalkboards in each classroom. At 11:55 a.m., the school-wide intercom crackled to life and the voice of the principal began to wish everyone a fun, happy and safe summer break. After a few brief remarks, he wrapped things up with a paraphrased quote from Abraham Lincoln: *"Whatever you choose to do this summer, do it well!"*

A moment later, the school bell rang, and students erupted in spontaneous cheer. Rushing headlong from every direction to their lockers, they slapped fives and gave out hugs, smiling ear to ear. In the midst of the mayhem, Charlie and the guys gathered in the hallway outside the main office. Once all together, they jumped down the steps, hooting and hollering, racing through the south doors of the building.

The sun shining down directly over their heads felt like good medicine and the turquoise blue skies confirmed that summer had indeed arrived.

"So long, Briarcliff Middle School. It was nice knowing you," declared Charlie as he walked backward looking at the building and giving a deferential salute.

"No more teachers, no more books," cheered George, ditching his sneakers to walk barefoot.

"Just think, DMarks, you've had your last visit to the principal's office here at the Alamo," chided BB.

"Ha! They're going to miss me."

"Well, you were one of their frequent flyers," tossed in George.

"Yeah, well, as far as I'm concerned, it was real and it was fun, but it wasn't really fun. High school's going to be so much better."

"We just completed middle school five minutes ago and you're already talking about high school? How's about we focus on what we've got here and now. We're on summer break my man," urged Charlie.

They walked along the sidewalk, through the grove of evergreen trees and out around the tennis courts in the adjacent Law Park. All four of them were on cloud nine, on a cloudless day. Wholesome summer air filled their lungs as the warmth of the sun raised goosebumps on their backs and shoulders.

They had made that walk a thousand times, but as they reached the south end of the park, they noticed something very different. A strong scent of stale motor oil, engine grime, and heavy machinery was in the air. Then, a few steps later, they saw why.

As they hugged the turn around the last tennis court, they stopped in their tracks with eyebrows raised. Parked alongside the tennis-basketball court was a huge steam shovel and a heavy-duty paving apparatus.

Keep Out signs were posted all around and the gate to the court was chain-locked. There had been a lot of talk around town about the need to overhaul the aging court. By all indications, work was about to begin.

"Call me crazy, but I'd say we're getting a new basketball court," surmised George. "That's some heavy artillery they've got there."

"Man, I sure hope this project won't take all summer," added Charlie.

"Time out! What genius decided to take this court out of commission at the start of summer break?" objected DMarks, rattling the gate to be sure it was locked.

"They probably had to wait for the temperature to reach a certain point before they could tear things up and resurface the court." Leave it to George to come up with the most logical explanation.

"I don't know what you're getting so worked up about. There's a perfectly good basketball court right in our backyards at Jackson Road Park," Charlie pointed out.

"You know that, and I know that, Charles, but hardly anyone else around town does. And I for one would like to keep it that way."

"I don't get it. Why does this get you so riled up?" asked BB.

DMarks rolled his eyes exhaling with a dramatic touch as he turned to address the group.

"Listen up, you bunch of corn nuts. If the basketball court here in Law Park can't be used this summer, people are going to look for another option. Then, before you know it, they'll be showing up on our turf and messing everything up for us. Catch my drift?"

"So you're against sharing the court at Jackson Road Park? Whaddya you think you own it or something?" teased Charlie.

"Raised by wolves," said BB. "I'm telling ya, the guy was raised by wolves."

"Oh, go eat bees," DMarks teased as he dive-tackled BB, which resulted in all four rolling around, wrestling in the grass.

For the guys, Jackson Road Park was their home away from home since kindergarten. It was a small gem neatly tucked into the west side of the Tree Streets neighborhood. There was a basketball court, a handball court a playground and a lazy brook. It was also bordered by Woyden's Swamp which offered a whole host of Tom Sawyer-esque possibilities.

Although they didn't want to admit it, DMarks had a point. An influx of kids from other parts of town could be tricky. The thought of it loitered in their minds as they continued their walk home.

A few minutes later, they reached the Pleasantville Road crosswalk where Mrs. Messina was on duty as the school crossing guard. To the boys, she was one of the coolest moms in town and they enjoyed seeing her each day.

"See you in September!" she called out, giving them all a fun-loving smile as she flipped her blond, waist-length braid over her shoulder. "Try to stay out of trouble this summer," she kidded.

The guys all chimed in with a happy response as they got back to discussing their plans for that afternoon. After a quick trip home to grab a bite to eat, they'd ride bikes back to the town pool in Law Park for an afternoon of fun in the sun.

One by one, they each peeled off to their own homes as they got to the heart of the Tree Streets.

"See you guys in front of my house in one hour," instructed Charlie.

"And, everyone, be on time. We don't want to waste a single minute of our freedom," ordered DMarks.

No sooner had Charlie arrived home when his mom pulled into their driveway in her VW Bug. It was the last day of school for her as well, and the car was packed with curriculum materials she had used with her first graders over at Todd School.

"Hi, Mom. Beautiful day," said Charlie, rushing to lend a hand. Loaded up with books, rolled-up maps, posters, and an oversized globe, they managed to knee the front door open while backing in with their arms full.

"Well, you sound extra happy. I wonder why? Something special happen at school today?" she teased.

"Yeah, they suspended us for the rest of the summer."

"Son, I'm going to have to have a talk with your father about this."

"I think he'll understand," Charlie responded. "By the way, can I have a grilled cheese for lunch?"

"Sure, buddy. Coming right up. In fact, I'll join you." Charlie smiled to himself. *I'm so blessed with the parents I have.*

"Okay, if me and the guys head to the pool after lunch?" he asked.

"The. Guys. And. I," corrected his mom.

"You coming too?" he teased.

"If you keep speaking like that, they might make you repeat the eighth grade," she warned as she skimmed a slab of butter into a hot frying pan.

A few minutes later, Mrs. Riverton put Charlie's sandwich on a plate and brought it to the kitchen table, along with a glass of milk and a bowl of Jell-O fruit salad from the night before.

"Thanks, Mom. You're the best." Mrs. Riverton just smiled back, reflecting on how quickly her only child was growing up. *How blessed we are to have a son like him.*

The two chatted for a while about the high points of the school year that was. They also talked about the things they looked forward to that summer.

After wolfing down his lunch, Charlie dashed upstairs and changed into his Adidas shorts, which also served as his bathing suit. Grabbing a pool towel from the hall closet, he bounded down the stairs and out the front door.

George and BB were just arriving on their bikes out in front of his house, but DMarks was nowhere to be seen.

"Where is that pudding pop?" fumed BB as the guys began to grow impatient.

"Yeah, he tells us not to be late then ends up being the guy who keeps us waiting," added George.

Charlie was just about to chime in when they spotted their friend in the distance, pedaling up the road. Squinting their eyes as he drew closer, their mouths dropped wide open in disbelief and envy.

"How the heck?" George wondered aloud.

"Am I seeing things?" asked Charlie, rubbing his eyes.

"What gives?" added BB.

There, before their eyes was DMarks, cruising up the street on a brand-new Orange Krate Stingray. Every kid in town wanted a bike like that. Nothing was cooler than those chopper-style handlebars, banana seat, and five-speed gear shift on the cross bar. This one even had shocks on the front wheel.

DMarks circled them a few times with a "yeah, that's right" look, then jammed his brakes and fishtailed to a skidding stop.

"What are you ladies looking at? You've never seen a Schwinn before?"

"How in the heck did you get one of those?" challenged BB.

"Oh, so you like my new set of wheels? It's called a reward for a job well done."

"Tell us," said Charlie, muttering to the others. "This should be good."

"It was pretty simple actually. I told my parents that if I brought home straight As, I wanted a new bike in return for the effort. They agreed. I got the grades, and we all took a little ride over to Jack's Bicycle Shop in Ossining."

"Who goes to their parents and gives them a demand about things like grades?" asked BB, shaking his head. "Don't answer that. You. Only you would try something like that."

"In case you ding-dongs forgot, we're living in what they call the *me* generation. You don't ask, you don't get. Simple as that."

The guys all rolled their eyes, wondering how he got away with stuff like this.

"Go ahead. Keep rolling your eyes. Maybe one of you will get lucky and find some brains back there."

BB reached out to land a dead arm, but DMarks managed to doge it.

"C'mon, guys, the pool's calling our names," urged Charlie with the brush of his hand in DMarks's general direction. Off they went in squadron-like formation.

Just down the road, in an attempt to be extra cool, DMarks popped a wheelie. Unused to his new bike, he lost control and veered off the road, plowing up a row of petunias in Mrs. Lividini's flowerbed. She happened to be sitting on her front porch and saw everything.

"That's going to cost you, Derrick Marks!" she called out good-naturedly.

"Sorry, Mrs. Lividini! Charlie will pop those right back up the next time he cuts your grass," DMarks replied, sweet as pie.

As they rolled along, they cut each other off and found ways to get airborne wherever they could. A few minutes later, they arrived at the pool and cable-locked their bikes to the chain link fence.

"Ahh, nothing like an afternoon swim," crowed DMarks stretching his arms up over his head. "God bless America, it's pool time."

The guys draped their pool towels over their shoulders and walked around to the entrance feeling carefree as could be. Then, just as they got inside the pool area, their backs went rigid. There, standing at ease in front of them, twirling his whistle around his index finger was James Dennis, one of the senior lifeguards.

Recently home from college, he was once again working the summer at the pool. Short, overweight, and always with a five o'clock shadow, he didn't seem to get along with anyone. He also was a stickler for rules and liked to brandish his petty authority over the kids who came to swim.

"Well, well, well," he carped. "The Four Musketeers are back for another summer of fun and games. Tell ya what, fellas, why don't you just turn around and leave right now. It'll save me the trouble of kicking you out later."

Most of the lifeguards were really nice. If you broke a rule like running on the pool deck, wrestling in the pool or jumping sideways off one of the diving boards, they'd kick you out for fifteen minutes. But for James Dennis, the minimum penalty was an hour.

DMarks wasn't in the mood for his early-on taunting. In fact, he was more than a little annoyed. Glaring back with grit teeth, he paused, locked in and came out with a daring response.

"What's up, Dennis?" he asked, raising his voice so that others nearby could hear.

The guys' heads snapped around, shooting concerned looks at their friend. Nobody referred to an authority figure by just their last name.

"Uh, I think you meant Mr. Dennis," Charlie whispered in a minor panic, elbowing him in the ribs. But it was too late. DMarks was going in for the kill.

"Tell ya what, I appreciate your suggestion, but we're kind of busy right now. Mind if we ignore you another time?"

The boys froze in place, eyebrows raised, eyes darting side to side.

"Major burn," gasped BB under his breath.

"We are so dead," squeaked George.

Talking that way to an adult was an audacious thing to do, but DMarks knew James Dennis was just a bully. Tough on the outside, weak on the inside. If someone stood up to him, he'd back down. And that's exactly what happened as the senior lifeguard just stood there gnawing on his whistle with barely controlled anger.

It was only a brief exchange, but in that moment, DMarks set the tone for that whole summer, at the pool and beyond.

"C'mon, guys, let's snag our regular spot near the diving boards," DMarks suggested.

As they walked away, Charlie hip-checked him.

"What did you have for lunch? Are you crazy talking to him like that?"

"Yeah, he looked like he wanted to slap you into last week," added BB.

"That was bananas," said George as they crowded in on their daring friend.

Even DMarks wasn't sure where it came from but acting on his gut instinct felt good. It also felt right standing up for himself. Even so, he shrugged it off with his typical self-confidence.

"That fat washout needs to mind his p's and q's. That'll teach him."

"Dude, you just put a giant bull's-eye on our backs for the rest of the summer," warned Charlie.

"Oh, chill out already. He thinks he's the man, but you can't just let people step all over you."

"I got to hand it to ya. You shut him up pretty good," said BB, jostling his shoulder.

"Yeah, I thought he was going to swallow his whistle." George laughed.

"Hey, it's like when Hank Aaron hit number 715 a couple months ago. When you get in a live situation, you swing for the fences." DMarks mimed hitting one out of the park with his sunscreen bottle.

"Just watch your step, man," added Charlie. "We've got a long summer ahead of us."

They found a spot near the diving boards, flapped their towels open, and spread them on the ground as placeholders.

"Who's up for a game of jump or dive?" asked George.

"Excellent idea, but no late calls," said BB as he, George and Charlie all spun and cast a stern glare at DMarks.

"Oh, give me a break, would ya? You act like we're playing for milk money or something."

They lined up at the diving board as the next guy in line called jump or dive once each player was in midair. The result was a steady display of belly flops, face plants, and awkward free falls with arms flailing. Each time someone smacked the water too hard the others would wince as though it had happened to them. On resurfacing, there was always a string of PG-rated curse words shouted into the bubbles.

A half hour later, they swam to the middle part of the pool for chicken fights. But just as they were getting started, Michelle and several other girls came strolling through the pool entrance. They waived to the guys and kept walking toward the diving boards. The guys were enjoying themselves, but the girls had hooked their attention, especially Michelle in her white bikini.

"Whoever invented bikinis...thank you!" whooped DMarks as he flopped below the water.

"I'm a Speedo kind of guy myself," said George, mock fainting.

"I'm fine with either!" declared BB as he peeled his eyes on their female classmates.

The summer tease had begun. Within minutes, the guys swam back to the deep end near where the girls had laid out their towels. Hoisting themselves out of the water, they whirled their heads around to fling the water off their hair.

"Summer up, girls! Let's make it one to remember," said DMarks. "Here, let me show you how to jam out with your tans out."

The girls all looked on with amused smiles as the guys crossed their arms wondering where their friend was going with this.

"First, it's important to position your towel properly so that you're directly facing the sun, like a sundial. Then, once comfortable, be sure to rotate your position every fifteen minutes to avoid sunburn."

"Since when are you an authority on sun tanning?" Charlie asked.

"Yeah, you usually look kind of medium-rare," chirped BB.

DMarks turned his nose up at his friends. "Funny, I don't recall asking for a cup of your opinion."

George was almost as amused as the girls. "Don't worry, maestro, no charge for those opinions. Please continue."

DMarks turned his attention back to the girls. "Now where was I? Oh, the most important part," he said, grabbing a tube of sunscreen from Andrea's bag. "Always apply plenty of lotion."

The girls looked on as he unscrewed the cap, wondering just how far he was planning to take this.

"Now, when applying lotion, it's critical to make sure it's evenly distributed. Who can I help here?" he asked, squeezing an overly generous amount into the palm of his hand.

Before anyone could respond, a younger kid came running by, plowing into the back of DMarks's elbow. The impact rocketed his arm up toward his face, slamming the handful of lotion right into his eye. Blinded by the lotion, which also stung like crazy, he spat out all kinds of bad words.

"Did he just curse in Italian?" asked BB.

"Sounded like it. I think he picked that up at the barbershop," confirmed Charlie.

"Adds new meaning to the phrase in your face," commented George.

DMarks grabbed his towel and tried to wipe his eye, but it only made things worse.

"Which kid was that? He's in for it! Wait till I get my sight back. I'm gonna—"

"Whoa, Kemosabe," said Charlie. "It was an accident. Besides, I think that was Will Morris's little brother. You lay a hand on him and you'll pay big time."

DMarks was steamed. He didn't know what was worse: the discomfort in his eye or the embarrassment he felt.

Always levelheaded, Charlie stepped in.

"We'll see you later, girls. I think we need to take this guy to the first-aid station."

"The lifeguards will save you," called out Meg.

"You're my hero," added Andrea, giggling.

"Maybe they can give you one of those eye patches like what pirates wear," Laura yelled after them.

"These chicks are lame," grumbled DMarks. "I try to do them a favor and I get sarcasm in return."

"Seriously. I can't believe they didn't appreciate your offer to rub them down with lotion," mocked Charlie.

"Who asked for your two cents?" DMarks complained as he stumbled over someone's beach bag. "Look at me, I'm wounded over here."

"Get a grip, would ya?" pleaded Charlie as he took DMarks's arm and led him into the lifeguard shack. One of the really nice lifeguards named Sue was on duty. She reached for her first aid kit right away.

"Yikes, Derrick, looks like you kind of missed your mark with the sunscreen," she said in jest.

DMarks was not amused.

Sue assessed the situation and asked the guys to bring him over to the sink. "We need to flush his eye with warm water."

"Sure thing, Sue," said Charlie, as they shuffled DMarks over.

"Great, now let's turn him around so he's facing away from the sink," Sue said, putting her hands on his shoulders and turning him 180 degrees. "Okay, now arch your back, and lean your head toward the faucet so I can run the water over your eye."

"Yeah, yeah. Let's get on with this already," DMarks replied impatiently. "I got things to do. Girls to check out."

Sue ran the water over her fingers until it was warm as the guys held him in place. Then, she pulled the faucet over and began to run it directly on his eye.

Everything was fine until George sneezed, causing him to nudge DMarks's face just enough so that his nose ended up under the faucet.

He instantly inhaled a major amount of water, heaving forward and coughing all over the place like a seal. The boys couldn't help themselves as they broke into waist-bending laughter.

After a few minutes of DMarks coughing and gasping, he finally got control. Sue guided him to a metal folding chair and put a hunk of cotton over his eye, wrapping a roll of gauze around his head.

Charlie and the guys thanked Sue and walked their friend out and back over to where they had been sitting. The girls saw them coming and they were ready.

"Wow, did they have to do brain surgery too?" asked Andrea.

"Can I sign your head thing?" asked Meg.

"Hey, give me a hunk of that cotton. I need some so I can remove my nail polish," added Laura as she reached over and tried to snatch a small swath.

"Very funny. I'll have you know that the average man could not handle the amount of discomfort I'm in."

"Oh, for crying out loud. It's just a little lotion. You'll be fine," said George.

"Here, let us position your towel correctly for you. Like a sun-dial," offered Michelle, tugging on the back of his towel.

"And can I rub some lotion on your back? I promise not to get any in your good eye," Andrea chimed in.

"I hope you're all having a good time because I'm not. Now someone get me a Coke before I die of thirst."

The good-natured George figured it was the least he could do as he got up and headed to the soda machine.

Eventually, everyone settled down and began talking about final grades, summer jobs, and family vacation plans. The whole summer was in front of them, and it was the best feeling in the world.

Before they knew it, Michelle's mom arrived in her Country Squire station wagon. She beeped the horn from the parking lot as Michelle gave her the high sign.

It was half past five and almost dinnertime. The boys said a quick goodbye, then picked up their towels, and headed for their bikes.

Charlie invited DMarks over for dinner thinking it might help him to feel better. "My mom's making steak and rice, your favorite. After dinner, we can watch *Good Times* and *Hawaii Five-0*."

"Thank you, Charles. Don't mind if I do. A full stomach will help my eye feel better."

They dialed their combination locks, unchained their bikes, and started home, wet towels draped around their necks. Summer was on.

Over on the far side of Law Park and completely unbeknownst to them, Skylar Northbridge sat casually on a bench. His six-foot-five, muscular frame was toned, tanned and relaxed in a white, untucked button-down shirt, faded Levi's and leather sandals.

He looked on with a broad, warm, smile through his well-groomed beard. *It's so good to see them again in person*, he thought.

For Sky, it had been a memorable Christmas in Briarcliff two years prior. Of his many assignments across the globe, getting to spend time with Charlie and the guys that Advent Season was his favorite. His heart filled with joy, seeing how they'd grown.

He watched as they rode over the hillside feeling a wistful kind of affection. Remaining in the moment, he ran his fingers through his thick, longish, sandy blond hair. Standing up, he took one last good look before the guys were out of sight.

He had intended to spend that summer in Briarcliff but a few unexpected circumstances resulted in a change of plans for him.

"If only I could be here full-time this summer," he whispered to himself, heaving a sigh.

2

CHAPTER

WORK IN PROGRESS

Whatever you do, work heartily as for
the Lord and not for men.

—Colossians 3:23

The gang had reached a point in life where it was expected they'd go out and find summer jobs. It wasn't just to earn a little spending cash; it also was to learn how to handle responsibility.

Charlie had multiple yard jobs all around the Tree Streets, where he did everything from cutting grass and edging gardens to trimming shrubs and pulling weeds. Unlike most others his age, he actually liked yard work, so he didn't mind pushing his lawnmower throughout the neighborhood.

Now in his fourteenth year, he had grown to about five foot nine, which put him on the tall side compared to most of his peers. But he was also beginning to fill out as he grew into his naturally broad shoulders. His thick, straight black hair was always neatly parted on the side, framing his kind blue eyes and angular face.

Bruce "BB" Brown had a paper route delivering the *Citizen Register.* Each day, he'd walk over to the Taconic Parkway overpass where the different sections of the paper were dropped off in bundles bound with burlap twine. It took about an hour to sort the different sections and assemble them all into each individual issue. Once done, he'd place them in his canvas shoulder sack then head out up Pleasantville Road on his route.

BB had also grown nicely into his athletic body. The girls loved how a thick cowlick on the front right side of his scalp set off his shy smile. He had standout abilities when it came to sports and old-school toughness as well. All the varsity coaches had taken note and tabbed him as one of those rare players who could potentially be drafted up as a freshman.

During eighth grade, the super-good-natured George Palmer had added a few inches to his lanky frame. His blond mop top could not be controlled no matter how much Brylcreem he used. Each summer, the sun would bleach it platinum, which made him stand out in a crowd all the more. His T-shirts and shorts hung from his long-limed physique like flags flapping in the wind. Even so, his reach and length were a unique asset whatever sport the guys might be playing.

When it came to kids and pets, George was quite popular as the neighborhood babysitter and dog walker. His daily routine took him from house to house taking care of animals, looking after kids and handling a few select errands as well. His gentle, patient ways kept him in demand and his friendly "wouldn't hurt a fly" smile set people at ease.

Derrick Marks had grown somewhat thickset throughout the schoolyear, especially in his stocky midsection and thighs. His low center of gravity would serve him well on the offensive line of the junior varsity football team that coming September. His coarse chocolate-brown hair had a mind of its own and created a unique contrast with his rosy cheeked babyface.

Of all things, DMarks somehow managed to get a job as a counselor at the summer day camp in Law Park. The camp itself was a tradition in Briarcliff that stretched all the way back to the 1950s. Campers enjoyed arts and crafts, field games, music, and swimming each day. It was run by Henry McBride, the recreation director, an amiable guy who always filled out his staff with local kids.

Back in those days, a little money was a lot of money. Charlie was paid about $1.75 for each lawn he cut. Similarly, George was paid anywhere from $1.25 to $2.50 per hour. BB did even better. In addition to a small stipend, he stockpiled tips on collection day. Camp counselors also received tips at the end of the summer. That meant DMarks would launch a charm offensive whenever parents were around. Henry found it amusing that he could be cranky around the kids all morning, then full-on Eddie Haskell when moms arrived at pickup time.

Even after depositing most of their earnings at People's Westchester Savings Bank, the guys still had plenty left over to spend around town. A package of baseball cards at Pete's Stationery was 25¢ cents and a piece of Bazooka Joe bubblegum only 5¢. A chocolate eclair or a toasted almond from the Good Humor truck was 65¢ cents and a bottle of Coke just 35¢ cents. So they were never at a loss when it came to the summer essentials.

For the most part, Charlie, BB, and George enjoyed their jobs, felt comfortable in them and had things under control. However, DMarks might have gotten more than he bargained for since Henry assigned him to lead 4B, or fourth grade boys, an age group notorious for being the most rambunctious of all. The result was a mismatch made in heaven.

Each day, DMarks would show up at 9:00 a.m., clipboard in hand, and let it be known that he was ready to dish out some old-fashioned discipline if necessary. Never mind that he himself was legendary for bending the rules when he attended summer camp as a kid.

The first thing camp counselors had to do each morning was check in with Henry to pick up their schedule for the day.

"Here's your schedule, Derrick," said Henry. "Arts and Crafts from 9:00 to 10:00 a.m., then field games from 10:00 to 11:00 a.m. After that, it's over to the hillside near Gooseneck Pond for a sing-along. Then lunch, then pool time."

"Wait, what? A sing-along? With who? With what?" complained DMarks.

"Tom Glazer's coming over with some of the high schoolers. They're going to bring their acoustic guitars and play a bunch of crowd-pleasers. You know, 'On Top of Spaghetti' and others like that."

"Oh, he used to come to the Todd School Gymnasium and give concerts when we were kids. In that case, I approve."

Henry paused, squinted and scrunched up the corner of his mouth.

"Hey, Marks. Tell ya what. You've got the whole rest of your life to be a pain in the neck. Why don't you do me a favor and take a day off once in a while?"

"Okay, okay. You can't blame me if the sing-along thing sounded a little too Kumbaya. I got a lot of rowdy kids in my group, and they get restless pretty fast. But this guy's fun. While they're laughing and singing, I can kick back a little."

"Ahh, well, actually, you're going to be up on the stage helping to lead the sing-along. In fact, I have a ukulele for you right here." DMarks looked at the miniature string instrument in Henry's outstretched hand, backing off at the sight of it.

"Say what? I won't do it. You can't make me!"

"Fine, Marks. If you'd rather that I dock your pay, I can easily arrange for that instead."

There were four things that got Derrick Marks's attention: sports, girls, food, and money. Henry had him checkmated. DMarks straightened up, ran his finger around the collar of his T-shirt, and swallowed hard.

"So are we in agreement?" Henry asked, dangling the ukulele in front of him.

"Yeah, sure, fine. But I'm telling you right now, I'm not happy about this."

"And I'm telling you right now, I don't care."

"I don't care," said DMarks under his breath, mimicking Henry with a sarcastic tone before storming off to meet his group.

DMarks liked kids. But he was easily aggravated, and his group quickly figured out how to push his buttons. Sometimes they'd tamper with his lunch when he wasn't looking. Other times they'd steal his whistle or hide his pool towel. At least once each week, they'd poach his camp schedule, which meant he'd have to ask Henry for another, which meant he'd get chewed out right in front of them.

Henry also scheduled a few field trips here and there. On those days, he usually needed extra staff and always asked Charlie to join his team on a per diem basis.

The most popular field trip destination was to Croton Point, which was two towns north of Briarcliff on the eastern banks of the Hudson River. It was a beautiful and fascinating place, jutting out into the vast Tappan Zee section of the waterway. Historically, it had been home to several Native American tribes like the Mohican and Iroquois.

Henry always made sure that Croton Point was the first field trip of the season. That way, he could kick things off in a big way. Everything was set for that Friday.

Campers were extra animated that morning as they boarded the three school buses parked outside the pool area. They knew it was just a short ride before they'd be hiking, swimming, and beachcombing.

The weather was ideal for a day at Croton Point. There was a mix of sun and clouds, which would provide a little shade from time to time. The air temperature was in the low eighties, and the water temperature was in the high sixties.

Planned morning activities included a botanist led tour focusing on native plant life, a dramatic aerial show from a local falconer who came with a few birds of prey and a display of turtles, snakes, and salamanders from the resident zoologist, which allowed kids a hands-on experience with some of the indigenous species from the area. It took the whole morning for the various groups to rotate through the different activities.

For lunch, the park superintendent barbecued hotdogs and hamburgers at the basecamp and also had bags of potato chips and pretzels. Row after row of picnic benches were filled to overflowing with young kids having the time of their lives. As they ate, Henry gathered the leaders to the side to talk about the afternoon hours.

"So listen up. The busses will be here by three o'clock. Until then, the rest of the afternoon is open. Once we break from lunch, gather your group together, and take a vote on what they want to do."

DMarks never had any intention of giving his group a choice on how to spend the afternoon. He had his fill of exploring and hiking and decided they'd stay by the basecamp and play kickball. Naming himself as all-time pitcher and umpire, he wouldn't have to exert himself.

Charlie sat Indian style with his group and asked what they had in mind. It was unanimous that they'd trek over and down to the curved northeast edge of the point known as Mother's Lap, so named for its calm, protected waters. It was the farthest spot from the basecamp and the hardest to get to. But if that's what they wanted, Charlie was not going to disappoint them.

"Okay, everyone, toss your soda cans in the garbage and let's make tracks," he instructed.

Moments later, they hiked off eventually coming to a sharp incline to a rocky beach about forty feet below. They took their time making their way down the bluff, grabbing on to exposed tree roots, dune grass, and whatever else they could to keep themselves from tumbling forward.

Once on level ground, they had to wade out into knee-deep water to get around the tip of the point before arriving at the perfect spot to swim, look for arrowheads, skim stones, and scavenge the shoreline.

The campers were having a great time in and out of the water, so Charlie found a comfortable spot where he could lean back on the barrier rocks while keeping an eye on things. A happy smile opened across his tanned face as he relived his own memories of visiting Croton Point during his younger years.

The sun-warmed rocks relaxed his body as his mind drifted back in time. Under different circumstances, he could easily have dozed off.

He remembered one time when they came across a huge striped bass stranded in a tidal pool of knee-deep water. With seagulls circling, he and the other campers used their bare hands to dig a canal between the tidal pool and the river so that the fish could swim free.

Another time, they were out swimming off the point when the Forbes Yacht cruised by. They waived and splashed which got Malcom Forbes to blow the foghorn a few times. They had been impressed with the size of the yacht, but they were even more excited by the bellowing sound of the foghorn.

Charlie was having a great time reliving some of his fond memories. Then, in a split instant, came the alarming sound of a camper screaming out in pain.

Springing to his feet, Charlie didn't even know exactly where to run. He just sprinted in the direction of the screaming. Sand kicked up behind him as his feet dug in and powered through with each stride. His heart was pounding and his mind was racing. *What could this be?* he wondered.

As he got closer, he saw one of the boys sitting at the water's edge, holding his foot in the air. Skidding to a halt, Charlie's eyes doubled in size. Blood was everywhere, on the rocks, on the sand, in the water, and on the boy's hands. A few feet away was the remnant of a rusty, jagged, partially submerged soda can. It had sliced a three-inch gash on the bottom of the boy's foot.

The look of fear on the young boy's face pierced Charlie's heart. The other campers gathered around, startled by all the blood.

Time was of the essence. Charlie knew a gash like that was a very serious thing. He had to pull himself together and act fast. Kneeling down, his hand grazed his chest. Through his shirt, he felt the cross with a crown of thorns pendant that Skylar had given him two Christmases ago.

Then, out of nowhere, he received an oddly familiar, warm kind of feeling along with a firm message from a curiously familiar voice.

"Charlie, take off your T-shirt and wrap that foot as tightly as possible."

Without hesitation, he sprang into action like an army medic, using his shirt as a tourniquet.

"Now, put him on your back and get him to basecamp right away!"

Charlie looked at the other campers all of whom were staring on with zombie-like expressions. None of them seemed to hear the voice.

"C'mon, everyone. Follow me!"

Lifting the boy up, Charlie took off with him piggyback style. The rest of the kids followed right behind. They took flight down the beach and around the northern tip of the point splashing water up to their faces as they ran.

All kinds of thoughts darted around Charlie's mind. *How much blood had he lost? Would he go into shock? What about tetanus?*

Charlie's hamstrings and calf muscles burned as he stormed the hillside, leaning forward, pumping his legs as hard as he could, sand shifting under his feet. Up and over the bluff they all went, straight into a headlong, heart-pounding sprint.

"C'mon, guys. Last one to basecamp's a rotten egg!" Charlie yelled.

DMarks noticed what looked like a small stampede in the distance. As it got closer, he was a bit perturbed seeing Charlie really putting out for his group while he just stood around rolling a kickball toward home plate. *It figures,* he thought.

Then, he began to realize that something wasn't quite right. Focusing his eyes, it looked like the boy Charlie was carrying was weak and pale.

Henry also noticed the group speeding along and assumed they were racing Charlie. Then, he looked closer and saw the T-shirt wrapped around the boy's foot, dripping crimson-colored drops of blood. Without hesitation, he rummaged through his duffle bag for the first-aid kit.

With a heaving chest, Charlie carefully unloaded the boy on a picnic bench. The other kids all fell to the ground exhausted, gasping for air. Charlie might have joined them except for the adrenaline rush pulsing through his veins.

Out came the mercurochrome, iodine, and gauze bandages as Henry cut Charlie's T-shirt off the boy's foot. The gash was deep and still leaking blood. Henry did his best to dress the wound, then wrapped it with heavy gauze.

"Charlie, stay here and apply pressure to the wound. I'm going to call for an ambulance."

"Can do, Henry."

As Charlie held the boy's foot in an elevated position, he spoke words of encouragement and reassurance to the frightened boy.

"It's okay, buddy. Henry has everything under control. You won't play kickball for a couple weeks, but you're going to be fine, okay? I promise."

Henry returned in a few minutes and kept an eye out for the ambulance. As the sun marinated Charlie's bare shoulders with comforting warmth, he didn't seem to mind that his favorite Bobby Murcer T-shirt was now laying in shreds by his feet.

Looking up at Charlie, the young boy noticed the gold pendant sparkling in the midafternoon sun.

"Where did you get that, Charlie?" he asked.

Charlie paused thoughtfully. "It was a gift from a friend. A very wonderful friend," he replied, patting it against his chest with the palm of his hand.

The young boy paused, staring directly into Charlie's eyes. "You're a wonderful friend, Charlie."

Smiling back with an inside warmth stronger even than the sun rays on his back, Charlie offered more words of comfort.

"You just sit tight, buddy. The paramedics are on their way, and they'll take good care of you."

The youngster looked familiar to Charlie. Then it dawned on him that it was Will Morris's younger brother.

"Your older brother would be proud of how tough you are."

"You know Will?" the boy asked.

"Sure, I know him. The whole town knows him. All league in football, basketball, and baseball."

"He's the best athlete in town. I want to be just like him when I grow up."

"So do all the rest of us."

Henry returned again after making a few emergency phone calls.

"Don't worry, buddy. An ambulance is on the way. I also spoke with your mom. She's going to meet you at the hospital."

A moment later, they could hear sirens approaching in the distance. When the ambulance arrived, Henry greeted the paramedics and gave them a brief rundown of everything that had happened.

The boy stayed surprisingly calm and composed as he was placed on a stretcher, then loaded into the back of the ambulance. Charlie remained by his side until the doors shut.

As the ambulance sped off with its alarm blaring and cherry top lights spinning, Henry looked at Charlie and realized he needed a shirt. Reaching back into his duffle bag, he grabbed something he thought might be Charlie's size.

"Nice work, man. See if this fits," he said, tossing him a brand-new Rec Department shirt with the word Staff written in large block letters across the back.

DMarks looked on. He was impressed with Charlie as always, but eight shades of green with envy. Every kid in town wanted one of those shirts, but mostly, they were only given to lifeguards.

"Wow, thanks, Henry," Charlie said, slipping it on. The shirt gave him a special kind of official feeling.

"You earned it, Charlie. If you ever want to give up your yard jobs, there's a full-time position for you on my team any day."

"I'll keep that in mind, Henry. Thanks."

After all the commotion, the time had come to gather up the rest of the campers so they could board the buses back to Briarcliff. No one really wanted to leave Croton Point. But after everything that had just happened, no one complained about it either.

Each bus filled up with kids cramming into seats as the wheels began to turn. On the short ride home, Charlie looked out the window and thought about the voice he heard and the instruction it gave him during the emergency on the beach.

That was so strange, he thought as he played the whole thing over in his mind. The voice and the incredibly warm, comforting feeling were strangely familiar. Then, as the bus rolled along, it struck him like a bolt of lightning. He sat straight up, eyebrows raised, hands gripping the top of the seat in front of him. *Was it you, Sky?* he wondered with whole-hearted enthusiasm.

The mere thought that Sky might somehow be back filled him with elated hope and expectation.

Why not? he reasoned. *God sent him for a purpose two Christmases ago, God can send him again.*

3
CHAPTER
BAND ON THE RUN

An Athlete is not crowned unless he
competes according to the rules.

—2 Timothy 2:5

The guys were usually done with their summer jobs by midafternoon. On most days, they'd meet at the town pool, arriving to the sounds of bodies splashing in the water, voices calling out, the lumbering clatter of diving boards and the occasional lifeguard whistle.

In addition to swimming, the guys would make time for a variety of other sports like home run derby, basketball, two-hand-touch football, running bases, and Wiffle ball.

It was all so simple. With just a basketball, a football, a baseball bat, a tennis ball, and a Wiffle ball and bat, they were set for hours. They didn't need bases; they used the handle of a baseball bat to etch them in the dirt. They didn't need boundary lines; they took off their shirts and used them to outline the playing field. They didn't need an even number of players; guys just subbed back and forth as designated runners or fielders.

One afternoon, in late June they were at the pool when the most dreaded of all summer sounds interrupted their fun. The droning hum of the PA system could be heard as it clicked on and warmed up, then the grating scrape of a fingernail dragging across the microphone. Sure enough, it was Doc Prewit, the pool superintendent announcing a half-hour adult swim.

For the kids, it was a minor form of torture to pull themselves out of the water so that mostly moms could have the pool all to themselves in their flowered bathing caps. Charlie and the guys decided to towel off and head outside for a game of touch football. There was a gang of sixth graders who also were looking for something to do, so Charlie invited them to join.

Once out on the field, Charlie and DMarks did odds-evens, tossing out one or two fingers to choose up sides. The game began, and everyone was playing hard. Charlie made sure the younger kids got plenty of passes so they could feel good about themselves.

Then, just as the game was taking shape, Will Morris and a bunch of his high school buddies emerged from the pine forest. They were big, they were tough, and as upperclassmen, they acted like they owned the whole town.

Instead of walking around the field, they marched straight through the middle of the game. It was an arrogant thing to do, but as far as they were concerned, it all tied back to the time-honored, age-related pecking order. They had to deal with it when they were younger, and now it was their pleasure to dish it out themselves.

Whatever the case, it didn't sit well with DMarks, who, in the heat of the moment did something that would become legend. Already in an irascible mood because of the high heat and humidity that day, he wasn't going to just stand by and let Will Morris and his minions get away with such a brazen show of disrespect.

Charlie, BB, and George all gulped hard as they saw their friend's eyes fire up.

"Hey! What do you muscle heads think you're doing? Can't you see we're playing a game of two-hand-touch here?"

Oh no, Charlie thought. Just what he was afraid of. Will Morris, who had been walking with his typical swagger, stopped in his tracks and turned, in a deliberate way to see who might have spoken to them like that. Locking in on DMarks, he flashed his locally famous death glare.

"This is the varsity baseball field, punk. And in case you didn't know it, we're the varsity. Keep running your mouth, and we'll throw you the heck off."

Will Morris stood about six-foot-four and weighed 220 muscular pounds. He was blessed with standout athletic ability and lettered in three sports. His sharp, good-looking features made him popular with the girls, especially since he recently began parting his longish black hair down the middle, as was the cool style of the day.

Narcissistic and self-absorbed, his summer wardrobe consisted of mesh shorts, cut-off T-shirts, a puka shell necklace ala Keith Partridge, and an American flag bandana tied around his forehead.

Despite his self-admiring ways, he also had an abnormal tendency to sweat profusely. That was particularly the case when he got riled up. The regrettable syndrome earned him the nickname of Wet Willy, which he absolutely loathed. No one ever dared used it in his presence for fear of physical retaliation.

"Hey, Shakespeare. 'Throw you the heck off' is bad grammar. Maybe you should repeat eleventh grade," yelled a defiant DMarks.

"Shut it, Marks," Charlie urged under his breath. "We don't need any trouble."

"Would you stay out of this and let me handle it?" DMarks replied, hiking up his shorts.

"Cool it, dude," begged BB. "This guy has a nasty reputation. Let's not tangle with him."

"Yeah, man. Let it go," added George, sliding his hand across his throat signaling to shut up.

"Can it, you bunch of thumbsuckers. If we let them get away with this now, they'll just keep it up all summer long."

"What did you just say?" growled the angry upperclassman. He scowled at DMarks. Beads of sweat breaking out across his cheekbones and upper lip.

Will's friends urged him to just let it go. They were more interested in their food from Joe Weldon's Deli. After thinking about it, Will spat in DMarks's direction and turned to walk away.

But DMarks was loaded for bear and bent on making a statement. He took a few steps, then hurled the football in a perfect spiral straight toward Will's head.

"Hey, Wet Willy. Show us what you got!"

The guys looked on in frozen shock with wide open mouths and stunned looks as the ball seemed to fly in slow motion on a perfect course for its intended target.

Once again, the angry upperclassman turned around just as the ball spiraled down and drilled him on the bridge of his nose. Stumbling backward, his bandana went flying as he spilled his Coke and his blood.

Charlie, George, and BB stood there, paralyzed in abject fear.

"What a moron! Didn't anyone ever tell you to never try to catch a football with your face?" DMarks heckled.

"Cut it out, Marks," urged Charlie.

"We are so dead," gulped BB.

Will's buddies helped him back on his feet. His nose, mouth, and chin were coated with blood. It took a minute or two, but he regained his bearings, wiping the blood away with his bandana.

DMarks knew things were about to get real. Instinctively, he took off running, heart pounding and adrenaline surging.

Tearing into the Pine Forest, he ran like the wind with Will Morris in hot pursuit. DMarks went flying down the footpaths, leaping over underbrush and fallen trees, then cutting hard through the tall reeds hoping he could shake the ever-more-angry upperclassmen.

In his mad dash, DMarks unwittingly cornered himself at the eastern edge of the Pine Forest which was bordered by the Pocantico River. With Will coming on fast, he had no choice but to jump in and swim across the forty-yard span.

The river was only about six feet deep, but the current was stronger than normal because of heavy rains the night before. He struggled to keep his course, but once he got to the other side, he reached up, grabbed a vine and pulled himself out.

He figured he'd have to keep running, but when he looked back, he saw a seething Will Morris come to a screeching halt on the other side of the riverbank. Dripping in sweat, his chest swelled with heavy breaths as he ran his wrist and forearm across his mouth.

Suddenly, a strong, breeze kicked up out of nowhere. It only lasted about ten seconds, but it was enough to blow the twelve-foot-tall reeds sideways. It also came with the scent of fresh-cut flowers. *What the heck is this?* wondered DMarks, looking all around. Then, he felt a serene sense of calmness and protection.

For Will Morris, it was the opposite. He stared DMarks down, grinding his teeth, sweat dripping off his chin. For some reason, he had given up the chase. But he also sent an unmistakable, non-verbal message from the other side of the river: *You might have won this one, kid, but you better watch your back this summer.*

For once, DMarks was smart enough to keep his mouth shut. Will pulled up the bottom of his shirt to wipe his brow, kicked a rock, and stormed off.

It took a few minutes for Charlie, BB and George to get the younger boys back inside the pool area. Once done, they sprinted in the direction of the Pine Forest fearing for what Will Morris might have done to their friend.

To their complete surprise, they practically ran right into him coming out of the woods. Stopping on a dime, they stared at him as though he was some kind wild animal escaped from his cage.

"Wh-What did you do with our friend?" stuttered Charlie. Will said nothing. He just shoved them out of his way and stomped on by.

"Huh?" said George.

"Let's motor, guys. He's probably bleeding and unconscious," urged BB.

The boys raced on, calling out to DMarks. There was no response. They kept running through all the familiar pathways and eventually ended up by the river. As they got there, DMarks was casually doing the breaststroke back across, calm as could be.

"Are you okay? Did he throw you in the river or something?" Charlie asked.

"Ha! The big ox never laid a mitt on me," replied DMarks.

Charlie bent down and reached out his hand to haul his friend out of the water.

"C'mon. What did he do to you? Gut punches? A knuckle sandwich? A half-nelson smack down?" BB wanted to know.

"I told ya, he never touched me. In fact, he never got within five yards."

"You mean to say we came running in here, ready to risk a beating ourselves, and he never touched you?" George said in disbelief.

"Yeah, that's right. Why do you seem so disappointed?"

"We figured we'd be carrying you out of here on a stretcher, you bigmouth joker," steamed BB.

"Gee, thanks for your concern. I'm really touched."

"So if the two of you never actually tangled, what exactly did happen?" asked Charlie.

DMarks was still trying to figure that out himself.

"Well, he chased me tooth and nail. A couple times, he was close enough for me to hear him breathing. So I kept running and when I came to the river, I jumped in and swam across.

"Yeah, then what?" begged Charlie.

"Then something strange happened. When he got to the river's edge, he put on the brakes and just stood there staring at me huffing and puffing like the big bad wolf."

"He just stopped? He gave up?" asked Charlie.

"I swear, Marks, you have nine lives," George said, shaking his head.

"Yeah. He called off the chase. Just like that," DMarks said, clicking his fingers.

Relieved, the boys headed back to the pool area. They were glad that their friend didn't get beat up, but they also knew that this wouldn't be the last they'd hear from Will Morris.

Despite it all, DMarks was feeling confident. He took a stand and backed it up.

"Who's up for some Wiffle ball. I plan on swinging for the fences baby," he said.

"You better get ready to climb the fences if you see Will Morris coming your way," answered BB.

DMarks ignored the comment. "By the way, what was up with that stiff breeze that blew through here a few minutes ago?"

"What are you talking about?" replied George.

"That gust of wind. You couldn't miss it. Almost blew me over."

"Maybe you should lay down for a while?" said BB, making a circular motion with his finger around the side of his head.

"Cut it out. I'm not making this up," DMarks bellowed. "It came with a really fresh smell of flowers too. I remember the scent from my days as an altar boy at St. Theresa's."

"Maybe Willy actually did pound him and now he's delirious?" suggested George.

"Oh, just forget it," declared DMarks.

He knew something out of the ordinary had happened but figured that he'd think about it later.

Charlie, however, was acutely interested. *Was it you, Sky?* he wondered.

4

CHAPTER

QUARTERMASTER

And do not get drunk with wine, for that is
debauchery, but be filled with the Spirit.

—Ephesians 5:18

Briarcliff had a much beloved summer tradition that took place every other Wednesday night from late June through the end of August. After the pool closed and the cooler, nighttime air set in, the lifeguards would set up a reel-to-reel projector on the sloped lawn in front of the middle school.

Families came with picnic baskets, blankets, and beach chairs eventually filling up the hillside amphitheater. Once the stars came out, a feature-length Disney movie would begin, projecting giant-sized images of Dean Jones, Annette Funicello, Shelly Fabres, and Kurt Russell off the huge, windowless façade of the building.

It was a wholesome slice of American pie as families settled in to enjoy each other's company and all that Mother Nature had to offer by way of summer evenings.

For budding teenagers however, there was an invisible line that began to come into play. Their perspectives were expanding, and most felt the urge to push the boundaries in search of new experiences. At the top of that list was sneaking beer.

Seventy-five cents would buy a quart bottle of Budweiser, Miller High Life or Schlitz. Part of the attraction was the thrill of breaking the rules and getting away with it. Of course, there also was a desire to look cool like the older kids.

To be sure, not everyone was all that interested. In fact, most who had tried beer thought it tasted terrible. But for those so inclined, a quick walk through the Pine Forest, across Route 9A and over to the High Health Deli was all it took.

Not surprisingly, DMarks had his mind made up. It was the last Wednesday of June, and he was determined to have his fun.

After finishing his dinner and saying a nonchalant goodbye to his parents, he slipped into the garage and carefully opened the driver's side door of his father's car. Sliding into the bucket seat, he pulled open the ashtray where his dad kept spare change for tollbooths and parking meters. Pushing coins around with his index finger, he plucked out three shiny quarters.

Breathing a little faster than normal, he pocketed the quarters, tiptoed out of the garage, and strolled across the front yard looking as innocent as a lamb.

A few minutes later, he met up with the guys who had already joined Michelle and a few of the girls in the neighborhood on their walk to the middle school.

It was a dazzling twilight as the sky turned blended hues of blue, orange, and silver. Although conversation flowed easily, DMarks was on edge, hardly talking the whole way there. No one thought much of the fact that he was uncharacteristically quiet, but once they got to Law Park, he got down to business.

"Yo, Charlie. I've got my three quarters. You in?" DMarks tossed the coins in the air as proof.

"Yo, DMarks. I told you. No, I'm not in," mimicked Charlie. "You and your three quarters are asking for trouble."

"What a surprise. Mr. Wonderful doesn't want to break any rules."

"No, I just don't want to do anything stupid. You, on the other hand, seem to be like a magnet for stupid."

"Go ahead. Spend your whole life in the on-deck circle. See if I care."

"The guy graduates from eighth grade and right away thinks he's the cheese," said BB, trying to grab the quarters from him.

"How many times do we have to save him from himself before he learns a lesson?" George sighed.

"Just give it up. He's hopeless," declared BB.

"I think you should listen to the guys," cautioned Michelle. "Besides, why are you in such a rush to drink your first beer?"

"Tell ya what, Ms. Robins, I function better without unsolicited advice," DMarks replied with a prolonged but playful stare.

"I'm with her," agreed Andrea. "Here we are, all of us having a fun time and you want to go off and do stuff like that?" She tossed a dismissive hand in his direction.

"Where have I heard this before?" asked DMarks. "Last call. Anyone who wants to join me, it's time to put up or shut up."

"Shuttin' up over here." Barrie laughed.

"I'm with you, sister," added Connie. The boys were amused listening to the girls caution DMarks in the same ways they had done so many times themselves.

"You're wasting your breath, girls," explained George. "It's who he is."

"You ain't kidding," said Charlie.

DMarks sighed and shook his head. "Looks like it's amateur hour again."

"Yeah, and you're the amateur. Again," countered BB.

"You guys just don't understand. You got to go out on a limb once in a while. That's where the fruit is."

"Wait, what?" asked Charlie. "Where did you get that one?"

"Sounds like a lyric from a John Denver song or something," added George.

"Just forget it. You guys are such a drag sometimes," DMarks said, stuffing his hands in his cut-off jeans, walking head down the rest of the way.

As the gang arrived at the park, they found a spot toward the top of the hillside. Getting comfortable, they sat side by side, leaning against each other like scattered books on a bookshelf. No sooner had they settled in when Charlie noticed Will Morris was close by sharing a blanket with Kristen Thomas.

Kristen was the prettiest girl in town with her silky blond hair and brown eyes. She also was known for having a super sweet disposition and a caring heart toward younger kids. Will didn't say a word when he spotted the guys, nor did he have to. They could feel the heat from his death glare.

Charlie nudged the others as they reluctantly made eye contact with the older adversary. The message he conveyed was unmistakable: *It's a long summer, and you're gonna regret tangling with me.* Then he flashed a callous smirk while pretending to snap something in two with his bare hands.

Kristen couldn't help but notice the peculiar interaction.

"What's with the Godfather hand signals? And why are you staring at those eighth graders?"

With beads of sweat popping up on his forehead, Will looked at her in a "mind your own business" kind of way. "I have a score to settle with those little brats," he declared, wiping his brow.

"Those guys? I used to babysit for some of them. Why on earth would you be having trouble with an innocent bunch of kids like that?"

"Let's just say they have a lesson coming."

"A lesson? What do you mean? You're twice their size."

"Look, when you mess with an older kid, you pay a price. That's the way it's always been. Okay?"

"A price? What price? Sometimes I wonder about you," said Kristen, shifting to the far end of the blanket.

Now Will was really sweating. The boys had been listening to all this, and before DMarks could say anything, they cupped their hands over his mouth and held him down until they were sure he wouldn't make matters worse.

Eventually, they let him back up as *The World's Greatest Athlete* rolled through opening credits.

As the movie played, DMarks kept scanning the area eventually spotting some older kids he kind of knew. This was his opportunity. He stood up and gravitated toward them, pretending to wave at other friends in the shadows along the way.

"Where's Cool Hand Luke going?" asked Andrea.

"I'm not sure, but I think he's making his move," answered Charlie.

"You mean for beer?" asked Michelle.

"10-4."

"I hope he knows what he's doing." Barrie sighed, popping a Fresca.

"Something tells me we're going to be saving his bacon later," fumed BB.

The gang looked on as he approached the older guys. All they could see were the silhouettes conversing. Within minutes, they turned to walk toward the Pine Forest with DMarks tagging along.

Sneaking out to buy beer with a bunch of tenth graders was heady stuff. As they rambled along, the iridescent glow of the full moon lit the way along the footpaths. The older guys were calm as could be. But DMarks felt a steady current of nervous energy coursing through him.

"Hey, Marks. Enjoy the summer while you can. Everything goes up a notch in high school," said, Bob who was an All-County offensive lineman on the Bears varsity football team. He seemed to want to help DMarks get the lay of the land.

"Take sports, for example. You have to go through tryouts, and there's no guarantee you'll even make the team."

"That was the worst," said Gary, another member of the varsity team. "I remember trying out as a freshman. It was the most nervous I've ever been. Then, I broke my collarbone in the first game and missed the rest of the season."

"Oh. And all those pretty girls you and your buddies showed up with tonight? Come September, it'll be like you never existed. The upperclassmen will be waiting, and once they make their move, it's all over," added Ralph, who also played on the offensive line.

"And as for academics, plan on a few hours of homework each night. Some teachers are pretty cool, but others just pile it on," cautioned Bob.

"And stay out of detention, man," cautioned Gary. "Unless there's a cute girl in there."

DMarks was feeling his oats and decided to chime in. "Thanks for the advice, guys, but three things I excel at are sports, school, and girls."

The older guys stopped, looked at DMarks, and laughed.

"Dude, you have no idea," said Gary.

"He'll learn. Probably the hard way," added Ralph.

Before long, they crossed 9A and were in the parking lot at the High Health Deli. They found a spot to lay low and began to focus on each of the cars that were pulling into the parking lot. Sooner or later, they knew a former babysitter or friend of an older sibling would hop out. Then all they needed was to put in the request for beer.

During the wordless waiting, DMarks grew restless.

"So, ahh, what happens next?"

The older boys looked at him with blank stares. "What's the matter? You worried about something?" asked Bob, knocking his shoulder. "We wait until someone over the age of eighteen comes by."

"I think our young friend might have flunked *Schoolhouse Rock*," chided Gary.

"Cut me a break, okay? I've never done this before. It wasn't that long ago when you mugs were in my shoes," DMarks pointed out.

Just then, a few guys who were home from college pulled up in an old Chevy Malibu. One of them, had been a swim instructor at the pool and also worked at Gooseneck Pond helping out with skaters during the winter months.

"I think that's Billy Blair," said Gary. "Hey, Billy!"

"What's up, guys? How's it going?" Billy asked.

"No school for two more months. It's going great," said Bob.

"I hear ya, man. What grade you guys going into come September? I lost track."

"Eleventh grade," said Ralph.

Letting out a deep breath, Billy just shook his head.

"Seems like it was just yesterday I was giving you guys swimming lessons at the pool. So what are you all up to tonight?"

"Well, actually, we were hoping someone could help us score a few quarts of beer. It's movie night over at the middle school, and we wanted to down some suds," explained Bob.

"Oh, man, I loved those movie nights. Got my first kiss there watching *The Ugly Dachshund*. What's your pleasure, boys?" he asked, collecting everyone's quarters.

"Four Buds, if it's not too much to ask," Gary replied, grinning.

"Uptight and outta sight." Billy gave a formal bow as he went inside. The guys slapped fives and got ready to sneak back through the Pine Forest. *This is so great,* thought DMarks.

A few minutes later, Billy was making the hand-off.

"Now, remember to pace yourselves," he instructed. The reason these bottles have screw tops is because you don't have to finish it all at once. If you get a little dizzy, just stash what's left, and you can come back and get it the next time."

"You're the best, Billy. Thanks, man," said Bob.

"Okay guys, be cool. See ya around town."

As soon as Billy left, DMarks's older companions turned to him.

"Hey, rookie," said Gary.

DMarks looked back with a "who, me?" face.

"The newbie carries the beer."

DMarks was about to protest, but then he thought better of it. He cradled the four quarts of beer against his chest with his freezing hands doing the best he could with the frosty bottles. Then, the group dashed back into the Pine Forest.

Eventually, they made it to a clearing near a large circular concrete encasement. It was about four feet high and ten feet in diameter, providing a popular spot to hang out. There were several others like it and they all housed now defunct pumps, which used to harvest water from underground springs.

The older guys shimmied up and sat with their legs dangling over the side. DMarks stood by and dutifully distributed the beer; then it was his turn to hop on. His heart started thumping, and his mind began to race. He was venturing deeper into uncharted territory as his normal overconfidence began to falter.

Bob, Gary, and Ralph tapped the tops of their beer bottles and raised a toast.

"To summer!" they cheered.

"And to our neophyte friend over here," added Ralph, looking at DMarks.

DMarks didn't know exactly what neophyte meant, but he assumed it was a sarcastic choice of words. It snapped him back to his brash self. Grabbing his bottle with both hands, he lifted it to his lips, tilted is head back, and took his first guzzle of beer.

As soon as his mouth filled up, his eyes practically popped out of their sockets. He knew in an instant it was a huge mistake. Completely unprepared for the bitter taste and carbonation, he heaved forward, spraying perfectly good Budweiser on the ground in front of them. Gasping for air, his eyes bulged wide as the full moon above.

The others enjoyed a good laugh. There were a lot of things DMarks didn't like, but nothing compared to the ire he felt when the joke was on him. He sat silently, steaming, waiting for the laughter to stop. Then, he clenched his bottle again and chugged.

It was a bold move, but when DMarks was mad, he was a force to be reckoned with. After downing about a third of the bottle, he looked at the others with indignation and belched out loud.

"What are you homecoming queens waiting for? You going to drink, or are you just here to howl at the moon?"

By now, his brassy behavior was starting to earn a measure of respect. The older guys looked at him, then each other.

"This kid's all right," Gary pronounced as they reached over to pat him on the back.

"Just one thing, Marks, there's no two-handed beer drinking around here. Just grab it by the neck and hold it with one hand. Okay?" instructed Bob.

"Yeah, that ain't a baby bottle," snickered Ralph.

DMarks pulled on the sleave of his T-shirt to wipe his mouth. "Got it."

About fifteen minutes later, a group of tenth-grade girls came wandering by. They stopped to chat and helped themselves to a few swigs of beer. After some small talk, they suggested the guys follow them to the movie night.

"Yo, Marks, why don't you put a lid on that beer and join us?" suggested Bob.

To his surprise, DMarks declined. "You guys go ahead wiffout me. I'm going to finish this Bud. Then I have to hook back up with my people."

The older guys all looked at each other with surprised, but amused looks.

"Think it's okay to leave him out here by himself?" Ralph asked.

"You mean wiffout us?" Gary mocked.

"Suit yourself, Marks, but don't overdo it out here all alone," Ralph warned.

"Yeah, yeah, yeah. Check you guys later."

Everything was fine as DMarks finished off his quart of Budweiser, sitting by himself in the moon shadows. He didn't feel all that different, except maybe a little bit bloated from all the beer.

Then, things began to change. His mind got fuzzy, and his whole body began to feel like rubber.

Get a grip, he thought, patting himself on the sides of his face. But it was too late, the ride had begun.

Leaning back on his elbows, he tried to chill. *That's better*, he thought. But then a woozy, unpleasant feeling began to rise up in his stomach.

He stayed as still as he could. "C'mon, Derrick, shake this off," he said to himself out loud. But he couldn't ignore what was starting to feel like the inevitable. *Uh-oh*, he thought.

A few seconds later, he gulped, gagged, heaved forward, and threw up all over his brand-new Converse All Stars. He was light-headed but not faint. Inhaling deep breaths, all he could think of was how much he wished he had a glass of water to rinse the awful taste in his mouth.

He knew it wasn't over. Moments later came the second wave of vomit like a freight train. Doubling over, he held his stomach. After swaying forward and backward for a while, he fell flat on his back, with legs dangling over the edge.

While DMarks was experiencing his trial by fire, Charlie and the rest of the gang were having a great time at the movie. Then, they happened to notice the older boys returning just the three of them.

"You guys," Charlie whispered, "how come DMarks isn't with them?"

Everyone sat up to cast an eye over the area.

"Where the heck could he be?" asked BB.

"No way he's off making out with someone," joked George.

"Charlie, I'm concerned. I think you should go talk with those guys to find out what's going on," urged Michelle.

"You're right, as usual. On my way." Charlie ducked low to avoid the light from the projector and crossed the lawn to where the older guys were hanging out.

As the group looked on, they saw one of them point toward the Pine Forest. A minute later, Charlie returned.

"What'd they say?" Michelle asked anxiously.

"The knucklehead stayed back in the woods to finish his beer. He's probably still there trying to pull himself together," moaned Charlie.

"You guys should borrow a flashlight from the lifeguards and go find him," suggested Andrea.

"Huh?" replied George, comfortably leaning back on a blanket next to Connie. He was loving life and didn't want anything to change. "It's time for him to stand on his own two feet."

"Or try to." Connie laughed.

"All for each and each for all. We have to make sure he's okay," countered Charlie.

Barrie put her hand on BB's arm. He caught her drift and got to his feet muttering under his breath.

"Marks would never leave sitting next to a pretty girl to rescue me."

"We'll be right back," said Charlie to the girls. "Those guys told me exactly where to go."

"Yeah, don't anyone move an inch," George pleaded, looking at Connie, thinking she looked so good in her patched bell-bottom jeans.

They went to ask for a flashlight from the lifeguards and then headed into the woods.

"This is just like that trampoline incident at Todd School a couple years ago," complained George. "I swear, he better be okay, or I'll kill him."

As they got deeper into the Pine Forest, Charlie shined the flashlight out in the distance. "Bingo! I see him. At least half of him."

They picked up their pace, making their way down the footpaths, and moments later, they were about twenty feet away.

"Hold on, what am I hearing?" asked BB.

"I'm not sure, but I think it's him, singing," said George.

"Ooh, da cat's in da cradle and da silver spoon, little boy blue and da man on da moon…" DMarks was crooning away into the night air.

"Wait. I know that song. Harry Chapin. He's singing that Harry Chapin song," said an incredulous George. "I left sharing a blanket with Connie so that I could listen to this moron butcher that song?"

"Seriously! And now it's going to be stuck in my head all night," BB shot back as they moved closer.

"Could he be any more off key?" said Charlie, wincing. "It's actually hurting my ears."

A few strides later, Charlie reached out and tapped DMarks's knee.

"You okay, buddy?"

"My brotherses! I's so happy you are here, are here," he slurred, not even sitting up to look at them.

George then grabbed his right foot to get his attention and ended up with a handful of upchuck. "What the… Gross!" he yelled, wiping his hand on D-Mark's T-shirt.

"Oh, boy," said Charlie, spotting the empty quart bottle lying on its side. "Tell me you didn't drink that whole thing by yourself."

Straining to pull himself up to a sitting position, DMarks swayed, looking at Charlie, and grabbed the bottle. Putting it up to his right eye, he squinted down into it.

"Umm, it looks berry empty in there. So probably yes, I did that. What you said." He then went right back to his fully reclined position.

"Great! He's bombed. Completely smashed," complained BB.

Suddenly, DMarks sat back up and began singing again. "When you comin' home, Dad, I don't knows when, but we'll get togedder den, son, you know we'll have a good times den."

"Would you can it with that song," pleaded George.

Then DMarks scanned his friends. "Ya know s-something... That's a sad song, a berry sad song," he said, jabbing his finger into George's chest. "Why won't his father come home?" asked DMarks. "Doesn't he love him?" Shrugging his shoulders, he added, "I dunno," before going flat on his back again.

The guys looked at each other trying to figure out their next move. Then DMarks spoke up from his horizontal position.

"Makes me think of my dad. All work, no play. I doesn't even remember the last time we even had a catch. A simple catch," he said with a major hiccup. The boys stepped back from his breath vapors, waiving their hands in front of their faces.

Charlie began to take charge.

"Guys, let's get him down and walk him out to the parking lot. Hopefully, he'll straighten up if we get him moving around."

He jumped up onto the concrete structure, put his hands underneath DMarks's shoulders, and leaned him forward.

"Hello, Charles. Where we going?" asked DMarks. "When does the movie start?"

"Actually, my man, the movie's almost over," Charlie answered.

"Yeah, but I have a feeling the show's about to begin," added George.

Charlie inched and shimmied his floppy friend forward, and BB and George caught him as he dropped to his feet. Draping his arms around their necks, they began to walk him to safety.

When they emerged from the Pine Forest, the girls grabbed their stuff and ran over to make sure everything was okay. They sat DMarks on the bumper of a car. He asked for a Coke. Barrie happened to have an extra can, handing it to BB not wanting to get too close to their wilted friend.

"Here, stupid. Drink this. It'll settle your stomach," BB said, yanking off the pull top and handing it to DMarks.

"Does anyone have any food?" asked Charlie. "I think he should try to put something in his stomach."

Between them, the girls were able to dig up some Funny Bones, PEZ, and Yodels.

"Girls always have the best snacks." George sighed, snatching a Yodel for himself.

DMarks promptly scarfed down a package of Funny Bones to go with his Coke, then belched long and loud.

"That felt good," he declared, rubbing his stomach.

By then, the movie had ended and the crowd was beginning to head to their cars. Parker Jones strolled by with Suzie Berkshire, who had her arm wrapped around his.

"Hi, Charlie. Everything okay, buddy?" asked Parker, sizing up DMarks's disheveled appearance.

"Hi, Parker. Yeah, we're good. Our friend just needs a little time to ah, to get his bearings."

"Get his bearings? He needs a set of navigational beacons, a good shower, and some new sneakers," scoffed the always unfiltered Suzie.

"Have a heart, Suz. We've all been there. He'll learn from this," said Parker.

"I'll say. When he wakes up tomorrow, that's going to be the worst seventy-five cents he ever spent," predicted George.

"Can we offer to drive him home?" asked Parker.

"You're the best, but we've got this," replied Charlie. "Better if he walks it off."

"Well, if you're sure everything's cool, we'll keep moving along. Tomorrow's a workday."

"Thanks for checking on us, Parker. And it's nice to see you, Suzie."

"You got it, Charlie," he replied, patting him on the back.

Before long, the lifeguards had packed up the projector and were coiling up the extension cord. Charlie, BB, and George got DMarks to his feet and slowly everyone started the short walk home.

"My aching head," muttered DMarks. He looked down at his sneakers and saw how messy they were. "What happened to my Cons?" he asked indignantly.

"He's kidding right? Tell me he's kidding," said BB.

"I feel like I swallowed a goldfish," DMarks said, crossing his arms over his stomach.

"Are you okay, DMarks?" asked Andrea, trying to show some degree of concern. "What happened in the Pine Forest tonight anyway?"

DMarks never passed up an opportunity to milk a situation.

"I made the mistake of helping some older kids get beer."

Charlie and the guys knew what was coming and just let him roll on.

"They kind of followed me back, so I took them to one of the concrete wells and we all hopped up and took a seat."

"Is that when you threw up on your sneakers, you dork?" asked BB.

"Oh, go eat onion grass," responded DMarks, shoving his friend.

"He's feeling better," said Charlie.

"Where was I? Oh yeah. The next thing I knew, they started chugging. 'Whoa,' I told them. 'Easy does it.' But they wouldn't listen. Meanwhile, I was kicking back, enjoying my Bud. The next thing I knew, they were heading to the movie with a bunch of girls who passed by."

"They probably didn't want you to throw up on them too," added George.

DMarks just looked on exhausted. He had run out of steam and couldn't muster the energy to respond.

The group meandered along, enjoying what was left of the night. Eventually, they made it to the Tree Streets as one by one the girls dropped off to their individual homes.

Outside DMarks's house, the boys helped straighten up their light-headed friend. He serpentined toward the front door, kicked off his sneakers, and left them on the doorstep.

"Don't forget to put your retainer in," whispered George as DMarks went inside, letting the screen door bang, causing the other boys to wince.

"We did our part. Now he's on his own," declared BB.

"Hope he goes straight upstairs to bed," Charlie added. "If he stops to talk with his parents, he's a dead man."

"Can you imagine what the conversation would be like with his dad?" asked George. "Mr. Marks is so strict."

"Totally. I don't mind saying. He kind of scares me," said BB.

The boys backed down the sidewalk, glad to see DMarks's bedroom light go on. "That's a good sign," breathed Charlie.

"Let's call it a night," suggested BB.

"Good call," said George slapping five.

The next morning, DMarks came downstairs for breakfast and was startled by the unfamiliar sight of his father sitting at the kitchen table.

"H-H-Hi, Dad. What are you doing here? No work today?"

"Hello, son. How are you feeling this morning?" asked his father as he took a long drag on his Marlboro.

"Oh, a little tired I guess," he replied. "It's still early."

Meanwhile, he had a splitting headache, his mouth was dry as saltines, and he desperately needed some aspirin.

"I was curious, son, when you left the house last night, did you happen to go into my car for some reason?"

His dad stared at him, blowing a smoke ring in his direction. DMarks's father was a senior prosecutor for the New York County District Attorney's office, and he had no qualms about putting people on the spot and making them sweat, including his own son.

DMarks gulped and went straight into panic-mode.

"Wh-why do you ask?"

"Because someone left the driver side door of my car open. As a result, the interior lights ran all night long, which killed my car battery. I'm waiting right now for Tony from Manor ESSO to come jump the car."

DMarks swallowed hard, eyes shifting back and forth, scrambling for a good answer, but he knew he better take The Fifth.

With his lawyerly skills of deduction, DMarks's father had already figured out what had happened, especially after he noticed the condition of his son's sneakers on the front doorstep.

DMarks couldn't talk his way out of this one. *Case closed, he's going to throw the book at me*, he thought.

"Son," said his dad, slowly stubbing out his cigarette in the ashtray, "it's a good thing I don't have to be in court this morning. My experience with cases like this is that there's no benefit to being lenient with anyone involved. The best lessons come when there's a price to be paid."

DMarks's head dropped to the point where his chin was touching his chest. *Here it comes*, he thought.

"Consider yourself grounded. You can leave the house to go to work. After that, it's straight home for the rest of the day and night until further notice."

"But…" DMarks dropped into a kitchen chair ready to plead for his freedom.

"Want to go for the whole rest of the summer?" his dad interjected. "Oh, and by the way, we'll be withholding your allowance until the brand-new pair of sneakers you ruined are paid for."

DMarks looked at his dad as he sat in silence. *I can't believe it. Summer break just started, and I've already been fined, grounded, and hungover.*

5
CHAPTER

GOLF BROS

Two are better than one, because they have a good return for their labor. If either of them falls down, one can help the other up.

—Ecclesiastes 4:9–10

Sneaking on the grounds of Briar Hall Country Club for twilight golf was a long-standing rite of passage in Briarcliff. The course was usually empty by dinnertime, so it was easy to play seven or eight holes before dark.

The south end of the course over by Tuttle Road was a comfortable distance from the clubhouse, which provided cover from pesky rangers who sometimes patrolled in golf carts looking for trespassers. Plus, there was a comfortable four-hole loop over there with a sprawling pond which had an island in the middle of it.

Charlie and the guys were regulars on weeknights. Sometimes, they'd kick off their sneakers and play in their bare feet. They loved the feel of the cool, velvety fairway grass.

Their standard routine was to spread out, tee up their golf balls and hit their first shots of the night simultaneously.

"On the count of three," said Charlie. "One, two, three."

They each drew their clubs back and up and over their heads, then uncoiled their flexible, athletic bodies with high arching swings.

Making contact at the same time, their golf balls went sailing fairway bound into the early evening sky.

"Well done, gentlemen," observed DMarks. "Maybe someday, one of you will outdrive me."

"Hey, Marks, was that one lump or two?" asked BB as he landed a dead arm with his elbow.

"Let's make it two," answered George, doing the same thing to DMarks's other arm.

"Cheese and rice! Was that necessary?" complained DMarks doubling over in pain.

DMarks stopped to rub his arms. As he reached his hand across his chest, he happened to glance toward the golf holes behind them. To his surprise, there was a golfer out by himself and coming their way fast.

"Son of a biscuit, we've got company," he said, standing up straight.

"Where'd he come from?" wondered Charlie out loud.

"Does it matter?" asked George.

"Geeze, we just teed off," complained BB.

Rule number one was to stop, drop, and roll if a club member or a ranger showed up. They left their golf balls out in the fairway and hustled to a glen of mountain laurels where they could crouch down out of sight.

"Well, this cramps our style," added DMarks. "Whoever this guy is, I don't like his timing."

"Just be patient, he'll play through in a few minutes and we can sneak back out," replied Charlie, always the voice of reason.

"He better not take our golf balls," warned DMarks.

As the golfer got closer, they noticed something familiar about him.

"Wait a minute, I think I've seen him before," Charlie said, craning his neck to get a better look.

"Me too," agreed George. "I just can't figure out where."

"Yeah, like on TV," added BB. "Wait a minute, I think he played ball for the Mets."

The guys all focused their gaze, putting their hands over their brows to block out the evening sun.

"And the Giants. It's Willie Mays!" said Charlie, trying to contain his enthusiasm. George popped up for a better look as DMarks immediately karate-chopped him back down.

Right there, on the other side of the fairway, was possibly the greatest baseball player of all time. The boys froze in awe; they were in the presence of baseball immortality.

This was completely unexpected as they stayed put, hunkered down, thinking they were out of site. But when Mr. Mays got out of the cart to hit his next shot, he noticed them right away.

"Hi, boys! You look like a pack of raccoons over there," he said with a warm, happy smile.

The boys couldn't believe that Willie Mays was actually talking to them. Rising to standing positions, they waived tentatively with glazed over looks in their eyes.

"Lovely night for golf," commented the home run hero. "Say, did you see where my second shot landed?"

Charlie gulped and then offered, "Actually, sir, it landed in the pond. But don't worry, we'll find it for you."

Without hesitation, they sprinted to the water. After a minor scrum, Charlie found a ball with a Mets logo and held it high in the air. "*Fore*!" he hollered, heaving it back toward Mr. Mays.

They also managed to snag about a dozen other golf balls that were there in the thigh-deep water. As they waded out, they were in a near worshipful state.

"Hold on there, I didn't hit that many shots in the water." Mr. Mays laughed at the sight of the fistfuls of golf balls the guys were griping. "Tell ya what though, I'm running low. How much do you want for the whole bunch you've got there?"

The boys didn't have an answer. They would have been happy to hand them over for free. Without hesitating, the former Mets and Giants star reached into his pocket and peeled off a twenty-dollar bill from his money clip. Charlie, BB, and George looked on, amazed at his generosity as DMarks snatched it out of his hand.

"I'll keep this safe for the boys, Mr. Mays," he promised. "You know how careless kids can be." As he went to tuck it into his pocket, George snuck behind DMarks and crouched down. BB gave him a quick shove and Charlie grabbed the bill as DMarks toppled backward.

The Say Hey Kid chuckled and went right on with his golf game, hitting a perfect wedge shot that landed and stuck a few feet from the flag pin. In return for the twenty-dollar tip they sprinted to the green fighting over who would tend the flag pin.

"Why thank you, boys. If you're not in a hurry to get anywhere, why don't you grab your clubs and join me? I think they allow five-somes at this hour."

"For real, Mr. Mays?" Charlie asked.

"Of course, golf is all about camaraderie." They sped over to grab their golf bags and hustled back, clubs clanking against each other.

"Mr. Mays, we're surprised to see you here. Are you a member of Briar Hall?" asked Charlie.

"No, but I'm friendly with the owner," he said leaning on his driver. "Nice little town you've got here."

"Thanks, Mr. Mays! There's lots to do, but mostly we play sports." Charlie laughed.

"Reminds me of when I was a kid."

"We were so glad when you came to the Mets. Are you happy to be retired now?" asked BB.

"Honest answer? Yes. I loved San Francisco but playing at Candlestick was tough. Ever been in the Bay Area when the sun goes down? It gets pretty cold pretty fast, even during summer months."

"Sometimes, we get to watch a Giants game and everyone on the field is wearing a sweatshirt under their jersey. I always wondered about that," added George.

"Well, if you ask me," said DMarks, "the Giants had no business ever leaving New York in the first place." BB clapped a hand over DMarks's mouth to keep him from saying something they'd all regret.

"We weren't too happy about it ourselves. I miss playing in the Polo Grounds. But that's life! Sometimes you get a curveball."

"Who's the toughest pitcher you ever faced?" asked Charlie.

"Oh, there were a lot. Sandy, Gaylord, Seaver, but the toughest, most intimidating had to be Gibson."

"I love watching Bob Gibson pitch. He practically falls off the pitcher's mound as he releases the ball," said DMarks, winding up his arm.

"Yes, he does. Throws a little chin music too," said the slugger.

"Well, Coach Nutson says the harder they throw, the faster the ball flies over the fence," said DMarks.

"That's right, son. Whoever your coach is, he knows what he's talking about. Hopefully, you'll be able to take that advice the next time an opposing pitcher tries to intimidate you."

"Ha! When someone's throwing heat, he just looks for a walk," added BB.

"Can it, Gingersnap! Don't listen to him, Mr. Mays. He doesn't know what he's talking about."

"You boys remind me of me and my friends growing up in Alabama."

As they got to the next tee box, number 24, took out his driver and literally knocked the ball out of sight.

"That thing took off like a Super Ball!" cheered George.

"I think it flew three hundred yards," exclaimed Charlie as the guys slapped fives.

Then, in the middle of this too-good-to-be-true experience, the boys spotted a ranger approaching in a golf cart. The closer he got, the more serious he looked.

The boys froze. They didn't know what the actual penalty was for trespassing, but they knew they were in for it. It was too late for them to try to hide.

The ranger slammed on the brakes of his cart and bounded out, making a beeline toward the group.

"Stay right where you are, you little autograph-seeking felons!" he shouted. "All right you four. I want names, phone numbers, and addresses," he snarled as he took out a notepad and pen.

Thinking on his feet, DMarks went on the offensive.

"Hang on, Sloopy. We're just helping Mr. Mays get around out here," he said, gesturing to the course.

The ranger looked at him, eyes bulging with indignation.

"Watch it, kid. I'll be having a little conversation with Detective Kaufman about this," he cautioned, reaching for his walkie-talkie.

"I'm sorry for this trouble, Mr. Mays. This will all be under control in just a minute. Please, go ahead with your golf game."

"I realize you're just doing your job, young man, but it would be rude of me to play on without my young friends here."

The ranger was caught completely off guard.

"Ah, umm, but Mr. Mays, this is a private club, and I happen to know that these boys are not members. It's my responsibility to turn them in."

"And you're to be commended on the fine job you're doing. But they're my friends. I'll be glad to pay a guest fee when I get back to the clubhouse."

He stepped forward and shook the ranger's hand, indicating everything was just fine. Looking like he just bit a lemon, the ranger turned to head back to his golf cart. As he climbed in, he gave the boys a glaring look, then floored it, rubbernecking as he drove away.

The guys looked at Mr. Mays, not knowing what to say. He just smiled and winked at them.

"Mr. Mays, how can we thank you for getting us out of trouble like that?" asked Charlie.

"It's okay, boys, me and my friends learned how to golf by sneaking on the Westfield Country Club at night. Some of the best days of my life."

The boys stood still, letting that sink in. "Wow, that's so cool to hear," offered Charlie.

"Thank you, sir, this was awesome," chimed in George.

"Yeah, we would have been in big trouble if it weren't for you," added BB.

"That's okay. I can tell you're all good boys."

"All I know is, it's a good thing you got in between me and that Barney Fife on a golf cart," said DMarks, running his mouth.

"Someone's gonna get an atomic wedgie if he doesn't shut up fast," growled BB. The boys landed a few charley horses, which further amused the baseball legend.

"It's almost dark, sir, and my dad will be picking us up soon. We better take our clubs and go."

"Okay, fellas, I'll see you out here another time soon."

The guys began walking away. A few steps later, Charlie turned and shouted, "Let's go, Mets!"

The boys were hyped up as they made their way to Tuttle Road, practically sprinting to where Mr. Riverton was parked. After stuffing their clubs in the trunk of the car, they piled in, exploding with enthusiasm, telling Charlie's dad about all that had happened.

"I wish I had been out there with you! I remember seeing him play in the Polo Grounds. One of the best ever."

"Third on the all-time home run list, right?" asked Charlie.

"Yep. But he also hit for average. For that matter, he fielded and ran the bases as well as anyone," added his dad.

"Dad, he was so nice to us. He even tipped us for fishing his ball out of the pond."

"Speaking of that twenty bucks, I say we use it at Joe Weldon's for lunch," announced DMarks. "It'll keep us going for the rest of the week."

"Deal," they all replied in unison.

With his arm comfortably propped on the window frame, Mr. Riverton drove along with a gratified smile.

"Any kid in America would love to have had the experience you boys had tonight. For that matter, any dad in America would have gladly traded places with you."

The boys couldn't stop talking about their experience as the car rolled along, windows down, wind cooling their sweaty shirts and hair.

But as they got to the bottom of Elm Road, the euphoria was harshly interrupted. Crossing the street right in front of them was Will Morris, American flag bandana in place and basketball under his arm. He happened to notice DMarks in the back seat and immediately delivered one of his spine-tingling death glares.

Mr. Riverton couldn't help but notice. "Wow, Derrick, what's up with Will Morris and that eyes-on-you thing?" he asked, turning to check on him.

DMarks was uncharacteristically rattled. "S-S-Search me, Mr. Riverton," he stuttered with a gulp, slumping back in his seat.

"Have you ever thought of witness protection?" George kidded.

"Yeah, we promise to visit you once a year," teased Charlie.

Sensing that maybe DMarks was in a bit of a pickle with Will Morris, Mr. Riverton offered some encouragement.

"We've all been in situations where we were at odds with someone, Derrick. But just remember, gutsy people have fire. Bullies? All they have is smoke."

In a rare moment of humility, DMarks thanked Mr. Riverton. He appreciated the encouragement.

Charlie touched DMarks's shoulder with his index finger and made a sizzling sound. "Yep, he's all fire."

"Yeah, don't get too close, you might get burned," added BB.

A few minutes later, Mr. Riverton pulled into his driveway and put the car in park. The boys all thanked him for the ride as they headed to the Riverton's front porch to hang out before calling it a night.

Conversation right away turned to Will Morris.

"What's up with that guy anyway? Why's he gotta be so intense all the time?" Charlie asked, leaning back on the porch swing.

"I think he gets it from his father," said BB. "Word is, he played linebacker at Wisconsin and could have gone pro. His claim to fame is that he made the cover of *Sports Illustrated* tackling Frank Gifford on the goal line during the 1953 Rose Bowl."

"Well, that says a lot right there. Linebackers are ass-kickers," said George, slapping his hands together. "Might explain why Mr. Morris goes around town like a bull in a china shop."

"That ain't all. He tore up his shoulder on that play, which ended any hopes of making it to the NFL," continued BB.

The guys sat in silence shaking their heads, each of them feeling a degree of anguish for what they had just heard.

Charlie sighed. "Wow, he was so close to living the dream, and then it was all gone in one single play."

"What do you suppose hurt more? His shoulder injury or missing out on a pro football career?" DMarks asked rhetorically.

As they thought about it, they each began to think a little differently about Will Morris. At least now, they could begin to understand him a little better.

"I guess the apple doesn't fall far from the tree," concluded DMarks.

"Yeah, and maybe that helps explain why Mr. Morris makes such a scene at Bears football games," added Charlie.

"Remember the Pleasantville game last season when he got so mad at how our team was playing, he yelled to Coach Hoffman to suit up the cheerleaders?" asked George.

"Yeah. Then, in the second half, the refs had him escorted out of the stands for almost causing a fight with some of the parents from Pleasantville," recalled BB.

"That kind of stuff has to be embarrassing for Will," George said.

"I could almost feel sorry for him," replied BB.

"And have you ever seen Mr. Morris driving around town? He's a total tailgater," said Charlie.

"One time, I saw him hang out his window, yelling at the car in front of him for not using their blinker," added George.

DMarks just sat and listened. The more he heard, the more he began to feel a measure of empathy. Leaning back on his elbow, he looked at the stars and semituned the others out. *I didn't realize Willy and I had so much in common,* he thought.

6
CHAPTER
RESCUE DOGS

Restore to me the joy of your salvation and
uphold me with a willing spirit.

—Psalm 51:12

Mr. Olson had a tender, mutually devoted relationship with his rescue dog, Taylor. The affectionate Chocolate Lab had done a praiseworthy job filling the void after Mr. Olson's wife passed away two years earlier.

Like most dogs, Taylor had a special ability to warm human hearts. Wherever he went, people wanted to pet him, which Taylor happily accommodated with a wag of his tale and a sloppy kiss.

That summer, a therapy dog program was being offered by Phelps Hospital on the grounds of the adjacent Rockwood Park. Mr. Olson happened to see an article outlining the details in the *Citizen Register*. As he read about the program, an energizing breeze flowed through the open windows and filled the house with the scent of garden blossoms. *Where did that come from?* he wondered.

As he paused to enjoy the breeze, he sensed a strong conviction to enroll Taylor in the program. Putting down the paper, he walked straight to the kitchen to use the downstairs phone. Placing the tip of his finger in the rotary disk, he dialed the hospital to reserve a spot in the beginner's class.

Smiling at the sense of purpose it gave him, he hung up the phone and recorded the time and place in his day planner. The first class was only a week away, and he was glad to have snagged the final spot.

That Saturday, he rose early, and in keeping with his regular morning routine, he fed and let Taylor out in the backyard. As Taylor stretched his legs, Mr. Olson made a pot of coffee along with his standard breakfast of bacon, two eggs over easy, and buttered toast. Normally, he'd linger at the breakfast table with his morning newspaper. But that day, he finished up quickly and took his dishes to the kitchen sink. He wanted to give Taylor a bath before therapy dog training class.

Good-natured to the core, Taylor was cooperative as could be. Mr. Olson drew the bath water and his four-legged family member stepped right in, tongue out and tail wagging. After a thorough shampoo and rinse, Mr. Olson patted him down with a few extra-large beach towels. For good measure, he also spritzed Taylor with some of his Hai Karate cologne.

"Taylor, old boy, if you meet someone special today." He leaned down to give him a kiss on top of his head. "That ought to help your chances."

They headed downstairs and out to the car. Mr. Olson opened the rear hatch of his spotless Chrysler Town & Country station wagon and Taylor jumped in, promptly curling up on his special throw blanket. Five minutes later, they arrived at Phelps Hospital. Grateful to find a parking spot in the shade, Mr. Olson cracked a few windows and hopped out with leash in hand.

Although it was only 9:00 a.m., the mercury was pushing seventy-five degrees and gaining about two degrees per hour. After clicking the leash to Taylor's collar, Mr. Olson took off his glasses and used his handkerchief to blot beads of sweat from the bridge of his nose.

Rockwood Park was resplendent that morning with sweeping, sun-drenched views of the Hudson River and the Tappan Zee Bridge. The rolling hillsides and open meadows were alive with the snapping whir of grasshoppers, the up and down pulsating of cicadas and the rustle of birds in the bush.

The cloudless skies were a deep cobalt blue, matched only by the yet more blue water of the mighty Hudson River in the distance. Moderate breezes off the river helped unlock the spicy aromas of Bottlebrush grasses, Pennsylvania Sedge, and Northern Bush Honeysuckle.

The seasonal sounds and fragrances transported Mr. Olson back to his happy days in Troup 18 of the local Boy Scouts. He paused to reflect, drawing a long breath through his nose.

Bending at his waist, he scrunched Taylor's ears. "Okay, boy, let's put your best paw forward."

The two mates walked side by side up the slight incline where a small crowd had begun to gather near an oversized registration tent.

"Hi, we're here for the therapy dog program," announced Mr. Olson at the sign-in table.

"Well, now, who do we have here?" asked the volunteer.

"This is Taylor. Best friend I've ever had." He paused briefly. "Other than my wife, God rest her soul."

"Well, if you can't be friends with a Chocolate Lab, then I'd say you can't be friends with anyone. Do you have his vaccination papers?"

"Sure do. We saw Dr. Moyer just last week. All his shots should be up to date."

"And, indeed, they are. Okay, if you can just join the others, we should be ready to get started in about five minutes."

"Roger that. Thanks!"

Mr. Olson and Taylor turned to walk away when all of a sudden and very uncharacteristically, Taylor began to pull and dig to the point where Mr. Olson struggled to keep control.

"Whoa, boy! What's gotten into you?" he asked a bit embarrassed by Taylor's willful display. "Easy, boy, you're supposed to be showing your best behavior."

Ignoring all the other canines present, Taylor pulled and tugged all the way to the other side of the tent until he came nose-to-nose with a beautiful female Collie, who seemed demure, but happy to see him. "Aha! Now I understand," said Mr. Olson. He knelt down to say hello to the Collie face-to-face. In the process, he noticed a very lovely-looking older woman holding its leash. She was looking down at the two dogs with a beaming smile.

Mr. Olsen rose back up, cleared his throat, then tried to apologize for any inconvenience.

"Please forgive my pup. He's not usually this forward."

"Actually, I'm enjoying this as much as they are," she said, nodding toward the sniffing, nuzzling couple.

"Well, that's a relief. My name is Jack. Jack Olson," he said, reaching out his hand. "And this is Taylor."

"Pleased to meet you, Jack Olson. I'm Mary Dalton, and this is Annabelle." She said hello to Taylor, patting him on his forehead. "Wow, Taylor, you sure like your cologne! If I didn't know better, I'd say you came here looking for a date." She peered up at Mr. Olsen.

"Well, he is an eligible bachelor," he replied with a slight blush.

"Very interesting. Annabelle's not spoken for either."

"Looks like love at first nuzzle."

They both laughed and slipped comfortably into a warm bit of conversation while waiting for the class to begin.

"So do you live around here?" asked Mr. Olson.

"Yes, born and raised in Ossining. I live over on Underhill Road. How about you, Jack, do you live nearby?"

"Yep. Briarcliff, born and raised."

"Well, now, we're a couple of real locals."

As Jack and Mary talked, Taylor and Annabelle continued to sniff and snuffle each other. All four were becoming fast friends.

A few minutes later, the instructor arrived, blowing her whistle and instructing everyone to line up with their dog. Her name was Mrs. Bridgewater, and it was clear that she took dog training very seriously. She was a stout, serious looking, middle-aged woman, dressed like a park ranger, complete with Smokey the Bear hat, protective sunglasses, beige cargo shorts, and rugged hiking shoes laced halfway up her shins.

Mrs. Bridgewater positioned herself out in front of the group and was flanked by a pair of huge Dobermans sitting at attention, stiff as statues.

"Good morning, everyone, and thank you for registering for my class. The name is Bridgewater. Mrs. Bridgewater," she said, standing squarely in front of the group with her thumbs tucked behind her belt buckle.

"Over the next few weeks, we're going to find out which of these canines are suited for therapy duty and which are not. Statistically speaking, only one-third of the dogs here today will make it all the way to certification. No offense to anyone or their dog, that's just a fact," she stated.

"Well, hello… It's nice to meet you too," whispered Mr. Olson, causing Mary to giggle out loud. In response, Mrs. Bridgewater shot a cold stare in their direction. They both felt like a pair of teenagers in trouble on the first day of school.

After a brief pause, she continued. "I've been training dogs for thirty years. Some learn quickly, some learn slowly, and others don't learn at all. It doesn't mean they aren't good pups. It just means they're not cut out for this kind of work. Sometimes, it has more to do with their owners," she declared, once again shooting Mary and Mr. Olson a look.

"Yikes! Run for cover," eked Mary out of the side of her mouth, as Mr. Olson tried to stifle a chuckle.

"These are my children, Captain and Tennille," she announced, pointing to her Dobermans. "They're smarter than most high school seniors around here and more loyal than your college roommates. They'll be helping me train this bunch of tail-chasers."

Mary and Mr. Olson tried to make eye contact with each other. "Mrs. Bridgewater has a future as a drill sergeant," Mary whispered.

"A future?" Mr. Olson whispered back.

"I see that some of the dogs present have a better attention span than their owners," scolded Mrs. Bridgewater.

After an awkward pause, she continued. "See that hospital over there? Five floors of people who could use some cheering up. You can send flowers, you can send a card, you can send a singing telegram, but nothing cheers them up like a warm, happy dog. So if you believe your pup has what it takes, I'll thank you for taking this class seriously."

"Well, since she put it that way..." uttered Mary, standing up a little straighter. She tugged on Annabelle's leash so she would too.

"There are four basic areas of obedience your dog will have to master in order to become certified. First is down-stay."

With that, she walked about then paces, turned, and called Captain to come. She then gave the down-stay command, which he immediately complied with.

"The second thing they'll need to learn is the importance of staying calm around sudden noises."

She walked over to Tennille and, without warning, blew her whistle. The dog didn't blink an eye.

"The third necessity is being gentle around patients."

She patted her thigh and Tennille immediately snuggled against her.

"Last is discipline for when things are dropped on the floor."

She reached into one of the side pockets of her cargo shorts and tossed two Milk Bones in Captain's direction. To everyone's amazement, he didn't flinch. Even Taylor and Annabelle seemed impressed.

"Are they dogs or robots?" Mr. Olson muttered, causing Mary to bite her lip to keep from laughing.

"Now, it's time for inspection."

People didn't know whether to be impressed, enthusiastic, or frightened. Mrs. Bridgewater began to walk slowly past each dog, sizing them up as she went. As she got to Taylor and Annabelle, she grumbled to no one in particular that she was impressed with the dogs but concerned with the owners.

After making it through the lineup, Mrs. Bridgewater circled back to the front of the group. Once again standing at ease with her thumbs tucked behind her belt buckle, she gave her verdict.

"Well, I feel better now that I've had an up-close look at some of my four-legged students. Now it's time for a few introductory drills."

For the next hour, everyone broke a sweat as Mrs. Bridgewater conducted various training exercises. As the time came to finish up the first class, she asked everyone to line up single file once again.

"It's apparent to me that some of the dogs here today have potential. Please be sure to practice these drills at home. I'd say it was a good first day, but there's always room for improvement. Unless there are any questions, class is dismissed."

No one dared ask a question. Instead, everyone exhaled in relief, milling around making acquaintances.

"Well, that was quite a workout," Mr. Olson said to Mary.

"Quite," replied Mary, fanning herself with a handout from the day's event.

"I think Annabelle and Taylor earned the rest of the day off."

"I think the same for you and I."

"It was a real pleasure meeting you, Mary. I'll look forward to seeing you and Annabelle next Saturday."

"Likewise, Jack. Remember to practice what we learned this morning with Taylor."

As Mr. Olson turned to walk to his car, he was surprised at how attracted he felt to Mary. It was completely innocent, but it made him feel years younger. He glanced down at Taylor, who seemed to be smiling back at him. *I wouldn't have met Mary if you hadn't dragged me over to Annabelle.* He grabbed Taylor's muzzle and gave it a little thank you shake.

As Mary opened the car door for Annabelle to hop in, she glanced back at Mr. Olson, wondering if he was spoken for. Then, looking down at Annabelle, she patted her head. "You still got it, kid," she whispered.

7
CHAPTER

DREAM TEAM

For God does speak—now one way, now another though no one perceives it. In a dream, in a vision of the night, when deep sleep falls on people as they slumber in their beds.

—Job 33:14–15

Charlie coasted down his driveway standing up on his bike pedals, leaning forward over the handlebars for maximum wind-jamming effect. The headwind in his face had blown his hair dry on the short ride home from the pool.

Sliding off his bike, he stepped on the kickstand and was greeted by the matchless scent of summer barbecue. He breathed in through his nose and filled his lungs. *Psych!* he thought, *Dad's cooking out.*

Stashing his bike in the garage, he hustled around the side of the house and straight to the backyard. A fun smile broke out at the sight of his dad standing on the slate patio wearing his KISS THE COOK apron. In his right hand was a pair of barbecue tongs. In his left, was a cold bottle of Michelob.

"Hello, son. How was your day?" asked Charlie's dad as he flipped a few things on the grill.

"Hi, Dad. It was a good day, thanks."

"Well, hopefully, it's about to get even gooder," his dad said with a chuckle. "Your mother bought enough food for an army."

"Are you surprised?" Charlie asked, glancing down at the grill. Just the sight of London Broil, chicken wings, and pork chops made his mouth water. *Oh, man, this is going to be awesome.*

"Is that Mom's homemade barbecue sauce?"

"The one and only. I'm about to flip this steak. Want to brush some on the other side?"

"Totally." Charlie picked up the Pyrex bowl filled with his mother's special recipe, top-secret concoction and began to slather it on.

"Make sure you brush evenly. We don't want any spots uncovered."

"Got it, 100 percent coverage." Grinning, Charlie spread on a thick coat.

"Nice work, son. I'd say you've got potential around a grill someday."

Charlie licked his lips as his stomach gurgled away.

"Dad, I'm so hungry I might come back for thirds tonight."

"Oh, this isn't for tonight. Mom's got some TV dinners in the oven. They should be coming out any minute."

Charlie noticed a crafty grin on his father's face.

"You almost had me," he said, smiling back.

Just then, Mrs. Riverton opened the back door so Barnes and Noble could greet Charlie. The two Boxers joyfully pummeled him as the three rolled around on the grass. After a few minutes, Charlie headed inside to wash up as the two super-rambunctious dogs trotted over to Charlie's dad, curious to see what he was grilling.

"Don't get any ideas, you two," said Mr. Riverton. Then, feeling sorry for them, he looked toward the kitchen window to make sure no one was watching. Seeing that the coast was clear, he sliced a couple of pieces of steak and tossed them to the grateful pups.

At the dinner hour, timing was everything for Charlie's mom. Her kitchen more closely resembled a war room with multiple workstations operating toward a collective goal. In one spot, there were sliced peppers, tomatoes, and cucumbers ready to be tossed for a summer salad. To the side was a mound of baked potatoes just out of the oven. Next to that was a batch of sunny-yellow corn on the cob. A huge plate of chocolate chip cookies filled out the crowded counter.

"Hi, Mom," Charlie called out, letting the screen door slam behind him.

"How was your day, buddy?"

"Pretty good. Standard stuff. I cut a few lawns this morning, then hung out at the pool with the guys."

"I hope you brought your appetite home with you. We've got a lot of food on the grill."

"I noticed. Are we having company or something?" His mom just smiled as she shook the Good Seasons salad dressing.

"Are we eating outside tonight?"

"That's the plan." She nodded toward the pantry. "Feel free to begin taking out the plates and silverware. Oh, and don't forget the vinyl tablecloth." The Riverton men were known for leaving a trail of her special sauce at the dinner table.

"Consider it done."

Charlie grabbed as much as he could and headed out to the picnic bench on the patio. After setting the outside table, he went back inside to help his mom bring out the salad and potatoes. As they stepped around the clamoring dogs, his dad was taking the food off the grill.

"Perfect timing once again," said his dad. "Honestly, I don't know how I do it." Charlie and his mom looked at each other smiling.

"You have a gift, dear," she deadpanned.

Once everyone was settled, Mr. Riverton asked for the Lord's blessing. Then it was all smiles as they passed around the plates of food and dug in.

There was something inexpressibly pleasing about eating dinner outside on a summer night. With daylight smoothly fading away, the setting angle of the sun cast a feathered glow all around. The night air was light and cool with just a hint of humidity as it swathed and refreshed everyone's faces, arms, and legs.

Even Barnes and Noble seemed relaxed as they lounged on the grass at the edge of the patio, all the while keeping eagle eyes out for any food that might fall from the table.

"We're proud of you, son. Your work ethic is outstanding," complimented Charlie's dad.

"Thanks, Dad. I really like yardwork. I feel lucky to get paid for it."

"Well, just be sure to keep putting your money in the bank so it can earn interest," cautioned his mom.

"I love it when they punch my bank book to show deposits and interest."

"By the way, what did Coach Cadman want to talk with you about when he called the other day," asked Charlie's dad, passing around a platter of corn.

"Oh! So cool. He's going to start a soccer clinic in town, and he asked if me and the guys might like to help out as junior coaches. It's part of some new thing called AYSO. American Youth Soccer something."

"Now that sounds promising. Soccer is the next big thing in this country, mark my words," predicted his dad. "That Kyle Rote Jr. is talented."

"Yeah, and Coach is the best. He makes everything fun and everyone always has a great time. Plus, I think Coach Nutson's involved too. He's the coolest. We love it when he lets us ride in his '69 Camaro with him."

"Well, just remember not to overdo it," cautioned his mom. "You already have all your yard jobs plus swim team," she added while standing up to collect plates.

"Plus Michelle," wise-cracked his dad.

Feeling full, all three began to take everything inside. Mrs. Riverton had every conceivable kind of Tupperware in existence, so all the leftovers fit snugly in their containers as she efficiently stacked them in the refrigerator. She claimed it was the elementary school teacher in her.

"Everything has its place, and there's a place for everything," she always said.

While his parents cleaned the dishes, Charlie took out the garbage. After everything was washed, dried, and put away, they all migrated to the den.

After checking out the listings in TV Guide, Charlie twisted the On button of their new twenty-one-inch color console TV. After warming up for a minute, the picture screen came alive and Charlie turned the dial to CBS.

As his mom and dad put their feet up, Charlie splashed down on his beanbag chair for the latest episodes of *Gunsmoke, The Partridge Family* and *The Six Million Dollar Man*. Barnes and Noble curled up against him.

His dad was half-watching and half-reading the *Citizen Register* as his mom worked on a crocheted blanket for the new hospice center at Phelps Hospital.

By 10:00 p.m., Charlie could hardly keep his eyes open. He had a thing with Barnes and Noble each night where they would tug at his shirt to help hoist him out of the beanbag chair. Once on his feet, he took his four-legged companions out to the backyard one last time for the night.

As he stood around, he looked up at the stars. There was no moon that night, so the heavens were awash with animated diamonds flickering away. *What a sky* he thought, which set him off thinking about his friend Sky.

Charlie knew he'd never have another friend quite like Sky. He wondered if somehow, he really was nearby. If so, why now? It had been over two years since his abrupt departure the day after Christmas.

He was too tired to think it all through, plus the dogs had already trotted back to the patio door, dog tags jingling in the dark. He yawned, stretched, and headed back inside.

Looking in on his parents, he said good night and headed upstairs.

"Night, buddy," said his dad.

"Sleep tight," his mom called after him.

After washing his face and brushing his teeth, he walked down the hallway to his bedroom. Drawing back the bed spread, he climbed in bed and got comfortable. Stretching out, he took in the manifest sounds of summer flowing through the screen windows. Then, he clasped his hands and closed his eyes as he whispered the Lord's Prayer. Before he knew it, he had prayed himself to sleep.

A short time later, he found himself standing completely by himself near the flagpole in Law Park. The fact that there was no one else around was odd and created a sweat-inducing, weird kind of feeling.

Normally, there would have been at least a few passersby, but there was no one to be seen in any direction. For that matter, no one was at the pool, not even the lifeguards. *Where was everyone?* he wondered.

He decided to walk around to see what was going on, but he couldn't move his feet. It was like they had become rooted in place. No matter how hard he tried, they wouldn't budge.

A sense of panic rose up in his head and his heart. Then, he heard a wonderfully familiar voice right behind him.

"Hey, buddy. Guess who?"

Charlie's heart soared with expectation.

"Sky!" he exclaimed as he turned around.

Standing right there was Skylar Northbridge, flashing his luminous smile. At first, Charlie thought he was seeing things, rubbing his eyes trying to bring them into sharper focus. Sky just looked down at him with his warm gaze, radiating affection for his young friend.

"Is it really you, Sky? Where have you been? When did you get here? Will you be staying this time?"

"Whoa, slow down, buddy, let's have a seat and catch up."

Sky reached out with his muscle-bound arm and draped it across Charlie's shoulder as they walked to a nearby bench.

"Sky, it's like you never left. I think about you all the time."

"And I think about you all the time Charlie. In fact, that's why I'm here."

"Really? What's up?"

"Word has it that some of the older guys are throwing their weight around."

How'd he know that? wondered Charlie. *Of course he knew that. He always knew about everything.*

"Well, now that you mention it, that's true."

Sky shook his head with a lengthy exhale.

"Some things never seem to change. A long time ago, I had a close friend named Joseph. His brothers all ganged up on him one time and sold him into slavery! It was all out of jealousy."

Charlie listened thoughtfully, so happy to be with his special friend in person again.

"One of them seems to have it out for DMarks. We don't really know what to do," said Charlie, throwing up his hands.

"Tell ya what, buddy, Matthew's gospel teaches us to love our enemies and pray for those who persecute us. I know that seems like a tall order, but it begins with showing patience, understanding, and forgiveness even when others might not be treating us very well."

"Okay, but I have to tell you, it got a little scary the other day."

"Understood. But try to remember that you're not alone in these situations. God is always with you, and you can turn to him in prayer any time of any day, no matter where you are or what you're doing."

"I'll try to keep that in mind."

Sky looked at Charlie with the deep affection of a devoted older brother.

"Nice job at Croton Point, by the way. If you didn't act the way you did, that young boy would have been in serious trouble."

"To be honest, I heard this familiar voice. Wait a minute—"

Before Charlie could continue, Sky interrupted. "So listen, I'm really busy with other projects this summer. Although I can't really stick around, I'll be there for you just the same. In fact, my boss asked that I keep an eye on Derrick."

"Gee, that would be great. He's in some hot water with a guy named Will Morris."

Sky smiled a knowing smile.

"Noted. And by the way, good call staying away from beer at the movie night."

"We told DMarks it was a mistake. Wait, how'd you—"

Once again Sky interrupted before Charlie could finish his thought.

"Now listen, since I can't really be here in person, I want you to try to stay tuned to my nods, tokens, and signs."

"Nods, tokens, and signs? I don't think I understand what you mean."

"Just keep your wits about you."

"But, Sky, I'm confused."

"By the way, I'm happy to see that you're wearing the cross with a crown of thorns pendant I gave you. Maybe you can share it with someone else someday."

"Share it?" Charlie grabbed the necklace through his T-shirt. "I haven't taken it off since you gave it to me two Christmases ago."

Sky looked on, radiating warmth toward his young friend with an incandescent smile.

"Now, getting back to those nods, tokens, and signs. Tell me more, I don't think I understand."

Sky reached out and put his powerfully strong hands squarely on Charlie's shoulders. Smiling at his young friend, he then began to fade away until he vanished completely.

In an instant, Charlie had the rudest awakening he had ever experienced. Confused and groggy, he sat straight up in bed. One second, he was looking out over the hills of Law Park, the next he was looking at the walls of his bedroom. *Was it only a dream*? he wondered.

Everything seemed so real and he was so happy to be with his heavenly friend. As he tried to gather his wits, he was sure it was more than just a dream. He felt Sky's warm presence, and it was all textured in a way that had extra layers of meaning.

But he was perplexed. It was like if a quarterback called a play that the team never really practiced.

Love our enemies? That's not in the playbook, he thought. As he mulled it over, he said a silent prayer. *I'm willing to give it a try God, but I'm going to need your help.*

He flopped over onto his stomach and eventually dozed off. A few hours later, the morning sun peeked through Charlie's bedroom window, bathing his face, gently waking him up.

His mind immediately ran through the details of his dream. He badly wanted Sky to be back for real and was certain they had visited together in a special way that night.

Hauling himself out of bed, he went downstairs for breakfast. The longer he was awake, the clearer his recall became of the things he talked about with Sky.

"Morning, Mom," he said as he walked into the kitchen. "I'll have French toast and scrambled eggs with a side of hash browns, please."

"I'm afraid the kitchen is closed today. You'll have to settle for Pop-Tarts and Tang," she replied, setting both on the table.

"Think I'm going to have to speak with management at this establishment," Charlie said, playing along.

"That would be me," she playfully swatted him with the dish towel, "but management is not accepting any complaints today."

Charlie smiled as he sat down. "Mind if I turn on the radio to get a weather report?"

"Go right ahead, but I already heard it's supposed to be overcast all day with a threat of afternoon showers."

"Yuck."

The radio dial had been turned to WRNW and his friend Howard was playing top forty songs. He was just about to change the station but something made him want to wait for the next song. It turned out to be a popular tune called "Rock the Boat" by the Hues Corporation. He had heard the song a hundred times before, but somehow, the refrain really resonated with him: "Rock the boat, don't tip the boat over."

After breakfast, he said goodbye to his mom, and he headed out to the garage to gas up the lawnmower and grab a rake. His first stop was the Moyer's house, and as he strolled down Simpson Road, that song kept playing in his mind.

He leaned his rake up against the picket fence, then pulled the ripcord on the lawnmower. Despite the racket it made, all he could hear was that song. Back and forth, he went across the yard when suddenly, he stopped in his tracks. *Could it be one of those nods, tokens, and signs from Sky?*

But if so, what did it mean? He thought it through and concluded that maybe "rock the boat" meant they were supposed stand up for themselves and rely on God's helping hand. He further reasoned that maybe "don't tip the boat over" meant they're supposed be willing to reconcile with others who mistreat them.

Charlie swatted a mosquito from his chest, grazing the cross with a crown of thorns pendant under his shirt. An immediate, warm, and profound feeling came over him. He stopped and looked around, thinking and hoping that maybe Sky was standing nearby. Not this time.

He finished raking up lawn clippings, then headed to the next yard on his schedule. As he walked, he reflected some more.

"Thanks, Sky," he said out loud.

8
CHAPTER

CAPE ESCAPE

For where two or three are gathered in my name, there am I among them.

—Matthew 18:20

Reverend Higgins kept a summer home on Cape Cod and hosted an annual youth group retreat. Over the years, it had become a much-anticipated summer tradition for kids at the Briarcliff Congregational Church.

The house was a classic Cape Cod saltbox. It had four upstairs bedrooms and a full bath, which was a perfect place for the girls to bunk. There were two bedrooms and a full bath on the main floor where Reverend and Mrs. Higgins stayed, along with Tom, the youth director. And the boys could comfortably sack out in the furnished basement.

The purpose of the yearly retreat was to help the kids get better acquainted with their Congregational faith traditions. At night, they'd sit around the fire pit as Reverend Higgins shared stories of the courage, determination, and faith of the original pilgrims, not just in getting to North America but also once they arrived. Invariably, he would build up to a rousing oration.

"The pilgrims were willing to risk everything. Even their lives so that they could rightly worship God! In fact, half of them didn't make it through their first winter. That's the kind of faith I want to have. That's the kind of faith we all should want to have!" As a direct descendant of the Mayflower, the Rev, as he was affectionately known, was passionate on this particular topic, his words echoing in the darkness.

There was no sleeping in on these retreat weekends. Each day was filled with fun activities and things to do. With about two acres of land, there was plenty of room for horseshoes, badminton and croquet during the day and flashlight tag at night.

Sunken Meadow Beach was only about a football field away, so walking or biking to the salty waters of Cape Cod Bay was easy. Some kids liked to scavenge for sanded glass and seashells, others threw frisbees and footballs, and most just hung out on the beach, swimming and soaking in the sun.

The air was seasoned with an aromatic scent of suntan lotion mixed with a briny ocean tang. Moderate waves rolled along the beachfront creating a seaside melody and the site lines opened up all the way to Provincetown.

When the tide was out, it was possible to walk over the tidal flats and sandbars almost all the way to the SS *James Longstreet* or what was left of it. The *Longstreet* was a Liberty ship used by the US Navy during World War II. Eventually, it was taken out of commission and anchored in Cape Cod Bay. During the 1950s, Navy flyers used it for target practice, leaving bare the rusted skeleton of a once proud vessel. Still, the kids found it cool to look at while imagining what it might have been like in its heyday filled with brave sailors.

One day, at extreme low tide, Charlie, Michelle, DMarks, and Andrea made the mile walk out to the Longstreet to take a closer look. As they strolled along dodging the occasional bay crab, they talked about how much fun they were going to have at the Wellfleet Drive-in Theater that night. A new movie called *Jaws* was showing.

DMarks was a bit of a film nut. "It's a film by a guy named Spielberg. I'm telling ya, he's going to be big someday."

"Poster looks cool, but what's it about anyway?" asked Charlie, skipping over a crab.

"It's awesome. This giant shark goes around terrorizing people. Swimmers, boaters, anything it wants. The whole town ends up afraid to go in the water. Right here on Cape Cod."

The girls rolled their eyes.

Andrea chuckled. "Sounds like your kind of movie."

"Wait, I don't want to get nightmares from this," squeaked Michelle, shielding her eyes from the sun to look out at the water. "Just how close can the sharks get?"

"Now, ladies…first of all, shark attacks are extremely rare. Second, if you do encounter a shark, just punch it in the snout. They can't stand that." DMarks demonstrated on Charlie's nose lightly.

Patting his hand away, Charlie asked him, "And how did you get to know stuff like that?"

Shooting him a fish-eye, DMarks said simply, "I know stuff, okay? I read a lot."

"Hard to imagine you reading for fun, DMarks," said Michelle, grabbing Charlie's arm and skipping through a tidal pool.

The four splashed along and soon they were within about forty yards of the Longstreet. However, the tide had begun to come in, so they couldn't go any further. What was left of the boat looked much bigger up close, and the sight of it made them wonder about all the places it had been and all it had seen.

Of course, DMarks was always on the lookout for an opportunity to show off in front of the girls.

"So this was used for target practice? Well then, watch me throw this rock right through that huge bombed-out opening in the middle part."

The water was now up to their knees. He looked at his target and used his best pitcher's wind-up and called out, "Fire one!" he let it fly. But he missed his mark, nailing the broadside of the ship instead. The result was a loud, reverberating clang, which caused a school of fish to stir and scatter from inside the hull.

"Did you see that? There had to be two hundred fish in there!" yelled an excited DMarks.

"Look at them all," shouted Michelle, quickly trying to get some pictures with her instamatic camera.

"If we had a net, we could catch dinner," exclaimed Charlie.

It was a phenomenal display of aquatic life. Then, in an instant, their spines jolted with lightning bolts of panic. Behind the school of fish was a dorsal fin cutting through the surface of the water and heading straight at them. DMarks's errant throw had stirred the bait fish and now they were easy prey for a local shark in search of a snack.

"Sh-Sh-Sh-Sh-Shark!" roared DMarks in a complete panic. Charlie grabbed Michelle's hand, and DMarks grabbed Andrea's as they made a mad sash for the nearest sandbar, kicking up water behind them. No one dared look back.

A few frantic seconds later, they made it to a tidal flat gasping for air, doubled over with hands on their knees. Heaving for air, they stood, bent over, drawing long breaths. Finally glancing up, all they saw was a harmless baby sand shark. Their finned visitor traversed slowly nearby wanting a closer look at them, nothing more.

Realizing that there was no real harm, DMarks resorted to his normal dramatics. "Girls, get behind me." He tried to corral them. "If that shark gets any closer, I might have to take it on with my bare hands."

"Oh brother." Charlie sighed. "Hang it up, Cousteau."

"I'm telling ya, if those things are hungry, they'll chase you right up onto shore," warned DMarks. He yanked his shirt off and got into a crouched position as though ready to wrestle.

That did it. Charlie walked up behind him and shoved him headlong into the water. The splash frightened the baby shark as it whirled away. DMarks reacted a little differently, getting up and out of the water in complete terror.

"Are you crazy?" he yelled at Charlie. "Those things have teeth!"

Charlie and the girls were laughing so hard that they couldn't even respond at first.

"Way to freak out, chicken of the sea," cackled Charlie.

DMarks was shocked at what his friend had done to him.

"I ought to tell the lifeguards about that little stunt. I can't believe you did that to me," he complained, shaking his hair in Charlie's direction.

"Oh, chill out. That little baby shark was more afraid of you than you were of it."

"Yeah, besides, all you have to do is punch them in the snout, right?" chimed in Michelle, miming karate chops in all directions.

Andrea took a little sympathy and handed him his shirt. DMarks looked at her and said, "I only had your safety in mind. I swear."

"My hero," she replied, throwing her arms around his neck in old-school fashion.

After all the commotion, they turned to head back to the beach as now the tide was coming in fast. Hurrying along, they didn't notice all the marine life coming out of hiding, and Michelle stepped too close to a ten-inch Atlantic Rock Crab. It clipped the bottom of her foot in self-defense.

The shock of the bite was almost as intense as the pain. Hopping on one foot, she screamed out loud as Charlie reached out to brace her.

"What happened? Are you okay?" He searched her up and down.

"Something bit me. It hurts, Charlie, bad. I think I'm bleeding." She held up her foot awkwardly.

Charlie knew exactly what to do. He looked at Michelle. "Here, hop on." *Here we go again*, he thought as he raced to shore, Michelle riding piggyback.

Michelle was a trooper, but when Charlie put her down on a beach towel, they realized how serious it was. Blood was flowing freely from the gash on her foot. Sometimes, the marine life carried venom as well.

"Man, those crabs are dangerous. We need to get you back to the house for some first aid," said Charlie. He once again took off his shirt and used it as a bandage. *First my Bobby Murcer Yankees shirt. Now my Walt Frazier Knicks shirt?* he thought.

DMarks helped get Michelle to her feet, and Charlie carried her to the bike they rode to the beach earlier. Setting Michelle on the crossbar sitting sidesaddle, he pedaled her back to the house.

Thankfully, Mrs. Higgins had a gift for homespun medicine.

"Quickly now, bring her up to deck so we can wash her foot with warm soap and water," she directed. Once she cleaned out the lesion, she treated it with Bactine and Betadine before bandaging it with gauze and mesh tape.

Charlie sat by Michelle the whole time, holding her hand.

Loving every minute of his thoughtful attention, she looked at him as he watched the bandages being applied. *Everyone should have a heart like his,* she thought.

Charlie was so relieved that it was nothing serious. Still, he hated to see Michelle wince in pain. *It should have been me who stepped on that crab.*

When she was done, Mrs. Higgins had Michelle rest on the deck with her foot propped up.

"There now, dear," she said, sliding a pillow underneath her foot. "This will help stem the bleeding." She looked at Michelle with a warm smile. "Let's give that foot some rest. You'll be fine in no time."

By then, it was late afternoon. As all the kids wandered back to the house, they took turn turns taking showers to get cleaned up and ready for dinner. Out back, Reverend Higgins lit some coals to prep the barbecue grill.

"What's for dinner, Rev?" asked DMarks.

"Burgers and dogs," replied Reverend Higgins, reaching for his Flour Power apron.

"Again? We had that last night."

The reverend wasn't having any of DMarks's attitude. "That comment just landed you on KP duty, mister. There are two dozen ears of corn over there on the picnic table. Start shucking."

DMarks turned his head to look at the overflowing bag of corn on the other side of the deck. He gulped, then drew his gaze back to Reverend Higgins.

"What? Wait a minute, I had a long day at the beach."

"And you're about to have a long night cleaning up after dinner if you don't watch it."

DMarks exhaled while shooting a glance at Charlie. "A little help here," he whispered out of the side of his mouth.

"You're on your own, my man," he breathed back.

An exasperated look spread across DMarks's face; then, a light bulb went off.

"How's about everyone shucks their own?" he offered brightly.

"How's about now you're taking out the garbage too," replied the reverend.

DMarks wisely gave up his cause and walked over to the bag of corn, shoulders slumping.

Looking on, the other kids were doing their best to hold back their laughter.

Game, set, match for Reverend Higgins, thought Charlie.

After a while, the Rev piled the burgers, dogs, and buns onto a platter, and Mrs. Higgins came out of the kitchen with some of the girls helping to carry all the side dishes. Everyone sat down for dinner and Tom, the youth director, invited them to hold hands as he offered a word of prayer and blessed the food.

"Dear Lord, we thank you for the ways you provide for us each day. Our hearts are truly grateful. We pray for faithful hearts in return that we might honor you with the lives you've given us. Amen."

The conversation around the table was lively, with the kids all sharing what they had done that afternoon. The crystal-clear skies and breezy night air seemed to energize everyone after a full day in the sun.

Once everything was cleaned up and put away after dinner, the group got ready to head over to the Wellfleet Drive-In Theater. The setting sun was putting on a show as it played off the sparkling waters of Cape Cod Bay. The temperature had also dropped enough so that everyone was wearing fleeces and sweatshirts.

Tom drove one car, Reverend Higgins drove another, and Mrs. Higgins was behind the wheel of the third. On the way down Route 6, Charlie noticed a huge billboard featuring Smokey the Bear and a bold print message reminding everyone that ONLY YOU CAN PREVENT WILDFIRES.

He'd seen that message a thousand times before. It was ubiquitous in the United States, especially during summer months. But somehow, it echoed in his head, and his heart in a different, more consequential way.

He couldn't understand why the commonly seen headline stuck with him like that. *We don't smoke, we don't go camping, and we don't play with matches. Why is this blanketing me like this?* he wondered.

He thought hard about it, but the ride was short and they were almost there. Then, it dawned on him. Maybe it was one of those signs, tokens, and nods Sky told him to watch for! Why else would a commonly seen message stir him like that?

But if so, what did it mean? Did it pertain to their summer skirmish with Will Morris and his bunch? Was this some kind of call for Charlie to prevent it from getting out of control?

He'd have to think about it another time. All three cars pulled into the parking lot and found spots right in front of the huge outdoor screen. The station wagons parked side by side with the windows rolled down so they could hear the speakers on the nearby stanchions.

As the movie began, the baker's dozen of youth groupers got comfortable, propping up against each other until each car looked more like an overstuffed sock drawer.

The tight quarters ended up being a good thing. No one was prepared for how scary the movie turned out to be.

"Whose idea was this?" groaned Michelle, upending her box of popcorn after one particular scene.

"I know. This music's gonna give me nightmares," muttered Charlie. "Bump bum, bump bum..."

DMarks wasn't bothered by the scary parts of the movie. "Hey, look on the positive side. It's not every day you get to go to an authentic drive-in theater. Besides, we're sitting in the back seat of a car with the prettiest, smartest girls in our grade. It can't get much better than this."

Charlie, Michelle, and Andrea all looked at DMarks suspiciously. It wasn't like him to toss out compliments like that.

"By the way, what's in bloom around here," he commented, leaning his head out the window. "You guys smell that?" He gave a huge sniff.

"Smell?" asked Michelle. "All I smell is fear."

"I smell church flowers," he said.

"So now you're becoming a flower child?" Andrea looked over at him, eyebrows raised.

"Did you get a little too much sun today, maybe?" asked Michelle as she nestled closer to Charlie and pulled his arm up, over and around her shoulder. Andrea did the same with DMarks.

Charlie had been paying close attention to the conversation. He leaned forward to look over at DMarks, who was all smiles, happy and relaxed as could be. Something was working on his friend, and he was beginning to think that he knew what it was.

9

CHAPTER

GOOD GIANTS

You are a hiding place for me, you protect me from trouble, you surround me with songs of deliverance.

—Psalm 32:7

The New York Giants football team held training camp each summer at Pace University in Pleasantville, which bordered the grounds of the Briarcliff High School. Since the practices were open to the public, the guys would sometimes ride their bikes up to the high school and make the short walk through the woods to where the Giants worked out each afternoon.

Once practice was over, there were coveted opportunities to interact with the players, which the guys took full advantage of. They knew all the key statistics and background of each player, which did not go unnoticed. After a while, some of them began to recognize Charlie, DMarks, BB, and George by name.

One afternoon, the boys ran into Lester Simpson, the massive offensive lineman at Weldon's. He recognized them right away and said hello as he waited in line to order his lunch.

After paying for their food, the guys left the deli and began to walk toward Law Park. At the same time, Will Morris happened to be approaching. He snuck up from behind and grabbed DMarks by his shoulders. Spinning him around, the angry upperclassman shoved DMarks up against a giant oak tree just outside Donato's restaurant. With fiery eyes, he locked in on his prey.

"What's that you've got there, Marks?" he jeered. "Awesome! An ice-cold Coke." He swiped it, took a long swig, then poured the rest out on the sidewalk. "Oops, I think I spilled your soda. Sorry, bro."

DMarks was partly startled, partly afraid, and partly furious. Charlie stepped in, asking Will to lay off. Keeping his eyes fixed on DMarks, Will thrust his right hand out and shoved Charlie so hard that his feet actually left the ground as he tumbled backward over a sidewalk bench.

"Stay out of this, Riverton. This is between me and your friend here, the comedian."

Will's chest was heaving with anger-filled breaths as he snatched the paper bag out of DMarks's hand.

"And what's in here, little buddy? Why, it's a roast beef wedge, with lettuce, tomato and mayo, just the way I like it." He chomped a huge bite off the corner, then tossed the rest on the ground. "Wow, that was good, but I don't want to finish the whole thing. Got to watch my weight. It's bikini season," he said, laughing derisively.

DMarks could only take so much. With fire in his own eyes, he grit his teeth and shot back at Will Morris.

"Hey, jerk, don't you know there are people starving in this world? That's a waste of perfectly good food," he barked actually attempting to shove the older, bigger foe.

Will narrowed his eyes and shook his head at DMarks.

"You just don't know when to shut up, do you?"

DMarks was about to respond when a gusty breeze engulfed him. It had a calm, comforting effect.

At the exact same time, he noticed Lester Simpson, all six-foot-eight, 340-pounds of him coming out of Weldon's. The two made eye contact, and the former All-American from Ohio State sensed that something wasn't cool.

The hulking Giant handed his bag of food to Charlie, putting his index finger to his lips, signaling for him not to say anything.

Then, as though God arranged for him to be in that place at that time, he stalked straight up behind Will without making a sound.

Emboldened by what was happening, DMarks began to direct the dialogue with Will.

"Hey, Willy, let me introduce you to my friend Lester. You know, Lester Simpson of the New York Giants. He's standing right behind you."

"Ha! You think I'm going to fall for that one? Besides, Lester Simpson's overweight and washed up."

Folding his arms and cocking his eyebrow the Giants star just patiently waited to see what else Will might have to say.

"Yo, Willy, I'm telling ya, you should just shut up and walk away."

"And I'm telling you, if you keep calling me that name, you'll be crawling away," he said while giving out a major wrist burn. They guys looked on twisting in shared pain.

"That had to sting," said BB.

"Yeah, especially since his arms are kind of sunburned," noted George.

Charlie just looked on as things played out.

"I'm telling ya, Lester Simpson is standing right behind you and he doesn't look happy."

"You're such a weasel, Marks."

"Suit yourself, but one of us is right and the other is you."

"Lester Simpson, really? Even if he was here, you think I'm afraid of him? I could outrun him on one leg."

"Oh? So what are you saying?"

"I'm saying that he's a fat lineman who can't run for squat. If you ask me, Coach Arnsparger should cut him."

That did it. Lester Simpson was a gentle Giant, but he wasn't going to take any more of Will's badmouthing. Reaching out with his hulking arm, he scooped Will up and carried him like a tackling dummy, over to a nearby bench.

The shocked look of fear on Will's face was priceless as sweat stains began to appear all over his shirt. Lester called on the boys to come stand in front of their foe.

"I'll give you ten seconds to come up with a really good apology for these boys." Will looked nauseous from fear and humiliation. In the heat of the moment, he froze up.

"Ten, nine, eight, seven, six, five, *zero*!" yelled Lester, stepping on Will's foot, applying pressure.

"I'm sorry," Will blurted out.

"Sorry for what?" asked Lester.

"I'm sorry you brats are such little jerks."

Lester leaned forward on Will's foot, shifting his considerable weight.

"Don't test my patience," he said, bending down to look Will in the eyes. "Now, how about you try that again.

Will was sweating hard. "I'm sorry for taking your food."

"And..."

"I'm sorry for roughing him up."

"Okay, now cough up five bucks so my young friend here can go back inside and get lunch."

"But a wedge and a Coke only cost two-fifty," Will protested.

"Yeah, but I figure they're going to need to visit the good-humor man later this afternoon. And I know you'd love to treat."

In a total fit of frustration, Will dug into his pockets and managed to produce five crumpled dollars. He spat on the sidewalk and handed the pile to DMarks.

"Why thank you, bikini boy. That's ever so kind of you," said DMarks, oozing with fake southern charm.

Will was about to swing at DMarks when Lester grabbed his arm and pulled it behind his back.

"Have a nice day, boys. I'll see you at practice soon."

"Thanks, Lester. You're the man," said DMarks as they headed back into the deli. Joe Weldon, who had been leaning in the doorway watching the whole thing, brushed his hands on his apron, and gave DMarks a playful swat on his shoulder.

He chuckled. "This lunch is on me."

"Dude, you totally played Willy," cheered BB as they stepped back up to the counter. "That was rad!"

"Gimme five," said George.

Outside, Lester wasn't finished with Will. "Tell me, what's your name? Willy?" he asked sincerely.

"Will. Will Morris," he answered, shaking out his wrist.

"Well, I'll tell ya what, I like to have a little company when I eat. How's about you hang out with me right here on this bench?"

Will didn't have much choice.

"So you think us offensive linemen are slow?" Will just sat there, head down, not saying anything. He knew that he had already incriminated himself. Lester casually sat back as he ate.

"You play football?"

"Yes, sir."

"What's your time in the forty-yard dash?"

"Fifty seconds, flat," he answered proudly, sitting up straighter.

"Full pads?"

"No, helmet and shorts."

"Say, what? I clocked a four-forty in full pads," said Lester, crunching on a potato chip for emphasis.

Will was amazed, and he began to lighten up a bit.

"What do you bench press?" inquired Lester.

"Two fifty," Will said, sticking his chest out. "Most of anyone on varsity."

"Not bad. How many reps?"

"Five."

Just as Will answered the question, a car drove by with a few teenagers who noticed Lester. "Go, Giants!" they yelled.

"Five reps at two-fifty? Shoot, I warm up with twelve reps at three-ten." Will was now officially impressed. Lester looked him up and down, plunging his fork into a pint of potato salad.

"You have good size. I bet you can move pretty well, too. What positions do you play?"

"Quarterback and linebacker."

"So you run the huddle on offense and defense?"

"Yeah, pretty much."

"Well, you can't do that without the right attitude. You've got to focus on the positives and encourage your teammates. That stuff you pulled with the younger kids back there? Not cool and it'll come back to bite you someday."

"But you don't understand. They asked for it."

"That's what I mean, if you let others get in your head, you'll lose your focus, and you won't be any good at calling or making plays. How are you going to handle it if someone on the other team late hits you or something? You've got to roll with that sort of thing and rise above it." Will laughed. "You make it sound so easy."

"I know it's not easy." He put a hand on Will's shoulder. "But if you look at it the right way, a good challenge brings out the best in us."

While Lester was talking, Will had extremely mixed feelings. No one had ever talked with him like this when it came to sports, not even his father.

"By the way, your name sounds familiar. Any relation to the Will Morris who played ball in Wisconsin?"

"Yeah, actually. That's my dad. He was a linebacker too."

"He's a legend in the Big Ten. When I was at Ohio State, I heard a lot of stories about how hard he used to hit. Glad I never had to face him."

Will's eyes welled up, hearing an NFL player talk about his dad that way.

Lester was content that he got his point across. Sensing a need to lighten the mood, he held out his bag of chips.

"Betcha can't eat just one," he said with a smile.

10
CHAPTER

DATE NIGHT

There is no fear in love, but perfect love casts out fear.

—1 John 4:18

Parker Jones and Suzie Berkshire first got to know each after his house burned down two years prior, just before Christmas. She being the ace local realtor and he in need of guidance finding a new home, the two visited countless open houses together before Parker found a place over on Scarborough Road.

Suzie was tall, blond, and stylish in a contemporary way. Her wedge haircut, made famous by Dorothy Hamill, seemed to accent her lively, cheerful personality. High energy on the outside, she a heart of gold on the inside. Her infectious zest for life made her popular around town, and her smile could be seen from a mile away.

Parker, on the other hand, was more reserved. After the loss of his parents and his experiences in Vietnam, he had somewhat of a self-shielded disposition. Standing about six-foot-three, he filled out his tall frame with an athletic physique. Each day, he maintained his army fitness regimen of push-ups, sit-ups, pull-ups, and jogging. He had a high IQ and always gave thoughtful consideration to anything he said or did. When he smiled, the corners of his creased eyelids bespoke of a kind and considerate disposition.

The handsome couple had become the talk of the town. To celebrate the anniversary of their first date, Parker made dinner reservations at Maison Laffitte, an ultra-high-end French restaurant on the northern edge of town.

On their way there, Suzie's hand trembled slightly, so she slid it under her thigh. But that seemed to trigger her foot to start tapping. She then rummaged through her purse, opened her compact to check her lipstick. Smacking her lips, she snapped it closed and stuffed it back in. With bracelets clattering, she then ran her fingers through her hair unable to keep her nervous energy at bay. *Get a grip!* she thought to herself.

As they arrived in the parking lot, Suzie cleared her throat and looked ardently at Parker.

"Umm, you know, people usually only come to this place for really special occasions," she hinted, batting her baby blues at him.

What's she up to? he wondered.

"Right, well, it was two years ago when we first started dating. I'd say that's pretty special."

Suzie's head tilted slightly as she squinted her eyes trying to read his expression. Ever the optimist, she was hoping perhaps that he might be planning to propose that night.

"That's what I mean, silly. Twenty-four months is a pretty long time for two people to be dating."

"And that makes me the luckiest guy in Briarcliff. Two whole years with one fantastic lady," he replied while getting out of the car so he could run around and open the door for her.

Suzie slumped in the passenger seat. *Ugh, he's a smart, gorgeous, capable man, but romantic he ain't.* Still, she stepped out and gave him a peck on the cheek with a big Suzie smile.

"Thank you, Parker. You're a complete gentleman."

He took her arm, locking it around his, and together, they walked through the colonial gardens to the front entrance of the elegant eatery. There, they were greeted by a tuxedoed, very French maître d'.

"*Bonjour, bonsoir*! So happy to see you." He bowed effusively.

"Hi. Reservation for Jones," Suzie piped up.

Parker smiled, shaking his head good-naturedly. *She's beautiful, smart and loveable, but subtle she ain't,* he thought.

Suzie was very successful and was used to being on her own and doing for herself. Parker drew energy and inspiration from her and her liberated ways, but that night, he wanted to take charge and was determined to fuss over her so that she could feel special.

"*Oui! Oui!* We have a lovely table for two near the south portico with a view of the Hudson River. *Spectaculaire vue!*" responded the maître d' with exquisite French flair. "Please, right this way." Tucking the leather-bound menus under his arm, he led them to their table.

The happy couple settled into the romantic alcove. Right away, Suzie reached out to hold Parker's hands, barely able to contain her delight.

The waiter arrived shortly after to take their drink orders.

"*Bonsoir.* Good evening. May I have the bartender prepare something for you?"

Suzie was about to blurt something out when Parker put his finger to her lips.

"Yes, thank you, sir. The lady and I will have Kir Royales with Perrier-Jouët, please."

"An excellent choice, monsieur," replied the waiter, clearly impressed with Parker's taste. "I shall return shortly," he said with a bow.

"Champagne? You ordered champagne for us?" Suzie nearly burst with joy. *Maybe he is romantic. Maybe tonight is the night.*

"I thought you might like that, plus, we have a lot to celebrate." *I love when she's happy*, he thought.

They enjoyed a few quiet moments before their drinks arrived. The waiter skillfully recited the specials for the evening and assured them he'd be back momentarily. Parker raised his glass and gazed at Susie. "It feels like I've been slowly finding my way to you my whole life."

Suzie felt dizzy from what she just heard and had to grab the sides of the table to keep herself from sliding off her chair.

Picking up the menu to fan herself, she tried collect her thoughts. "I... I'm not usually speechless like this."

"I've noticed," Parker replied with a smile.

"It's just, well, that's the most romantic thing anyone's ever said to me."

"And you're the only person I've ever wanted to say that to." He reached over to caress her hand as they sipped their champagne.

When the waiter returned, Suzy motioned to her menu and said, "For an appetizer I'd like—" Parker once again put his finger to her lips.

"The lady will start with chilled gazpacho, followed by the chicken croquette. For myself, I'd like the brie with cranberry chutney, followed by the filet mignon."

"And how would monsieur like his filet prepared?" inquired the waiter.

"However the chef recommends," replied Parker.

The waiter nodded back, giving Parker a gratified look. "Excellent choices, monsieur, *le plus excellent*." He bowed as he left to head back to the kitchen.

Suzie was intoxicated by Parker ordering for her with such confidence. She looked around to see if any of the other diners noticed, smiling proudly. As they continued to hold hands and chat, her mind weaved in and out of focus. *At this rate, maybe I'll ask him to marry me!*

Before long, their food arrived. With each bite, they agreed that it more than lived up to its vaunted reputation. As wonderful as the food was, they both knew that they could be equally happy eating TV dinners off their laps. After a decadent dessert of pears belle Hélène and chocolate souffle, they strolled onto the back patio.

The stars were glimmering in the moonless sky and the air was filled with the scent of honeysuckle. They leaned against each other, gazing out at the river. In that moment, Parker felt a beautiful, floral breeze.

"May I have this dance?" he asked.

Suzie glanced sideways at him, wondering if the champagne might have made him a bit tipsy.

"But there's no music."

"You don't hear it?" he asked, looking deep into her eyes.

After a long, curious pause, she began to catch on. "Oh, wait a minute, maybe I do, faintly."

He took her in his arms and began to softly sing "Your Song" by Elton John. Suzie went into a full swoon, nestling against his chest.

"I hope you don't mind that I put down in words…how wonderful life is, when you're in my world," whispered Parker in her ear, dipping Suzie backward and kissing her softly.

As he pulled her back up into his arms, his mouth spoke spontaneously what his heart was feeling.

"I think I'm in love with you, Suzie," he professed for the first time.

Suzie's eyes lit up. "I know I'm in love with you," she replied without hesitation. "I like your last name. Maybe we can go halves on it someday?"

"Someday," Parker replied, wiggling an eyebrow at her.

Suzie couldn't contain herself and rocked him with a passionate, prolonged kiss right in the middle of the patio. Soon, Parker was the one arched backward.

Inside the restaurant, the other diners had witnessed the entire scene and broke into spontaneous applause, a few of them standing. Even the waitresses and waiters stopped to enjoy the affectionate embrace.

Always one to celebrate romance, the restaurant owner himself broke open a vintage bottle of Grand Marnier.

"*Vive l'amour!*" he shouted going from table to table filling liqueur glasses so that everyone could toast to life and love.

Suzie and Parker, oblivious to the world around them, were lost in their own magical moment. Finally looking up, they noticed all the smiling faces and raised glasses.

"Wait, what just happened?" Suzie asked.

"Love. Love just happened." He grinned, pulling her close for another deep kiss.

11

CHAPTER

FORGIVE US OUR TRESPASSES

If we confess our sins, he is faithful and just to forgive us our sins and to cleanse us from all unrighteousness.

—1 John 1:9

Charlie loved taking care of the Cuthbertson's yard. The husband was an avid golfer, and he had a putting green out back. He was also a generous tipper and often invited Charlie to take a few puts with him.

After cutting their grass, he rode his bike up town to the Manor Barbershop. It was so hot that day, he thought about getting a crew-cut like in his younger years.

Squeezing the hand breaks on his bike, he skidded to a stop on the sidewalk outside. Wheeling the front tire of his bike into the bike rack, and footing the kickstand, dialed the combination on his lock, and secured his bike.

There was no way to enter the barbershop unnoticed. Not only did the bell hanging above the door ring out each time someone arrived, the family of Italian barbers themselves were always so happy to greet everyone.

"Charlie! *Mio giovane ragazzo.* Long time no see," welcomed John, the head barber.

In return for the friendly attention they always gave him, Charlie made it a point to learn a few phrases in Italian.

"*Lavoro, lavoro! Fare soldi.*"

"Ah, you work, you make money." Nick nodded.

"You a good boy," added Nat.

Charlie just smiled as he looked for a recent issue of *Sports Illustrated* on the magazine table. But all he could find was the current issue of *Time Magazine.* It had a bold headline that read The New Quest for Peace with a cover-sized photo of Anwar Sadat. He didn't think anything of it at first as he picked it up and found a seat to wait his turn. It wasn't his normal reading material, but his parents had been encouraging him to learn about current events.

"It's a good thing you here, Charlie. If your hair gets any longer, they make you wear a bathing cap at the pool," teased Nat, "like your cutie pie girlfriend."

Over in Joe's barber chair, Mr. Smythe was sitting comfortably, engaging him in warm conversation. The gentle and quiet barber had become his favorite, so Smythe always waited until he was available for a clip and trim.

"I'm afraid I don't have as much hair as I used to," said Smythe, running his hand over his balding pate.

"You no worry. I cover things up for you." Joe laughed, dropping his barber towel on top of his head.

"Not sure that will be possible, my friend. I used to have waves. Pretty soon, all I'll have is beach."

Nat signaled Charlie to let him know it was his turn. He got up and settled into the barber's chair. *Here it comes,* Charlie thought as Nat draped an apron over him.

Spinning the chair around, Nat looked right at Charlie, comb in one hand, scissors in the other. "I give-a you first haircut right in this very chair. Remember that, Charlie? Sat you on a leather block."

All four of the barbers claimed to have given Charlie his first haircut and each time he came in, they all told him so. By now, Charlie was used to playing along.

"Sure do," he replied. "The razor made me cry. But then you gave me a lollipop." *They'll be doing this when I'm forty.* Charlie smiled to himself.

"So tell me, what's all this lavoro?" asked Nat.

"Oh, just a bunch of yard jobs around the neighborhood. You know, grass cutting, gardening, trimming."

"A landscaper! Ats a noble profession, Charlie. My grandfather and my father were the two best landscapers in Pisa."

"Our hometown. God bless!" shouted Joe as all four barbers stopped to make the sign of the cross.

"Not sure I'd go so far as to refer to myself as a landscaper," said Charlie.

"You gotta start somewhere," said Nat, reaching out, cupping his hands and pitching his shoulders. "You and me, we do similar work. I clip hair and you clip grass."

As Joe finished up, he dusted the back of Mr. Smythe's neck with talcum powder. Smythe got out of the chair, patted Joe on the shoulder, and pressed a ten-dollar bill in his hand.

"Bless you, Mr. Smythe," he said, clasping his hands in a prayer-like way.

Mr. Smythe then stopped at Nat's chair. "Charlie, maybe you can come do some yard work at my house. Mrs. Smythe always has a list of projects to be done."

"Sure thing, Mr. Smythe."

"How much do you charge per hour, son?"

"Oh, about a buck-fifty."

Mr. Smythe drew back and looked disapprovingly at Charlie. "That will never do, young man. If you come to work for me, it will be two-fifty per hour and not a penny less."

"Gosh, thanks, Mr. Smythe. I'll put the difference in the offering plate at church."

"Well, good then. I'll have my better half phone at your house later today," he said.

After paying at the cash register, he waived to the barbers and wished them well. As Mr. Smythe walked across Pleasantville Road to where his Lincoln was parked, the barbers all looked at each other, raised their eyebrows, and pursed their mouths into matching downward smiles.

"Who woulda thought that mean paisano from a few years ago would end up being mayor of Briarcliff?" asked Nat.

"And the nicest man in town," added Joe, as all the barbers bent their heads in agreement. "*Vai a capire*! Go figure," said Nick, snapping his towel.

A few minutes later, Charlie was done as well. As he paid at the register, John told him to take two pieces of Bazooka Joe from the large glass canister. "One for you. One for the girlfriend. You can blow bubbles together."

"Kiss first. Bubbles second!" shouted Nat.

Charlie did his best to smile as the brothers always managed to make him blush. "Thanks, guys. See you next time."

"He a good boy. Gives me hope for the future," said Joe, looking at his brothers. "You three? Not so much."

Charlie could hear the laughter as he stepped outside. Then, just as he slid his foot across the kickstand, the headline on that issue of *Time Magazine* came rushing back to the forefront of his mind. *It might have pertained to the Middle East, but it could apply right here in Briarcliff too,* he thought.

He turned his bike and got ready to ride. Then, he was halted again by the thought that maybe the magazine cover had a special message from Sky. It was easy for him to conclude that Sky would want them to seek peace with Will Morris. But both sides had to be willing. Then, it was almost as though he heard Sky's voice interject. It wasn't audible, but it was very real: *If Egypt and Israel were trying to make peace, so can you guys.*

It occupied his mind as he hopped on his bike and rode down through the town center, passing by Janniello's Market and Manor Wines, where Tom and Fran were setting up for an afternoon wine-tasting.

The sun warmed his skin as he glided along carefree with the wind refreshing his face. As he rode along, he hummed the theme song used by the New York Yankees during their broadcast games. Then, out of nowhere came a shocking and very rude awakening. Will Morris jumped out from behind a tree and practically clotheslined him. Charlie jammed on his brakes, heart pounding, uncertain of what just happened.

"Nice haircut, Riverton. Did you get that over at the beauty parlor?"

With a racing mind, Charlie was too frightened to make eye contact. All he could think to do was to try to inch his bike forward to move around the menacing bully.

"Not so fast," said Will, grabbing Charlie by the arm practically cutting off his circulation. "Listen up, gingersnap. You and your chump friends better wise up quick or one of these days, you're gonna end up in the emergency room over at Phelps Hospital. Got that?"

Charlie tried not to show it, but he was genuinely scared. He couldn't believe how brazen Will was being right there in the middle of town. Usually, there were people all around, going from store to store. *Where is everyone?* he wondered.

"Don't think that your little friendship with Lester Simpson's gonna save you all summer long," growled Will.

Then, he snatched the Yankees cap right off Charlie's head and flung up the sidewalk.

"See that hat, Riverton? Better stay clear of me, or the next time your hat goes flying, you'll still be wearing it."

The fear Charlie felt was changing over to humiliation and anger. He wanted to strike back, but he knew that would be unwise. He also wanted to follow Sky's guidance and instruction, but in the heat of the moment, that didn't seem quite possible.

Then, like an answer to prayer, Parker Jones came walking out of Wonderous Things jewelry and gift shop. He was carrying a small box. Parker spotted Charlie and sensed right away that something wasn't quite right. Changing directions, he walked straight over, dress shoes clip-clopping on the brick sidewalk.

"Hi, Charlie. What's going on?" he asked, stepping up to face Will Morris nose to nose, with unblinking eye contact.

"Great to see you, Parker. Everything's fine, thanks for checking in. I just have to pick up my hat over there, then I'm heading to the pool." Charlie felt kind of pleased by his effort to keep the peace instead of snitching out Will.

Parker was an especially perceptive individual. He had to be in order to have led a whole battalion in Vietnam. He also had nerves of steel which he put to work staring Will down.

The standoff seemed to last forever. But as angry as Will was, it was rare for a teenager to show disrespect to an adult back in those days. Rivers of sweat began to stream down his forehead and off his brow. Swallowing hard, he stepped backward with a clenched jaw, then turned to walk away.

Parker put his hand on Charlie's shoulder.

"Wow, Parker, you came just in the nick of time," said Charlie.

"What's going on with him?" He nodded in Will's retreating direction.

"Oh, we just seem to be getting in each other's way these days."

"Listen, Charlie, every town has a guy like him. Hopefully, he'll wise up before someone gets hurt."

As the two chatted, Charlie noticed the small package Parker was carrying.

"What's the occasion?" he asked.

"Oh, this?" asked Parker, breaking eye contact with Charlie.

"It's nothing," he answered, suppressing a grin.

"Something special for Suzie?"

"Ahh, kind of… I think she'll like it." He looked back up to see Charlie flashing a huge, telling smile.

"Okay, guess I'll see you around town then. Thanks again, Parker. You're the man."

"Okay, buddy. Have fun at the pool."

"We always do."

Charlie glided through the main village area outside the long row of shops. As he zipped along, he deliberately steered his bike over the sheet metal trap doors in the sidewalk, which provided a springy bounce while making a loud rumbling noise.

Eventually, he came to the steep incline near the police station and let his feet of the pedals as his momentum took him the rest of the way ever faster.

"Hey, slow down, Charlie! I don't want to give you a speeding ticket," yelled Officer DiLoreto who was washing one of the squad cars out front.

When Charlie arrived at the pool, he headed inside to where DMarks, as usual, was holding court by the diving boards.

Apparently, the custodians had left a small window at ground level partly open over at the middle school. To DMarks, it was an invitation for the group to take a trip down memory lane.

"Memory what?" asked BB.

"Memory lane, you dork. Don't you have any sentimentality?"

"Ahh, no. As a matter of fact, I don't. And by the way, you have no business using SAT words like that."

"What is this, *Mister Roger's Neighborhood* all of the sudden?" teased George.

"What are you up this time?" asked Charlie.

"What I'm up to, Charles, is this. We all know what the middle school was like when school was in. Let's take advantage of this opportunity to see what it's like when school's out."

Somehow, the notion caught everyone's attention.

"Ya know, it would be kind of cool to sneak inside for a quick visit. I know it's only been a few weeks, but I kind of miss the place," confessed George.

"Are you guys forgetting that the school is off limits? That's why they posted No Trespassing signs," warned Charlie shaking his head side to side.

"Here we go. Briarcliff's very own Richie Cunningham doesn't want to break any rules in the name of having fun," heckled DMarks.

"Rules are there for our own safety." Charlie wasn't taking the bait.

"Great. So let's just hang around here and do the same old thing."

As DMarks chided his friend, Michelle and a bunch of the girls came walking by.

"Ladies! Anyone up for a little adventure this afternoon?" inquired DMarks

"Is this the episode where you take out your Binaca in case you might get kissed?" teased Andrea.

"You have a one-track mind," declared Robin.

"Whoa, whoa, whoa. I think you're getting a little ahead of yourselves, although I like where you're going."

"Okay, spill. What do you have in mind?" asked Michelle, looking way too cute in her cut-off jean shorts.

"My associates and I were thinking about taking a self-guided tour of the old middle school."

Looking at each other with half smiles and tilted heads, the girls thought about the idea. They had no specific plan for the afternoon.

"It would be kind of cool going in and out of our old classrooms," said Gretchen.

"That's the spirit! The only question is whether or not any of these Goody Two-shoes will be joining us." DMarks shot an expectant look at BB, Charlie, and George.

Michelle arched her eyebrows at them. "What do you think? It'd be something different."

"C'mon, Charles. I'll even autograph one of the No Trespassing signs for you," said DMarks.

"I don't feel right about this, but someone has to be there when this pork chop gets everyone in trouble," cautioned Charlie.

"Okay then, welcome to the team. Now listen up. Here's the plan. BB and George, you head over to the middle school and act real casual while you scope out the area. Then Charlie and I will follow. Once we make sure that no one's watching, we can roll into action."

"At what point do you self-destruct?" joked Charlie.

"Okay, I'm just going to let that one pass," huffed DMarks.

He turned to the girls. "Give us five minutes, then start walking. Got that?"

"10-4 BJ and the Bear," said Michelle.

Looking at the guys, he nodded his head. "One for the money, two for the show. Let's make tracks."

"Umm, I don't think that's how the saying goes," mentioned George, which earned another impatient look from D'Marks.

"Duh!" he replied with a flick of his finger to the back of George's ear.

The plan rolled into motion and moments later, everyone regrouped outside the band/orchestra room trying to stay out of sight. DMarks slid through the window first so he could help the girls land on their feet inside.

"You better watch your hands," warned Robin, holding her jean skirt with both hands.

"Yeah, no monkey business," added Andrea.

"Ladies, please, I'm only interested in your safety."

One by one, they all shimmied through with Charlie going last. The sensation of being in the empty school building surrounded by the sounds of silence were at first fascinating. Giggling and glancing at each other, they tiptoed out into the main commons area.

Being there brought on a rush of evocative feelings. The air was cool and motionless. It was almost like they were in a strange, vaguely familiar time warp. Yet in their minds, they could see all the familiar sights and hear all the sounds that had been part of their everyday lives for the last three years in what otherwise was a constantly kinetic place to be.

Stepping tentatively, they wandered downstairs looking and acting like burglars peering in and out of classrooms and darting in and out of the shadows. As if in church, they were trying to laugh silently and failing, which only made them laugh louder.

It would be major trouble if they were caught inside the school building. But the sense of adventure and the thought of getting away with it was enough to suppress any hint of caution. Rambling along, they eventually ended up in the hallway outside Mr. Saltzman's shop room and Mr. Webber's art room.

"Look, guys. We made all our Christmas presents in these two rooms each of the last three years," said Gretchen.

"I can still remember the first cutting board I made in shop class," recalled George. "Nearly lost a fingertip on that sanding machine."

"And those macramé plant holders we made?" asked Robin. "My mother loved hers."

On their way over to the other wing of the building, they each instinctively stopped at their old lockers and dialed the combinations. DMarks stayed out in front of the group acting like a ranger on lookout.

As they passed by the auditorium. BB walked over to the entrance doors, closing one eye and squinting through the vertical gap where the heavy double doors met. It looked empty inside. Gripping the door handle, he gave a cautious tug. To everyone's surprise, it was not locked. They rushed to file in, as the doors closed with a whoosh behind them.

The auditorium was cavernous and was used for school plays and musicals, special assemblies, local elections, community meetings, and more. The rows of seats could fit about 250 people in front of a huge stage framed in smartly carved mahogany. Tall half-moon windows lined both sides of the space and welcomed daylight streaming through which illuminated the dust they were kicking up.

DMarks hopped on stage and stood front and center. "To be or not to be, that is the question," he bellowed, arms outstretched.

"First, he sings Harry Chapin. Now he's quoting Shakespeare?" snorted George.

"Is that Shakespeare? I thought it was the Fonz," replied Andrea.

"You guys have no culture," kidded DMarks, heading back behind the heavy curtain.

The rest of the group glanced back up the aisle at the doors, wondering if they were going too far. But backstage had always held a special appeal, darkly lit, mysterious and rambling with all manner of backdrops, spotlights, hooks, and gaffs. They all migrated in that direction.

"Remember when we'd have to get up on this stage with the Glee Club and sing for parents during back-to-school nights?" asked Michelle.

"Torture, pure torture," complained George.

"Check out all these props. I think they were left over from the last Senior High Variety Show," noticed Charlie. Among other things, they found a fake skeleton, a full set of knight's armor, an extra-large rocking horse, and a few director's chairs.

As the group rummaged around, Michelle stumbled across a large trunk. She opened the lid, which released a musty, musky scent from stored costumes and pulled out a Cleopatra wig and headdress. "How do I look?" she asked slipping it on, turning to Charlie in a regal way.

"The queen of Egypt meets Popeye," he responded as he reached in to put on a sailor's cap and neckwear.

Everyone got into the act. DMarks was walking around in a full-length fur coat and turban while Andrea donned a baseball jersey and cap. Gretchen wrapped a boa around her neck and put on a pair of sleeve length white gloves. BB opted for a top hat and cane and shuffled a little dance for everyone. George grabbed a cowboy hat and leather vest with a sheriff's badge.

They threw caution to the wind and began having laugh-out-loud fun as they each made-up silly lines based on the different costumes they were wearing.

DMarks found some levers in the wings of the main stage. Shoving them upward the whole area was suddenly lit with spotlights.

Almost simultaneously, the double doors at the back of the auditorium flung open. It was one of the janitors making his rounds, pulling his bucket-on-wheels with keys jangling off his belt.

The gang was jolted back to reality as they froze in place.

"Ditch it!" yelped DMarks.

Everyone scattered and crouched behind whatever props they could find. But it was too late, they were in clear sight.

"Hey! What are you kids doing up there?" the janitor called out.

"Quick you guys. Drop the costumes and follow me," said DMarks as he flung off his fur coat and sprinted out stage left. They each jumped up and followed along with costumes flying everywhere.

DMarks shoved the horizontal bar on the emergency exit door, and they fled down the three-story exterior fire escape, feet pounding on the metal-grate steps. Once on the ground, they bolted around the back of the building and raced toward the pool.

As they zipped inside, James Dennis was there, twirling his whistle around his index finger.

"Something tells me you've been up to something," he snorted.

"Yeah, well, we're an up kind of bunch," spat out DMarks without breaking stride.

Some of the girls ducked into the bathroom. The boys dove right into the pool to hide underwater hoping the janitor might give up his pursuit.

Once the coast was clear, they all met up on the hillside behind the diving boards.

"I've heard of exiting stage left, but that was literally exiting stage left," said George.

"I got to hand it to you, Marks, if you hadn't thought to use the fire escape, we would have gotten in a ton of trouble," BB congratulated him.

"Thanks for getting us in and out of trouble," quipped Charlie. "Now, about that autographed No Trespassing sign…"

"Hey, no one got hurt. No damage was done," boasted DMarks.

"Yeah, well, I think that was enough excitement for the day," said Michelle.

"I'm with you," affirmed Robin.

They each felt a strange combination of exhilaration and guilt for having broken the rules. Everyone agreed that the next time they'd step foot inside a school building it would be the first day of ninth grade come September.

12

CHAPTER

SUMMER BROTHERS

Iron sharpens iron and one man sharpens another.

—Proverbs 27:17

Going out after dinner during daylight savings was automatic. There was so much to do and being outside during twilight hours came with a different kind of multisensory experience.

Since the pool stayed open till dark, Charlie and the guys often rode over to Law Park after dinner. Not many people swam at night, so they had the pool mostly to themselves.

That summer, they noticed an older couple who came to the pool several nights each week. While the husband mostly used the diving board, the wife swam laps.

The boys were impressed with the advanced skills the husband had on the diving board. Charlie marveled at his concentration, executing perfect swan, pike and back dives, one after another.

One night, the guys were playing Marco Polo when Charlie felt a strong desire to introduce himself.

"Guys, let's take a break. I want to go say hello."

"Of course he wants to go make some new friends. Never mind that we're in the middle of a game here," complained DMarks.

In response, Charlie buried DMarks's face with an impressive hand splash. He then swam to the other side of the pool underwater so that he wouldn't have to listen to any harassment.

When he reached the diving area, the older gentleman was standing by the three-meter board looking out at the water, contemplating his next dive.

"Excuse me, sir, I wanted to introduce myself. My name's Charlie, Charlie Riverton," he said, hoisting himself over the side of the pool and onto the deck. It was a point of honor among the boys to never use the ladder.

"Hello, young man, my name is Walter Ransom. It's nice to meet you," he said, extending his hand.

"My friends and I were admiring your diving skills. You get such lift off the board and your form is perfect."

"You're very kind, Charlie. Thank you. I've been diving since I was your age or younger, and trust me, that's a very long time," said Mr. Ransom, laughing heartily.

"Where did you learn to dive?"

"Well, Charlie, all credit goes to my uncle. He taught me how to swim and dive when I was a young child. Seems like yesterday, but that was back in the 1920s."

Charlie was intrigued. Mr. Hunt covered the Roaring Twenties in his social studies class last semester.

"Every afternoon, he'd walk me and my brothers through the woods to the Briarcliff Lodge."

"The Lodge? You mean where the King's College is today?"

"The one and only. What a grand place it was. The grounds, the views of the Hudson River, the food. My uncle always said that only the best was good enough for Briarcliff!" *Uncle?* The wheels were turning in Charlie's head.

"It was quite a place. So many famous people coming and going all the time. We used to love watching Babe Ruth hit golf balls."

"*The Babe?*" Charlie was about to ask another question when he was pegged in the back of the head with a tennis ball. He spun around to the sight of his three buddies looking innocent as could be. Shaking his head, he returned his attention to Mr. Ransom.

"Yes, sir. Such a nice man. Sometimes, he'd buy hot dogs and ice cream for us kids."

Now Charlie's mind was racing. "Are you from Briarcliff, Mr. Ransom?"

"Originally, yes. I grew up on Scarborough Road in the large white house across from the main entrance to King's."

"The replica of Mount Vernon? That's such a cool house."

"Yes, that's the one. My mother's sister, Georgianna Ransom, married my uncle Walter. Walter Law. He founded Briarcliff Manor, and he also built and operated the Lodge."

Charlie was bowled over. An actual descendant of Walter Law right there, right in front of him. His curiosity was totally peeked when a sudden splash broke his focus. It was DMarks landing a perfect cannonball just a few yards away.

"I remember the time Uncle Walter arranged for the Olympic swimming trials to be held in the giant Roman pool at the Lodge. It's just a big old pond now, but in its day, it was quite a showplace. Johnny Weissmuller himself came to compete." Charlie looked at the man speechless. *Tarzan?*

"Esther Williams used to stay at the Lodge, too. She was beautiful and we used any excuse to watch her swim. She gave us kids diving tips."

"Where do you live now, Mr. Ransom?" Out of the corner of his eye, Charlie spotted the guys moving toward them. Sporting flowered bathing caps they must have pulled out of the Lost and Found, they did a series of mock water ballet moves, squirting water from their mouths and splashing their feet. He folded his arms and turned his back to them.

"Actually, we live in South Carolina, but each summer, we come up this way to beat the heat. Dr. Cook at The King's College is kind enough to let us live in a suite of rooms in the old Briarcliff Lodge building while classes are out."

"I've never actually been inside the Lodge building, but it's awesome to look at whenever we ride our bikes through campus."

"It was one of my uncle's pet projects way back at the turn of the century. He spared no expense."

Charlie was completely absorbed by every word.

The man continued, "Me and the missus like to come down here to the pool for night swimming. I can recall doing the same at Gooseneck Pond right over there before this pool was built." He pointed to the left.

"Wow, well, we don't swim in Gooseneck anymore, but we play hockey there during the winter months."

"Glad to hear. That was the place to be on winter afternoons when I was a boy."

Charlie felt like he could have listened for hours, but the rest of the guys were unrelenting.

"Yoo-hoo, Charlie!" cooed DMarks. "We're waiting."

"Mr. Ransom, it's really nice to meet you, sir. Maybe you can give me some pointers on the diving board sometime."

"Great way to meet girls," said Mr. Ransom with a broad, gracious smile.

They shook hands. Then Charlie ran down the deck to bomb his friends with a huge can opener.

"Welcome back, Charles. Now that you've done your good deed for the day, maybe we can all get back to what we came here for?" chided DMarks.

"Hey, Marks, why don't you find your Off button and use it," said Charlie, dunking him as the boys gathered in a huddle.

The normal fun and games resumed for a while more, but before long, they decided to towel off and head out on their bikes around town.

On their way out of the pool area, they made cattails with their dampened towels. BB had a gift for twisting his so tight and flicking it so sharp that it made a taut snapping noise. It was no fun being stung by a cattail, so the guys had to stay on their toes as they raced to their bikes.

Up the hillside, they rode and over the ridge near the war memorial. As they sped through Law Park, DMarks noticed some of their classmates being dropped off at the Parish Hall at Briarcliff Congregational for dance class.

"Guys, check it out. We're in our bathing suits and those poor suckers are in suit suits," observed DMarks.

"Man, if my mom made me go to dance class, I'd intentionally sprain an ankle," said BB.

"I say we take a closer look," suggested DMarks.

They rode over to the back side of the Parish Hall and ditched their bikes behind a row of evergreens. Ducking down, they shimmied along, commando style on their knees and elbows. Peeking in the tall, rectangular windows they saw girls in nice dresses and white gloves sitting on one side of the meeting hall and boys in their Sunday shoes, sitting on the other side looking nervous.

"The guys all look so uncomfortable," said Charlie.

"Well, how would you feel if you had to get up, walk across the floor, and ask a girl to dance right in front of everyone?" whispered BB.

"I heard that Mr. Richards, the instructor guy, has them go up to the chaperones and introduce themselves and say all these 'How do you dos'," said George. "I think they have to bow or something too."

"Poor bastards," added DMarks.

The guys could hear everything through the screen windows. As "Time in a Bottle" by Jim Croce began to play, they cackled at how some of guys inside got tongue-tied asking girls to dance.

Meanwhile, unbeknownst to them, Reverend Higgins was walking around the grounds, "putting the church to bed" as he liked to say. When he heard some murmuring in the bushes across the parking lot. He stopped to see what was going on.

Realizing that someone was up to no good, he slipped off one of his shoes, then ran in across the pavement so they'd think he was walking instead of running. The boys tried to scatter, but thanks to the reverend's clever approach, he was already just a few steps away.

"Stop right where you are!" he shouted, but they kept running. "Go ahead and run, but you have to come back to your bikes sooner or later. I'm prepared to stay here all night if I have to," he continued loudly, bending down to put his shoe back on.

After a brief but panicky standoff, Charlie knew they had to come clean. Shamefaced, he came out from behind a glen of evergreens.

"Why, Charlie Riverton, I'm surprised at you," the reverend admonished, hands on his hips and shaking his head."

I'm sorry, Reverend Higgins, we meant no harm, we were just trying to—"

"Stop right there, mister. I know what you were up to. You were making fun of your friends. Well, the joke's on you. The fact is, you don't know what you're missing. I remember dance class myself. That's where I learned to polka."

The boys bit their tongues to keep from laughing. The idea of putting on a jacket and tie to stand around sipping punch and asking girls to dance was incomprehensible to them, especially as an alternative to swimming and riding bikes and popping wheelies.

"You kids these days. You don't get it. That's how we used to win over girls back when good manners counted."

The guys looked down to avoid eye contact with Reverend Higgins.

"As first offenders, I'll let you off the hook this time. Now get on your bikes and stop disturbing the peace around here."

"Thank you, Reverend Higgins," said Charlie as the boys sped off, relieved that no one was going to call their parents.

They cruised up Pleasantville Road and down to the Tree Streets, taking a detour to the basketball court at Jackson Road Park. Coasting to a stop at center court, they were riding high on adrenaline from wiggling off the hook outside dance class.

"We still got an hour before curfew. What should we do?" asked DMarks.

Realizing that they were directly across the street from the Roman's house, they decided on ding dong ditch.

For whatever their reasons, the Romans didn't seem to enjoy the sights and sounds of kids playing in the neighborhood. That was especially the case on Halloween night, when they stiffed all the trick-or-treaters.

Sneaking across the street, they made their way up the walkway to the house and rang the doorbell. After that, it was every man for himself as they each sprinted off, diving into the shadows.

Mr. Roman answered the door. When he saw that no one was there, he stepped out onto the front stoop to look around. Sporting an intense frown and shaking his fist in the air. It was clear that he was not amused.

The boys were huddled in the dark, filled with nervous energy.

"Let's do it again to see if the old lady answers this time," whispered DMarks.

"Nah, let's move on. So many doorbells, so little time," BB whispered back.

"Dude, have you forgotten about the time they called the police because we were making too much noise playing basketball?"

"My man, you have to let that go," Charlie said in a hushed tone.

"Nothin' doin'. I'm going back for a little revenge." DMarks crawled out of the shadows and up to the front door.

"His day-glow swimsuit might not have been the best choice for this caper," observed BB.

What they didn't know was that Mr. Roman suspected someone was up to no good. After returning inside, he went out the back door and tiptoed around the side of the house. In his right hand was a rotten tomato he had snatched from his vegetable garden.

He peered around the corner of his house, watching and waiting. Then, just as DMarks's pointed finger was about to ring the doorbell, Mr. Roman jumped out and threw a perfect strike, nailing DMarks right in the eye.

Down he went, not knowing what hit him. When he put his hand to his face, he saw red ooze and assumed he was bleeding. In a panic, he got to his feet and stumbled back across the street to where the guys were.

"That's right, you better run! And don't come back or you'll get worse!" yelled Mr. Roman.

"I'm hit," DMarks yelled as he dropped to the ground like a scene from *Combat.* "My eye. How bad is it?"

The boys came rushing over to him. It was dark, and it did look like he was bleeding.

"Guys, this looks serious," said Charlie. "Someone get a bike light so we can get a better look."

George hustled over to grab his bike and tilted the light down toward DMarks's face.

"I can't believe I took one in the eye again," he complained as he laid flat on his back.

"Geeze, it's the same eye from the suntan lotion incident," said George.

"I'll probably never see out of it again. Quick, someone call an ambulance."

"I think I see blood, you guys. Maybe we should get him to the hospital," declared Charlie.

"Wait a minute," said BB after taking a closer look. He reached out and swiped his finger across DMarks's cheekbone. Then, he sniffed and tasted the tip of his finger. "That's not blood. You got pegged with a tomato you pansy."

"What the heck are you talking about?" replied DMarks.

"The old man beaned you with a rotten tomato."

The guys looked at BB. "You sure?" asked Charlie.

"Trust me, my grandmother grows tomatoes in our backyard each year. I know what they smell and taste like."

The guys were relieved, so they treated themselves to a huge laugh at DMarks's expense.

"You deserve an Academy Award for that performance," declared George.

"Yeah, for a while there, you had us thinking you were actually hurt," grumbled BB.

"I can't believe you let Mr. Roman Chef Boyardee you," teased Charlie.

DMarks felt humiliated and more than a little bit embarrassed. "I'll show that old man who he's messing with," he said through grit teeth.

Getting to his feet, he stood staring at the house, breathing deeply with a wild look in his eyes. His mind ran the gamut of payback possibilities: toilet paper in his trees, shaving cream all over his windows, a deflated car tire or two.

But then, he was distracted by a strong, floral breeze. In an instant, his state of mind seemed to completely flip. He was overcome with a sense of guilt, as an uncharacteristic feeling rose up from his heart.

The guys looked on as DMarks's body language shifted right in front of them.

"What's up with him?" asked BB.

"Beats me," replied George. "Oh, DMarks, hello?"

But Charlie sensed something special was happening as he looked on with an understanding gaze.

"I'll be right back you guys," DMarks said, wiping his eye with his T-shirt. "I need to go apologize."

The boys looked at each other in shocked silence, wondering if they had heard him correctly.

"What? You've never apologized for anything in your whole life," scoffed BB.

"Yeah, not even that time when you hit Mrs. Kramer in the mouth with a hockey puck and knocked her two front teeth out," remembered George.

While the others were chiding DMarks, Charlie stood back, took it in and smiled on the inside. Something was working on his friend's heart and mind.

"Sometimes, a man's got to do what a man's got to do," countered DMarks.

BB and George looked at each other with raised eyebrows.

"What a space cowboy," said George.

"You ain't kidding," added BB.

DMarks straightened himself up and walked with purpose to the Roman's front door. This time, he knocked instead of ringing the doorbell.

A fearsome looking Mr. Roman opened the door. His posture suggested that he was ready to take on the whole village. They guys couldn't hear what was being said, but DMarks's hangdog posture said it all as the older gentleman stood at attention, arms crossed, listening. After a lengthy pause, he reached out for a handshake. Looking relieved, DMarks clasped hands.

As he made his way back across the street, he pulled his T-shirt up to his eye one more time to wipe his face.

"There," he said. "I'll sleep better now."

"The way you're acting, I'd say a good night's sleep is exactly what you need," declared George.

"Yeah, and maybe think about calling in sick tomorrow from work," added BB.

"Easy, guys, that took more guts than ding-dong ditch in the first place," noted Charlie.

They stood around on the basketball court, sorry that another day had come to a close and talking about what they wanted to do the next day.

Charlie looked up at the stars. *Keep it up, Sky,* he thought.

13
CHAPTER

CAREER CLOSET

Stay dressed for service and keep your lamps burning.

—Luke 12:35

"Got to dress for success!" bellowed Reverend Higgins bounding down the steps to the church basement and into the area occupied by the Career Closet. He and Mrs. Higgins had become very active with this special cause which collected quality, secondhand business attire for people in need of proper clothes for job interviews.

The Briarcliff Congregational Church had a lot of great outreach projects, but this was one the parishioners really got behind with their time. The Career Closet accepted clothing donations all week long, which church volunteers would sort based on size, style, and color. Mr. Olson was one of the supervisors.

That morning, the church basement was a beehive of activity with at least two dozen volunteers carrying out different tasks. People were coming and going, dropping off items, lugging, racking, and stacking. Even with the cool basement air, people were working up a sweat.

"It's amazing the quality of the clothes people drop of," remarked Mrs. Higgins. "Some things seem brand new." She was handy with a needle and thread so her job was to find items that needed minor repair. A few nights each week, she'd take an armful back home to work her magic with the help of her trusty Singer sewing machine.

Reverend Higgins and his seemingly boundless energy kept things lively and lighthearted. After all, people were donating their time, and he wanted them to feel appreciated.

"You're doing God's work," he'd shout out periodically.

That morning, he spotted a suit that he liked and felt would fit him perfectly.

"Say, I need another dark suit for Sunday services, I might just make a donation and bring this home for myself," he declared, holding the jacket up to his chin to show Mrs. Higgins, who quietly shook her head.

"George, you donated that suit yourself last month. Now put it back where you found it and get to work, please."

"Who knew I had such good taste in suits?" he boasted.

Mary Dalton, who attended St. Theresa's Church just up the street, heard about the Career Closet from Father James Crowley. She had a whole attic full of clothes from her days as an English and language arts professor at Briarcliff College. Wanting to contribute, she meticulously laundered, ironed, and boxed them up, then headed over to the Congregational Church.

After finding a parking spot, she took her car key and unlocked the trunk. There was no one outside so she'd have to lug the overstuffed box to the drop-off station herself.

Mr. Olson, who had been trying to fix an old Atlas electric fan took a break to carry an overflowing box of rejected clothing items outside to be discarded.

As Mary got to the door, she balanced the box she was carrying between herself and the wall of the church building. Reaching down, she then grabbed the doorhandle and flung if open, pivoting and shuffling in backward.

At precisely the same time on the other side of the door, Mr. Olson had turned to back out through the doorway with the box he was carrying. Neither one saw the other coming, and in an instant, they collided like bumper cars, dropping everything. Clothes were scattered all over the floor around them.

"I beg your pardon," said Mr. Olson, catching Mary around the waist to keep her from falling.

Mary spun around, ready to give a few choice words about who could be so clumsy. Then, she saw who it was.

"Pardon granted. Hello, Jack." Running a hand through her hair, she got her bearings. "Please forgive my rather inelegant entrance."

"Mary! Is that you? I didn't recognize you without Annabelle."

Laughing at themselves, they bent down to gather up the overturned boxes of clothes.

"I'll have you know that at one time, these items were considered to be semi chic, teacher's attire," noted Mary, as she repacked her box.

"Well now, I'll have to get our best fashion expert on this. I'm sure whatever you've got there will fly off the rack."

"I like that better than seeing them attract moths in my closet."

"Your moths' loss is the Career Closet's gain," Jack improvised, picking up her box and motioning for her to follow him.

"So is this where you attend church, Jack?"

"Yep. Baptized, confirmed and married here."

Married? she thought with a start.

"Well, that sure covers the bases," she said, feeling a bit deflated that he was taken.

"And is the Career Closet one of your volunteer projects?"

"Why, yes, it is. When someone goes on a job interview, they've got to show up and show out. Hopefully our efforts here can help a little, especially with the way kids dress these days."

"I totally understand. While I was still teaching up the hill at the college, you never knew what the kids would wear to class. Tie-dyed shirts, jeans, sandals, you name it."

"Don't even get me started. I'm an IBM man." He tugged on his sensible navy-blue tie and invited Mary to join him for a cup of coffee.

"Don't mind if I do. I'm a bit coffee thirsty this morning."

Mr. Olson poured two cups from the huge urn in the corner of the basement room.

"Let's go outside and find a place to sip."

"Love to."

They headed up the stairs, both making a great show of letting one go before the other to avoid a collision. Once outside, they strolled to the area in front of the church known as God's Half Acre and found a spot on a weathered, wooden bench under a huge sugar maple.

The shade felt good in the heat of the midsummer day. *She looks so pretty in that floral sundress*, thought Mr. Olsen as they got comfortable.

While sipping and chatting, he had a schoolboy's urge to slide closer and maybe even hold her hand. *I wonder if she'd mind? Wait, what am I thinking?*

"You might like to know, this bench was given in memory of Walter Law who founded Briarcliff and built our sanctuary building," he blurted out, composing himself.

She smiled. "Wow, this might be the most important bench in Briarcliff." *We only met last week, but I feel so drawn to him. Maybe I should move closer? But wait, he mentioned being married.*

"When we were kids, we'd wait right here for Mr. Law to arrive at church in his chauffeured car. We'd run up and when he got out, he'd give us nickels."

"A king's ransom back then."

"It sure was. We'd pool our resources, putting half in the offering plate, then go up town after church to the penny candy store with the rest."

"I loved the penny candy store when I was little. You're talking about the one above Birratella's Garage? What was your favorite treat?"

"Cherry shoelaces. No, wait a minute. Bottle Caps. Bottle Caps for sure."

"I was more of a Candy Buttons gal. Loved picking them off those sheets of paper and letting them melt in my mouth. Then again, I sure loved nibbling on Rock Candy from time to time."

"Life was so simple back then," Mr. Olsen replied, stretching his arm along the back of the bench. *Oh good heavens, you can't put your arm behind her like that,* he thought, cringing.

"Simple, but full. Everything seems so complicated these days."

"Nobody seems to agree on very much anymore," said Mr. Olson, shaking his head.

"I know. If a bunch of Martians landed in America, then watched the nightly news, they'd skedaddle in a hurry."

"I have to agree. So tell me, do you miss teaching?"

"At times, yes, terribly. I loved working with the students and developing relationships with them, helping them through the coursework and college life in general."

"Right, yes, it's the people you end up missing the most."

"But then, other times, I'm glad that I retired. It was time. The workload kept getting bigger and bigger, and it was a challenge for me to muster up the energy to get the job done."

"Oh, yes. I concur," he said, noticing that she wasn't wearing anything on her ring finger.

"And family? Other than Annabelle, any children, brothers, sisters…er, husbands?"

You clumsy oaf! he scolded himself.

"Actually, I married my high school sweetheart. He was the most wonderful person. So wonderful, he enlisted in the Air Force. I never saw him again after he left for war in 1940. But I did receive the Silver Star he was awarded after his plane was shot down in the Pacific theater."

Jack's eyes suddenly welled up, recalling his own experiences in battle. "Mary, I'm so sorry. I didn't mean to bring up a hurtful memory," he said, patting her on the shoulder.

"Oh, that's okay, Jack. It was an early lesson in life. The longer one lives, the more acquainted one becomes with grief. Then again, I've also learned that the longer I live, the more aware I become aware of God's many blessings. It's all part of life in this crazy world," she let out a big sigh. "How about you? Do you miss driving over to Armonk each day?"

"Well, IBM was a fantastic place to work all those years and it was very exciting to design and launch new products. They're working on something right now they're calling a personal computer or PC for short. It won't be ready for another five years, but it will sit right on your desk and allow you to do calculations, typing, filing, all kinds of things we do manually. Can you imagine?"

"Gosh, if I had something like that, maybe I'd still be teaching."

"Right, yes. I'm sorry that I won't be there when it launches. But companies like IBM realize their lifeblood is new, fresh ideas and perspectives. So for me, it was time to turn a page."

"Imagine that, they value fresh, young perspectives over knowledge, expertise, and experience," said Mary with a chuckle.

"Life works in strange ways. A few years after I retired, my wife suddenly passed away."

"Oh, Jack, I'm so sorry."

"Thank you. You learn how to cope. At first, I was lost. But gradually, I discovered that life moves on...and in a blessed way, it all somehow took on a deeper, richer sort of meaning. God is there to help if you let him."

Looking down in a silent, reflective pause, they both gripped their coffee cups with two hands nervously twisting them in circles. *Well, that explains things*, Mary thought.

After a pause in their conversation, they glanced up simultaneously, as though by fate. Their eyes met in a sustained gaze.

Looking away shyly, hearts beating a little faster, they clutched their Styrofoam cups a bit tighter. Instinctively, they both had the same idea at the same time to shimmy toward the center of the bench. Once again, they bumped each other, this time splashing coffee on ground.

Mr. Olson turned red as the daylilies all around the bench where they were sitting. Mary smiled back with the glow of a thousand fireflies, green-blue eyes blinking affectionately. They stayed put on that bench in their own little world, neither in a rush to go anywhere. Then, leaning shoulder first, Mary gave Mr. Olson a little nudge as they both began to giggle.

Mr. Olsen cleared his throat. "Well, I guess I'm obligated to take you to dinner tonight, what with all the clothes you donated."

"Dutch treat?" Mary offered.

"Dutch never!" said Jack. "There's a new place that opened over by the A&P. It's called 105Ten."

"I love that restaurant. Meet you there?"

"Nothing doing. I'll pick you up at six."

Elated, Mr. Olson jumped to his feet. "Well, I better get back inside or risk a demotion from my own self."

As Mary rose, their eyes met again. Then, as Mr. Olson turned to head back to the Career Closet, Mary called out to him.

"Aren't you forgetting something?"

He turned and looked at her, wondered what she was referring to.

"You don't know where I live!"

14

CHAPTER

TURF WAR

For you equipped me with strength for the battle; you made those who rise against me sink under me.

—Psalm 18:39

Jackson Road Park fit snugly along the western edge of the Tree Streets neighborhood. Charlie and the guys considered it to be their home turf, and they were always quick to point out who called the shots if guys from other parts of town showed up.

The centerpiece of the park was a regulation-sized basketball court, which the boys also repurposed for street hockey, Wiffle ball, skateboarding, and more. There was also a kid's playground and a handball court. Beyond that was an expansive area of marshy woodlands known as Woyden's Swamp.

During morning hours, the playground area was the domain of small children and their mothers and babysitters. A few of the moms would hit tennis balls against the handball court as their little ones played on the swing sets, sliding ponds, and jungle gyms. By early afternoon, they tended to move to Law Park and the town pool.

One day in early July, the guys decided ride over to Jackson Road Park for a game of basketball. They also invited a few others to join them so that they could have a five-on-five, full court game.

After shooting around, Charlie and DMarks were voted as captains. Even though they were the closest of friends, picking teams was all business. They walked toward each other like gunslingers while everyone else gathered around at midcourt. With Clint Eastwood–style squinted eyes, they looked each other straight-on, neither one blinking.

"Call it," snarled DMarks.

"Evens."

"Once, twice, three—shoot," they said in unison, tossing out one or two fingers. Evens it was.

"Dang," whined DMarks. "I'm zero for this summer at odds and evens."

The only thing at stake was bragging rights for the rest of that day. Still, the two teams battled back and forth to a score of 24–24 off one-point baskets. Neither team could break it open, and with the standard win-by-two baskets rule in place, the game had no end in sight.

As the guys fought for each bucket, showing off all their best moves, Will Morris and a bunch of his friends showed up typically loud and aggressive. They walked straight through the park entrance, dribbled their basketballs onto the court, and began to shoot around. The fact that there was a full-court game in progress meant nothing to them. It was as though they didn't even notice.

The physical presence of the older boys out on the court made it impossible for the game to continue, so DMarks called timeout.

"Yo! What do you lambchops think you're doing? We're playing a game here."

At first, Will wanted to pummel DMarks for talking that way to him and his gang. But one of the kids there was his girlfriend's younger brother, so he had to lay off. The rest of them just ignored the exchange and kept shooting around.

As DMarks looked on, he began a slow boil.

"Are you guys deaf? I said we're playing a game here. Now get off the court and wait your turn!"

Still no reaction from the older boys. Charlie and the guys tried to encourage DMarks to let it go, but they could tell he was not going to back down.

Hawking up some major phlegm he spat in Will's direction. His aim was either beyond terrible or absolutely perfect. The spit hurled through the air a good ten feet and landed right on Will's brand-new suede Puma Clydes.

That did it. Will flashed his death glare as he stomped toward DMarks. Charlie did his best to hold on to the messages he believed Sky had channeled to him. In an attempt to defuse the situation, he asked Will if the older guys could just wait to use the court until they finished their game.

"Tell ya what, Riverton, why don't you and your little friends go play Spud or something?" Will fumed, shoving Charlie away.

Grabbing DMarks by the back of his neck, Will hauled him off the court.

"You've been shooting your mouth off for long enough," said Will, nose to nose with DMarks. "Here's the deal. If a bunch of older kids show up and want the court, they get the court. That's the way it's always been. Got it?"

DMarks was ready to fight. Now, even Charlie was getting fired up by what was happening as he stepped in to defend his friend.

"You want the court? Play us for it," Charlie said, glaring at Will. "We can shoot to see who gets the ball."

Will Morris looked at Charlie. Then he looked at his friends, then back at Charlie. "One. Last. Time. Riverton. Older kids get priority."

"That was then. This is now, so put up or shut up," came the out of character response from the good-natured Charlie.

"Tell ya what Riverton, you seem to be getting a little heated up. I think you need to cool off a bit."

With that, Will grabbed Charlie, tucked him under his arm like an overgrown puppy and walked him over to the brook by the side of the court.

"Here you go. This should cool you off," he sneered as he heaved Charlie into the brook, laughing out loud. The rest of Will's cronies were slapping fives and cackling like a pack of hyenas.

Meanwhile, Charlie felt a rare surge of bad anger. *Love your enemies can wait,* he thought as he hauled himself out of the water. George and BB had to make flying tackles to restrain him.

"Easy, buddy. Nothing good's going to come out of you trying to fight that big ox," said BB.

"Where is he?" seethed Charlie. "I'll tear him limb from limb."

"Buddy, he's twice your size," cautioned George, as he wrapped his arms around Charlie's legs.

"That fathead won't know what hit him," ranted Charlie, trying to wiggle away.

"Well, you'll know what hit you! He's not in the mood, man. You have to chill," pleaded BB.

"When I get done with him, he'll never throw anyone in that brook ever again."

"Okay, my man, we all know you're the toughest nut in the woods, but let's settle down," urged DMarks who could clearly see that this particular battle was lost.

Dragging Charlie along, they regrouped on the other side of the handball court.

"This is exactly what I said would happen when they took the court out of commission over in Law Park," declared DMarks.

"I hate to admit it," said BB, looking at Charlie and George, "but he was right."

"If we're going to protect our turf, we need a plan," pronounced DMarks.

"I don't know if we should mess with them right now," George cautioned. "Let's just go to the pool or something."

DMarks shot him an exasperated look. "Now listen up you guys and listen good. You can't go through life in retreat. If we don't make a stand, we won't just regret it for the rest of this summer. We'll regret it for as long as we live."

"Okay, a little dramatic, but I hear ya," added BB.

They stayed off to the side of the court trying to process the complete frustration they were feeling. After about a half hour, Charlie had mostly dried off in the heat of the summer sun. As they got up to leave, they noticed the older boys kicking back under the glen of huge willow trees by the brook.

"Ha, those fat, ugly jerks play for a half hour and they need a break already," observed DMarks.

"C'mon, let's ride over to the pool," said Charlie.

They walked across the court to where they had left their bikes without saying a word. Then, just as they were about to swipe their kickstands Charlie noticed that DMarks was nowhere to be seen.

"What the? Where'd he go?"

They looked back toward the basketball court and saw the single, most daring and utterly hilarious thing they had ever witnessed.

The older guys had left their basketballs at half-court while they lounged by the brook. Realizing the willow trees provided a natural blind, DMarks stopped to empty his bladder on Will's brand-new basketball. For good measure, he wet down the others too.

"I can't believe what I'm seeing," said Charlie. "And right in broad daylight!"

"I think he's gone stark raving crazy." BB laughed.

George was completely speechless. The boys had to hold on tight to their bikes to keep from falling over with laughter. As he zipped up, DMarks casually walked to his bike.

"The court's all yours!" he shouted to Will and his buddies. "Remember, the key to basketball is teamwork. Make sure to pass the ball around on offense."

As DMarks got to where the guys were, they genuflected in his direction, still spitting out laughter.

"I swear, Marks, I don't know if you're the bravest, nerviest person I know or you're just not right in the head," said BB, slapping him on the back.

"I think it's a little of both," said George.

DMarks had gotten the last laugh that day. But he was at least a little bit conflicted. He rode alongside Charlie.

"I'll ask forgiveness in church this Sunday."

"Way to rock the boat," Charlie replied.

15

CHAPTER

WE HOLD THESE TRUTHS

Blessed is the nation whose God is the Lord, the
people whom he has chosen as his heritage.

—Psalm 33:12

Briarcliff held a town parade each year on the Fourth of July. All the marchers gathered in the parking lots at People's Westchester Savings Bank and St. Theresa's Church on the north end of town.

With a hearty dose of red, white, and blue spirit, the participants trooped down through the town center, over to the Tree Streets and back around to Law Park. There, near the war memorial, commemorations, and the placement of memorial wreathes took place along with a keynote speech.

That year, Reverend Higgins, who had served in the navy, was named honorary Grand Master of the parade. He could not have been more in his element, leading the way decked out in full Scottish regalia. As he marched, he puffed heartily on his shepherd's pipe, tapping his walking stick to the ground in perfect cadence with the beat of the drum corps.

A few steps behind him were Parker Jones and Mr. Olson. They were both dressed in formal military attire and displaying solemn discipline, distinguished war heroes that they were. Next came Mayor Smythe and the Village Board of Trustees. They were each waving handheld American flags as crowds of spectators cheered them on.

Everyone got goosebumps as the Minuteman Marching Band passed by. Mr. Camilli, who fought on the ground in Europe during World War II, helped direct the parade and made sure that everything honored the occasion properly.

Following behind the marching band were school board members and any other elected or appointed officials in town. The Brownies and Girl Scouts, along with the Cubs and Boy Scouts came next. Trying not to step on their heels were twelve Little League teams, each player in full uniform, marching three by three.

Anchoring the procession was the Volunteer Fire Department and the Woman's Auxiliary. Fire Department apparatus, including the hook and ladder, pumper trucks, and the ambulance all rolled along, gleaming in the sun from a fierce washing and polishing session at the station the night before.

Charlie's parents staked out a spot at the corner of Pleasantville and South State Roads. They were joined by DMarks's, George's, and BB's parents, everyone laying out blankets and lawn chairs side by side.

Each time the procession came to a halt, they took the opportunity to catch up on things around town. The annual Family Fun Day event was about six weeks away, and they were all involved with planning and organizing.

"I'm helping with food this year. I think we should set up by the library. That way, we can use their refrigerator if needed," said Charlie's mom.

"They couldn't have picked a better person for that job," confirmed Charlie's dad, pointing a flag in her direction.

"Lucky you. They've got me on field events," bemoaned DMarks's father. "The last thing I need is to stand out there in the hot sun herding kids all afternoon. Not to mention I have to buy and refrigerate five dozen eggs for the egg toss."

"Stop complaining, dear. It will do you well to be out there with the youngsters," said DMarks's mom.

"It would do me much better to be working on my golf game. How'd I get signed up for this in the first place?" he groused, rummaging through their picnic basket.

"Well, actually, you skipped the planning meeting, so we gave you the job no one else wanted," said Charlie's dad with a wry smile.

"We're in charge of pool events," piped up George's mom, "and what a list we've got. Family relays, the greased watermelon chase, the rowboat race, diving for pennies, you name it."

"That's the best job of them all," said BB's dad. "We're on parking detail."

"That's a thankless job if ever there was one," replied DMarks's father. "If I were you, I'd work out preferred parking for anyone who might be willing to shed a few bucks."

The apple doesn't fall far from the tree, Mr. Riverton thought.

As Parker and Mr. Olsen marched by, the whole parade route was treated to Suzi Berkshire loudly proclaiming, "Oh, how I do love a man in uniform!" Mr. Olsen couldn't resist a small smile, but Parker didn't break form or stride.

In time, the parade made its way back to Law Park where the honor guard stood at attention. All the spectators had found their way into the park as well.

This year's honorary speaker was Mr. Olson. He was the only person in Briarcliff still living who fought in World War I. Mayor Smythe asked him to speak as a show of appreciation for his service, but it was Mr. Olson who could not have been more appreciative of the opportunity.

The Stars and Stripes flew on the giant flagpole as a gently persistent breeze caused it to fold and flap making a faint snapping sound.

After a twenty-one-gun salute, Mr. Olson approached the podium. He paused to scan the audience looking for Mary but was unable to see her among the hundreds of faces in the crowd. *I know you're out there somewhere*, he thought. Clearing his throat, he began his remarks.

"It's an honor and a solemn privilege to be here with you today. As we approach our nation's bicentennial, and with the people whose names are engraved on this war memorial close at heart, we're reminded of the critical sacrifices so many have made in the name of freedom and in the name of America.

I myself went overseas in World War I, but I was fortunate. I was blessed. I made it home." As he spoke those words, he was momentarily overcome with a gush of emotion recalling soldier friends who were cut down in the prime of their lives.

Composing himself, he looked out at the crowd. To his great joy, he spotted Mary looking on, blinking her eyes and smiling. The sight of her caused his heart to soar.

"Excuse me." He coughed, looking down at his notes. "I seem to have lost my place." *And my heart!* he thought. Smiling back at Mary, he went on to talk about the price of freedom.

"When I hear America's teenagers advocating for peace as a better alternative to war, it gives me hope for the future. And remember, you don't have to be a soldier to serve your country. The original patriots fought first with their minds and with their pens and with their convictions—convictions focused on God, family and liberty."

May I also suggest that we all fall asleep counting our blessings tonight." He paused, looking back at Mary, who shot him a thumbs-up gesture. Then, with both hands gripping the podium, he looked out at the crowd and finished his speech.

"The United States has a unique place in all of recorded history and it's up to each one of us to do our part on a daily basis to make sure our next chapters as one nation under God are prosperous for all Americans, everywhere." He concluded with a clarion call to become involved with civic and volunteer activities.

"Thank you all and may God continue to bless America!"

After an enthusiastic round of applause, Father James Crowley took to the microphone to recite the honor roll. He then offered a benediction as the bugler blew taps.

With the ceremony concluded, Mr. Olson stepped away from the podium and began making his way through the crowd looking for Mary.

"There you are. I didn't know if you'd make it."

"Well, I guess I can't resist a man in uniform," she said coyly.

"Good to know. Maybe I'll wear this to our service dog training class."

"Actually, I'm not sure Mrs. Bridgewater would approve. She likes to feel in charge, you know."

"Right. You're right as usual."

They smiled affectionately at each other. It didn't matter where they were or what they might be doing, life seemed a little richer, a little better when they were together. There was something special blossoming between them, and they both felt it.

"So what time are we due over at Sleepy Hollow Country Club tonight?" she asked, reaching out to touch one of his medals.

"The Smythes are expecting us at six bells. Okay if I pick you up at 5:45?"

"Deal, 5:45 it is."

He reached out for her hand as they strolled down the gentle hillside toward Gooseneck Pond. Feeling young and free, she kicked off her shoes and went barefoot. Law Park was packed with others reveling in the spirit of the day, but for Mr. Olson and Mary it was as though they were the only two people there.

They found a bench donated by the Rotary Club in a shady spot and continued holding hands as they sat and relaxed. They chatted effortlessly about favorite memories from past Fourths of July.

As usual, time flew by. After a slow walk to Mary's car, Mr. Olson reached out to open the door for her.

"Till later," she said as she slid into the bucket seat of her stylish, dark green Mustang convertible. "Yes, bye for now," he said, closing the door and giving it a good pat.

As she drove past him, he could see his house across the street from Law Park. *That car would look good parked in my driveway.*

As Mary exited the lot, she glanced up at his house. *Well, I'll be. Jack has a two-car garage.*

16
CHAPTER

READY OR KNOT

Live as people who are free, not using your freedom as
a cover up for evil, but living as servants of God.

—1 Peter 2:16

Sleepy Hollow Country Club was renowned for their annual Fourth of July celebration. Each year, the expansive West Lawn of the former Vanderbilt mansion came alive with colorful, patriotic spirit.

Flags and bunting were on display everywhere. Streamers and garland festooned the portico of the main clubhouse and red, white, and blue table settings perfectly accented the buffet tables which all overflowed with summer fare.

Energetic children wearing Uncle Sam hats and Tricorn caps scampered throughout the grounds waving sparklers and pinwheels. The main event was a world-class fireworks spectacular that so lit up the sky it could be enjoyed by people up and down the Hudson River from Piermont to Peekskill.

The day itself was a midsummer gift, filled with spirit-lifting sunshine, low humidity, a comfortable 82 degrees, and a refreshing breeze off the water which gently brushed the grounds.

The Smythes were long-time members at the club and they loved playing host to friends from around town. Joining them that year were the Rivertons, Reverend and Mrs. Higgins, Mr. Olson and Mary, Parker and Suzie, Coach and Peggy Cadman, and Dr. and Mrs. Cook. Charlie was also happily there with Michelle.

Mr. Smythe tried to greet everyone as they arrived, but the crowd was so large and the space so wide open that he had to search around to find his guests.

"Well, hello, Reverend and Mrs. Higgins. How are you this fine evening?" asked Mr. Smythe.

"Happy as a clambake, Winthrop. Thanks for asking," the reverend replied with his usual enthusiasm.

"I'm glad to hear that. Speaking of clams, I hope you'll sample some of our raw bar selections tonight."

"Sample? Been back two times already. Not quite as good as the clams I rake out of Cape Cod Bay, mind you, but more than adequate by this New Englander's standards."

"I'm relieved to hear that, especially since those clams you enjoyed came from Long Island Sound," replied Mr. Smythe.

"I'd say you flatlanders have some mighty fine stock," the reverend replied.

Mrs. Smythe loved to personally walk her guests around the serving tables so they could see all the different food choices including an expansive spread of desserts. Once that was accomplished, she left it up to everyone to make themselves at home.

"Just remember to pace yourselves. I expect everyone to go back for fourths," she said good-naturedly. As the Smythe party began to find their way to their reserved table, each had a full plate and a big smile. After everyone settled in, Mr. Smythe asked if Dr. Cook would offer a blessing.

"Why, that would be a happy privilege, Winthrop," answered the well-known president of the Kings College. "Heavenly God, thank you for the courage and the blessings you bestowed on our founders as they won liberty for this great nation. Thank you for the ways in which they lit the torch of freedom for future countries to follow. Grant us what we need to maintain those liberties through Jesus our friend and Savior. Amen."

Mr. Smythe thanked Dr. Cook, then raised his glass to propose a toast. "Here's to our country's birthday. One flag, one land, one heart, one hand."

The conversation around the table was cordial and lively. Coach Cadman knew that he'd have Charlie on junior varsity basketball that coming school year so they were busy talking about the various players who would be going out for the team.

Classmates and lifelong friends, Peggy and Suzie chatted away. Suzie did most of the talking with sweet-natured Peggy mostly listening, smiling, and nodding.

On the other side of the table, Mary and Mrs. Higgins were deep in conversation. Cut from the same well-bred cloth, they enjoyed talking about family, pets, and community involvements.

"I'm so pleased that you're taking Annabelle to therapy dog training. I'm a Candy Striper at Phelps Hospital, and we can use all the patient support we can get," mentioned Mrs. Higgins.

"It's kind of a funny thing. I'm recently retired and was looking for opportunities to become more involved around town. Then out of nowhere, this splendid cause just randomly showed up in my life. I had no prior notions about doing something like that, but when the opportunity presented itself, I had this overriding sense that Annabelle and I should take the plunge."

The thoughtful Mrs. Higgins paused to look across the table at how happy Mr. Olson seemed to be. It was almost three years ago when he lost his wife and everyone was so worried that he might have lost his will to go on without her.

"Are you sure it was a random thing? God has subtle ways of directing our lives."

Mary liked the sentiment. "Right. Father knows best."

Meanwhile, at the far end, Mr. Olson, who was talking with Parker Jones, noticed that he seemed preoccupied and anxious.

"Everything okay, soldier?" he asked.

"Me? Oh yes, fine. Why do you ask?"

"Oh, no particular reason. Other than that you just put ketchup and mustard on your lobster tail."

"What? Oh geez," he said, giving Mr. Olson a defenseless look.

"Okay, then. At ease, Lieutenant."

"Yes, sir, thank you, sir," replied Parker with a quick salute.

Suzie, Coach, and Peggy began to reminisce about times when they used to come to Sleepy Hollow Country Club while growing up in Briarcliff.

"Remember when the Glascott brothers hosted that graduation party?" asked Suzie.

"How could anyone forget?" replied Peggy.

"After dark, they hijacked golf carts and led everyone up to the sixteenth green," recalled Coach Cadman.

Suzie winked. "Yeah, but it got really fun afterward when people started jumping in the pool for a midnight swim."

Peggy winked back. "You're right. And a few didn't have bathing suits!"

While the adults were all engaged, Dr. Cook, who loved young people, naturally focused his attention on Charlie and Michelle.

"Tell me, you two, how in the world are you?" he asked, using the intro greeting from his popular daily radio broadcasts.

"Fine thanks. And you?" Charlie responded, putting his arm along the back of Michelle's chair.

"Thank you for asking. We're actually heading to the Poconos next week. Looking forward to our annual summer retreat."

"Oh, I love the Poconos," said Michelle. "My friend has a home there."

"Small world. We'll have to look them up sometime. Hope you both are enjoying your summer break so far."

"So far so good. I work most days until early afternoon. Then I meet up with my friends at the pool."

Dr. Cook was active in the community and well liked around town. Michelle decided to ask him for some advice.

"Dr. Cook, are there any Bible lessons on how to deal with older boys when they act like jerks?" she asked. Charlie cocked an eyebrow at her.

"That's an interesting question, young lady." Dr. Cook paused to consider it. "As a matter of fact, yes. The Bible has a lot to say about situations like that. Any particular reason why you're asking?"

Just as Michelle was about to continue, Charlie jumped in. "Well, you see, there's this group of older guys and they've been giving some of us a hard time this summer."

"Those older boys are grade A, first-class troublemakers," interrupted Michelle, earning a quick tap on her foot under the table from Charlie.

"I see. Well now, I guess it could be said that any town or village that ever was had a few local bullies. But it still presents a predicament." He leaned back in his chair, folded his arms, and cupped his chin.

"Well, when we tried to stand up for ourselves, this one guy they call Billy the Butcher took our basketballs and punted them into the swamp at Jackson Road Park," Charlie said.

"Billy the Butcher?" inquired Dr. Cook.

"Yeah, he's like six-two, has a crew cut, and he's a really dirty player. Always gets a lot of fouls. That's how he got his nickname."

"And then one day, the leader of the group went schizo and threw Charlie in the brook! I'd like to see them pick on someone their own size," interjected Michelle again.

Charlie was glad for her support but shot her a look to signal that he'd take it from there. Dr. Cook exhaled, tilting his head downward in thought.

"Let's see, if we were in Old Testament times, the rule of law was 'an eye for an eye.' Funny thing though, that approach will only make the whole world blind."

Charlie smiled as he listened intently.

"Now that we're in New Testament times, the example Jesus provided would have us strive for peace."

Charlie and Michelle leaned in to capture every word the esteemed college president and pastor was saying.

"Psalm 34 comes to mind for situations like this," Dr. Cook said, leaning forward. "When the righteous cry for help, the Lord hears and delivers them out of all their troubles. Like anything else,

Charlie, I'd say you should offer this up to the Lord in prayer. Then, all you have to do is watch for nods, tokens and signs."

Charlie froze at Dr. Cook's comment. *That's the same phrase Sky used in that dream from a couple weeks ago.* Dr. Cook, who knew Sky well from his last visit to Briarcliff, gave Charlie a knowing smile.

Charlie was amazed at the stunning parallel.

"God hasn't brought you this far to drop you now," he assured Charlie. "His heavenly host is always ready to get involved on behalf of those who believe."

"I sure wish Sky was here," he said wistfully as Michelle gave his hand a squeeze.

"Tell ya what, Charlie, Sky's a very special kind of friend. Even though he might not be with us physically, it always feels like he's close by."

"I totally get that. Sometimes, I feel like he's still there, almost like he's trying to communicate with me."

Dr. Cook listened, nodding his head with that knowing smile again.

"Well, God channels special messages to us in all kinds of ways," he replied. "A dream, a song lyric, a speech, a billboard slogan. You name it, God can use it."

Charlie felt himself physically absorbing every word Dr. Cook was saying.

"You know, Charlie, there's been a struggle going on between right and wrong ever since the dawn of creation. But you know what else?" He gestured to the setting sun over the Hudson. "God's plan always triumphs in the end. That doesn't change the present reality, but it should give you hope to carry on."

"Thank you, Dr. Cook, I'll definitely think about the things you mentioned."

"Very good then. I think I'll visit the desert table," said Dr. Cook. "And remember, walk with the King and be a blessing!" Charlie and Michelle smiled at him, recognizing his signature radio show closing tag line.

Sitting directly across the table, Mr. Olsen mentioned to Charlie that Taylor recently found himself a lady friend.

"Wow, Mr. Olson, that's awesome. Tell me more, how'd they meet?"

"Well, I took Taylor to therapy dog class. He spotted Mary's dog Annabelle right off the bat, and it was love at first woof."

Mary beamed at the memory. "And I've been thanking Annabelle ever since," she said, leaning into Mr. Olson and locking arms with him.

"Taylor's such a good soul," said Charlie. "He deserves a good companion."

I'm so glad we rescued Taylor two Christmases ago, thought Charlie. Then he paused and thought for a moment. *I can't believe Michelle never realized I named him after James Taylor for her.*

Michelle looked on with her warm-as-the-sun smile. *What a coincidence, Mr. Olson's dog has the same name as my favorite rock star.*

From way down at the other end of the table, Suzie called to the Smythes.

"This is amazing!" she gushed enthusiastically. "Thank you so much for having us."

"Not at all. Mrs. Smythe and I are delighted you and Parker could join us."

"How's construction going with the housing units you're building over on North State Road?" inquired Parker.

"Excellent. The first two developments were quite successful and there was demand for more, so we're breaking ground north of the Briar Lanes bowling alley."

"That's fantastic news," said Parker as he raised his mug to him.

"Yes, yes, indeed. Each morning after the six o'clock mass at St. Theresa's, I put my hard hat on and head over to the construction site."

"I think that's just wonderful. And thank you for making my real estate office the exclusive sales agent," said Suzie, raising her wine glass to him.

"You're welcome, Suzie. There's no one else I'd rather work with."

Mrs. Smythe asked Charlie's mom how she was enjoying her summer break from teaching.

"Well, on the one hand, I miss those first graders, I really do. On the other hand, I kind of need this time off. It gives me a chance to hit the reset button."

"I understand, dear," mentioned Mrs. Smythe, patting her hand. "Before I married Winthrop, I was a schoolteacher myself just down the street at the Washington Irving School. Summer break was divine."

The conversation continued around the table, lighthearted, and cheerful, with plenty of laughter and warm voices rising up and into the evening air. With nightfall approaching, it was almost time for the fireworks show to begin.

Charlie and Michelle broke away from the larger group and cozied up next to each other on a bench made for two on the far southern edge of the lawn. He felt so proud to have her as his girlfriend and told her that she looked extra pretty that night.

As darkness set in, a single flair was set off to signal that the show was about to start. Within minutes, the skies reverberated with a glittering display. The colors were breathtaking as deafening explosions created a rolling thunder which echoed off the hillside and the massive fieldstone clubhouse.

As everyone looked out over the valley at the fireworks, Parker took Suzie by the hand and led her back to the West Lawn area, near where they had been sitting during dinner. As they stood all by themselves, he looked at her, drew the deepest breath of his life and got down on one knee. Glancing up, he took out a small velvet box, opened it carefully, and began to propose to Suzie.

But it was dark where they were. Moreover, the club had turned off all the house and exterior lights so as not to interfere with the fireworks display. The nonstop bangs and blasts further compounded Parker's predicament making it impossible for him to be heard.

Suzie looked down at him, unable to see that he was holding out a ring box. "What?" she yelled, completely clueless to the fact that this was the moment she had been waiting for her entire life.

"I can't understand a word you're saying. And what are you doing down there? You're going to get a grass stain on those brand-new Khakis, and then I'm going to have to scrub them by hand."

Parker had been nervous about proposing to Suzie. Now, given the way things were going, he realized that he might have made a tactical error trying to propose during the thunderous light show. His mind raced, and he began to sweat, wondering if he should retreat. But then, a flowery breeze washed over him calming his rattled nerves.

With renewed confidence, he straightened himself up, took Suzie by the hands, looked deeply into her eyes, and asked her to marry him once again. But the noise and the darkness got in the way a second time. She couldn't understand what he was trying to say.

"Military you? Oh! You mean this reminds you of your days in Vietnam?"

Suzie felt bad, thinking the fireworks must remind him of the battles he fought in.

"It's okay… I *understand*," she said, overemphasizing her pronunciation in a way that an emergency room nurse might try to talk a patient down from a traumatic experience.

Parker winced in exasperation.

"No! Listen to me!" he yelled, cupping his hands over his mouth. "Will. You. Marry. Me?" he repeated pointing at her, then to himself.

"Carry you? Carry you where?" she asked impatiently. "You weigh a hundred pounds more than me. Just how am I supposed to carry you anywhere?"

Parker looked down and rubbed his forehead, then tried one more time.

"I said, will…you…marry…*meeeee*?" He waved the little box dramatically back and forth in front of her.

The diamond ring sparkled off the fireworks as Suzie's expression sling-shotted to a look of stunned amazement. She finally understood what Parker was saying. Parker just looked back, with a huge relieved smile and nodded.

Suzie, for once in her life, was at a loss for words. She tried to collect herself to reply but was completely tongue tied.

"I… I… I… Wow!" She knew that didn't come out right. She tried again. "I mean, I… Uh-huh! I mean I… I… Woo! No, I mean, I do! Yes!"

But this time, Parker couldn't understand what she was saying. "What?" he yelled, cupping his hand to his ear. "What did you say?"

"Yes!" she repeated emphatically. "Yes!" She pulled his face close to hers and screamed, "Yes, I will!" at the top of her lungs.

At that very instant, there was a lull in the fireworks just before the finale. Everyone turned to see what the shouting was all about.

Normally, Suzy would be kicking herself for falling into another embarrassing situation. But there she was, embracing Parker in a beautiful, passionate kiss that would have been the envy of Hollywood's greatest leading men.

Parker smiled and looked into her glistening eyes.

"There's only one thing I want to change about you," he said, pulling her close. "Your last name."

As the onlookers began to grasp what was happening, they broke out in spontaneous applause just as the fireworks finale reached its crescendo.

A few moments later, Reverend Higgins strolled over and cleared his voice. "I'm available here and now if you'd like to get hitched under the stars."

"And I can reserve the honeymoon suite for you right here at the club," added Mr. Smythe.

Parker was grinning with sheer joy. But the wheels were already turning in the mind of the take-charge Suzie.

"Thank you, but not on your life," she protested, hooking her arm around Parker's waist. "We have a lot of planning to do."

She had waited this long, and she was going to have the traditional wedding she'd always dreamed about.

Mr. Olson came over and saluted Parker. "Well done, soldier." Parker saluted him back, then reached over for a back-slapping hug.

Off to the side, Michelle and Charlie were taking it all in, holding hands. "That's the most romantic thing I've ever seen," said Michelle.

"So far," cut in Charlie, giving her a little hip check.

17
CHAPTER

THE LAND IS OUR LAND

Behold, I have given you authority to tread on serpents and scorpions and over all the power of the enemy, and nothing shall hurt you.

—Luke 10:19

Going back to the late 1800s, the Woyden family owned the entire area that eventually became known as the Tree Streets in Briarcliff. Descendants of the original family still lived in the manor home on the south end of the neighborhood. Just off their backyard was an expansive meadow where waist-high wild grasses grew across rolling hills.

On the other side of the property, running parallel to Route 9A, was the area known as Woyden's Swamp. It was heavily wooded and full of brambles, reeds, sweetbriars, and vines so thick the guys would sometimes swing on them like Tarzan.

The lowland grounds were damp, spongy, and prone to flooding after summer rainstorms. If the rain was heavy enough, portions of the swamp would turn into a virtual lake where the boys could swim in waist-deep water for a day or two until the waters began to recede.

Over the years, the guys spent a lot of time exploring the swamp, creating secret passageways, secluded hideouts, and a well-appointed treehouse, which they dubbed School's Out. Perched about fifteen feet above the ground in a huge Twin Oak, it was their pride and joy. Sometimes, they'd even have sleep overs in it. They swore each other to a strict code of silence. School's Out was their private hangout, and they didn't want anyone sniffing around.

Over by the Pocantico River on the other side of the swamp, they had a second, much more modest hangout. It was nicknamed The Hub because of all the hubcaps they'd pick up from cars speeding by on 9A, which they hung on nearby tree branches.

The Hub was located at a spot on the river they called Root Beer Rapids, so named from the brownish mud-clay bottom which made the water look darker than normal. The Hub was nothing more than a glorified lean-to, with matted down areas to lounge on.

Sometimes, they'd kick back and chill out on the cushy beds made from tall reeds, but The Hub also offered some fun sporting opportunities. One of their favorite pastimes was to build dams in the river, then capture perch, catfish, and sunnies with their bare hands. Catch and release, of course.

That section of the river was also very wide, which allowed for rock-skimming competitions. BB had the best arm and usually won. No one would ever top his record of twenty-one skips.

One day, they were kicking back talking about different things.

"How cool is it that Arthur Ashe won Wimbledon? First African American to do that. And he beat Jimmy Connors, which ain't easy," said Charlie.

"Classy guy, classy game," replied BB.

"I think he actually lives near here. Mount Kisco or something," added George.

"Makes me proud," said DMarks. "He represented America well."

It was peaceful out by The Hub. The sounds of birds chirping and river currents lapping against rocky embankments created a relaxing backdrop.

"Looks like President Ford's going to run for reelection," mentioned Charlie.

"I think he should. He's a good man," DMarks declared. "He'll stand up to those Russian troublemakers."

"I don't know. It's so strange. He's a good guy for sure, but he was appointed president, not elected president," said George.

"Right? I like the guy, but who is he? This is so weird," declared BB.

"Who is he? He's the leader of the free world, that's who. Plus, he has our own Governor Rockefeller from Pocantico Hills as vice president. How cool is that?"

Their conversation was interrupted by the sound of revved up minibikes coming through the swamp. There were a pair of older brothers in the neighborhood who liked to ride down the network of pathways the boys had established.

These guys were different from the other upperclassmen around town. They were really nice to the younger kids and seemed to take a genuine interest in Charlie, DMarks, BB, and George. Plus, the Kawasakis helped keep the scrub vines from growing back. Anyone else was not welcome.

The boys got up from their straw mats and ran to say hello.

"Hi, Bobby. Hi, Doug," yelled Charlie, waving.

Downshifting their bikes, they came to a quick stop.

"What's happening, guys? Is this where the girls are hanging out today?" asked Doug.

"Actually, this is where we come when we want a little privacy from them," answered DMarks.

"Girl troubles?" asked Bobby.

"Ha! Could there be such a thing?" DMarks replied.

"Very definitely!" Bobby and Doug replied in unison. "Wait till you get to high school."

"You guys usually only ride at night. What brings you out at four in the afternoon?" inquired Charlie.

"Yeah, we finished up early today on the maintenance squad at the high school, so Mr. Conacchio let us have the rest of the day off," replied Doug.

"So what's shakin' this afternoon with you guys?" asked Bobby.

"Oh, we're just hangin'. Probably going to head to the pool for a quick dip before dinner," said Charlie.

"Right on, boys. Well, be cool," said Bobby.

"Let the good times roll," added Doug.

The two brothers gave the guys a peace sign and rode off deeper into the swamp.

Unbeknownst to any of them, Will Morris had snuck into the swamp and was only about forty yards away, hiding behind a tree. His friends had been bugging him about when he was going to drop the hammer on DMarks, Charlie, and the guys. He continued watching as he worked himself into a slow boil. With sweat beads popping up all across his forehead, he sharpened his eyes, waiting to pounce.

"You guys had enough hanging out over here? If we leave now, we can be at the pool by 4:15," suggested Charlie.

Everyone agreed so they walked back toward The Hub to get their shirts and sneakers.

"One of these nights, we should try camping out over here for a change," suggested BB.

"Great idea," replied George. "We have fresh water, a fire pit, a comfortable place to sack out... What else do we need?"

Just then, the boys heard a crushing, crunching, swooshing sound in the brush behind them. They all turned, thinking maybe it was a deer. But to their alarm, it was Will Morris coming at them like Dick Butkus about to demolish a running back.

"You're mine, Marks!" he growled. The boys took off in an all-out sprint. Their fleet-footed speed and intimate knowledge of the winding swamp trails was their only defense.

In a matter of seconds, the boys happened to flee right past where Bobby and Doug were taking a break, sitting on their mini-bikes. Sensing that something was wrong, they kicked their bikes back on and rode out to put themselves between the boys and whatever danger there was.

Double-clutching, they raced ahead at maximum speed quickly coming in view of a rabid-looking Will Morris. When they were about ten yards in front of him, they spun out their wheels holding their throttles in place and spraying Will with mud, sticks, and small rocks.

Putting up his hands and turning his head, Will had no choice but to retreat a few steps. The barrage was so heavy, it caused him to stumble into a thorny batch of sagebrush.

"What the heck is wrong with you guys?" he bellowed pulling prickers out of his arms and legs.

"Sorry, bro, we had to spin out or we would have run you over," explained Doug.

Will was enraged. "Yeah, sure, you're just trying to help those little punks," he fumed.

"Whatever do you mean?" Bobby asked in a sarcastic, innocent way.

Will was drenched in sweat and muck. He pulled his shirt up to wipe his face. "I'll deal with you two later," he snarled as he took off running again.

Bobby and Doug slapped fives.

"That should give our young friends a nice head start," said Bobby.

"Rock on, bro," added Doug.

When Charlie and the guys reached their bikes, they hopped on and began to pedal. Realizing they had escaped, Will slowed down and gave up the chase. He was winded, he was cursing, and he was sweating.

A few minutes later, the boys arrived at the pool, giddy with laughter from their close call with Will.

"We're safe now." George beamed.

"Man, we owe Bobby and Doug," said Charlie.

"Did you see how filthy our sweaty friend was when he came out of the swamp. What a chump," said George.

"All I know is he was one crazy dude back there," declared DMarks. "Did you see the look he had in his eyes."

"Right? Like a rabid animal," observed Charlie.

As they walked over to the hill behind the diving boards, Charlie started thinking. He tried to square what had just happened with the lesson from his recent dream, he wondered if it all tied together somehow. *Was it time maybe to hold out an olive branch?* he wondered.

18

CHAPTER

SWIM TEAM

Do nothing from rivalry or conceit, but in humility count others more significant than yourselves. Let each of you look not to his own interests, but to the interests of others.

—Philippians 2:3–4

The Briarcliff swim team was a big deal all summer long. Tons of kids participated ranging in ages from seven to seventeen. Plus, the pool facility in Law Park was one of the best in the county, so Briarcliff hosted a lot of meets.

That year, there was a new coach who was a member of the Fordham University swim team. Every Tuesday and Thursday, he'd arrive at 4:00 p.m. for practice, which began with twenty-five laps just to warm up. After that came drills, races, and endurance training. If everyone practiced hard, there'd usually be a game of water polo as a reward.

On practice days, everyone tried to take it easy, especially with regard to the amount of food they ate. Coach Devin expected all members of the team to be at their best when they hit the water.

On one particular day, however, DMarks went a little overboard while visiting Weldon's for a late lunch. In addition to his normal roast beef wedge, he also got a pint of macaroni salad, a pint of potato salad, a package of Ring Dings and a bag of Ruffles.

"What are you pregnant or something?" chided BB.

"Yeah, what's with all that food?" asked George.

"Those brats at summer camp stole my lunch again. I haven't eaten since breakfast and I'm starving," he complained as he tore open his bag of chips.

"Outsmarted by a bunch of camp kids again?" joked Charlie.

"It's not a fair fight. There's ten of them and only one of me."

"Do the other camp counselors have this problem?" asked BB.

"Shut. Up. You," DMarks replied, throwing a fake punch.

"All I know is, eating that much food before swim team practice is a bad idea," cautioned Charlie.

"I'll bet two Cokes that he hurls in the men's locker room before warm-ups are over," wagered BB.

George laughed. "That's a sucker bet if there ever was one."

DMarks didn't care about the razzing. He just wanted to fill his stomach, fast. The guys looked on shaking their heads as they chilled out up by the flagpole in Law Park.

"Don't say we didn't warn ya." Charlie sighed.

Stretched out and leaning back on their elbows, the grass was soft and cool to lounge on. Looking down at the pool and all the activity that was going on, their minds filled with memories of when they were younger, learning to swim with kickboards. Each of them would have been content to stay put where they were for the rest of the afternoon, but a half hour later, it was time for practice to begin.

Coach Devin blew his whistle to get everyone's attention.

"Let's go. Look alive. It's lap time!"

Everyone dove in for warm-up laps, one after another, using kick turns each time across the pool so that the whole team could keep a steady pace. DMarks lagged behind from the moment he hit the water.

"What's the matter, Marks? If you swim any slower, you'll be going backward!" yelled Coach Devin. "C'mon. Pick up the pace."

Normally, that kind of talk would have been a prime source of motivation for DMarks, but that day, it didn't make a difference. His huge lunch was weighing him down. He swam as hard as he could, but before long, the rest of the team was lapping him. Pretty soon, he was doing the sidestroke just to make it back across the pool.

"I know who's not swimming the anchor lap against Pleasantville this weekend," said Coach Devin for all to hear.

In addition to the swim team, there also was diving team which was coached by a really nice college girl named Bev. That year, she had an abundance of girls on the team but needed more boys in order to be competitive at meets. After warm-ups, she made an announcement to the swim team and invited any interested boys to follow her to the diving area for instruction and practice.

All she got in response were blank stares. Deflated, she turned to walk away. Unbeknownst to any of his friends, George had been thinking about trying out for diving team. He took a deep breath to calm his nerves, then glided through the water to the side of the pool. Without saying a word, he hoisted himself out of the water and hurried to catch up to Bev who was well down the pool deck.

"W-W-What the?" stammered DMarks. "He never said anything about going out for diving."

"I think he's sweet on Deirdre and hopes he might get to know her better. She's the number one diver on the team," replied Charlie.

"Deirdre? She's way out of his league," said DMarks.

"He deserves credit for trying. I'm kind of proud of him actually," said BB.

When Bev noticed that George was coming her way, she drew a deep breath, putting her hand to her mouth. She used to babysit for him and could not have been any happier.

"George! This is great. It's so good to have you with us."

"Th-Thanks, Bev," he stuttered in a nervous way, realizing that there was no turning back now. "I've kind of been w-working on a few dives."

His knees felt shaky and it was hard for him to think in complete thoughts. It helped a little as he glanced back at the guys and noticed they were giving him enthusiastic thumbs up signs.

"Love it. Glad to have you," said Bev, putting her hand across his shoulders.

"Nice to have another boy on the team," said Deirdre. George turned red as a Coke can in response.

That afternoon, diving instruction focused on proper technique for the three-step approach on the diving board.

"Everyone thinks the dive is judged by what happens once you're in the air, but the judges will be watching you from the moment you step onto the board. It all begins with great posture, head up and eyes straight forward," pronounced Bev.

She then demonstrated proper techniques right there on the pool deck and asked everyone to pair off to work on a few dry runs. Since Deirdre was an experienced diver, she asked her to coach George along.

Dierdre smiled and gave him a few pointers.

"Okay, let's start with the basics. First of all, stand straight up, chest out, shoulders back." George almost fell in the pool when she demonstrated.

"Chin up, three short steps, then kick your right leg up, both feet down, and let the board launch you up and into the air. Got it?"

"I... I think so. Can you show me one more time?" He hoped the boys were catching all this between laps.

"Okay, and another thing to remember, when you launch off the board, you have to go straight up and straight down. You can't dive forward, you'll make too big of a splash. The judges don't like that."

After ten minutes of practicing the three-step technique on the pool deck, it was time for everyone to move to the diving boards. For the first time, George discovered what it meant to have butterflies in his stomach as he waited his turn.

Then, as if on autopilot, he stepped onto the diving board, gripping the railing bars on either side. He was numb, too numb to even notice the severe case of cottonmouth which had set in.

"Whoa, whoa, what dive should I do?" he asked, looking down at Deirdre.

"Whatever you want. How about a simple Pike?" she replied.

George looked across the pool and spotted the guys watching. Charlie twirled his finger in the air, signaling he should do a one-

and-a-half somersault, which they all had been working on that summer. It wasn't an easy dive, but it looked really cool and it would be impressive if he could pull it off.

The idea connected with George. It was bold and it was risky, but what a way to make a statement if it worked. He decided to go for the gold.

Shaking out his arms and hands, he pulled his right knee up to his chest, then his left, drew a deep breath, and began his three-step approach.

Everything was fine as he launched off the board and into a nice, tight somersault. But mid-dive, he panicked, causing him to come out of his tuck too soon.

George's face and torso smacked the water hard, causing everyone in the entire pool area to turn their heads to see what had happened. Charlie and the guys winced with pain as their friend crash-landed.

Sinking down beneath the surface of the water, George began to realize the full extent of the epic mistake he had made. As much as his body hurt, his ego hurt even more. He wished he could stay down at the bottom of the pool like in *The Incredible Mr. Limpet.*

When he finally surfaced, all he could hear was laughter coming from every direction. To make matters worse, he had a bloody nose. Swimming to the side of the pool, he started to haul himself out of the water. As he glanced up, he noticed that the one person who wasn't laughing was Deirdre.

"That was so awesome! You almost nailed it. We can work on how to stay in your tuck until it's time to release," she reassured him. "Here, let me help you," she said, offering him her towel.

But George's humiliation got the best of him as he dashed past her and into the men's locker room. Collapsing onto one of the wooden benches he reclined back and pinched his nose to stop the bleeding. Charlie and the guys rushed in behind him.

"I like it. He took a calculated risk and went for it," gushed DMarks.

"Seriously, no way I would have been brave enough to try that. It's one thing when there's only a few of us messing around, but to do that in front of the entire diving team took guts," added Charlie, handing him some paper towels.

"Give me five, buddy," said BB, putting out his hand. "Better to aim high and fall short than aim low and win."

George appreciated the encouragement, but he felt like he could faint from embarrassment.

"Tell me when it's 8:00 p.m. I'm not leaving here until closing time," he declared.

"Umm, we've got like three and a half hours before the pool closes, my man," BB told him.

"I don't care if I have to skip dinner tonight. I'm staying right here."

"Buddy, we understand how you feel, but I'm telling ya, you're going to score points from that one," encouraged Charlie.

The guys hung out with George until the bleeding stopped. Once he was sitting upright and thinking a little more clearly, they did some reconnaissance in the pool area. Bev came over, concerned about George.

"How's he doing, guys?

"Well, I'd say we have a shot at getting him out of there before dark," answered Charlie.

"That bad, huh?" she lilted, leaning her chin on her clipboard.

"Yeah, it's bad," added BB.

"He has to know that all of us have been in that sort of situation before. I remember the time we had a meet at Torview, and it all came down to me and my fourth dive. I launched off the board, blanked, and came crashing down flat on my back.

"Did that really happen, Bev? Can I tell him that?" asked Charlie.

"It absolutely happened, and it cost us the meet."

"Wow, Bev, thanks. Give us a few minutes. Let us see what we can do," affirmed Charlie.

As the guys were about to head back into the locker room, Deirdre came rushing by holding a bloody towel to her face.

"What the heck is going on around here?" DMarks wanted to know. "Is this a blood drive or something?"

BB nodded. "I never thought of swimming as a full contact sport."

Charlie hushed them. "Are you okay, Deirdre? What happened?"

Through the towel, Dierdre explained, "After my practice dive, I swam back to the side of the pool with my eyes closed because the chlorine was stinging them. I didn't realize how close I was and banged my nose on the ladder."

"Ouch!" the guys replied in unison, dipping their heads and rubbing their noses.

As Bev took Deirdre to the first-aid station, the guys rushed inside to look in on George.

"Hey, buddy, I think you're fine to come back outside. In fact, I think you'll want to," said Charlie.

"Why, is the *Citizen Register* out there with a camera or something?"

"C'mon, man, we wouldn't steer you wrong," promised BB.

George was listening, but he wasn't budging. DMarks finally stepped up to try to snap him out of it.

"All right, now listen up. First of all, you can't stay in here all night, James Dennis would never allow it. Second, your nose stopped bleeding a while ago, so it's time to get back in the game. Third, you don't need an ambulance. Fourth, you have to shake this off and just be glad you were brave enough to try that dive in the first place."

Charlie and BB looked on and nodded their approval.

"We're with him," they echoed.

After a few minutes, Charlie got George to the mirror so he could clean up his face. He tossed the tissues in the garbage can and headed outside, keeping his head down not wanting to make eye contact with anyone.

"I'm such an idiot." George sighed, shaking his head as he came back into the daylight.

Then, he came face-to-face with Deirdre, who was holding a tissue to her nose. "You okay, George?" she asked with a look of genuine concern.

"You got a bloody nose too? What happened?" George stuttered.

Instead of answering, she handed him one of the Cokes she was holding.

"Look at us," she said. "We look like we just came from a rugby match."

George felt his spirit rising.

"Not the best place for us to donate blood." He laughed.

"You know what? I think we make a good team." She grabbed his arm as they walked right past Charlie, DMarks, and BB on their way up to Law Park.

The guys looked on, happy for their friend.

"Note to us. Less Marco Polo and more time on the diving boards," pronounced DMarks.

"Man, maybe I'll try blowing a dive in front of a bunch girls," said BB.

"Whatever it takes," said Charlie, playfully snap-whipping him with his towel.

19
CHAPTER
SUMMER LOVE

Let all you do be done in love.

—Corinthians 16:14

Charlie and Michelle had something special for two people their age. They had been going out since sixth grade. Everything felt natural and easy between them "like it was meant to be," as they'd say once in a while to each other.

A couple times a week, Charlie would walk over to Michelle's house after dinner. They had a special routine where they'd arrange two adjacent Adirondack chairs but facing in opposite directions. That way, they could look at each other as they chatted, forearms resting side by side on the armrests, pinky fingers intertwined.

They loved watching day turn into night and listening to the radio as the stars came out.

"My grandmother used to take me out in the backyard at night whenever she visited. We'd look up, and she'd always say it was like God scattered ten thousand diamonds in the night sky," said Charlie.

"I love that. And my grandfather used to take me out and show me the different constellations. That's Perseus right above us," replied Michelle.

"Perse-who?"

"Perseus. He killed Medusa and rescued Andromeda."

"Ah. Sounds romantic."

"Very."

One night before leaving his house, Charlie called WRNW-FM, the local station in Briarcliff. He spoke with a new, young DJ named Howard Stern and requested that he play "You've Got a Friend." Michelle loved James Taylor and that was her favorite song.

After arranging their chairs and tuning in the radio, they sat holding hands, talking about everything and nothing at all. Each time a song ended, Charlie leaned toward the radio with a raised eyebrow, in anticipation of the dedication. He wasn't sure if or when his request would be honored, but he wanted to be ready.

He tapped his fingers in an anxious cadence on the wide, flat arm of the chair as his right foot fidgeted and jostled, bouncing up and down. Then, at about half past the hour, an appreciative grin spread across his face as he leaned back to listen in.

"Well, folks, we got another warm sticky night here in Briarcliff Manor," said the DJ. "It's eighty-four degrees with 95 percent humidity. But ya know what? I'm hoping things are about to heat up some more. That's right, I got a beautiful young couple hanging out under the stars over on Jackson Road. Here's the song that put James Taylor on the map. I'm told it's also a good song to make out to. This one's for Charlie and Michelle. You kids have fun over there."

Michelle bolted upright with blinking, dilated eyes, trying to assimilate what she just heard. "Did… Did… Did you…?" Charlie just smiled back, giving away the answer.

"You are the single, most thoughtful person I've ever known." Michelle giggled as she bent across the arms of their chairs for a tender kiss.

"Wow, remind me to call my friend Howard the next time we do this," he quipped.

Michelle grinned. "You've come a long way in the music appreciation department."

"I had a great teacher." Charlie leaned in for another gentle kiss.

They continued listening to the radio when "Don't Let the Sun Go Down on Me" by Elton John began to play. High-spirited as always, Michelle jumped up and asked Charlie to dance. He happily accommodated, and they swayed smoothly in the moon shadows.

"Is this dancing, or are we just kind of hugging and swaying?" asked Michelle.

"This is about as close to dancing as I've ever gotten." He pulled her closer.

"But don't you like it if you're out to dinner somewhere and there's a band and you see your parents get up to dance. You know, old-fashioned, like in the old days?"

"I guess so, but I'm getting a little concerned about where this conversation's going."

"I just think it looks so romantic." She smiled up at him. "Maybe someday we can go to dance class."

"I was afraid you were going to say that."

"C'mon, lots of kids go." She toyed with the gold heart on the necklace he had given her last year on her birthday.

"Tell ya what. There isn't much I wouldn't do for you, but suits, dancing, punch bowls?"

"It was just a thought."

"A scary thought. A very scary thought."

Charlie grabbed her hand and they sat back down, this time together in one chair. They went on to talk about hopes and concerns for high school, where they wanted to go to college, and what they had in mind for possible careers.

"My dad and I have talked about different kinds of jobs. I've got a couple things I'm thinking about."

"Tell me," Michelle said eagerly.

Charlie explained that, in his heart, he wanted to be a phys ed teacher and a coach. "I like the school environment, and I really like sports. Plus, I've been able to help out coaching younger kids in the flag football and Saturday morning basketball leagues. It's a blast."

"I can so see you doing that."

"Coach Cadman said he'd take me to see Springfield College where he went to school to get his degree."

"That's awesome. Coach is the best."

"What about you? What's in your heart?"

Michelle also knew what she wanted to do. She loved to travel and was great with math and calculations.

"I'm going to be an airline pilot so I can see the world! UMass Amherst has a good school for aeronautical engineering. If I go there and you go to Springfield, we'll only be about a half hour from each other."

"If that's the case, I think I'll be applying for early admission."

Michelle liked the sound of it all, laying her head on his shoulder as he ran his fingers up and down her forearm.

"What's it like having a younger brother and sister?" Charlie asked.

"Well, most of the time, it's awesome. They kind of look up to you and think you're cool."

"I always wished I had a brother or sister to pal around with."

"You'd be such a great big brother. You kinda are to your crew."

"I don't know how good I'd be, but I love it when the younger kids want to hang out with us over at the pool. Sometimes, we let them join us for jump or dive."

"I've noticed! And you always make it easy on them so they can feel cool around you older guys."

"How did you develop your love of travel?" Charlie asked.

"Well, my parents both enjoy going places, but my dad sometimes takes me on business trips, too."

"What's your favorite place to visit?"

"Southern California," she answered without hesitation. "Love the beaches there, plus the weather's always great." Michelle kicked off her clogs and tucked her feet under Charlie's thigh.

"So I've heard," he agreed, tickling her toes.

"You should go someday. There's so much to do and you run into movie stars sometimes."

"Have you met anyone famous?"

"Well, the last time I was there, we met Goldie Hawn coming out of Giorgio's on Rodeo Drive."

"That's so cool! Was she nice?"

"Yes, very. It was just a quick hello."

"I have family in Fort Lauderdale, so we go there a lot whenever we take a vacation."

"I love Florida too. Sometimes we go to Miami on winter break."

The thick, humid night air seemed to slow down the passage of time which was fine with them as they basked in the trouble-free enjoyment of each other's company.

"By the way, I've been meaning to ask, have you heard from your friend Sky lately. Seems like he would have kept in touch somehow. I mean, it's been a while since the last time he was in Briarcliff."

Sitting up a little straighter, Charlie thought about how best to answer the question. "Have I heard from Sky? I guess you could say that, yeah."

"Did he write? Did he call you on the phone?"

"Not exactly," Charlie answered, scratching behind his ear.

"What was it? Did he talk to you in a dream or something?"

"Let's just say we've been in touch lately. I don't suppose we'll be seeing him this summer, but you know what they say, long distance is the next best thing to being there."

"Well, say hi for me."

Michelle put her arms around Charlie's back, locking her fingers together as "Sister Golden Hair" by America finished playing.

Then came Howard Stern's now familiar voice.

"Hey, uh, Charlie and Michelle. How's it going? Hopefully, you're locking lips about now, but in case you need some more mood music, here are a few more songs from James Taylor."

"Wow, I feel like a celebrity." Charlie laughed.

"Okay, Mr. Celebrity. Let's not disappoint Howard," said Michelle as she cozied up with her light-up-the-night smile.

20
CHAPTER

SCOUT'S HONOR

Be strong and courageous. Do not be frightened and do not be dismayed, for the Lord your God is with you wherever you go.

—Joshua 1:9

Charlie's mom spotted a delivery of fresh Maine blueberries at the A&P, so she purchased a batch to make a pancake breakfast the next day. There weren't many things Charlie enjoyed more than homemade blueberry pancakes, so he had extra spring in his step when he came downstairs and into the kitchen that morning.

"Hello, best mom in Briarcliff."

"Best? An *A* for effort would be plenty good enough for me." Mrs. Riverton wagged her spatula at him.

Eyeing the platter full of luscious-looking pancakes he slid a few onto his plate. Taking a seat at the kitchen table, he began to meticulously coat the top of each layer with butter, before smothering them with maple syrup. His stomach churned with anticipation as he took his fork and cut a triangular section from the triple decker delight. With salivating tastebuds, a huge smile broke out across his face as the first forkful melted in his mouth.

Without hesitation, he cut out another section and wolfed it down. It was only as he went in for his third mouthful, that he finally noticed his father sitting on the other side of the table. "Oh, hi, Dad. Didn't notice you over there."

"I guess your old man can't compete with your mom's blueberry pancakes."

"I forgot it was Saturday. Nice to see you at the breakfast table."

"Why thank you, son. By the way, are you planning to share any of those?"

"Sure, Dad one for you, three for me," he continued, gobbling away.

"Gee, thanks," his father dryly responded. "It's probably for the best. My waistline hasn't been cooperating lately," he said, giving his stomach a firm pat.

"So what are you and your friends going to do today?" asked Charlie's mom.

"We've been thinking about riding our bikes up to the Girl Scout camp to see what's up that way."

"That's practically all the way to Chappaqua. It'll take you at least a half hour to get there," cautioned his mom.

"Well, we don't have to be in a hurry, it's Saturday."

"Just be careful, Charlie. Some of those roads are pretty narrow and watch out for blind corners," cautioned his father, nodding at him over the top of his newspaper.

Over on the far northeast edge of town was Camp Edith Macy, a retreat for the Girl Scouts of America. DMarks reasoned that there must be girl scouts up there and claimed to have heard that they liked to sunbathe by Echo Lake just inside the grounds.

"There's a ton of woods and a beautiful lake over there. Your grandfather and I spent many a Sunday afternoon fishing and relaxing," his dad told him. "Just remember, it's all private property, so no shenanigans and mind the No Trespassing signs."

"Right, I promise, we'll steer clear of any areas that have No Trespassing signs," replied Charlie, wincing. *Did they somehow hear about how we all snuck into the middle school a couple weeks ago*?

"Okay, buddy. We know you'd never be found someplace you're not supposed to be," said his dad, looking pointedly in his direction. Charlie stopped chewing as his dad's words sunk in, making him wonder if his parents knew more than he realized. He tried to think fast, like DMarks would.

"Before I meet up with the guys, I was thinking that I'd wash and wax your cars. Are either of you going out anytime soon?"

"That's awfully good of you, but only if you let us pay you," said Charlie's mom.

"The Turtle Wax is on the shelf in the garage above the spare tire," interrupted his dad, winking at his mom.

Charlie tried to analyze the exchange as he went back to his pancake breakfast. Whether they knew about the middle school escapade or not, he was happy wash and wax his parent's cars for them.

He finished off what was on his plate, pushed back from the table and gave a prolonged exhale.

"Wow, that was good. Thanks, Mom."

"You're welcome, son."

Barnes and Noble gazed at their bowls, disappointed that there were no leftovers for them.

"Sorry, guys," said Charlie, scrunching their ears. "I'll get you back at dinner tonight."

Into the garage he went to grab a bucket and a sponge, then out to the driveway. The morning air and sun felt great as he uncoiled the hose and dragged it over to the two parked cars. First, he sprayed down his mom's VW Beetle, then he turned the hose on his dad's Caprice Classic.

As he soaped up both cars, the radio was on in the background. His mind wandered to a few years down the road when he'd be asking to borrow one of the cars to pick Michelle up for dates and school events.

Just as he was finishing up and putting the hose away, the guys arrived in front of his house. Wasting no time, he hopped on his bike as the four of them sped off. There was a sense of adventure as they rode out of the Tree Streets.

They talked, pedaled, and laughed all the way to where Washburn Road connected with Old Chappaqua Road. It had already been a long haul, so they decided to take a break and rest up in the shade.

"I swear, Marks, there better be tons of bikinis up there. The hilly part's still in front of us," BB growled.

"Suck it up, slacker," DMarks responded.

"Our bikes only have three gears. Your Stingray has five. Want to trade?" huffed George, throwing himself on a patch of grass.

"Just wait till we get to where the girls are laying out in the sun. That'll cure you guys of all this whine-itis."

"No one's whining. It's just that you've got us going over hill and dale and we want to be sure this isn't some wild goose chase," replied Charlie, cupping a blade of grass in his hands and blowing through it to create a whistling sound.

"Easy, easy," DMarks assured them, "what could possibly go wrong?"

After chilling out for another few minutes, they pressed on. Several miles later, they crested the last hill and could see the camp entrance in the distance.

"Hold on, fellas, I think we should ditch our bikes in the woods, then go the rest of the way on foot," declared DMarks.

It was a reasonable suggestion, so the boys followed his lead. They were entering private property and had to stay out of sight from that point on.

"Follow me. We can sneak along the water's edge until we get up to where the cabins are," instructed DMarks.

With no paths to follow, they had to make their way through thorny brambles and all kinds of vine-covered underbrush. It was slow going as they pushed branches out of their way, stepping over downed trees and climbing up and over all sorts of rock formations.

As they rambled through a thick patch of evergreens and scrub growth, they noticed a quiet buzzing sound. Then, within seconds, it throttled up to a furious, humming reverberation.

The guys must have disturbed a hornet's nest as a cloud of angry bees began to swarm around. There was only one thing to do.

"Quick, guys. Into the lake!" yelled Charlie.

They took off sprinting and dove in, swimming underwater as far as they could. Eventually, they broke the surface gasping for air.

They were already half-way across the lake, so they kept swimming until they came to the other side.

As they waded out of the water, they were out of breath, but they were also out of danger. Miraculously, no one got stung.

"Man, that was a close call," said Charlie bent over, hands on his knees, chest heaving.

"Thank goodness for that lake," added George, trying to catch his breath. "We'd all be covered in welts by now."

They peeled off their saturated T-shirts, wrung them out and looked around. There was nothing but deep woods, more hills, and hundred-foot-tall trees. It felt like they were in the middle of nowhere. Squinting hard, they could just about see cabins over on the far shoreline of the lake.

"Great. Now what?" asked BB. "There's a million gallons of water separating us from the Girl Scouts and a swarm of bees between us and our bikes."

"Relax, Gidget. I say we hang out over here in the sun. By the time we dry off, the bees will be gone, and we can head back," responded DMarks. "A little downtime never hurt anyone."

Charlie, George, and BB shrugged in agreement, as they hung their shirts on low-hanging tree branches.

"Hello out there!" yelled Charlie, cupping his ear as his voice rebounded back. "Now I know why they call this Echo Lake."

"Any girls out there?" hollered DMarks.

One by one, they all got comfortable leaning up against grassy hummocks and tree trunks.

"Hey, Marks, you know what's good-looking and hangs out in the woods?" asked BB.

"Tell me."

"I have no idea, but apparently, it ain't Girl Scouts! Why we ever followed you out here, I'll never know."

"Yeah, there's a reason why I never joined the Boy Scouts. You know why? Because I don't like the woods," complained George. "Now you've got us stuck out here with no sign of life or bikinis in any direction."

Only Charlie had a positive spin on their predicament.

"Guys, let's just try to make the best of this. At least it's a change of pace for us."

"Thank you, Charles," offered DMarks. "I appreciate your practical point of view."

They kicked back in the picturesque setting but boredom set in fast. DMarks felt compelled to liven things up, so he began to tell a story he once heard as a kid.

"Any of you guys ever hear of the Phantom Gravedigger?"

"What? Shut up," scoffed BB.

"Yep, it happened right here at this lake about a hundred years ago."

"Can it, dweeb," dismissed George.

DMarks kept at it. "About a mile over the hillside right behind us, is the Far Ridge Cemetery in Chappaqua. Apparently, the gravedigger was a hardworking, honest man. But his wife wanted more, so she took up with a banker over in Mt. Kisco."

"Oh brother," interrupted Charlie, motioning for him to wrap it up.

"When the gravedigger found out about his wife's betrayal, he turned to the bottle to drown out his pain. Every night, he'd sit out in these woods and knock back a fifth of bourbon after work."

"I'm going to knock you out if you don't shut your face," ordered BB.

"Ha! You and what army?" DMarks replied. Undeterred, he carried on with his story.

"Then, one day, he started early, finishing a bottle with his lunch. That whole afternoon, he was drunk out of his mind."

"Wait, did he sing Harry Chapin songs while he drank?" joked George.

DMarks let the interruption go. "Where was I… Oh yeah. The poor bastard started heading home through these very woods." DMarks paused, spreading out his arms to remind them where they were. "But he was so drunk, he took a wrong turn and ended up down here by the lake. No one knows what actually happened, but that was the end of him. Or was it?"

Now the boys were actually sitting up and paying attention. They didn't know if this story was for real or not.

"Is he being serious?" asked George, eyes darting between Charlie and BB.

"Umm, then what happened?" BB asked, glancing around with anxious eyes.

"When they found him, it looked like he had been hit in the back of the head with a blunt object." DMarks karate-chopped his hands together loudly causing George to flinch. "The locals thought maybe his wife had swung at him with his own shovel, toppling him into the lake."

"Geez. What a way to go. Then what happened?" a very jumpy BB wanted to know.

"He drowned. Whaddya think happened? A day later, he was found face-down over by the waterfall. A tree branch had snagged his suspenders. Otherwise, he would have gone over the falls. Splat!"

"Wait, what happened to his wife?" asked Charlie.

"Apparently, she had a little too much of the good life and ended up at an institution. Some said she lost her mind because of the guilt she caried around."

"And what about the gravedigger. Is he buried around here?" asked George. "We're kind of surrounded by dirt mounds." He pointed out scanning the area.

"Yeah, in an unmarked grave, or so I'm told."

"You mean you don't know?" asked Charlie.

"Well, the details are kind of murky. But that, my tenderfoot friends, is the legend of the phantom gravedigger."

The boys were genuinely spooked.

"For real, Marks?" challenged George, folding his arms.

"How do I know? I wasn't around back then. All I know is what I've heard. Legend has it that he still walks these woods, looking for his wife."

"Maybe that's why there's no one else out here? I mean, there's nothing out here," Charlie said as his voice trailed off.

"I'd say that's a good deduction, Charles," answered a smug DMarks.

The boys looked at each other with anxious glances.

BB gulped. "Um, do you think it's safe to try to get back to our bikes?"

"Safe or not, let's get out of here," George urged.

As they each got up to grab their still-damp shirts, they heard the sound of snapping twigs and heavy footsteps rustling in the leaves, coming in their direction. Their blood ran cold. Before they could even turn around, they heard a grim and gravelly voice.

"You boys looking to join the Girl Scouts?"

Slowly they turned. Right there, a few yards away, was a huge, hulking man with a long, unkept beard, a filthy-looking John Deer baseball cap, and a lazy eye bearing down on them. He was wearing a red flannel shirt with sleeves cut off at his shoulders and a pair of dark blue work pants held up by thick, red, sweat-stained suspenders. Covered in dirt, he looked like he had been out in the woods for months. He cocked a half smile and cackled a menacing snicker as he balanced his right forearm on a huge shovel.

"Code red!" yelled DMarks. The boys dropped their shirts and dove into the pond, swimming at an adrenaline-filled pace that would have broken Olympic records.

The man with the shovel just stood there laughing. A moment later, a few others from the camp maintenance crew showed up.

"You have to stop scaring kids like that," commented one of them. "I was just having some fun. Look at those little fellers go."

The boys got to the other side of the lake, sprinted to their bikes and took off down Chappaqua Road. At least the way home was mostly downhill.

When they got to the bend in the road, they stopped to catch their breath. Straddling their bikes and leaning over their handlebars, they began to feel safe.

"What the heck was that?" asked an out of breath BB.

"I don't know, but that was scary."

"Kind of cool. We actually met the Phantom Gravedigger," crowed DMarks. "I'm using this for Truth or Dare."

Charlie was thinking in a more practical way.

"There goes my Digger Phelps Basketball Camp T-shirt," he lamented. "I'm zero for three with favorite shirts this summer."

"Was that the one Coach McLaughlin gave you for being Diggers' sixth man?" asked George.

"Yup. I'll never see it again thanks to Mr. Girl Scouts USA," he replied, nailing DMarks with a perfectly landed dead arm.

"Dang, that shirt was a keeper. Too bad, man," added BB.

"Yeah, I don't care how many Girl Scouts there might be up there, I'll never go near that stupid lake ever again," said George.

"I'm with you," agreed BB.

They all looked at each other and then broke out laughing, a bit delirious with relief. Shirtless, the four headed back down the last hill, crisscrossing their bikes and doing imitations of their horror-struck faces back in the woods.

"Dude," Charlie rode close to DMarks, "you were so like this." He opened his mouth as wide as possible in a silent scream.

"And, BB." George laughed. "You were shaking like a little girl."

"Was not!" BB shot back. "And what about you? Your eyes were popping out of your head, big as jawbreakers."

Laughter trailed after them all the way to the pool, just in time for their third dip of the day.

"Last one in's a dead gravedigger," challenged DMarks, launching himself off the deck with a Tarzan scream.

21

CHAPTER

SUMMER OF SHOVE

A friend loves at all times and a brother is born for adversity.

—Proverbs 17:17

One afternoon, the guys were at Jackson Road Park, trying to decide what to do.

"I have an idea," offered George. "Let's build a ramp by the brook, then jump it on our bikes like Evil Knievel."

The guys were immediately intrigued by the possibilities. *Wide World of Sports* had recently televised the famous motorcycle jump over the Caesar's Palace fountains, which they all thought was super cool.

"He doesn't step up with big ideas very much, but when he does, he delivers," said DMarks.

"Best idea of the summer," said BB, giving him a thumbs-up.

"I think we have a winner," declared Charlie.

They set out collecting materials from the swamp. First, they made a foundation of logs and rocks. Then, they laid branches and reads to make a ramp. After setting everything in place, they tamped it down, packing mud in all the gaps and crevices.

Once complete, they took turns walking up and looking out across the brook, just like Evil Knievel always did on his motorcycle.

But once they got a look, they each gulped, realizing that maybe this wasn't the greatest idea.

Now that the moment of truth had arrived, none of them wanted to be the guinea pig as excuses began to fly instead of bicycles.

"I'd do it, but I have to protect my good eye," professed DMarks.

"I can't do my paper route on crutches," affirmed BB.

"I get airsick," mumbled George.

Finally, Charlie stepped up. He looked things over and determined that once he got airborne, he'd be about four feet above the brook. If he could hit the ramp with enough speed, he'd stay dry, but he still had to nail the landing. This was no easy challenge and unlike anything they had ever done.

"We didn't go to all this trouble to chicken out now. I'll do it."

DMarks was so impressed with Charlie's nerve that he offered to let him use his Stingray. Charlie nodded solemnly. Without saying a word, he grabbed the chopper-style handlebars and began walking the bike to the top of Maple Road. The boys followed along in silent support.

At the top of the hill, George broke the tension. "Atta-boy," he said, slapping Charlie on the back.

"You got this, man," encouraged BB, grabbing Charlie by the arm.

After a brief pause, DMarks chimed in. "Yo, Charlie, if you crash and die, can I have your Yankees autograph collection?"

BB immediately nailed him with a dead arm. "Shut up, dork. This takes guts."

"I was kidding. Just trying to lighten things up," he replied, grabbing his arm, folding over in pain.

"I don't give a Donald Duck. This is no time to joke around," scolded BB, this time administering another dead arm with his elbow, which really killed.

Charlie was oblivious to the whole spat. He just kept walking, head down. When he got to the top of the hill, he turned around to look at what was in front of him. Patting Sky's cross with a crown of thorns pendant under his T-shirt, he took a few long, deep breaths and furrowed his brow in deep concentration.

Clenching his jaw, he sharpened his eyes and got on the bike. After riding around in a few wide circles, he shifted into fifth gear so he could pedal downhill as fast and as hard as possible. At the end of the fifth circle, he locked in and headed down Maple Road, standing up as he pedaled. At the bottom of Maple Road, he cut into the park. Leaning left, he was on course with the jump only about twenty yards in front of him. There was no bailing out now.

He could actually hear his heart pounding as the bike tires swooshed through the grass. A moment later, he was airborne. Instantly, it was as if time went into slow-motion as he glided through the thick summer air. All he could think of was to stay vertical to the ground for a safe landing. A split second later, he hit hard on the other side of the brook. His momentum propelled him forward across the grass and hardpan before he came to a skidding wipeout.

It all happened so fast that Charlie couldn't immediately realize what he had done, but he definitely knew to say a silent prayer of thanks. The others raced to his side with arms raised, cheering and celebrating the first-of-its-kind accomplishment at Jackson Road Park.

Charlie was exhilarated, but once was enough as far as he was concerned. They crowded him, patting him on the back and raising his hands high above his head.

"Never a doubt!" hollered BB.

"That's my boy!" yelled George.

"If you weren't so *you,* I'd nickname you Evil!" roared DMarks, sneaking a close glance at this bike to make sure there was no damage.

"I can't even remember what I just did." Charlie's knees were shaking as he stepped away from the bike, happy that he didn't break an arm or a leg.

"C'mon, guys," pronounced DMarks. "Let's find some shade, sip some Gatorade and relive Charlie's glory."

"I'm telling, ya, when we look back on this summer, that will be the coolest thing of all," declared BB.

"If this were a movie, they would have gotten a stunt man," said George.

"I think he should be able to keep the Stingray for the way he pulled that off," added BB. "Nice and clean."

"Whoa, whoa, whoa! Let's not get crazy over there," replied DMarks, shoving his friend from the side.

The guys were on a natural high from what Charlie had just accomplished. Then, out of nowhere, it was all rudely interrupted by the sounds of Will Morris and his foulmouthed pack of cronies heading in their direction.

They each felt a fight or flight feeling surge inside. Charlie chose flight.

"Let's not have any trouble today guys," he urged.

"Yeah, no hot garbage with these bums today," said BB.

Incredibly, DMarks agreed. He then further shocked his friends by quoting a verse from proverbs.

"I'm with Charlie. The Bible says that a soft word turns away wrath but a harsh word stirs up anger."

The comment caught Charlie's attention as he listened along with a sunny grin. BB and George stared at each other curious to hear more.

"Did I just hear what I think I heard?" asked George.

"I was just wondering the same thing," replied BB, cupping his hands to his ears.

DMarks glared back at them, "Yeah, that's right, I've been spending a little time reading my Bible at night. Don't look so surprised."

"And what got you to pick up your Bible?" asked BB.

"I was hanging out at Greenie's house the other afternoon and we were kind of bored. So his mom suggested we read our Bibles and I took her suggestion to heart. Mrs. Greenberg's the best."

Just then, DMarks was once again distracted by an incredibly clean flowery breeze. He inhaled deeply, letting out a deep breath, "Ahh…"

The guys all looked at him.

"What's with you?" asked BB.

"Can I help it if I like the smell of fresh cut flowers," responded DMarks.

"What the heck are you talking about?" asked George.

"You didn't get a whiff just now?"

"Okay, you're starting to scare me," answered BB.

"Buddy, I hate to tell ya, but you're a few sandwiches short of a picnic," added George.

"Oh, mug off. You guys don't know what you're missing," replied DMarks, pretending to gather in more of the scent with his arms. "It smells like a flower shop around here."

"Yeah, and Jeremiah was a bullfrog," chided BB.

At the same time, their older adversaries had arrived with their typically rude swagger and bluster. DMarks looked in their direction. Then, he got up to walk over to them. Charlie, BB and George all grasped at his ankles to hold him back, but it was too late. Then, to their amazement, he went right up to Will Morris.

"The court's all yours. Have fun."

Bouncing a basketball very slowly, Will glared back at DMarks, wondering what he was up to. Not trusting that he wasn't playing some kind of trick, Will reached out, grabbed him, and shoved him so hard, DMarks tumbled all the way across the court and onto the grassy area on the side.

Charlie and the guys looked on, expecting an eruption from their friend. Instead, DMarks got back on his feet, brushed himself off and looked at the guys.

"C'mon, let's go swimming."

The fact that he didn't get mad or say anything back seemed to get Will all the more angry. He stood there, bursting with sweat, grinding his bubble gum and boring in on DMarks.

"What, no wise-guy remark? No name-calling?"

Will's buddies thought something was fishy too. They just stood and looked on, basketballs tucked under their arms.

DMarks didn't answer, which further dialed up Will's anger. Instead, he just walked to his stingray with the guys following close behind.

"What was that? Were you sleepwalking or something?" asked BB, talking sideways to him.

"Yeah, keep this up, and they're going to send you to the Funny Farm," added George.

"You heard the man. It's pool time!" Charlie happily chimed in.

They all hopped on their bikes and began to ride down Jackson Road. Charlie pedaled up alongside DMarks.

"Didn't see that one coming. I'm proud of you."

"Thank you, Charles. And I'm proud of you for that jump you made."

DMarks rode along self-confident as ever, but he was distracted and quiet. *What's gotten into me?* he wondered. *I feel like I'm arm wrestling…with myself.*

22
CHAPTER

PLAYLAND

So whether you eat or drink, or whatever
you do, do all to the glory of God.

—1 Corinthians 10:31

For Charlie's fourteenth birthday, his parents took the guys to Playland for a night of fun and rides. Michelle and some of the other girls joined as well.

Playland was the ultimate summer destination. Located about twenty minutes down-county from Briarcliff in the village of Rye, the quaint amusement park was built in the early 1900s on the shores of the Long Island Sound. Famous for its Dragon Coaster, there were also arcade games and loads of refreshment stands overflowing with cotton candy, taffy, ice cream, and penny candy.

Mr. Riverton drove the guys and Mrs. Riverton drove the girls. After parking in the massive lot, everyone made a beeline to the admissions window underneath the art-deco façade.

The air was filled with carnival music and the scent of fried dough. Mr. Riverton bought unlimited rides tickets for each of Charlie's friends. As he handed them out, Charlie's mom laid out the ground rules for the evening.

"Okay, everyone, you can go anywhere you'd like in the park, but be sure to check in with us regularly. We want to be sure you're safe."

"Mrs. Riverton and I will camp out by the benches at center gardens. If anyone needs anything, that's where to find us," added Charlie's dad, taking a candid photo of all the kids standing together.

"C'mon, everyone, let's start with the Dragon Coaster," suggested Charlie.

"I call the front seat!" declared DMarks. They all took off running.

"There he goes again, calling shotgun," complained BB.

"Let him have it. He'll be crying for his mother after the first hill," predicted George.

DMarks took out his Binaca and spritzed a few shots in his mouth.

"Ahh, never leave home without it," he crowed.

"Dream on, bed-wetter. You're going to need way more than fresh breath tonight," added BB.

"Oh, shut your face."

"I don't know what it will be or when it will happen, but something tells me he's going to put on a show tonight," predicted George.

Arriving at the Dragon Coaster, they filed in boy-girl taking their places in the two-seaters. The ride operators passed through, pulling the crossbars down across their laps. The girls all latched onto the arms of whoever they were sitting with. After everything was secure, the cars lurched forward and the ride began.

DMarks naturally figured out how to sit with Andrea who was obviously anxious when it came to roller coasters. As the cable pulled the coaster up the super-steep first peak, the cranking noise intensified. Sensing an opportunity, DMarks made his move.

"I think we should make out. If this thing goes off its rails, I'd hate to go to my grave without ever having kissed you," he said, throwing an arm around her shoulder.

Feeling panicky, Andrea actually consented but only briefly. The coaster was about to begin its descent. As it inched forward,

DMarks turned to glance at what was in front of them. His eyes almost popped out of their sockets as they went swooping down.

He screamed in a high soprano octave as Andrea stuck her fingers in her ears, laughing uncontrollably. Now it was DMarks who was grabbing Andrea's arm, holding on for dear life.

The ride only lasted a few minutes, but it was up-down, all-around, open-air exhilaration. As the coaster came skidding to a halt, everyone jumped out and headed straight to the back of the line to do it again.

"My head is spinning," Michelle leaned into Charlie for support.

"I know! Isn't it great!"

DMarks shuffled down the gangplank to the ride exit with his arms folded across his abdomen. The ride had made him nauseous, turning him a whiter shade of pale for the whole group to see.

"What's up with you? You look seasick," BB called over from the line.

"I think I'll sit this one out. The night is young."

"Ha! What a chicken," clucked George, flapping his arms.

"Revenge of the Dragon Coaster," declared Charlie.

DMarks couldn't even respond. All he wanted to do was get to the nearest bench. No one was sweeter than Andrea, and she decided to stay with him out of concern.

"How's about you wait here. I'll get you a Coke. It'll settle your stomach."

"Grab me a chili dog too!" yelled DMarks as he sprawled across the bench.

"Umm, you sure that's a good idea?"

"A chili dog is always a good idea," he said, waving her on.

The night air helped DMarks to feel better. Thanks to the incoming tide, the breeze off the Long Island Sound was sweet-smelling and caused the temperature to drop a few breezy degrees.

By the time Andrea returned, DMarks had his sea legs back. Swiping the Coke and chili dog right out of her hands he devoured them in under a minute. True to form, he stood up and belched, tossing the soda fountain cup in a nearby trashcan.

"Thanks, that hit the spot," he said. Giving Andrea a big wink. "I'll pay you back at Ye Olde Mill."

Ye Olde Mill was Playland's version of a lover's lane. Playfully tugging on the tassels of her peasant blouse Andrea tilted her head, responding with a "We'll see…"

Just then, the rest of the group came sprinting by on their way to the next ride. DMarks grabbed Andrea's hand and got right in stride with them.

In between rides, there were dozens of games to be played at the Arcade, like the water pistol horse races, the shooting range with real BB guns, and shuffle bowl. Of course, there also were sports games which the boys naturally gravitated toward.

The first booth they stopped at was the basketball free throw. Charlie spotted an oversized teddy bear he wanted to win for Michelle. That meant he had to make ten out of twelve shots. It was a low margin for error, but he was up for the challenge.

Charlie glanced at Michelle, who flashed one of her beaming smiles. After stepping up to pay, the man at the booth put twelve basketballs on the counter as everyone gathered around.

"You got this, Charles," said DMarks, slapping him on the back. "Just remember that sweet form Coach Nutson taught you. Cocked arm, full follow-through and a flick of the wrist as you release the ball." DMarks demonstrated dramatically for the girls.

"This guy's going to lose money on Charlie tonight," said BB, nudging Robin.

"You won't be welcomed back after you knock these shots down," added George.

Charlie spun a ball around in his hands to get a feel for what he was working with, then he promptly hit his first three shots.

The booth operator indicated that three out of three earned anything he wanted from the first row of souvenirs. He looked at Michelle and nodded for her to pick whatever she liked. There were a bunch of vintage 7UP bottles with stretched out necks. She liked the psychedelic throwback look, so she snagged one.

He then swished his next three shots with ease, earning an upgrade for Michelle from the second row of souvenirs. This time, she traded in her 7UP bottle for a framed mirror with a picture Leif Garrett on it. The girls all came over for a closer look.

Charlie was on fire making three of his next four shots. All he needed was to make one out of his last two.

Taking a slow, deep breath he locked in his concentration. At the same time, DMarks had picked up the last ball and began to spin it on his finger trying to show off.

His timing could not have been worse. He lost control of the ball, which hit Charlie's shooting hand just as he was letting go of his eleventh shot. The ball clanked off the rim, leaving Charlie with one last chance and no margin for error.

Charlie nailed him with a fiery stare.

"What?" replied DMarks, acting clueless about what he had done.

BB was not happy. "If he misses this last shot, I'm putting you on the Dragon Coaster and tying you into your seat for the rest of the night you meatball."

Charlie snatched the last ball, focused his shooting eye, and let it fly. It bounced high in the air off the rim and came straight down, swishing through the net for his final basket. He took the mirror from Michelle and asked the man to replace it with the giant teddy bear.

Michelle nearly melted, hugging it close.

"Now I have two bears, my Briarcliff bear and this stuffed one."

"I hope you plan on keeping them both for a long time," answered Charlie, as they leaned in for a brief kiss.

After Charlie's triumph, the group wandered around taking in the sights, eventually ending up by the north end of the park which had a huge stage for live performances. Just as they passed by, a traveling performing group called Up With People came out to begin that night's show.

"Check it out!" said Michelle. "They performed at the middle school last year."

Up with People featured about fifty teenaged kids who trekked around the country on a goodwill tour. The song they opened with was "Hooked on a Feeling" by BJ Thomas. The first line really got DMarks's attention—"*I can't stop this feeling deep inside of me…*"

As he stood listening, he mulled over the things he had been thinking and feeling of late. It was like something was slowly, patiently working on him. *I have to get my head on straight about this,* he thought.

Then, as the song ended, he shrugged his shoulders. *But not tonight!*

"C'mon, you guys. Let's stop for some soft ice cream," he suggested.

While everyone else was content with regular chocolate or vanilla, DMarks had to go deluxe—sprinkles, chocolate sauce, walnuts, the works.

"Do you believe this guy?" asked Charlie.

"Yeah, I've seen the end of this movie before. It's not pretty," replied BB, stepping back a few feet.

Then, to everyone's amazement, DMarks took a handful of hot-buttered popcorn and sprinkled it over his cone.

"That's just gross," declared Barrie. "When you get sick later, make sure you don't do it next to me."

"Try it, you'll like it," chided DMarks, giving the cone a big lick.

"Seriously, are you trying to short-circuit your tastebuds or something?" asked Robin.

"On the contrary, my tastebuds are standing up and applauding right now."

"I bet they'll be asking for a refund pretty soon," warned George.

"Okay ladies, who wants to join me on the tilt-a-whirl?" DMarks asked as he dashed off in the direction of the next ride. Only Andrea seemed to be game to follow along. The rest sat on a bench and finished their softs serve.

"Did he skip lunch again or something?" asked Charlie.

"I don't know, but with all he's had to eat tonight, he can sure skip lunch tomorrow," answered BB.

A short while later, they headed for the bumper cars, followed by the mind scrambler. By then, things were finally starting to catch up with DMarks.

"Does he seem a little woozy to you?" Michelle asked Charlie.

"Why do you ask? Is it the pale-green complexion or the way he's holding his stomach?" Charlie responded.

A moment later, and sensing he was about to throw up, DMarks dashed to a nearby garbage can. Bending over at the waist, he began to wretch his guts out. At one point, he heaved so hard that he practically fell in.

"That's vile!" shrieked Barrie as the girls all looked away. Meanwhile, the boys winced and twisted but overall saw this as quality entertainment.

"Man, he's thrown up more times this summer than I have in the last three years," noted Charlie.

"Smooth, Marks. Very smooth," said BB. "You're gonna need a bigger can of Binaca!"

"I don't know what your problem is, Marks, but I bet it's something very hard to pronounce." George laughed.

As Charlie looked on, he felt his cross with a crown of thorns pendant shift underneath his blue Izod shirt.

"Tell ya what, guys, we've only got about another half hour before we have to leave. You jump on a few more rides, I'll stay here with Mr. Upchuck to make sure he's okay."

"But, Charlie, it's your birthday. One of us should stay instead," suggested BB.

"Nah, you guys go ahead. All for each and each for all."

"You're the best, Charlie," said George. Grabbing Meg's hand to head to the next ride, he noticed she was carrying the Leif Garret mirror.

"Hey, wait, how did you get that?" he asked.

Blushing, Meg admitted she used her charms on the guy at the basketball free throw stand after they had all walked away.

"I just love Leif," she crooned.

When DMarks finally came up for air, Charlie walked him to a bench near the beachfront.

"I'm so sorry, man. Usually my stomach can take anything I throw at it."

"Dude, I'm the one that's sorry. Feeling any better now that you spilled your guts out?"

"Actually, yes. But no more rides for me."

"Or food."

"Deal."

The two buddies sat next to each other looking out on the Long Island Sound.

"What a great summer it's been already," commented Charlie.

"Yeah, give me five."

"Maybe later after you wash those hands."

"Right. Good call."

After a few quiet moments, DMarks broke the silence. "So I've been thinking…does it feel like maybe this summer's taking us some place?"

"What do you mean?"

"Like, do you kind of feel that maybe some things are happening for a reason? Like that song we just heard from Up With People. I've heard it a hundred times, but tonight, it's like it was written specially for me."

Charlie sat back with a look of satisfaction.

"There have been a few things that made me wonder."

"I just feel like we're on a path to something," said DMarks, giving Charlie a sideways look.

"Like someone's guiding us along?"

"Yeah. That's right. Like someone up there is looking after us."

"Well, the Bible says that God takes a personal interest in each of our lives."

"So I've heard."

They sat quietly for a while more, then Charlie spoke up again. "Reverend Higgins has a motto. Something like 'better faithful than famous.' Not sure what made me think about that."

"I like it. Can I quote you?"

"Might be something for us to remember with all this stuff from Will Morris."

"How so?"

"I mean, if things keep escalating, one of these days, we're going to end up in the headlines. Might be better if we tried to call a truce with him instead of becoming the talk of the town."

"You're a better man than me, Charles. Any other words of wisdom?"

"Nope. That's all folks."

"Good, 'cause I'm down for a slice of pizza," said DMarks as he bolted from the bench.

Charlie laughed and shook head. "He's like the human version of the Uncola," he said, shaking his head.

23
CHAPTER
TROUBLED WATERS

A time to love and a time to hate; a time
for war and a time for peace.

—Ecclesiastes 3:8

The following day gave new meaning to the "dog days of summer." By late morning, the mercury was pushing into the low nineties and humidity levels were running equally high.

In spite of the hazy, hot, and humid conditions that afternoon, Charlie and the guys gathered at Jackson Road Park for a pickup game of basketball. They all played shirtless as their arms, shoulders, torsos, and backs glistened with sweat in the hazy sunlight. Because of the heat, they played a win-by-one game to twelve points. After that, they gladly retreated to the shade-covered area near the brook.

Right away, the conversation turned to their feud with the older boys. Jumping to his feet, DMarks voiced his opinion.

"I know that I kept my cool the other day. But part of me thinks the time has come for us to take a stand," he declared pounding his right fist into the palm of his left hand.

"I hate to admit it out loud, but I think he might actually be right," affirmed George.

"Here's the deal. From now on, if they come on our turf and mess with us, there has to be a price to pay. Simple as that," said DMarks.

"Doesn't sound that simple to me," complained George.

"Hey, it's the American way," affirmed DMarks.

"Time out, buddy. I know I got pretty heated up after I got thrown in the brook, but I've been thinking about all this. I had a conversation with Dr. Cook on the Fourth of July, and he explained how resorting to force doesn't always get the result you want," said Charlie.

"By the way, Charlie, I know that must have sucked getting tossed in the brook, but you looked really cool flying through the air," offered BB.

"Gee, thanks, I feel so much better," Charlie deadpanned, swatting at BB.

DMarks, who wasn't pleased with the side conversation, gave an exaggerated exhale.

"My associate Charles over here tends to focus on a New Testament kind of outlook. You slap him across the face and he'll turn the other cheek. I, on the other hand, think it's time to handle things in an Old Testament kind of way. You mess with us and you'll get it right back and worse."

Charlie, BB, and George raised their eyebrows at each other.

"I understand where you're coming from," interrupted BB. "And trust me, I'd like to punch those jerks right in their snot lockers. But they're twice our size. How are we supposed to fight and win against them?"

DMarks paused again for dramatic effect. "The wise man outthinks his opponent," he explained.

"Okay. Time out. You lost me quoting Kung Fu or whatever that was," complained BB.

"Yeah, want to mansplain that for us?" said George.

DMarks started over. "How do we fight and win? We make a plan, and we use our superior knowledge of Jackson Road Park and Woyden's Swamp to gain an advantage. We can outwit, outfox, and outmaneuver those Tootsie Pops any day of the week."

Charlie nodded along. *Rock the boat, don't tip the boat over,* he thought as he looked around hoping for some confirmation from Sky.

"You have to think like Muhammad Ali," urged DMarks. "Stick and move. Rope-a-dope. Float like a butterfly and sting like a bee," he said, throwing a right uppercut for emphasis and hopping around.

The boys were getting hooked by the rhetoric and began to buy-in.

"So what are we going to do? We're going to study them, then we're going to strike. And then we're going to keep on striking until they retreat."

"Okay, hold on," said BB. "How do we get from where we are right now to the point where they're waiving a white flag?"

"I have a plan, but I just need a little more time for it to fully hatch," DMarks grinned devilishly.

"Oh boy. Here we go," said George with a sense of anticipation.

The words were barely out of DMarks's mouth when they heard a ruckus of loud yelling and bad language. Out of nowhere, Will Morris and his partners in crime were charging straight at them in full stride from the woods on the other side of the basketball court.

"Run for it!" yelled DMarks.

Without a moment to spare, the boys fled into the swamp, charging down their network of pathways. Never had they run so fast in their entire lives, pumping their arms, chests heaving for air.

Within minutes, they found themselves at the hindmost end of Woyden's Swamp. Bent over, hands on knees, completely winded, they looked at each other with hearts pounding and fear in their eyes. They were cornered. Pinned between the Pocantico River and the menacing gang of upper classmen closing in on them.

"I guess this is it. Plan or no plan, we stick together," urged DMarks.

"All for each and each for all," affirmed BB.

"They can punch me anywhere they want, just not my nose. Please, no more bloody noses," implored George.

As they each prepared for the worst, Charlie's hand happened to brush against the cross with a crown of thorns pendant under his shirt. At that moment, a warm feeling came over him with a strong conviction to head south along the riverbank.

"C'mon, guys, follow me."

As they scurried along, he remembered a small dam they made out of rocks the last summer near The Hub. If they could get there in a hurry, they could escape across the river and over to South State Road.

A minute later, they reached the rocky footbridge and scooted across near where the God Answers Prayers sign stood.

With Will leading the way, the older boys were in hot pursuit. But when they got to the river's edge, he came to a skidding halt. His partners in crime all looked at him wondering what he was waiting for. With valuable time ticking away, he just kept looking down at the river, hesitating to go across.

As Charlie, DMarks, BB, and George dashed along, Will finally took a deep breath and reached his foot out to place it on the first bunch of rocks. But just as he began to transfer his weight forward, a freakishly strong current swept by without warning and washed the rocks downstream.

What had been a viable footbridge a moment ago was gone in an instant. Already leaning toward his front foot, Will lost his balance; and as he was about to splash into the chest-deep water, he cried out for someone to grab him. In the nick of time, two of his sidekicks reached for his outstretched arm and hauled him back to solid ground.

Will's gang stood around kicking rocks, cursing, and spitting over the missed opportunity to pound on Charlie and the guys. They were unsure of what to make of Will's craven display, as he tried to convince them that he freaked out because he didn't want to get his sneakers wet.

Meanwhile, from down the riverbank, Charlie and the guys saw that the chase was off.

"Man, that was some nice thinking, Charlie," said George thankfully.

"We were dead meat until you thought of that old crossing dam we built," said BB.

"Not for nothing, did you guys see how that current just suddenly showed up and wiped it out right after we got across?" asked DMarks. "It was like God's invisible hand just reached down and whoosh." He mimed, grabbing at the air.

"Yeah, what a coincidence," said George.

"A coincidence? You think that was a coincidence?" asked DMarks.

"Okay, how about a lucky break?"

"Open your eyes, man! Stuff like that doesn't just happen by accident."

BB and George had to admit DMarks had a point. Charlie smiled knowingly.

They trotted across Route 9A and over to South State Road and safety. It would be a long walk home, but that was way better than if Will Morris and his gang had caught up to them.

"I guess I need to finalize my plan sooner rather than later," offered DMarks. "I didn't see them as the kind that would launch a sneak attack like that."

"Seriously. What's with them?" complained BB.

"Yeah. A sneak attack in broad daylight?" added George.

"I never knew life in Briarcliff could be so hazardous," said DMarks with mock irony.

Charlie reflected as they walked. *Thanks, Sky. That was a close one.*

24
CHAPTER

TRUTH OR DARE

Whoever goes about slandering reveals secrets, but he who is trustworthy in spirit keeps a thing covered.

—Proverbs 11:13

Charlie, DMarks, BB, and George had been like blood brothers since kindergarten. During their younger years, there was always a Saturday night sleepover. Gradually, that transitioned to just hanging out on non-school nights and watching TV, going to a Bears varsity game, or maybe to the movies. Whatever the case, they were inseparable, and it was always just the guys.

Now that they were almost in high school, a lot of their evening activities seemed to include girls. On the one hand, they considered that to be a good thing. A very good thing. For them, girls were beautiful, fun, lively, and smart. They were attracted to the girls in their grade in ways they couldn't even describe.

But there was still something about interacting with them that was a little bit scary. The fact that girls seemed totally comfortable being around boys was not lost on them. It made them feel like they were on an uneven playing field. Then again, it had been taught in school that girls mature faster than boys so at least there was a reasonable explanation for it.

One Friday night, Michelle invited the core group of girls for a slumber party. She also invited Charlie and the guys to hang out until curfew. At around 7:00 p. m., they walked over to Michelle's house. Already, their minds were going a little haywire, and their hearts were beating a little faster. Just before they got to the front door, DMarks took out his Binaca, opened his mouth wide, and spritzed a couple shots.

"Watch out, Andrea. Here I come," he uttered in a self-confident way.

"In your dreams," said George.

"You know something, Marks?" revealed BB. "I'm starting to feel really jealous of all the people who have never met you."

"All right, break it up you guys," said Charlie. "We need to be cool for Michelle's parents."

"Yeah, let's keep things real," added George, cracking his knuckles. "Lots of opportunities tonight."

"And who exactly do you intend to set your sights on?" inquired DMarks.

"No one in particular. My plan is to find someone who looks like they might be interested, then hope they're braver me."

"Honest answer. Can't beat that," said Charlie. "And who might *that someone* be?"

"Who else?" George patted down his wispy blond hair. "Diane."

"I like your taste, my man," replied DMarks, "but give it up. There's no way."

"I figure that the longer the evening goes, the more attractive I'll become, especially if you guys all peel off with someone, and then it's just her and me."

"Right, the awkward-sympathy kiss angle," added BB, giving him the thumbs-up.

"What about you, hotshot?" DMarks looked at BB.

"Well, I've noticed lately that Robin has been kind of extra friendly. And in case you haven't noticed, she's already sporting her midsummer tan and it's *dy-no-mite*!"

"Oh, we've noticed!" the boys all said in unison.

"Well, good luck with that one," DMarks said, dripping with sarcasm. BB promptly flicked the back of his ear. In retaliation, DMarks turned, and belched in BB's face.

"Way to be cool, you rejects," scolded Charlie. "Are we done yet?"

They all straightened up then rang the doorbell. Michelle's mom and dad swung the door wide with a welcoming, "Hello, boys! C'mon in. Nice to see you."

"And it's very nice to see you, Mr. and Mrs. Robins. I know that I speak for all of us when I say that you have a very lovely home," said DMarks.

Michelle's dad picked up on the Eddie Haskell schtick right away.

"Why, thank you, Derrick. And I know that I speak for Michelle's mom when I say that there better not be any monkey business tonight. If you even think of sneaking beer, I'll personally deliver you to Detective Kaufman."

DMarks straightened up as the boys stifled laughs.

"Do we see eye to eye?" asked Michell's dad, zeroing in on DMarks.

"Yes, sir. Thank you, sir. No, sir… I mean yes, I understand."

"Good boy. Okay then, the girls are downstairs, I'm sure they'll be glad to see you."

The basement at Michelle's house was a cool, wood-paneled hideaway, with shag carpeting and an oversized corduroy pit couch positioned in front of an old Zenith television set. Michelle had stacked all her favorite albums on the record player which dropped one after another filling the room with favorites from Carol King, James Taylor, Carly Simon, Three Dog Night, and Joni Mitchell.

As the boys made their way down the carpeted stairs, they could hear the girls thick in conversation.

"Did you hear that they're not going to renew *The Brady Bunch!* That's so lame," lamented Meg. "I'm still crushing on Greg."

"I know. I loved watching that show. It always came on right before *The Courtship of Eddie's Father*," added Diane.

The girls all moved to one side of the huge sectional couch when the boys arrived, so they could get comfortable on the other.

"Personally, I'm crushing on Nurse Dixie McCall from *Emergency*," said DMarks, whistling a catcall.

The guys semi-awkwardly mixed in, filling cups of soda and grabbing fistfuls of Fritos, Ruffles, and Cheese Doodles.

"Whatever happened to the old shows like *The Rifleman*, *My Favorite Martian*, and *Mister Ed*?" DMarks asked.

"A little thing called color TV happened, you lamebrain. Who wants to watch black-and-white shows when they're making them in living color now?" explained George.

As the boys bantered, the girls leaped to their feet and began to dance to The Loco-Motion, the popular new single from Grand Funk. In the middle of the song, they reached out to grabs the guys by their hands to get them to dance with them. In response, and with horrified looks, they grabbed couch pillows to swat them away.

"Why do girls feel compelled to dance all the time?" asked George.

"I know! Put on a song and they get up and dance. What is with them?" said BB.

"I think they call it a 'girl dance' or something," added Charlie.

Only DMarks saw it as an opportunity as he jumped right into the middle of the pack to show off his moves. First, he did the robot, then he took a stab at the lawnmower before switching to the funky chicken.

After the song ended, everyone collapsed back onto the couch. The guys had to admit, it was a pretty good icebreaker, and it seemed to result in easier conversation. Then, just as they were feeling comfortable, someone suggested a game of Truth or Dare.

Once again, the girls were way ahead of the boys, and they launched right into it with Michelle turning to DMarks and firing away.

"Tell us who you like, or you have to knock on Mr. Hershey's door and ask for a glass of water."

Mr. Hershey was an acclaimed painter who lived over on Valentine Road. He was known as a gentle, quiet man, but he was lanky, gaunt and ghostly looking. He was also a complete recluse, seldom seen outside in daylight. The idea of knocking on the door at his always dark unkept house was more than a little scary.

"Who do I like? Why would I divulge something like that? It takes away my tactical advantage," he said, giving Andrea an exaggerated wink.

"DMarks, is your eye still bothering you from the sunscreen accident?" Andrea asked.

"Wait, I saw that! It's Andrea. You're flirting with her right now," teased Michelle.

"Correction, Charlie's angel. I'm not flirting, just being extra nice to someone who's extra good-looking," explained DMarks.

Andrea loved the attention, winking back and flipping her long, silky hair in his direction.

"Okay, I guess you're off the hook then," said Michelle. Next, she picked BB. "Tell us who you've kissed or you have to run across Woyden's horse field in the dark."

The Woyden property was an expansive area on the south end of the Tree Streets. It had a huge manor home, stables and property the size of two football fields where their horses roamed free. It was frightening enough to run across the field in broad daylight. Doing it at night would take an Olympic amount of courage.

"Who have I kissed? I'm still stuck in the batter's box," protested BB.

"Liar! What about your cousin's neighbor on Long Island? I heard you made out with her on the beach one time," said Diane, making a kissing sound.

"How the heck did you know that?" BB asked, blushing red.

"When your cousin visited for Thanksgiving, she told me."

"Busted!" shouted Michelle. BB was embarrassed, but at least the truth was out, so he wouldn't have to take the dare.

Diane decided to get into the act and turned to Charlie. "Tell us your deepest, darkest fear, or you have to sing 'Billy Don't be a Hero' in front of us."

Charlie paused, taking the question seriously.

"My deepest, darkest fear? That Michelle's dad might get a transfer to another city and move his family out of Briarcliff."

Charlie's answer stopped everyone in fascinated silence.

"Leave it to him," muttered DMarks.

"I meant it," emphasized Charlie. "Ask me an honest question, and I'll give you an honest answer."

"I have no doubt, Charles, and I predict a bright future for you working at Hallmark."

Michelle got up and slid in next to Charlie on the couch, giving him an affectionate kiss on the cheek, tussling his well-groomed dark hair.

"This guy! I think he's made of apples cause he's sweet as pie."

"See what happens when he says something like that?" grumped DMarks, looking at Andrea. "His girlfriend puts on her love-face."

"Maybe you should be taking notes," Andrea said with a mock huff.

The only boy left was George, so now Diane locked in on him.

"Tell us the last time something made you cry or you have to kiss the person on your left," she said impulsively before realizing that she was sitting directly to his left.

"Aha! Coincidence? I think not!" bellowed DMarks, egging on the situation.

"I'll gladly take the dare," said an emboldened George, leaning over, eyes closed and smiling. Diane was happy to comply with her own truth or dare declaration.

After going around the room so that everyone got their turn, they switched to an energetic game of Twister. On the surface, the boys acted like they were uninterested, but in reality, they were psyched for an opportunity to get physically closer to the girls. For their part, the girls mock complained trying to move away, only to inch back closer and closer as the game played on.

After Twister, more snacks, and a couple girl dances, they played Charades. DMarks insisted on going first.

Standing in front of the group, he began to mimic extreme anger. Some thought he was a grizzly bear; others guessed a boxer.

"No, wait, a lion tamer?" asked Robin.

"I got it! He's just being himself!" yelped BB.

DMarks faked silent laughter. He then changed course and mimed playing different sports, but that didn't work either. With his patience wearing thin, he went into the bathroom and splashed water on his face. When he came back out, Charlie, BB, and George had it.

"He's Wet Willie!"

"Great choice of a subject, but, man, you have to up your game," heckled Charlie.

"Very funny. I'd like to see you cupcakes get up in front of a crowd and act something out."

"We would, but it's the girl's turn," pointed out George with relief.

"Lame excuse. What would you guys do if you didn't have me around to razz all the time?"

"Hard to imagine what that would be like, but I'd be game to check it out," jeered BB.

DMarks said nothing in response. BB's comment stung him. Everyone seemed to notice as he got very quiet for the rest of the game.

Thankfully, Don Kirshner's Rock Concert was about to come on the TV, so everyone jumped back on the pit couch, this time in more of a boy-girl way.

The gang enjoyed watching some of their favorite bands in concert, but all too soon, Mr. Robins called downstairs to let the boys know it was time for them to head home. The whole gang exchanged group hugs as Charlie, DMarks, BB, and George headed upstairs and out the front door.

"Good night boys. Hope you had a nice time," Mrs. Robins.

"We had a very pleasant evening. Thank you for allowing us to enjoy your lovely home," replied DMarks.

Mr. Robins chuckled. "Think you covered that on the way in, Derrick."

"Would you just give it a rest already?" mouthed Charlie, shoving him out the door. "Do you honestly think they buy that stuff from you?"

As they headed down Jackson Road, DMarks felt that curious, sweet-smelling breeze kick up. Along with it came an unfamiliar feeling. *What is this?* he wondered. *Whatever it is, I like it.*

As they walked, he tried to pinpoint the emotion. It was different from anything he had felt before. *Is this what gratitude feels like?* he wondered.

Feeling inspired, he spoke up, "I've been thinking. We spend a lot of time giving each other a hard time, like the way BB blindsided me with that comment during charades," he said, giving him a flat tire in retaliation as they walked along.

"Maybe we should ease up on that stuff. We have too much to be thankful for to spend all our time make fun of each other."

"Wait, what? Where did that come from?" asked George.

"Yeah, were you abducted by Martians or something?" teased BB.

"That's what I mean. Can you guys ever cut me some slack? I'm serious. There are people who will go to bed hungry tonight. There are people who don't even have a bed to sleep in tonight. And then there's guys like Wet Willy who go around angry all the time. We don't realize how blessed we are."

The boys all stopped to focus on their friend, surprised by his show of humility and concern for others.

"I mean, God goes to the trouble to bless us with all the comforts we could ever want, and we just go on our merry way."

As the boys stood there trying to process what their friend was saying, DMarks himself was unsure of what was happening. Still, the words reflected what he was feeling, even if it was a bit out of character for him.

"Okay. I apologize for what I said back then. But it's not like I meant it," responded BB.

"Yeah, yeah. And I admit that sometimes I deserve it," added DMarks.

"Sometimes?" asked George in an exaggerated way.

"Okay, okay, most of the time," confessed DMarks. "But I'm working on it."

Charlie looked on with a perceptive smile. "Pour it on, Sky," he whispered under his breath.

25

CHAPTER

SNAKE, RATTLE, AND ROLL

When justice is done, it is a joy to the
righteous but error to the evildoers.

—Proverbs 21:15

As Charlie rode his bike to town, he noticed a bumper sticker on a passing car that was popular that year. It read, "Sorry for driving so close in front of you." He got a chuckle and brushed it off as a flip way of asking people not to tailgate. But as he got to Weldon's, the message began to resonate with him.

Parking his Schwinn Racer in the sidewalk bike rack, he wondered if it might be one of those signs, tokens and nods Sky told him to watch out for. *Could it be some kind of danger signal?* he wondered.

This whole situation with Will and his squad had reached a boiling point. Should they try to put some distance between themselves and the older guys? Charlie walked into the popular deli, head down, brow furrowed in deep thought.

"Everything okay, Charlie? You're looking kind of serious," asked Mr. Weldon.

"Oh, it's nothing, sir," Charlie tried to brighten up. "Guess I've just got a few things on my mind."

Mr. Weldon broke out a big smile. "Charlie, you're too young. Leave the worrying to us old guys."

"Hey, watch who you're calling old," complained Paulie, one of the deli workers, giving Mr. Weldon a gentle elbow behind the counter.

"By the way, Charlie, the Yankees are starting to rally. Maybe they'll surprise us and make the playoffs," said an optimistic Mr. Weldon.

"Now that's a happy thought."

He paid for his roast beef wedge and Coke, then left Weldon's still in deep thought. He was feeling confused. They had to stand up for themselves, but how? They already had enough close calls to last them for the whole summer.

After mowing a few lawns, he joined the guys hanging out at Jackson Road Park. They hadn't even been able to start a game of basketball when Will Morris and his gang came strutting along. They were making a lot of noise, dribbling their basketballs, talking loudly, and acting like they owned the whole neighborhood.

"Here they come. Like clockwork." George sighed, hanging his head.

"It's too hot to deal with these jerks today. Let's go find some shade," suggested Charlie, standing up, brushing off his shorts.

They headed to The Hub. Kicking off their sneakers, they sat on banks of the Pocantico River with their feet dangling in the cool currents.

"This sucks," said BB, flinging his arm sideways to skip a rock in the river. "I hate having to go into retreat mode whenever those goons show up."

"It doesn't seem fair," lamented Charlie.

"But this is how it's always been. The older kids rule," said George snaping a stick and tossing it into the water.

"Maybe that's the way it's always been, but I say we don't have to take it." answered DMarks. "There's got to be a way. I'm not saying we have to fight them or something, but I know we can push back and win."

"You talk a good game, but where's that plan you promised?" asked BB.

"I'm still working on it. But don't worry, you won't be disappointed."

As the boys sat and talked, they noticed a visitor in their midst. It was a ringneck snake, slinking and slithering along. DMarks grabbed it and held it up for a closer look. With a cocked eyebrow and an affirming nod, he turned to the others.

"Well, well, well. What do we have here?" he asked out loud. "You guys know what this is?"

"Yeah, a long, fat ringneck snake," answered George.

"Wrong, my wayward son," said DMarks, pausing for effect. "It's kryptonite."

"What on earth are you talking about?" asked BB.

"It's just a harmless snake," echoed George.

Even Charlie was clueless as to where his friend was going with this. DMarks exhaled, muttering under his breath about the amateurs he had to work with. He stood up and paced back and forth in front of them.

"Now pay attention, class," he said for effect. "Our friend Willy happens to have an extreme snake phobia," he said, holding the snake up letting it sway back and forth.

"What?" exclaimed Charlie, sensing a great opportunity to land a blow without throwing a punch.

"Yep. His little sister told my little sister. And just like that, we have a tactical advantage."

The boys perked up, sitting up straight, giddy over all the possibilities that rolled through their minds.

"I say we take this little fella out to the basketball court and see if he'd like to make a few new friends," suggested DMarks.

"Then what?" asked Charlie.

"I'm gonna make an offer Willy can't refuse," said DMarks in a husky voice

"Sly, cunning, totally wicked. Should be illegal. I love it!" BB guffawed.

"Oh, man, this is going to be good," added George.

"What do you think, little ringneck man?" DMarks asked the snake, looking into its eyes. "Up for some slime?"

Laughing, the boys jumped up, put on their sneakers, and all but raced to the basketball court, confidence growing with each step they took.

Out of the swamp they came and straight to the middle of the court, interrupting the game in the same way the older guys had done with them. As anticipated, Will was incensed, locking in on DMarks and striding humorlessly in his direction.

"What's shaking, Willy?" asked DMarks, immediately throwing major fuel on the fire.

"What's shaking? I'll tell you what's shaking. You're gonna be shaking as soon as I get my hands on you."

DMarks showed amazing composure as Will stormed toward him.

"Lighten up, honey bun," he taunted back, counting Will's steps before he'd make his move.

"Oh, you are so dead," growled Will through clamped teeth, sweating profusely.

Waiting until the last second, DMarks seized the moment.

"By the way, Willy, did you know this is the time of year when snakes love to come out of the swamp to say hello to park visitors in person?"

The mere mention of snakes stopped Will Morris in his tracks, just a step away from DMarks.

"Yep, all kinds of snakes, too," he said, making a hissing noise.

Right before everyone's eyes, Will's anger flipped to out-and-out fear. He froze, looking at DMarks with a frightened gaze.

"As a matter of fact, we came across one just a little while ago."

Will's eyes darted back and forth in a panic.

"Whoa… Whoa… Where did you see it?"

"Back in the swamp near the river."

Feeling relieved, Will's swagger returned in an instant.

"And where's the snake now, Ace?"

DMarks shot a sly wink at Charlie, BB, and George.

"Right here," he said, reaching into the side pocket of his gym shorts, pulling the snake out and holding it up in Will's face.

The sight of the eighteen-inch snake twisting and coiling right in front of his nose was so terrifying to Will that he wet his shorts right in front of everyone.

Charlie, BB, and George collapsed in laughter.

BB laughed. "I guess they don't call him Wet Willy for nothing."

The older boys didn't know what to make of it. Their leader afraid of a harmless snake. Meanwhile, DMarks was in the driver's seat and he knew it.

"What's the matter, Miss America, afraid of a little snake?"

Will couldn't think or talk. All he could do was backpedal with a panicked look in his eyes and sweat pouring off his forehead. Confused and embarrassed, his clueless friends reluctantly followed alongside him like frightened puppies.

"That's right, Willy, take your ball and buzz off. This is our park, and don't you ever forget it."

The boys didn't know what was better: seeing Will in a petrified state of horror or listening to DMarks when he was on a roll.

"And remember, this little guy has a whole family that would be glad to make your acquaintance. Think about that the next time you step on our turf."

Still walking backward, eyes glued on DMarks, Will picked up the pace of his retreat. DMarks reached out with the snake, acting like he was about to start a chase, which sent them all fumbling, bumbling, and banging into each other as they tried to turn and run.

The guys all enjoyed a sense of triumph as they mock-waived goodbye to their adversaries.

BB started a chorus of the popular song by Stream. "Nah, nah, nah, nah—nah, nah, nah, nah. Hey, hey, hey, goodbye!"

"Game, set, match," declared Charlie.

"And that's a wrap," affirmed George.

With Will Morris and his friends out of the picture for the rest of that afternoon, DMarks looked back at Charlie, BB, and George who were laughing and saluting. He took a bow then walked to the edge of the swamp to let the snake go.

"Live long and prosper," he said, letting it slither out of his hand and into the brush. "I owe you one."

26
CHAPTER
THEN CAME YOU

Above all, love each other earnestly.

—1 Peter 4:8

The growing, mutual affection between Mary and Mr. Olson was on a fast track. Each time they got together their feelings seemed to blossom a little more.

It helped that they had a lot in common. In addition to their love of dogs, they also enjoyed Victorian literature, big band music, *The New York Times* crossword puzzle, rooting for the New York Mets, and in particular, sunsets over the Hudson River.

They established a standing Friday evening date night at Rockwood Park earlier in the summer. After a 6:30 p.m. rendezvous, they'd make the short walk up the hillside to the spot where they first met. Mr. Olson would unfold a cozy, quilted blanket, and Mary would unpack a picnic basket full of lip-smacking delicacies from Janniello's Market.

Mary's selection of gourmet foods, along with great conversation and the company of their four-legged friends, was close to heaven on earth for all of them.

"What's your favorite sunset color?" asked Mr. Olson, happy to hear Mary's view on literally anything.

"I'd have to say the Maxfield Parrish blues and silver-azure linings on the far horizon."

"Ah, yes. Hard to beat," said Mr. Olson as he waited for Mary to ask him as she kept gazing off toward the vanishing point of the distant skyline.

"Eh-hem," Mr. Olson mock-coughed, trying to get her attention.

Turning to him, she said, "Is everything okay? Here, have a sip of lemonade. It will help clear your throat." She poured him a glass from the giant thermos.

"Gee, thanks, but I'm not very thirsty at the moment."

"Okay then. Help yourself when ready." Mary went back to the glorious sunset developing in front of them.

"Ah, um, it's customary when someone asks a question like that, to ask it back so they can offer their own opinion."

"What did you say, dear? Oh! Of course." She laughed. "Will you ever forgive me? What's your favorite sunset color?" She reached out to pat his hand.

"Well, now that you asked, I'm going with the ginger-auburn on the distant vista." He paused, looking fondly at her. "It's the same color as your hair," he said, tucking a strand behind her ear.

"Ha! What makes you so sure that's my real hair color?" she asked, stroking it self-consciously.

He paused and smiled, "Well, everything else about you is so real."

She returned his smile affectionately. "What a very good answer. Thank you, dearest."

Both breathed deeply and slowly exhaled into a blessedly relaxed state. The river always cooled and humidified the night air in and around the sweeping hills of Rockwood.

"I never tire of looking out at the Sleeping Giant," Mr. Olsen said, tracing his finger along the silhouette of The Palisades along the west side of the river. "I wonder though, has it ever been decided in which direction he's laying?"

"I've always thought his head is repining northward. That way, he can keep an eye on what's happening at West Point."

"Good point, no pun intended! I concur."

"There, that settles it."

"Oh, the joy of one less thing to worry about. I feel a tremendous weight off my shoulders," said Mr. Olson, giving an exaggerated shrug and then leaning back on his elbows.

Mary moved closer to lay her head on his chest. Taylor and Annabelle were propped up against each other as well. The four of them sharing a blanket was sublime, thought Mr. Olsen. Although their conversation was always effortless, it was equally wonderful when no words were exchanged. Just being together was sufficient for them.

As daylight faded away over the western horizon, it was time to fold up the blanket and gather their things. The dogs walked happily beside them, tails wagging and tongues flopping.

"Here, Mary, take my hand. It's getting dark, and I don't want you to stumble."

It was a little ritual Mr. Olsen suggested each time they left Rockwood, and which Mary always obliged with a glowing smile. She loved the old-fashioned gentleman that Jack was. He loved the way she received his bashful attempts at chivalry.

On the way home from Rockwood, they always stopped at Pizza Beat to pick up a small pie. Even there, they were simpatico: thin crust, light on the cheese, peppers, onions, and extra mushrooms. Then, it was back to Mr. Olson's house where they'd light a few citronella candles on the porch and enjoy their pizza with a couple of Heinekens.

Seasoned engineer that he was, Mr. Olson had figured out how to get reception on his black and white Philco TV out on the porch. He turned the dial to WOR for the Mets game and adjusted the rabbit ears. While he was setting up the TV, Mary grabbed two frosted mugs from the freezer and a couple of Dixie paper plates.

"Is there anything better than the aroma of a fresh, hot pizza waiting to be devoured?" she asked.

Mr. Olson sat down and pulled the tabs off the aluminum cans of Heineken. "Not that I'm aware of, although freshly opened cans of beer are a close second," he said, pouring them into the chilled mugs.

He handed Mary her Heineken and gazed at her. *How blessed I am to have found a beautiful companion who loves pizza, beer, dogs, and the Mets.*

"Oh, Jack, Rusty Staub's on deck, can you please turn up the volume? He's my favorite."

"Actually, I was going to switch over to *The Rockford Files.*" He feigned looking at his watch. "It's almost nine o'clock."

"You wouldn't! You scamp, rogue, mischief-maker."

"You saw right through me," said Mr. Olson with a warm smile. "Of course I'll turn up the volume. Let's go Mets!"

What a good sport, she thought. *I think he might actually prefer to watch James Garner instead of Rusty Staub. Thank goodness he can put up with my love of the Mets, dogs, beer, and pizza.*

Although they had never talked about it, they were both very well aware of the terrific chemistry between them. She often caught him looking at her, seemingly lost in thought.

At the same time, he noted that she always had a supply of his favorite things like lifesavers, licorice, and chiclets. Both were reasonable, rational, highly educated people who liked to live responsibly. They seemed to be on the same page about everything from politics and sports to church and community.

As they sat together that particular night, an uncommonly warm, rich feeling blanketed them both. Suddenly, Mr. Olson heard what seemed like an oddly familiar voice.

"It's time to act on what God placed in your heart."

He was taken aback and almost responded audibly, catching himself at the last second. He tugged at his ear wondering if he was hearing things.

"Did you just hear something?" he asked Mary.

"Only that Seaver struck out the side and the Mets are blanking the Expos."

Strangest thing, he thought. He knew that voice from somewhere. But what really got his attention was that it seemed to encourage him to do exactly what he was thinking and feeling. He thought about it for a few minutes and then let it go.

"What's in bloom out there, by the way. It smells lovely," he asked.

"My dear, the only thing that's in bloom this time of year is crabgrass, elderberry, and common purslane."

"Funny thing. I could swear I smelled altar flowers on that breezy gust a moment ago."

"What breeze are you referring to? The air is completely still tonight."

"You didn't feel that?"

"Dear, just look at those candles. Their flames aren't even flickering."

Mr. Olson took off his glasses and wiped them clean with his napkin. *That's the strangest thing.*

The two sat, swaying back and forth. Then he heard that voice again.

"It's ordained in heaven, Jack. Green light."

He was confused and momentarily sidetracked. *What on earth?*

His fingers drummed on the arm of the porch swing as they swayed forward and backward. Pursing his lips, he looked out into the dark trying to understand.

Then it all became clear. *Of course!* All his friends had prayed for him after his wife passed away two and a half years ago. Mary's the answer to those prayers.

He sat up straight and centered himself. It seemed a bit reckless and engineers didn't do reckless things. After all, they had only known each other a short time. Still, he knew what he had to do, what he wanted to do.

After taking a deep breath and clearing his throat, he turned to Mary.

"Since it's in-between innings and Rusty Staub isn't due to bat again for a while, there's something I wanted to ask you."

He was so nervous that he couldn't think in a linear way. But his lips kept moving and the words were flowing. He was on autopilot.

"I was just thinking... Um, well, I was wondering, ahh... What are you doing with the rest of your life?"

"Well, that's a funny question. I realize that I should have a plan, but honestly, I'm only thinking about the here and now, my dear."

"What I mean is..." he said, bracing his hands on the swing seat for support.

"Jack, the Mets are holding onto a one run lead, the fireflies are mating and the night air is nothing short of divine. I'm focusing on the moment and I don't think I could be any happier than I am right here with you on this porch swing. As for the future, *c'est la vie*."

She leaned up against him, pulling his arm up and over her head, down across her shoulder. While this was not exactly the answer he was looking for, he loved the way she nestled against him. After a long pause, he decided to rephrase his question.

"Um, what I mean is, would you like to...that is, if you're available...um, is there any way you'd consider... Oh, good heavens! I'd like to spend the rest of my life with you if you'll have me!"

Mary shot straight up and turned to look him in the eye with a focused, resolute gaze. His eyes welled up as he fixed right back on her.

"Jack, are you proposing to me?" she asked with gentle, loving anticipation.

He was too choked up to talk. All he could do was nod his head in confirmation through moist reddened eyes. She broke into the most joy-filled outburst of her life. Her entire body was pulsing with happiness. She cradled his face in her hands, then kissed him ardently.

"Does that give you your answer?" She kissed him again and then again.

He pulled back playfully. "I'm not sure. Maybe you can restate your position?"

Mary exuberantly threw her arms around him and started all over again.

"The answer is yes, you silly, handsome, young old man. Yes! Yes! Yes!" They embraced on the porch swing like a pair of teenagers in love.

"You make my whole life one big smile," he softly whispered into her ear.

"And I'll love you Jack Olson with all that I have for as long as the Lord permits."

"I think this calls for a couple more Heinekens," he suggested.

"And a couple more kisses," added Mary.

Mr. Olson headed back to the kitchen, feet barely touching the ground. In a flash, he was back with two more mugs of ice-cold beer.

"This gives us a lot to plan, but we can talk about the details another time. Let's just soak in this moment. I'm just so happy being with you, my dear, sweet, adorable Jack."

As they sat entwined, Taylor and Annabelle came trotting over.

"Oh, look, our family came to congratulate us," Mary said, smiling her playful smile.

"Look at those two. Puppy love at its best. I guess we can thank them for fixing us up in the first place," said Mr. Olson.

"Why yes, I think you're right. Thank you, Taylor," Mary said, reaching down to pat him on his forehead, "for being so forward with my Annabelle." She then rested her head on Mr. Olson's shoulder, and he tilted his head against hers.

"True rescue dogs," he said softly.

In that moment, there was nothing more either one needed. Life itself was perfect.

27

CHAPTER

SWAMP THINGS

Therefore encourage one another and build each other up.

—1 Thessalonians 5:11

Charlie didn't talk very much with Michelle about the troubles he and the guys were having with Will Morris. But what she did know fueled a growing concern. She hated things that weren't fair. Fairness and honesty were a thing with her, and she insisted that she and the girls get involved.

Charlie mentioned it to DMarks, BB, and George one afternoon at the pool. DMarks focused his eyes and listened intently, absorbing all that Charlie had to say. After thinking about the possibilities, he surprised everyone by welcoming the offer.

"Now this idea has potential. Tell your girlfriend I like the way she thinks."

"Huh? You want the girls to get involved with this?"

"I think my plan might have just found it's missing ingredient. Can they meet us here tomorrow afternoon?"

"I guess. I'll ask. But I know that they like to watch *General Hospital* sometimes."

"Tell them they can watch the idiot box some other time. We need them here at three o'clock sharp."

Charlie looked back at his friend. Clearly, the wheels were turning and he had something up his sleeve.

"Yes, sir," he replied, kicking his heels together and offering a formal military salute.

"Oh, man, this is going to be good," DMarks said, rubbing his hands together.

The next day, everyone gathered at the Jackson Road playground, girls included. DMarks stood and addressed the whole group in an overly formal way. Everyone played along, not knowing exactly how to react.

"Now, ladies, we're about to take you where few have gone before." The girls wriggled with barely contained zeal.

"Aye, aye, Captain," Connie responded.

DMarks immediately put his finger to his lips to shh her. "Easy does it, honeybee."

Pacing back and forth, DMarks came back to form.

"We're going to give you girls temporary access to a top-secret place, but just for this mission. After that, it's off limits without our prior consent. Got it? Good."

Then, using his basketball as though it was a Bible, he had each girl lay their hand on it as he swore them to secrecy on all they were about to see.

"Okay then. Follow us," he instructed as he led them down their network of secret pathways.

"Sheesh, does he think he's taking us to the bat cave or something?" whispered Michelle.

"Yeah, is he going to blindfold us maybe?" kidded Andrea.

DMarks spun around like an army drill sergeant. "Hey! I heard that. This isn't the time. Now get focused and no fooling around," he barked.

The girls stifled some giggles and followed along in and amongst the tall reeds, eventually coming to a clearing. There, right in front of them was a magnificent twin Oak and their treehouse hideout.

DMarks stopped to notice the awestruck looks amongst the girls. Then, projecting a self-important posture, he once again reminded them of their oath.

"Ladies, I present to you School's Out," announced DMarks. A makeshift No Trespassing sign was nailed to the side of the tree.

"Cool name for a treehouse." Michelle nodded. "I like it."

"So this is where you guys go when you want to talk about us," Andrea asked. The boys smiled and began climbing the two-by-fours they had hammered into the side of the tree.

"Okay, one at a time, up you go," he ordered. "Oh, and one very important thing. Make sure to step in the middle of the two-by-four at the top rung."

The platform of the treehouse sat snuggly in the center of where the trunk branched off in two different directions. It was about fifteen feet off the ground, had a roof, built-in benches, and a lookout perch. It also had a trapdoor on the other side with a knotted rope that could be dropped for a quick escape. Various amenities included a transistor radio, a pair of binoculars, a canteen, and a Swiss Army Knife. In addition, there were odds and ends collected from the swamp, like a quartz rock, unique feathers, a muskrat skull, and a raccoon tail.

Climbing up and in, one by one, the girls were absolutely amazed with it.

"Can you guys build something like this for us?" asked Robin.

"Sorry, ladies, this is one of a kind," answered DMarks. He knocked on the ramshackle plywood roof for good measure.

"I can't believe this is the first time you've brought us here," complained Connie. "Look at this view! I can see all the way to my backyard."

"Never mind about all that stuff," admonished DMarks. "We need to get down to business. Now gather around."

Everyone knelt down as he unrolled a handmade map showing the network of the pathways they had created throughout the swamp.

"Now listen up. We know two things. First, that Willy and his thugs usually show up each day around three-thirty. Second, he thinks he's God's gift to the female population of the world."

Charlie, BB, and George's eyes darted side to side wondering where their friend was going with all this.

"Right, got it. So what's the plan?" asked Michelle.

"Here's what I want you girls to do," he said, putting his index finger on the map. "We're going to position you at the beginning of Snake Path. Then, when you hear them arrive, start walking until you get to Cattail Turn. See that here on the map?"

"Got it, Snake Path to Cattail Turn," repeated Michelle, tapping the side of her head.

"You'll be out of sight from the basketball court, but within hearing range. Once Willy and his dopey friends arrive, give them about a minute, then start calling out to them. Say that you're all sitting by the river and that they should come and join you."

"We can do that!" Andrea replied enthusiastically.

"They'll stop what they're doing to follow your voices," he explained.

"I like it! Should we wear camouflage?" asked Michelle.

"Don't get ahead of me, sister," growled DMarks.

"Okay, okay," Michelle replied bubbling with delight.

"Once they begin to head into the swamp, turn around and go left on Rocky Road," he said, tapping his finger on the map. "That will take you down Hidden Lane and straight back here to School's Out. Climb up, lay low, and don't make a sound. They'll never see you."

"I like the element of danger," said Robin, with look of fun anticipation.

"While you guys are drawing them into the swamp, we'll be hiding behind the handball court. Then, we can sneak over to their bicycles and do our thing."

"Oh, that's good." Connie nodded. "Devious, but good."

"He's smarter than the average bear," Andrea added.

"And what are you guys going to do?" asked Michelle.

"First, we'll grease the pedals. Then, we'll loosen the brake grips so that if they manage to get going, they won't be able to control their bikes."

"You definitely have a future as a professional criminal." Andrea laughed.

"What if something happens and this whole thing backfires?" asked Robin.

"Can it, dream girl. If something happens, there's only one thing to do. We go Chuck Norris on them," said DMarks, standing up and doing a few quick karate chops.

"Wow, Marks, you're really feeling your oats with this whole thing," commented Charlie.

"Shut it, Charles. This is my operation. Got it? Now, any questions?" He scanned the group making eye contact with each of them.

"One question. Where are the tools we'll be using to mess with their bikes?" inquired BB.

"I have everything we need in my old Daniel Boone lunchbox hidden near the park entrance."

"You thought of everything," replied George.

"The man pays attention to details," added Charlie.

"It's what I do," answered a confident DMarks.

Michelle giggled. "I feel like we're in an episode of *The Mod Squad*." giggled

"Okay then. Let's synchronize our watches."

Everyone climbed down from the treehouse and got into position. The girls stayed on Snake Path, and the boys crouched behind the handball court. In a matter of minutes, Will and his heavies showed up right on schedule. They hopped off their bikes and let them fall to the ground over by the park entrance.

Eyeing the empty court, Will felt a pang of suspicion.

"I wonder where those brat punks are?"

"Maybe they finally learned their lesson and found a new place to hang out," said Bruiser White, one of Will's gang.

"Maybe they moved to Pleasantville," chuckled Joker Plunkett, the group funnyman.

The boys could hear every word.

"Pleasantville? That one's gonna cost 'em," DMarks whispered, mimicking a knife to his heart.

On cue, the girls began to call out to Will at the appointed time.

"Oh, Will! We've been waiting for you. Why don't you come join us over by the river?" called out Michelle.

"Yeah...we're just hanging out in our bikinis," added Connie. "Working on our tans."

"Good one," whispered DMarks as they stayed in hiding. "Now I want to join them myself." He grinned.

Will had no idea who was calling to him, but it didn't matter. The voices belonged to girls and any kind of attention from girls got his interest like nothing else.

DMarks cautiously extended his hand from behind the wall of the handball court holding out a makeup compact he stole from his mother. Tilting the mirror, he could see that the older guys were taking the bait. They left their basketballs bouncing around on the court and headed toward the swamp in a charmed state.

"Hi, girls! Where are you?" Will shouted out, parting tall reeds with his hands.

"Youhoo. Over here," Robin answered.

"Follow me," Will ordered as they trekked further into the swamp.

Per DMarks's instruction, the girls counted to ten, then took off to School's Out. They climbed up into the tree house, delighted with the job they had done.

"We faked them out good," whispered Andrea, hands raised like a prize fighter.

"That was far out," Connie added with a nod.

Looking at his Timex, DMarks signaled the guys to roll into action. They scurried over to the older boy's bicycles and went to work disabling their brakes and layering on a generous amount of 10W-40 to their bike pedals. After finishing the job, they took the older guy's basketballs and tossed them into the brook as an additional "gotcha" moment.

Meanwhile, Will and his friends were struggling to find their way through the thickets and underbrush. Every few steps, someone would let go of a branch that would whip back and smack the next guy in the face, leading to an outburst of bad words and promises of payback.

By the time they made it to the riverbank, everyone was irritated and exasperated. To make matters worse, there were no girls to be seen anywhere. They stood there like the stooges they were, lamely calling out. But silence was all that greeted them.

Back in the treehouse, the girls had a bird's-eye view of everything that was happening and could hardly contain their excitement. They had played their parts to perfection. As Will and his flunky friends stood there looking around and feeling more and more wary, they noticed an odd sight coming their way on the currents of the river.

"What the? Those look like basketballs," noted Joker.

"Don't be stupid. How would a bunch of basketballs just come floating along way out here?" asked Bruiser.

Will dashed over to the riverbank to take a closer look. Enraged and breaking out in a massive sweat, he looked back on the others.

"Those are basketballs all right. *Our* basketballs! Now get in there and fish them out," he barked.

The basketballs had made their way downstream from the brook near the basketball court, which filtered into the Pocantico River. Although it was not planned, the timing was perfect as Will surmised they had fallen into some kind of trap.

"Hurry up! Let's get out of here," he snarled.

They grabbed their basketballs as Joker threw them out from the river, one at a time.

"Whoever pranked us is going to pay," Will hollered, punching his fist into the palm of his hand.

As they reached the clearing near the court, they noticed Charlie, DMarks, BB, and George casually standing over by the park entrance.

"Did you water rats have a nice swim?" asked DMarks.

Will exploded with rage. His face was bright crimson and veins were bulging in his neck. He and the others took off in a headlong sprint as the DMarks and the guys turned to bolt up Maple Road.

"You punks think you can outrun us on our bikes? This time we've got you!"

DMarks and the guys got to the crest of Maple Road, then turned to look back just as Will and his gang got to their bikes. They each hopped on, using the handlebars to pull themselves into a standing position for power peddling. Instantaneously, their feet slid off the pedals causing them to slip and land hard on the cross bars.

Down they all went, collapsing sideways, each one of them on the ground, seeing stars.

Charlie, DMarks, BB, and George cringed as the older guys practically blacked out.

George groaned. "Right between the bells."

"A fate worse than death!" yelled BB.

"They're gonna be singing soprano in church this Sunday," added Charlie.

The guys slapped fives and assumed their mission was accomplished, but DMarks had one more thing in mind.

"Follow me, gentlemen," he said in the tone of a proper English butler. Down the hill they went, marching right up to where Will and his bully friends were groaning and twisting on the ground.

"Now for the piece de resistance," purred DMarks. He sidestepped the temporarily out-of-commission older boys and took their unopened Gatorades.

"May I suggest that in the future, you lollipops wear cups when riding your bikes?"

Charlie, BB, and George had to give it to him. Another legendary play by DMarks. As they walked away, DMarks bent down and patted Will on the top of his head.

"Nighty night, Willie. You'll feel better when you wake up."

28

CHAPTER

THE HARDER THEY FALL

I can do all things through Christ who strengthens me.

—Philippians 4:13

One night, after watching TV with his parents, Charlie let Barnes and Noble out in the backyard. He gazed in awe at the star-filled sky as the dogs trotted around. There was no moon that night, so each star shined brighter than normal with its own unique sparkle and flicker.

"You are amazing, God. Thank you," he whispered, fixing his eyes on the far horizon. *Creator, sustainer and orchestrator of all things. I can't even begin to comprehend,* he thought.

As the dogs stretched their legs, he began to reflect a little further in the muted nighttime darkness. *Whatever happened to carefree summers?* he wondered.

Charlie didn't like to be at odds with anyone. At the same time, he didn't like feeling bullied either. In spite of it all, he had no malice toward Will Morris and was still hopeful everything could be resolved in a fair way. But there were no easy answers. As he stood under the stars, he prayed for guidance.

After bringing Barnes and Noble back inside, he said good night to his parents and made his way upstairs. Although his mind was restless, he was physically spent. It was going on 11:00, and he needed a good night's sleep.

The next morning, he awoke to a ray of sunshine bathing his face with a warm shaft of light. Collecting his thoughts, he tossed off the bedsheet, stretched his arms high above his head, and opened up a gaping yawn.

After a quick breakfast, it was off to his scheduled lawn jobs for the day. Going from yard to yard, he recalled childhood memories of playing capture the flag, army, flashlight tag, and other kid games around the neighborhood. It was fun for him to see younger kids doing the same things he had done with DMarks, George, and BB.

Later that afternoon, the guys were at Jackson Road Park. It was just the four of them so they played a couple games of Around the World and horse. As they shot baskets, Charlie tried to make the case that maybe it was time to hold out an olive branch to Will Morris.

Not surprisingly, DMarks wasn't buying it. Tucking the basketball under his arm, he began to lecture about how this was all part of an important life lesson for them.

Charlie just shook his head. "I swear, it's like you actually put in time and effort toward being difficult."

"It's my way of balancing out the universe, Charles. You're on one end of the spectrum, I'm on the other." He chucked the ball at Charlie's chest.

"You don't get it," Charlie said, raising his voice, chucking the ball right back. "Why do you always have to have a cow over everything? Reasonable people can disagree but still get along."

BB and George couldn't figure out which side to go with. Then George stepped up and chimed in.

"I'm a lover, not a fighter, so I'm game to give Charlie's idea a try." He patted him on the back.

"And besides, the Bible tells us to overcome bad by doing good. Reverend Higgins preached on that just last week. Sometimes God asks us to do the opposite of what we might be feeling. But he knows what's best," Charlie added.

"I kind of like Charlie's perspective on this. Let's take the high road," said BB. "Besides, if we respond to them by being nice, it'll mess with their heads."

"All this talk about compromise makes me want to puke! We don't need compromise. What we need is guts." DMarks was fired up. "Compromise is for the weak. It's a dirty word. Besides, you can't compromise with someone who won't even talk with you."

"He's got you there, Charlie," noted BB. "I don't think Henry Kissinger could get Wet Willie to chill long enough to have a civil conversation with us. And by the way, Marks, no more puking this summer. Please!"

"Everyone has a point where they're willing to let go of past differences," pleaded Charlie.

"Umm, the only problem is we're talking about current differences," said George.

"True. And Willie is currently pretty ticked off," added BB.

Charlie was clearly not getting anywhere, so he decided to give up his argument for the time being. It was a hot, humid day, and he didn't want to debate anymore.

The sun was out with hardly a cloud in the sky, yet it was so hazy that it almost seemed overcast. With the heavy, moist air, even the mosquitos were taking the afternoon off.

After a while, they decided to head back to The Hub. Lounging in the shade, they dangled their feet in the cool currents of the Pocantico River, saying hello to the occasional perch, trout, and sunny that swam by. Conversation as usual, focused on sports and girls, girls and sports. Once in a while, the topic would switch over to food.

A short time later, they heard the jingling signal of the Good Humor Man out on Jackson Road. BB, George, and DMarks jumped up to answer the bell.

"It's so hot, I'm getting two Italian ices. One to eat and one to roll across my forehead." DMarks laughed.

For Charlie though, the hazy, hot, and humid weather made him a bit sluggish. He was too comfortable to move so he decided to stay put.

"See you guys when you get back. I'm gonna grab a few z's." He leaned back against a grassy knoll and dozed off.

A few minutes later, his catnap was interrupted by the sound of something big coming in his direction. His eyes popped open as he shook his head to help wake himself up. Jumping to his feet, he scanned the area to see what it might be. But whatever it was, it stopped each time Charlie turned his head while looking around. Assuming it must be a deer, he began to settle back down.

Then, just as he got comfortable, the noises started up again. This time, something was flat-out charging in his direction at a high speed.

He still couldn't see through all the tall reeds and brush, but it was cutting a wide swath. He looked straight ahead with a pounding heart. Then, his worst nightmare came into focus right in front of him.

A mere thirty yards away was Will Morris, gunning for Charlie like a crazed animal. Unbeknownst to the boys, he had been spying on them the whole time. He was really after DMarks, but he was happy to settle for Charlie.

Charlie froze. Then, he heard Sky's voice.

"Quick, Charlie, get over to School's Out. Hurry!"

With no time to think, he took off in his bare feet running like the wind. Even so, Will Morris was closing in on him.

"You're a dead man, Riverton," he growled.

This is getting so old, Charlie thought. As he ran, he once again heard from Sky.

"Cut left under the giant Willow tree by Possum Path."

Again, without any hesitation, Charlie sprinted in that direction as his left shoulder brushed along outer edge of the dangling tree branches. After Charlie sped by, something remarkable happened. A huge tree branch swung around from out of nowhere and walloped Will across his face. Down he went, hitting the ground hard.

Charlie kept running. *Thanks, Sky!*

Will was stunned by the blow, but he got back on his feet, shook it off, and restarted his pursuit.

By then, Charlie had reached School's Out and started climbing. He had hoped to make it there before Will saw him. No such luck.

"You can run, but you can't hide, chipmunk!" yelled Will. He had a bloody lip and a welt on his chin, but he focused in on getting to the huge Twin Oak.

"So this is where you girlie scouts go to hide out," he snarled from the base of the tree. "I hope you have a pair of wings because the only way you're going to avoid a pounding is if you can fly."

Will started to climb up the two-by-fours. Charlie's heart was beating at warp speed. His only hope, once Will got up there, was to open the escape hatch and use the knotted rope to climb down. His mind raced as he backed up toward the rear of the treehouse.

Then he remembered the propeller step. DMarks had devised a special boobytrap for times like this. The last two-by-four only had one nail in it. If you didn't toe it squarely in that spot, it would spin like a propeller, causing the intruder to lose his footing.

"Say your prayers, punk," barked Will Morris as he unwittingly put his full weight on the right side of the propeller step. In an instant, the angry, fierce look on his face converted to hopeless panic and fear as he fell straight down in a blunt thud.

Charlie cautiously leaned out of one of the treehouse windows. Will was flat on his back, seeing stars, lying in a small cloud of dust.

"You okay, Will?" No answer.

Charlie shimmied down the knotted rope and walked around the tree to take a closer look. The fall had completely knocked the wind out of his adversary, but he'd be okay.

"I'm really sorry for what happened, Will, but maybe we can talk about it sometime over a Coke?"

Will opened one eye in a daze. Instinctively, he tried to reach out to grab Charlie's ankle, but his grip was limp as a lazy catfish.

"I guess not," Charlie said, shaking his foot away.

He then tiptoed around the flat-out upperclassman and headed over to the basketball court area, where the guys were finishing up their Good Humors.

"What was all that ruckus we heard back there?" asked BB. "You get chased by a muskrat or something?"

"You won't believe me if I told you."

"Try us," urged DMarks, licking away at his Italian ice.

"I was minding my own business hanging out at The Hub when Will Morris came crashing through the swamp, coming right at me."

"No way! Then what?" begged George.

"What do you think? I took off running, but no matter what I did, I couldn't shake him."

"For a big guy, he can really motor," added BB.

"Then, I heard a voice tell me to cut past the giant willow tree on the way to School's Out. Just as I passed by, a huge branch kind of reached out and wind-milled him upside his head. It was like the tree was trying to help me or something."

"What, like in *The Wizard of Oz*, only friendly?" probed DMarks.

"Right. When the branch thwacked him, he went down, hard."

DMarks looked on with a knowing smile. *Intervention from our heavenly friend?* he wondered.

"That bought me some time, but he must have seen me climbing up to School's Out. So he got up, said a few bad words, then started to hustle over."

"Oh, this is about to get really good," said George, remembering that he himself was the one who put the single nail in the last two-by-four.

"I was cornered. It was curtains for me. Then, he reached the propeller step."

"And that was the second howl we heard?" concluded DMarks. "I love it."

"Man, that was a close call," said BB. "Had I known that you were being chased I would have dropped my Nutty Buddy and come running," he swore with a chuckle.

"He's still lying there. Should we check on him?" asked Charlie.

"Are you kidding? He'll only want to pound us all the more once he comes around. I think our work here is done," concluded DMarks. "Nice job, Charles. Someone up there likes you."

"I say we chill out at the pool for the rest of the afternoon," suggested BB. "All in favor?" Not wasting any more time, the boys rode off to Law Park where they took part in their normal array of fun and games in and out of the pool.

Later that night, after dinner, the Rivertons were once again gathered in the TV room. Charlie watched *Happy Days* as his parents read.

"What are ya reading, Dad?" Charlie asked.

"Oh, I found a random book at the library that seemed interesting. Essays by a person named Josh Billings."

"Never heard of him," replied Charlie. He reached over to turn the volume down.

"He was a nineteenth-century humorist and essay writer. Kind of like a lesser-known Mark Twain."

"Oh, cool. Definitely heard of him."

"There's an interesting essay here on how to deal with people who treat us badly."

"Really? What does he say?"

"The essay is titled 'There Is No Revenge So Complete as Forgiveness.' Very similar to the message found in Romans 12:20. I'll tell you this, son, if you decide to pursue a career in the business world like your old man, you'll want to keep that lesson handy."

"Actually, Dad, it's pretty relevant to dealing with upperclassmen right here in Briarcliff."

Then, it struck Charlie. *Was this another one of those signs, tokens, and nods from Sky? What are the chances Dad would accidentally find a book with a theme like that?*

"Is Derrick still having trouble with Will Morris?"

"Pretty much, yeah," Charlie looked down, shaking his head. He was intrigued by the thought Sky might be communicating with him through this essay.

"Why are older kids such jerks sometimes?" he asked his dad.

"I think It's just the natural pecking order of things."

"Well, it's gotten pretty intense a few times. At least no one's had to go to the hospital. At least not so far."

"You boys be careful," said his dad, closing the book he was reading, looking at Charlie earnestly. "Maybe try turning the tables by responding with kindness when they get out of line."

Just what I've been thinking, Charlie thought.

29
CHAPTER
FAMILY FUN DAY

Let no one despise you for your youth, but set the believers an example in speech, in conduct, in love, in faith, in purity.

—1 Timothy 4:12

Family Fun Day took place each year on the third Saturday of August. It was one of the most anticipated events of summer and always attracted broad community participation.

Kids in particular went all-out, decorating their bikes for a mini parade through Law Park. Some fastened streamers to their bike seats; others laced red, white, and blue crepe paper through the spokes of their wheels; still others attached horns and bells to their handlebars to add a little joyful noise to the colorful scene.

A lot of the local clans dressed in a coordinated way. Some even wore specially made T-shirts with their names printed on back. That year, the Fergusons had shirts that said with WISHFUL THINKING on the front and a picture of the Family Fun Day trophy on the back. Even the lifeguards got into the act, dressing in different get-ups complete with hats, glasses, and props.

Some families were large enough to participate on their own. Others merged together in order to have the requisite number of participants. Charlie and Michelle encouraged their parents to create a Riverton-Robins team, which was an easy decision since they were already good friends.

As people arrived, Mayor Smythe greeted everyone over the loudspeaker.

"It's my distinct pleasure to welcome one and all to Briarcliff's annual Family Fun Day, a tradition that our community has enjoyed since 1935. Last year's champions, the Kennedys, are ready to defend their title, and it looks like Henry, our illustrious rec department leader, was able to arrange for perfect summer weather."

Spontaneous applause broke out with raucous whistling from a few of the dads.

"Now I'd like to ask everyone to face the flag for the Pledge of Allegiance."

Old Glory could be seen from every direction as it flew at full mast on the soaring flagpole in Law Park. Mr. Smythe filled up with emotion at the sight of hundreds of people of all ages standing with hands over hearts, reciting the Pledge in unison.

"Thank you, everyone. Well done!" he said, spreading his arms wide to the crowd. "On behalf of the village Board of Trustees, I'd like to wish you all good luck. Now, break clean and let the games begin!"

Smiles, handshakes, and pats on the back were exchanged everywhere as families got organized for the field events. Henry's staff was stationed all around with whistles, stop watches, measuring tapes, and clipboards.

The sack race always got things started. It was a good way to let younger kids get involved early on. Dozens of school-aged children happily stepped into burlap bags and got ready to hop across the turf. As the race began, dads ran alongside snapping pictures and calling out words of encouragement. Somehow, it always ended in a pile-up at the finish line with dozens of giggling youngsters rolling around on the ground.

Next came the three-legged race. Suzie meticulously tied her right leg to Parker's left leg.

"Hey, not so tight. You're going to cut off my circulation," Parker complained.

"You want to win, don't you?" scoffed Suzie, giving the knot an extra tug.

This race was a little different because participants had to go fifty yards down and back. Some never quite got the hang of it. Others stumbled making the turn. But that year, Parker and Suzie kept it together trotting arm-in-arm to win first place.

The fifty-yard dash was usually dominated by middle school aged boys. They loved competing against each other, but they loved showing off in front of girls even more. Some took their shirts off to try to look extra cool, but it was to no avail that year. Out of nowhere, a sixth-grade girl speedster who was new in town ran like the wind and won the race by a good ten yards. Charlie and DMarks were amazed.

"Can you imagine sending her on a fly pattern? It'd be an easy touchdown every time," Charlie declared.

"I have to agree. Not even BB could guard her," concurred DMarks.

"Speak for yourself," BB replied, flicking the back of DMarks's ear as they hoofed over to the softball toss.

This was the time for the dads to shine as kids crowded around to watch and cheer. Leading up to Family Fun Day, Will Morris's father had actually been coming down to the ballfield after dinner to practice throwing softballs. He never did lose his competitive fire from his college football days.

A lot of the fathers played baseball when they were young, so most were able to reach back and hurl the ball from home plate into centerfield. Will's dad with his great athletic size and muscular arms heaved it all the way to the warning track.

He was comfortably in the lead until Mr. DePalo, who once was a pitching prospect of the New York Yankees, stepped up to take his turn. With ease, he threw the ball over the fence.

Once the cheers died down, Mr. Morris, who was not happy, insisted that there be a throw-off.

"One ball each, man to man," he growled with an intense look in his eyes.

The other participants and the crowd of onlookers felt awkward, crossing their arms, looking down, and generally at a loss for how to respond. None more so than Will Morris.

This sort of behavior from his dad was nothing new. But somehow, in that particular moment, Will saw it in a different way. For the first time, he saw it for what it was. Shamefaced, he approached his father, meekly trying to get him to let it go. But all he got in return was an unyielding, "Mind your own business, Junior."

Mr. DePalo wasn't the least bit put out, so they flipped a coin to see who would go first. Will's dad won. Snatching a softball from Henry, he walked silently to home plate psyching himself up with stoked intensity.

After a few deep breaths, he got a short running start, reached way back, and threw the ball with an impassioned roar as he released it. Sailing high and far, it bounced once and landed on the other side of the centerfield fence.

Proud of his throw, he looked at his opponent with a "beat that" kind of taunting stare.

Henry then handed a ball to Mr. DePalo who was standing behind home plate, loosening up his arm, swinging it in a circular way. He looked toward the outfield, then took a few steps, and let it fly. This time, the ball flew over the outfield fence and landed in the Pine Forest on a fly.

"I think we have a clear winner," Henry declared, raising Mr. DePalo's arm up in the air.

Everyone applauded, except Will's father, who stormed off in the direction of the tug of war event. Will walked quickly behind him breaking out in an uncontrollable sweat, embarrassed by the lack of sportsmanship.

"Dad, you made a great throw. Why wouldn't you shake hands?"

Will's father stopped and turned around, looking like he might pummel his own son.

"No one ever remembers who came in second. Never forget that son," he snarled.

Will was crestfallen. He stepped back and felt something vital shift deep inside. He was ashamed by how intense his dad got over a friendly competition but also realized that maybe he was looking in the mirror. Stuffing his hands in his pockets, he walked off the field in a daze. Head down and shoulders slumped, he made his way home.

For the tug of war, Henry and his team always created a sprawling mud pit over which the fate of entire teams hung. No one wanted to end up in the muck, so participants really dug in. When the Tree Streets team brought down the lifeguard brigade, Charlie and the guys laughed with great pride seeing James Dennis fall face-first into the mud.

DMarks laughed. "He won't be blowing that whistle for a while."

"Look at him. He's covered in mud," howled BB.

The watermelon-eating contest followed. Nothing tasted more like summer than freshly sliced watermelon. But nothing made hands and faces stickier either. Thinking ahead, Henry's team ran a garden hose up from the pool area so that kids could wash off afterward. Most took a good long drink of water while they were at it. No one was surprised when DMarks's younger sister took the hose and tried to spray Henry.

Charlie and Michelle were content to let her younger siblings lead the way in the various field events so that they could concentrate on the egg toss.

"Now, when I toss the egg to you," Charlie said in full-on coaching mode, "remember to catch it with soft hands. Got that? Soft hands." He mimed catching an egg in midair.

"Got it, Coach." Michelle winked.

"Also, you have to sort of reach out to catch the egg, then pull your hands back as it gets to you for a soft landing."

"Right, can do."

"And when you toss it to me, you have to lob it underhand, nice and easy."

"You mean, I'm supposed to throw it like a girl?" Michelle asked in a mock-upset way.

"I mean, don't throw it like you would on Halloween night, okay?"

"Ahh, right. That makes sense."

Next to Charlie and Michelle were Andrea and DMarks in a gathering lineup of twosomes. DMarks was giving Andrea a similar line of coaching, although with a little more game-time intensity.

"Remember what I told you, wind up like you're bowling, take an easy step forward, follow through, and let it fly," he said while hiking up his tube socks.

"Okay, but the sun's in my eyes. I can hardly see you," she said, holding up her hand to shield the sun glare.

"Just toss it in the direction of my voice. I'll take it from there."

Henry took the bullhorn and got things organized.

"Let's have everyone stand opposite your partner and form two parallel lines. The rules are simple. After each toss, take one giant step backward. If you drop the egg at any time, you're out. Okay then. Ready, set…let 'em fly!"

At first, it wasn't that difficult tossing the eggs back and forth, but before long, there was fifteen feet and more between the participants. With each step, more and more teams were eliminated.

Happily Charlie, Michelle, DMarks, and Andrea were among the teams still alive when things got really challenging. Now, the remining participants were a good thirty yards apart.

"You're doing great, Andrea! We got this. Just remember what I told you," he said, shaking his arms out like a prize fighter.

"And you remember what I told you. I can hardly see with this sun glare."

On the count of three, Michelle and Andrea tossed their eggs. Both eggs flew close to each other and slightly off course. DMarks moved to his right to make the catch but bumped Charlie in the process. Charlie was able to make a clean grab, but as DMarks fell backward, his egg came plummeting down, hitting him in the eye and exploding on impact. His face was instantly covered in sticky yellow ooze.

"My eye! I can't believe she hit me in the eye!"

"What is it with you this summer? That's the third time you took one in that same eye," said Charlie, fighting back is laughter.

George laughed. "Maybe you should start wearing protective goggles like from science class."

"Maybe more like an astronaut helmet," cracked BB.

"I swear, that girl is dangerous. She tried to blind me."

"Let me give you some advice. It's never a good idea to catch an egg with your face," said Charlie, referencing what DMarks said to Will Morris two months ago in that exact same spot.

"Oh, you're a regular riot," complained DMarks, flinging egg yolk at him.

Michelle laughed. "I've heard of having egg on your face, but this is ridiculous."

As DMarks got to his feet, a few of the lifeguards came over to check on him. It wasn't serious, but he'd definitely have a shiner for a few days. They walked him to the first-aid station at the pool. Once inside, they asked him to tilt his head backward over the sink so they could rinse him off.

"Oh no, you don't. They tried that on me before, and it didn't work out too well. Just give me a wet towel."

DMarks sat on a metal folding chair, hunched over, holding an ice pack on his eye seriously annoyed.

"Second time I've been in here this summer," he groused.

"I guess I need a little practice tossing eggs," said Andrea, peeking inside.

"Here's a better idea. How's about find a new partner."

"Oh, don't be so dramatic. Want something from the refreshment stand?"

"Yeah, a new eye."

"Oh brother. You'd think they're giving out Academy Awards or something."

After a few more field events, things came to a climax with a giant game of Simon Says. All the moms and dads participated. Dozens and dozens of couples jostled into position, lining up to face Mayor Smythe.

"Simon says stand on one foot. Simon says hop on one foot. Put your other foot down."

Just on that alone a quarter of the participants were eliminated right from the start. Charlie's mom being a schoolteacher was an excellent listener. She outlasted everyone that year and took a bow as the last person standing.

As the afternoon sun began to lose some of its heat, everyone headed inside the pool area for the aquatic events. Someone dressed in an Uncle Sam costume appeared from out of the men's locker room and paraded over to the high dive. Nodding to the applause of the onlookers, he sprang off and completed a well-executed cannonball.

The ovation was loud enough to hear on the other side of town. It got even louder when he climbed out of the pool, took off his top hat, and fake beard to reveal it was none other than Father James Crowley from St. Theresa's Church.

"My friends and I used to jump off the Broadway Bridge into the Harlem River when we were kids. Gosh that brought back fun memories," he recalled.

As the ovation died down, "Seasons in the Sun" began to play over the loudspeaker, and everyone turned their attention to the middle section of the pool. Clad in matching striped swimsuits and ponytails wrapped in colorful yarn, the Water Ballet Club showed off their skills and precision with a beautiful routine.

Charlie and the guys were more than a little impressed. Almost all the girls they knew were in the club, so they made sure to provide the loudest and most enthusiastic support.

With people still clapping, the lifeguards headed over to the deep end and began flinging fistfuls of pennies into the water. This was another event the older guys shined in. They all stood along the edge of the pool, boxing each other out to make sure they hit the water first. Everyone got one dive and whoever came up with the most pennies won.

Bev, the diving coach, was in a particularly proud mood that afternoon. She arranged for a special exhibition from George and Deirdre, who had worked together for weeks. Using both diving boards, they executed several difficult dives in unison. Although they were embarrassed by the applause, they were happy to be diving together and smiled as their friends rushed over to pat them on their backs.

"Dude! Nice spinning what-cha-call-it," said Charlie.

"Yeah, and no bloody noses this time," cheered BB.

The husband-wife rowboat races followed. All the kids thought it was so crazy to see rowboats in the pool. Husbands paddled in front, and wives gave direction from the back. No one seemed able to coordinate both, so most boats zig-zagged along like bumper cars. At one point, Mr. Schutte lost his paddle, so he leaned over the front of boat and propelled it with his hands and arms, still managing to cross the finish line first.

After a series of relay races, the pool events ended with clown diving, which the upperclassmen and a few dads lined up for. Not only could they get the most spring off the diving boards, they were the most daring.

After a half hour at the first-aid station, DMarks emerged, once again wearing a huge eye patch and more gauze. He stormed over to where he left his towel just inside the exterior pool fence near the deep end.

Reaching down to pick up his stuff, he was suddenly arrested by a foreboding sense of apprehension. He froze in place as the eerie feeling washed over him.

Unnerved and alarmed, he slowly stood back up. Standing there, still as a statue, he scanned the area, trying to get a read on what this bleak premonition could be. But it was unlike anything he had ever experienced and couldn't even get to first base trying to grasp it.

A moment later, Charlie came by.

"What's up with you? You look like you saw a ghost. And by the way, nice eyepatch."

In a calm but penetrating way, DMarks turned to look searchingly at his best friend.

"Check that. You don't look like you saw a ghost. You look like a ghost. You okay, buddy?"

"Does anything feel a little strange to you? I mean, as in, standing right here in this spot. Does anything feel odd to you?"

"Huh? Everyone's having a blast. What the heck are you talking about?"

"I don't know, but when I walked over here, I got this creepy sense that something's not right."

Charlie gave him a joshing. "Shake it off, Cyclops. The barbecue's about to start. I'll meet you over there."

As he turned to head up the hill, Charlie realized his friend was serious. He patted him on the back and looked him in the eye.

"I'm talking food. Barbecued food. C'mon, it'll make you feel normal."

DMarks stayed put, but nothing came to him. "Yo, Sky, this doesn't feel right. If you're out there, hit me up," he whispered.

With the enticing scent of grilled chicken in the air, people began to migrate up the hillside and into Law Park where Henry and his team had begun a giant cookout. In addition to all the great food sizzling on the half-drum grills, there were vats of Kool-Aid, platters of corn on the cob, bags of chips, and ice cream cups in tubs of ice for the taking.

Soon, the picnic benches were overflowing with people eating family style, elbow to elbow while laughing and reliving the various events of the day. Plates were piled high with great food and hearts were filled with good cheer.

Mayor Smythe once again took to the loudspeaker to preside over the awards ceremony. Different-colored ribbons were given to first, second, and third place finishers in each event. That year, the Lupos won the Family Fun Day Trophy, which they could keep on display for twelve months.

As sunset approached, a touch of cool air arrived with it like a friendly reminder that September was just around the corner. People began reaching for hooded sweatshirts and windbreakers. Not long after, families one by one started to collect their things to leave for home.

One car after another backed out of their parking spaces, headlights competing with fireflies, and kids leaning out of rolled-down windows calling to their friends.

Charlie and the guys stayed around to help the lifeguards straighten out the pool area. There were kickboards dotting the pool deck, a few wandering lifesavers floating around in the water, stray T-shirts that had been left behind, and even some sneakers scattered round about, none of which seemed to complete a matching pair. *James Dennis is going to need a bigger Lost and Found bin,* Charlie thought.

After everything was put away, the guys began the walk home through Law Park. By then, darkness had set in. After such a full day, they had plenty to talk about as they walked along.

"Can you imagine if Sky had been here to participate today?" Charlie asked.

"That's a pretty random thought. Where'd that come from?" replied BB, picking up a dropped first place ribbon and pinning it on his shirt.

"Yeah, it's been over two years since he was seen around here," said George.

"Whatever. With his size and strength, he would have single-handedly won the tug-of-war," said DMarks. "He was such a cool guy. I wish we could see more of him."

"Maybe he'll come back this winter to help at Gooseneck Pond," suggested BB.

Charlie and DMarks shot telling smiles to each other.

"I always felt safer when he was around. Like everything was going to be okay," affirmed DMarks.

"If we all live to be one hundred years old, I bet we never meet someone like him again," added George.

The four musketeers made their way past the war memorial and almost to the edge of the park. With their voices fading behind them, Skylar Northbridge stepped out from behind a huge maple tree. Even in the dusky nightfall, he cast a glowing presence.

Looking around in a reflective, 360-degree way, he could hear the echoes of the day lingering in the air. Realizing how much he missed direct interaction with the boys, he wished he could have spent that summer in Briarcliff.

"What a special place," he said to himself, hands tucked into the pockets of his faded Levi's as a summer breeze flowed through his white, loose-fitting button-down shirt.

Smiling inside, he was proud that the boys were growing up and learning to find their own way. He looked off in their direction with a wistful smile.

"I'm still here for you. I'll always be here for you," he said in a hushed tone. "Even in ways you can't always see."

30

CHAPTER

RESCUE SQUAD

And as you wish that others would do to you, do so to them.

—Luke 6:31

The last week of August had arrived all too soon. For the guys, it was starting to feel like a last-ditch sprint to the Labor Day finish line. With the end of summer in clear sight, they shoehorned as much as they could into each day and night.

In anticipation of the new school year, Charlie and his mom paid a visit to Books N' Things for school supplies. As they drove over to the Chilmark Shopping Center, Mrs. Riverton tuned the AM dial to News Radio 88.

"Do we have to listen to news all the time? It's so boring," Charlie grumbled, slouching in the passenger seat.

"We've had this conversation before, buddy. It's important to know what you think and why you think it. There's a lot happening in the world and good or bad, you need to be aware."

"I guess so, but most of the news seems so depressing."

"Look on the bright side. These news stations give sports updates too."

"Even more depressing. The Yankees are about to be eliminated from the postseason."

"Well, it could be worse. You could be a Mets fan."

"I get that, Mom. They're in, like, fifth place. But you understand what I mean, sometimes I don't think I want to know what's in the news."

"Well, Charlie, it's very true that we live in a fallen world. But that doesn't mean we should turn a deaf ear to what's going on out there. And by the way, sit up straight, please.

"At the top of the hour, the announcers began to run through the headlines for that day. Apparently, President Ford was planning to offer amnesty for conscientious objectors of the Vietnam draft. It caught his attention and suddenly, he was interested and engaged.

He wondered once again if it was time to call for a truce with Will? After all, they'd be seeing him every day in the hallways of Briarcliff High School pretty soon. Could they forgive, forget, and offer amnesty to each other?

Wait a minute. Is this one of those nods, tokens, and signs from Sky? he wondered, inclining his head toward the radio to listen more closely.

His mom glanced over at him as she coasted along in her VW Bug.

"Everything okay?" she asked, squeezing his forearm.

"Ye-yeah, Mom. I'm good…" his voice trailed off.

"Well, that wasn't very convincing," she said, tapping the steering wheel.

Charlie thought about opening up a little more to her about some of the challenges he and the guys had been having that summer with Will Morris. He also wanted to tell her that he believed Sky was back and helping them along but in a different kind of way.

"Things good with you and Michelle?"

"Yeah, fine. She's the best."

"And everything's cool with you and the guys?"

"Yeah, we're tighter than ever. By the way, Mom, don't say 'cool.'"

"What, I'm too old? Ha! Well, let's see, Barnes and Noble are good. Girlfriend is more than good. Your mother and father are fine. It must be work. Everything okay with your yard jobs?"

"Yes, Mom. I swear, everything is fine."

"Your father and I are very proud of you, Charlie. Hard to believe you're starting ninth grade next week. Seems like just yesterday I was walking you to kindergarten at Todd School."

"To tell you the truth, Mom, I'm a bit restless about making the jump to high school. Last semester, we were kings of the hill. Next semester, we'll be nobodies."

"Now, Charlie, that's not true. It will be a pretty big adjustment, granted, but you make it sound like doomsday."

"I guess, but it feels a little weird at times."

"You're fortunate to have a good core of friends, and I'm sure you guys will figure out how to roll with the punches." Charlie winced at that one, thinking of how badly Will would like to punch them out.

Once inside Books N' Things, they picked up a supply of Bic pens and No. 2 pencils, a five-subject loose-leaf binder, and some book covers featuring logos from various colleges and universities. His mom also browsed the best-seller section, picking up a copy of *Centennial*, the new historical novel by James Michener.

They paid for everything at the cash register, and then Charlie held the door for his mother.

"What's for dinner tonight, Mom?"

"You haven't even had lunch and already you're thinking about what's for dinner?"

"Well, you always have something for me to look forward to."

Charlie was about to put in a request for chicken and rice, his favorite, when he spotted something that made him lose his appetite.

Will Morris was pulling into the parking lot, and there was no place for Charlie to hide. His mind scrambled as he picked up the pace, walking briskly toward their car. He even challenged his mom to a race.

"Last one to the car's a rotten egg!"

"What's the hurry? The sun feels great."

"Me and the guys want to go to the pool," he said, reaching for the door handle, hoping to get in before Will saw him.

As Charlie slipped into the passenger seat, he slid way down as far as he could go. But Will was only a few parking spaces away, and

Charlie was in plain sight. He also was the latest recipient of the Will Morris death glare. Trying not to make eye contact, Charlie began to rifle through the shopping bag full of school supplies.

Unaware of what was happening, Mrs. Riverton stepped on the clutch and shifted the car into reverse. Then of all things, DMarks's mother came out of the pharmacy next to Books N' Things, so Mrs. Riverton stopped to say hello.

As the two moms chatted, Charlie squirmed in his seat. Swallowing hard, he peered up just slightly to see if Will was still there. His blood ran cold as Will was very much still there, on the other side of the walkway, starting at Charlie with a sardonic half grin. He made a fist with his right hand and pounded it into the palm of his left hand. Then he turned to head into Books N Things himself.

Charlie almost blacked out. *C'mon, Mom, wrap it up,* he thought. Finally, they pulled out of the parking lot on their way back to Briarcliff.

Once home, he ran up the stairs two at a time to change into his bathing suit. Then, on his way out the door, he scrunched Barnes's and Noble's ears and promised them a long walk later in the day.

Hopping on his bike, he road to the end of his driveway just in time as the guys showed up for the short to ride over to the pool.

"September's closing in fast you guys," said Charlie as they weaved back and forth, riding alongside each other. "I just came back from picking up school supplies."

"You ain't kidding." BB sighed. "Where the heck did summer go?"

"I know. Such a rip-off," grumbled DMarks.

"Only you could conclude that two and a half months of school vacation was a rip-off," pronounced George.

"Stuff it, tater tot," replied DMarks, deliberately bumping George's back tire.

George got his revenge by cutting DMarks off and almost running him into a garbage can.

"Hey! Watch it amateur. That one's gonna cost ya," threatened DMarks.

"Yeah? You and what army?" replied George.

Eventually, they arrived at the pool. The banter continued as they locked their bikes to the chain-link fence near the deep end of the pool.

As he dialed the combination to his lock, DMarks stopped abruptly. Squinting his eyes, he tried to focus his attention. Once again, he was startled by another foreboding premonition. He stood up straight and looked around trying to pick up some hint, some clue of what was happening. *What the heck is going on?* he wondered. *What is with this spot?*

Charlie happened to glance over at him. DMarks looked back as if to acknowledge that he was picking up that same kind of cautionary message.

Again? Charlie mouthed.

DMarks nodded back, wondering what it could possibly be. But no clear answers came. The two approached each other looking eye to eye. Charlie tried to understand and wanted to pick up on what his friend was feeling, but nothing came to him.

They looked around some more, then began a pensive walk to the pool area. James Dennis was by the entrance, chomping away at his whistle. He gave them an expressionless nod. The guys brushed right past him and kept walking to their normal spot near the diving boards.

As they hung out in the late August sun, Charlie decided to take another shot at the subject of reconciliation with Will. After listening to the news in his mother's car that morning, he hoped that maybe his luck would be better this time.

He picked his spot in the conversation and laid out his case. The guys listened politely and waited for Charlie to finish before they reacted. Then, one by one, they spoke up.

"You make a good case, Charles," said DMarks. "But a truce between us and Wet Willie? I just don't see that happening." He slammed the cap back on the sunscreen bottle.

"Why not? Earl Monroe and Clyde Frazier were adversaries for a long time, but look what happened when they became teammates on the Knicks," responded Charlie.

"Good one, Charlie," said George, looking at DMarks.

"Yeah? And look what happened when Roosevelt and Churchill teamed up with Stalin. They trusted that madman and now look. The Russians are still causing trouble all over the place," lectured DMarks.

"Touché. Score one for DMarks," added BB.

"So let me get this straight, Charlie. You happen to hear a news report on the radio, and you somehow think your old friend Sky was sending a message through the headlines?" asked George.

"That's right. God communicates with us in different ways," he replied, fiddling with the corner of his towel.

"Dude, I know you're a church-going man. We all are. But this is a little out there for me," said BB.

George interrupted, "Yeah, but Charlie takes this stuff to heart. Prays a lot, reads his Bible, never misses church. If he thinks that way, there's got to be something to it."

Feeling encouraged by George's endorsement, Charlie kept going. "It's other stuff, too. Like sometimes I happen to hear a song, and it's almost like the lyrics are speaking to me,"—he motioned to all of them—"to us!"

"How come the rest of us aren't getting this secret decoder ring message thing?" asked BB.

"Maybe you need to adjust your antennae," said DMarks, meaning it.

The guys spun their heads around. DMarks looked right back at them. "What? You guys think I'm beyond this sort of thing? I can totally relate to what Charlie's talking about. Been getting hints and hunches lately myself."

"Wait, what? You? You!" asked BB, pointing a finger at him.

"Come again on that?" said George as the guys got up to walk to the diving board.

"Yeah, me," responded DMarks, shoving BB into the deep end. "There, why don't you soak for a while."

DMarks felt a weight off his chest by finally saying something out loud about his similar experiences and growing faith. BB and

George were acting shocked, but Charlie gave his irascible friend a happy look.

"We can continue this conversation later," affirmed DMarks.

After their normal progression of pool games, they headed to the tennis courts for a six-inning game of Wiffle ball, which took most of the rest of the afternoon.

Around 5:30, they began to head home. That night was the last of the summer movie nights, and they planned to make the most of it.

After dinner, the guys all met up outside Charlie's house, then walked around the corner to Michelle's where she and some of the girls were waiting. From there they all walked over to Law Park, so happy together.

Will Morris also had plans for that night. He and Kristen Thomas arrived for the movie night just before dark, laying their blanket down in a spot toward the back of the hillside. Kristen put out a few snacks and they quickly got comfortable leaning up against each other.

"When does football practice begin?" she asked.

"Next week. Double sessions. Can't wait to see which rookies puke in the woods," he said with a cynical snort.

Pulling away, Kristen looked back at him with dismay. "What's that supposed to mean? Do you actually like seeing people suffer? And oh, by the way, what you just said was disgusting."

"Ease up, would ya? It happens every year. No one dies."

Trying to change the subject, Will asked when cheerleading try-outs began.

"Not until the first day of school. I'm excited to see who comes out for the squad this year."

"And you're captain?" he asked sweetly, coaxing her back to leaning against him.

"I sure am," she said proudly. "I've been waiting for this opportunity for a long time."

"Well, I hope you get some good-looking babes on your squad."

"Is that all it is to you? The girls on the cheerleading squad work hard on our routines and all that matters to you is how we look?"

"Whoa, whoa, whoa." He raised his hands in defense. "I didn't mean that the way it sounded."

Kristen shot an angry glare his way and busied herself with some of the snacks she brought.

"Oh brother," he moaned. "I'm getting the cold shoulder and this stupid movie hasn't even begun," he muttered.

"What did you say?" asked Kristen, crossing her arms.

"Oh, nothing. Nothing at all," replied Will as sweat beads sprung up across his forehead.

As Will went into damage mode, Charlie and the guys arrived with Michelle, Andrea, Connie, and Gretchen. They unwittingly found an open spot on the grass just in front of where Will and Kristen were sitting.

Will began to grind his teeth at the mere sight of them. The movie began a few minutes later, but not even *Herbie Rides Again* could shake him out of his anger.

Kristen felt his hot exhale on her forearm.

"What's eating you?" she asked.

"It's those little felons over there. They've been giving me trouble all summer," he complained, pounding his fist into the ground.

"Haven't we had this conversation before? Besides, they're just a bunch of middle school kids having fun. You're not setting a very good example."

"Oh yeah? See this welt on my chin? That's because of Riverton over there. He looks like such a nice kid, but I'm telling ya, he's dangerous. And in case you're wondering, it isn't fun falling out of a treehouse."

"Huh? What are you talking about? Are you blaming him for falling out of a treehouse? And what treehouse are you referring to?"

Will realized that if he gave her an honest answer, he'd have to confess that he'd been harassing Charlie and the guys all summer long.

"Never mind. I'll tell you another time."

"Actually, I'd like to know what you're up to. I've known Charlie since he was a first grader."

"That little trickster? He almost killed me when I was chasing him through Woyden's Swamp."

"And why exactly were you chasing him?"

"Because he needed a lesson. Okay?"

"He's the best kid in Briarcliff. Don't you remember Christmastime two years ago? When he took on that campaign to help others? What on earth could you be upset with him for?"

By now, Will's shirt was practically matted to his back with perspiration.

"Would you just forget it and enjoy the movie?"

Kristen's lips pursed in disappointment as her head tilted downward.

"Maybe you're the one who needs a lesson," she said, pulling the blanket out from under him and storming off with her picnic basket.

To Will's dismay, the scuffle caused people to turn and giggle at the sight of him all alone with a bag of Fritos and a bottle of Orange Crush.

"Fine! Be that way," he called after.

DMarks turned to see what the commotion was. He was startled to see how close they were sitting to their nemesis. His head told him to just ignore it, but his mouth was already engaged.

"Hey, Willy, what gives? Did you forget to brush your teeth or something?"

"Real funny, Tinkerbell. How would you like to lose a few teeth?"

"Hey, Chilly Willy, I was just trying to make sure everything's okay." Will sat up straight and keyed in on DMarks.

"You know what, Marks? You've got a beating coming to you. Maybe I'll give it to you right now."

"Time out. Now take a deep breath, and tell me what you plan to do. Detective Kaufman will want to know exactly how this went down."

The guys were not surprised by DMarks's cockiness, but this time, he had really crossed a line.

That did it. Will jumped to his feet. When DMarks saw the look in his eyes, he realized he'd gone too far and took off like the

Road Runner cartoon. As Will launched forward, BB resourcefully stuck out his foot causing him to trip, landing in the middle of the Lebenson's chips and salsa two blankets over.

BB's move gave DMarks a vital head start, but there was going to be a price to pay.

"You little punk," snarled Will, rolling over to administer a major wrist burn. "Better watch it. There's more where that came from," he warned.

Getting to his feet, Will scanned the landscape and took off in search of DMarks. This time, he would finally settle their summer-long scuffle.

BB was practically hyperventilating in pain.

"Way to take one for the team," said George, pulling him to his feet.

"C'mon, guys, let's book. If he gets to DMarks before we do, this could get ugly," urged Charlie.

"Uglier!" called out Michelle.

"What gives? We come here with you for the last movie night of summer and then you ditch us?" asked Gretchen.

"Yeah," chimed in Andrea. "This feels like déjà vu."

"Sorry. Duty calls," apologized Charlie.

"Everyone stay exactly where you are. We'll be back as soon as possible," pleaded George, winking at the girls with praying hands.

The guys took off sprinting, not knowing which direction to go in.

"Here we go again. We've got it made in the shade with some of the prettiest girls in our grade and Marks has to blow it for us," complained George.

"Let's find him before Willy does so we can pound him first," replied BB.

DMarks was running as fast as he could trying to stay away from any of the lamplights throughout the park. Around the tennis courts he went, up the hillside past Gooseneck Pond, and all the way to the War Memorial where he slid under the rhododendrons to hide.

The guys made their way out onto the ballfield behind the middle school. Stopping to catch their breath.

"When we were kids playing hide-and-go-seek, he always hid near the War Memorial underneath the rhododendrons. I bet that's where he went," suggested Charlie.

"Good call. Let's check it out," said BB.

Past the pool area and up the hillside they went. DMarks saw them coming and shushed them as they got closer.

"Over here. Slide in and keep it zipped." They hunkered down, winded from their sprint.

"And no breathing," DMarks added.

It looked like they had shaken Will off their trail for the time being. Still, it was dark, and they couldn't tell for sure exactly where he was. One thing they did know, he hadn't gone back to watch *Herbie Rides Again*. He was out there somewhere in Law Park, prowling and stalking and sweating.

"Man, you really pushed his buttons this time," whispered George.

"Seriously, Marks, if we get out of this alive, you're dead," warned BB, still rubbing his arm from that wrist burn.

"You're ending this summer the same way you started it. Front and center on Will's hit list," added Charlie.

"Shut it. All of you. Just stick with me, and I'll get us out of this."

"Like the way you saved us from the Phantom Gravedigger?" deadpanned BB.

"What is with you, guys? Seems like you lost a few pounds of manhood since the last time I saw you."

DMarks stood partially up and visually studied the area as they waited things out. They could either try to sprint out of Law Park and back to the Tree Streets or they could run as fast as they could back to the movie night. In either case, it meant being out in the open and potentially exposed to Will Morris.

Waiting it out was excruciating. Just when it seemed like their nerves couldn't take it anymore, they saw Will's silhouette tiptoeing around down by Gooseneck Pond. He was dashing in between trees and coming in their general direction.

"*Mister Roger's* didn't prepare me for this," George nervously murmured.

"Now what, Marks? We're sitting ducks if we just stay here," added BB, pinching his arm hard as payback for the mess he'd gotten them into.

Shrugging him off, DMarks instinctively reached down and picked up a small rock.

"Okay, I'm going to toss this toward the library," he whispered. "When Willy hears it, he'll take off running in that direction. Once that happens, follow me down to the pool and over the fence. We can hide by the first-aid station. Charlie, say a prayer."

"You and that first-aid station. They're going to start charging you rent for all the time you've spent there this summer," cracked George.

"How can you joke at a time like this?" asked DMarks, clipping the back of his head.

"Stop it, you two," whispered Charlie, smacking DMarks's hand away.

DMarks looked down as though he was saying a prayer. Then, with great caution, he stood up and winged the stone like he was throwing to home plate from centerfield. The rock skittered across the parking lot pavement, which got Will's attention.

The guys looked on as he scampered toward it. Then, they made their move dashing down the hill, over the chain-link fence and into the pool area. But in their haste, George's shirt got caught on the top of the fence, making a loud shredding noise and causing him to crash into the fencing with a noisy, springy clatter. It caught Will's attention and he was back on their trail.

Perfect, just perfect, thought DMarks, mentally picking out his coffin. Will began charging toward the pool. As he got over the ridge of the hill, he saw them dashing down the pool deck.

"Now I've got you!" he yelled as he charged to the fence, easily scaling it with his great athletic ability. It probably wasn't DMarks's best idea to hide inside a fenced-in area that was also lit with security lights. The boys knew they were cornered with their backs literally against the wall of the first-aid station.

"Remember, we're all in this together," said Charlie, breaking out in goosebumps.

They looked on as Will landed squarely on the pool deck. He was only about fifty yards away. Exhaling heavily in a crouched position, he spotted them right away. Standing up a little straighter and smiling in a devious way, he began to sprint in their direction.

Even at a distance, they could see his eyes were programmed to destroy. With sweat dripping from his forehead, Will focused on his prey. As a result, he didn't see the kickboard someone had left on the pool deck. After just a few strides, his right foot planted on top of it, twisting his ankle and causing him to tumble headlong into the deep end of the pool.

The boys immediately spotted an opportunity. With Will in the pool, they had a shot at freedom.

"C'mon, guys. Here's our chance," shouted DMarks.

They got up and ran right past where Will had fallen in the pool. Leaping onto the fence, they gripped it with their hands, digging their feet into the chain links. But just as DMarks was straddling the top of the fence, a fresh floral breeze encompassed him. Looking back at the still waters of the pool, he realized that Will hadn't resurfaced.

"Guys, wait up. He's still down there. Do you think he's hurt?"

"It's a trick. Don't fall for it," called BB who was already on the other side of the fence.

"Wait, what if he really is hurt?" asked an out-of-breath Charlie, bent over with his hands on his knees, also safely on the other side of the fence.

"He's been down there a while. What the heck is he doing?" asked George, leaning against Charlie, trying to catch his breath.

Still unsure what to do, DMarks heard a familiar voice.

"He's drowning, Derrick. Get in there and help him!"

DMarks looked at his buddies with an urgent look. "He needs help. I have to make sure he's okay."

Bewildered, the guys instinctively climbed back over the fence and onto the pool deck.

Will finally surfaced. He was completely panicked and out of breath.

"Can't swim! Can't swim!" he shouted, as he submerged again.

Without hesitation, DMarks yanked his shirt off and dove in to help. Will surfaced once again, flailing and calling for help. Charlie dove in to help DMarks while George grabbed the gaff from the lifeguard station. BB looked around for a flotation device. Working all together, they were able to tow the oversized upperclassman to the shallow end of the pool where they propped him up on the steps to stabilize him.

By then, Will had swallowed a lot of water and was only semi-conscious. The boys did their best to revive him.

"Quick, BB. You're the fastest. Run over to the movie night and get the lifeguards," ordered DMarks as he cradled Will's head.

Shaken but focused, Charlie, George, and DMarks did everything they could to care for Will. They were functioning on pure adrenaline. They knew this was serious, and yet their minds blocked them from thinking about what seemed like the worst-case scenario.

This can't be, thought DMarks. "C'mon, Will, you got this," he pleaded. "Open those eyes and breathe," he said, patting him on the sides of his face to help him regain consciousness.

George and Charlie stuffed kickboards behind his broad, muscular back to buttress him in an upright position. It was all they could do as his whole body began to shiver.

Panic-struck, the guys looked on as the strongest, toughest kid in town lay motionless. His lips were blue, and he was turning paler by the minute.

"This is not good. I think he's going into shock," Charlie observed.

"Shock? Is he even breathing?" George asked.

DMarks put his ear to Will's chest. "Will, buddy, you've got to hold on. The lifeguards will be here soon."

Just then, Will stirred, coughing up a gut full of water.

"That's a good sign. Go ahead and cough up some more," exclaimed DMarks.

Then, DMarks heard that same uniquely likeable and familiar voice. "*You're doing great, Derrick. Keep it up.*"

They could hear the lifeguards hustling in their direction. With keys jangling, they opened the gate to the pool area and ran through. Sliding into the waist deep waters of the shallow end of the pool, they surrounded Will and assessed the situation.

"Okay, Marks, let's let the pros take it from here," said James Dennis.

"No way, Dennis. I'm staying right here," said DMarks, cupping the back of Will's head with his hands. "C'mon, big guy," he whispered. "Stay with us. You got this," he encouraged.

The senior lifeguard didn't like being defied, but he did like the way DMarks was so committed to doing the right thing. Signaling for one of the other lifeguards to call an ambulance, he got down in the water opposite DMarks and helped support Will Morris and his brawny torso.

"Have you taken his pulse?" asked James Dennis.

"Yeah. It's only about fifty. This isn't good, man. This isn't good."

"What happened here? Was there any trauma?"

"No. No trauma, just took in a lot of water when he fell in the pool."

"How's his breathing?"

"Shallow. Very shallow."

"Why haven't you done CPR?"

"Why? Because I have faith." He looked heavenward. *I know that was you talking, Sky. I'm trusting what you said.*

James Dennis looked at DMarks all the more impressed. A few minutes later, the ambulance arrived with siren blasting and lights whirling. Now it was the EMT's turn to splash into the water. In unison, they lifted Will out of the pool and onto a gurney.

As they wheeled him out of the pool area, DMarks hustled alongside holding on to Will's hand and offering words of encouragement. Will kept falling in and out of consciousness.

"You're going to be fine. Can't keep a good man down."

Just as he was being loaded into the ambulance, Will gave DMarks an exhausted but clear thumbs-up. Siren wailing and lights flashing, the ambulance sped away into the night. By then, there was a major crowd of bystanders looking on, including Michelle and the girls. They wanted to go to Charlie, and the guys to make sure they were okay, but they were not allowed into the pool area.

Charlie saw the concerned look on Michelle's face when she spotted him soaking wet in street clothes. Although he was shaken up, he managed to give her an "okay" signal.

The guys huddled together with anxious looks. They were starting to shiver, in the night air, dripping with pool water.

"Wow. That was a close call," said George.

"You ain't kidding," added BB. "Who would have thought that the best athlete in Briarcliff didn't know how to swim?"

They stood there side by side, trying to absorb everything that had just happened. Nothing much was said. It was something so out of the ordinary that they were all in a state of shock themselves.

Finally, BB spoke up, "How'd you know he was drowning?"

DMarks exhaled, then looked at the guys.

"You won't believe this, but just as I was about to jump off the fence, this flowery breeze made me stop."

George and BB gave him a skeptical side eye, but Charlie smiled back.

"Then, there was this voice," he continued. "It specifically told me that Will was drowning, and we needed to save him."

"C'mon, Marks. You're putting us on," said BB.

"I speak the truth." He gave them the Boy Scout salute.

"How come none of us noticed this breeze or heard this voice?" asked George

"I don't know, but I'm not making this up. I swear."

Charlie nodded to him in an understanding way.

"You came up big tonight, bro."

"Thanks, man," replied DMarks, reaching out to slap fives and feeling a huge sense of relief.

It could have all gone so wrong, he thought, head down.

A few minutes later, James Dennis came walking over with an arm full of towels. The guys gladly draped them across their shoulders.

Although angry that he had to stop the movie, the normally crabby lifeguard surprised the guys with a considerate tone.

"First, I want to say that I'm proud of the way you saved Morris's life. Looks like you actually paid attention during Advanced Water Safety, Marks. You even remembered how to take his vital signs."

DMarks nodded his head in thanks and, to the guy's relief, kept his mouth shut.

"We'd be hauling him off the drain in the deep end if it weren't for you. It took guts to do what you did," said the senior lifeguard.

The boys looked on thankful for the positive words.

"Second, I want to say that I'm really ticked off that you would have been inside the pool area after closing time. I don't know what you were thinking, but it shows what pea-brained, reckless little felons you are."

The boys looked down, digging their sneakers into the deck and resisting the urge to talk back.

"You realize this can't go unpunished, right?" asked James Dennis, hands on hips.

They looked on, not saying a thing, pulling the towels more tightly around their shoulders.

"I have no choice. You're outta here for the rest of the season. I don't want to see you at this pool again until next Memorial Day."

The boys looked at each other. This was not good news. At the same time, they were relieved that their punishment wasn't more serious.

"Now get the heck out of here before I think of something else to hold against you."

Not in the mood to protest, the boys turned quietly and began walking away. As they got to the pool exit, James Dennis called to them.

"One last thing. Good luck with your freshman year," he said with an affirmative nod. A half grin opened across the side of his face. In that moment, it seemed that their summer-long cold war was over.

The boys walked home through Law Park. They were wired from what had happened, but no one felt like talking. As they reached the Tree Streets, BB and George peeled off toward their houses.

"I guess we should call it a night," said George.

"Yeah, see you guys tomorrow. Oh, and Marks, good job saving Will from drowning," added BB, giving his friend a robust pat on the back.

"Yeah, man, you saved his life," added George, with a big wave.

"It was a group effort. We all earned a good night's sleep," replied an uncommonly self-effacing DMarks.

The nighttime sounds of summer were fully animated as Charlie and DMarks walked along in silent thought. The two were so close that just walking side by side, there was a sense of completeness.

Then, Charlie heard Sky's voice.

Pass it along.

At first, Charlie wasn't sure what to make of it. *Pass what along?* he wondered.

Then it hit; Charlie looked at his friend.

"You know I think you're a knucklehead, right?" asked Charlie, play punching him in the shoulder.

"Join the crowd," answered DMarks.

"But I love ya, anyway."

"You're all heart, Charles."

"Here, I have something for you."

Charlie stopped, reached under his T-shirt, and took off the cross with the crown of thorns pendant Sky had given him two Christmases ago. He held it in his hand, looking at it as the rare gift it was. Then, with a full heart and smile to match, he handed it to DMarks.

"Here, this is for you."

For once, DMarks was without words. In fact, he was thankful for the dark of night so that Charlie wouldn't be able to see that he was fighting back tears.

"I don't think I can accept this. I know how much it means to you."

"It would mean even more to know it's blessing you the way it blessed me."

"But, Charlie, this came from Sky, your special friend."

"Buddy, I want you to have it, and I happen to know that Sky would approve."

DMarks's eyes welled up again as he looked at his best friend. He reverently slipped the pendant over his head.

"I'll wear this every day, and I promise to make Sky proud."

"You better. He seems to be watching you closely these days."

They smiled and embraced briefly, slapping each other's backs.

"I love you, man," said Charlie.

"I love you back," replied DMarks.

31
CHAPTER
HOMETOWN HEROES

Above all, keep loving one another earnestly,
since love covers a multitude of sins.

—1 Peter 4:8

What happened at the pool with Will Morris was way out of the ordinary in Briarcliff. If he had drowned, it would have left a permanent scar on the hearts of everyone who ever lived in the small, close-knit village. Instead, people talked nonstop about the fortunate outcome.

Two days later, a reporter from the *Citizen Register* called the Marks residence. "I got it," bellowed DMarks as he walked into the kitchen and snatched the receiver from the wall-mounted phone.

"Hello?"

"Hi, I'm a reporter with the Citizen Register, and I was hoping to talk with Derrick, please."

"You're talking to him."

"Oh, great, we'd like to do a feature article for our evening edition covering the incident in Law Park." DMarks leaned against the wall with a pleased grin, imagining all the attention and recognition he'd get in the hometown newspaper.

"What did you have in mind?"

"If I could meet you and your friends later this morning in Law Park, that would be great. Can we say eleven o'clock?"

"Yeah, sure, fine. I'll get the guys together, and we'll see you then."

"Why thank you, young man."

"No problem."

He hung up, then dialed Charlie and the others. They all agreed to meet in an hour.

Charlie, BB, and George showed up in their normal summer daytime attire. DMarks, however, was sporting a button-down shirt, neatly tucked into a pair of pressed khakis. He also had combed his hair with a generous amount of Brylcreem.

"You don't even dress this well for church. What gives?" asked George.

"Yeah, who stole my friend," kidded Charlie.

"I figure this lady might want to snap a few pictures, and I wanted to look my best," replied DMarks as he turned around so they could appreciate his whole appearance.

"Oh, brother. You could have told us you were going to dress up so that we don't look like schlubs next to you," complained George, tucking his shirt into his shorts.

"We should have known he'd turn on the high beams for this," carped BB, wetting his palms to slick down his bedhead.

"Seriously, man, now us guys are going to look like we don't care or something," protested Charlie.

"Let's just make this into a learning experience, shall we?" replied DMarks in a teacher-like way.

"Maybe you can learn how to get a few grass stains on those pants," threatened BB.

"Yeah, and maybe we can muss up his hair so it looks more like his normal crop," added George, reaching out his hand as DMarks ducked and weaved.

"Ah let it go. It's not worth the aggravation," said Charlie.

"What? There's a lot of eyeballs that are going to see my pearly whites when this article comes out. I wanted to put my best foot forward."

"Well, just don't put your best foot in your mouth," warned BB.

The guys hung out on a picnic bench overlooking the pool. It was the end of the season, but there was still a lot of summer fun happening down there. They each exhaled a long sigh and shook their heads as the reality of their pool suspension sunk in.

Before long, the reporter arrived, pencil and pad in hand, instamatic camera hanging from her neck.

"Hi, boys. Nice to meet you."

The boys politely stood to say hello and shook her hand.

"If you wouldn't mind, I'd like to start by snapping a few pictures. Can you gather together for me? Maybe over here by the flagpole."

The boys stood stiffly as if in a police lineup. The reporter was amused by how serious they looked. Laughing, she suggested they lighten up.

"Hey, this is a big moment. You should be proud of what you did. Relax and enjoy the spotlight."

She held the camera to her eye. "Great, okay, say cheese." DMarks stood up straight, sticking his chest out, mugging for the camera.

"Thanks, boys. That's great."

She then opened her notepad to a blank page and tapped the tip of her pencil to her tongue.

"So tell me what really went down the other night. How'd you end up in the pool area after hours?"

Suddenly, DMarks's realized this wasn't just some feel-good photoshoot for the afternoon paper. The *Citizen Register* sent an actual reporter and she was already digging for the facts. Not wanting to be in the paper for the wrong reason, he gave a blunt response.

"No comment."

With an open look of surprise, the reporter gathered herself and pressed on. "Umm, okay. Ahh, why did you guys leave the movie before it was over?"

"No comment."

The guys drew back from their friend glaring at him, wondering why he was being so rude. The reporter was also taken aback. She tried another angle.

"Is it true you guys are suspended from using the pool for the rest of the season?"

"No comment." DMarks crossed his arms.

"How did you happen to see the older boy struggling in the deep end?"

Realizing that she wasn't going to give up, DMarks drew a deep breath and gave his version of what happened.

"It's like this. They were showing *Herbie Rides Again.* Since me and the guys had already seen the movie when it was in the theaters, we decided to leave early. As we walked through the park, we noticed some…some activity in the pool."

"Right, okay. But how did the older boy get in there in the first place?"

"What does that have to do with anything? A life was saved by a bunch of kids who were out on a summer night. We saw an emergency, and we took action, at great risk to our own selves, I might add. Everything turned out fine. End of story."

"So the older boy, Will, just happened to somehow stumble up and over the fence, landing in the deep end, just as you four happened to be walking by in the dark?"

"Something like that. We fished him out of there, then the lifeguards called for an ambulance."

"Wow, well, that was awfully courageous of you guys."

"Well, the way I look at it, courage is like muscle. Use it or lose it."

The boys just looked at DMarks, openmouthed and shaking their heads.

The reporter looked back with an amused but impressed smile.

"Can I quote you on that?"

"Permission granted."

"I was told that maybe you guys had some kind of a summer-long feud with this Will Morris, the boy you rescued, and that he might have been chasing you through the park?"

"Look, lady, it's a small town. Kids knock heads around here all the time. It's no big deal."

"So this is just a 'boys will be boys' type thing?"

She flipped a page in her notebook and stared straight at DMarks, her pencil poised in the air.

"That about sums it up. Any other questions? No? Great. It's a wrap. Thanks for coming."

"I guess that covers it, unless you other boys have anything you'd like to add," said the reporter, looking at Charlie, BB, and George.

Just as Charlie was about to say something, DMarks interrupted. "Well…thanks for everything. Come back and visit again next summer."

"Thanks," replied the reporter. "If I have any follow up questions, I'll call the police desk."

That last comment landed like a thud. Suddenly, DMarks became very polite.

"We'd like to thank you for your time. We know how busy you are and coming here like this is very nice of you."

"Just part of my beat," she replied. *What is with this kid?* she wondered.

"And by the way, maybe you should just put our picture in the paper. No need to write anything up."

"But I'm a reporter," she said, giving him a quizzical look.

"Yeah, yeah, but you must have more important things to report on."

"Nonsense. This is gold. Everyone in town will want to read about the four accidental heroes who saved," she looked from one to the next, "the local bully."

The reporter tapped the eraser end of her pencil on her chin. Her instincts told her there was more to this story, but she wasn't getting it from these guys. The boys waited for her to walk down the hill and then the three of them dead-armed DMarks.

"That was rude, even for you," said BB.

"Yeah, you need to get your bolts tightened," quipped George.

DMarks doubled over, rubbing his arms. "I didn't like her sniffing around in our business like that."

"Ha! Scared of being in the local paper? Sounds like your courage muscle needs to work a little harder," chided George, landing a major charley horse on DMarks's left thigh.

"We're already kicked out of the pool for the rest of the year. Football practice starts in a few days, and don't forget, we have no idea how Will Morris is going to treat us when he gets out of the hospital. We don't need any more heat. Got me?" lectured DMarks.

"I hate to admit it, but he's got a point. We should never have ended up inside the pool area in the first place and if word got out that we were being chased by Wet Willy, that would not be good," admitted George.

Since it was close to lunchtime, the guys headed uptown to Weldon's. As they strolled past the police station, Sergeant Whiting was outside. He smiled broadly and gave them a formal salute.

"Nice work, boys. You saved a life, and you should be proud."

The boys saluted back and thanked him as the gravity of what had happened began to sink in a little more.

They got a similar greeting walking past Whigg's as the ladies who worked inside came out to give them pats on the back. Pete and Mrs. Pete at the stationary store even offered them free bubble gum.

DMarks grinned. "I could get used to this."

Then, a few steps further down the sidewalk, Charlie reached out to open the door at Weldon's. Just as they were about to stroll in expecting more fanfare, Will Morris came walking out. All four guys took a giant step back and froze in place, filled with shock and fear. *This can't be a good thing*, thought Charlie.

Will was equally surprised but never showed it. He stood expressionless, looking down at his young foes not saying a word. This time, it was the boys who broke out in a panicked sweat.

Then, during the unnerving silence, DMarks felt that fragrant breeze, which had become so familiar to him all summer. It flowed over him, and with it came that same, resonant voice. *"This whole summer was fated for this moment. It's your move, Derrick."*

Feeling inspired, DMarks looked at Will and broke the silence.

"So ahh, pretty eventful summer, huh?"

During his brief hospital stay, Will had time to reflect on things including his general outlook on life. He looked back, paused, then grinned a thankful smile.

"Glad we made it through alive," he said.

It wasn't much, but that brief response triggered the massive release of a whole summer's worth of stress and pressure. After a guarded pause, Will kept the conversation going.

"You guys going out for JV football?"

"We've waited our whole lives to play JV football," answered DMarks. "See this right here?" He pointed to himself and the others. "Thunder and lightning in football pads."

"Well, listen up. It's a big step from what you're used to. You're gonna be facing some guys that are a lot bigger than you. Just remember to play your position, know your plays, and keep your head up."

"Thanks, Will. We appreciate the advice," said Charlie.

"And start working out now. You don't want to show up for double sessions out of shape. You'll be puking in the woods all day."

"Trust me, we've seen our share of throw-up this summer, and we don't want any more," said BB, shooting a glance at DMarks.

"Any other words of advice?" asked George.

"Yeah, if you can, keep a spare set of cleats in your locker. That way, on days when it's raining, you'll have a dry pair for the next practice."

"Right on, Will," said DMarks.

The guys couldn't believe that they were having an actual conversation with Will Morris, let alone receiving important advice from him.

"So, ahh, how was it over at Phelps? We heard they kept you in the hospital for a day or two after the pool…um, accident…incident…swimming thing," Charlie finally got the words out.

"Well, I hated to be stuck in a hospital room like that. Worst of all, I had to wear this geek hospital gown. Every time I got out of bed, it felt like I was mooning someone."

The boys laughed out loud, then quickly caught themselves, not wanting to anger Will. But when he joined in, they all laughed together, even louder.

"There was one good part, though. Mr. Olson's dog kept me company. Climbed right up in bed and slept next to me each afternoon."

"Taylor? He's the best." Charlie grinned.

"Yeah, and he has a little girlfriend named Annabelle. She's pretty awesome, too."

Will then reached out and put his hand on DMarks's shoulder, tilting his head down and looking him in the eyes.

"You're a tough little sucker, Marks. You don't back down. That came in very handy at the pool the other night. I have a lot of respect for that."

DMarks stood speechless, almost getting emotional. Finally, he was able to choke out a few words.

"Gee, thanks, Will."

The two maintained eye contact as a smile opened up across Will's face. He paused, looked down, then looked back at DMarks.

"Tell ya what. Call me Willy."

Now, everyone was smiling.

"C'mon, you guys," said the upperclassman, opening the door to Weldon's. "Your lunch is on me today."

The guys all looked at each other like it was Christmas morning, Halloween and their birthdays all rolled into one.

"Thanks, Will. You're the man," said BB.

"So cool, Will," added George.

"This is great, Will, but really, it's not necessary," said Charlie as DMarks interrupted him.

"Now we're talking," DMarks rubbed his hands together in an exaggerated way. "I knew there was a reason why we saved your life," he chirped.

The boys flinched, thinking DMarks's wise guy routine was going to ruin everything, but Will just motioned that it was cool.

"Hey! You guys coming or going? Air-conditioning isn't free, you know," called out Mr. Weldon.

As the door swung shut behind them, Will jabbed at DMarks, flicking his ear.

"It's a good thing I'm such a nice guy," Will said, beaming a transformed smile.

Later that day, BB threw the evening paper on each of their doorsteps with a loud "Huzzah!"

The boys were thrilled to see they were frontpage news. Their phones began to ring off the hook once families around town saw the evening paper.

Getting your name in the local paper was a big deal. If the article also included a picture, that was really major. Thankfully, even with her suspicions, the reporter did right by the boys. Her article portrayed them as heroes, and for the next week or so, they were treated like royalty around town.

For the guys, it felt like everything was flowing in the right direction as they edged closer to their first year of high school. The annual end-of-summer touch of melancholy was in the air. Even so, the season was ending on a high note for them.

32
CHAPTER

WE DO!

So now, faith, hope and love abide these three,
but the greatest of these is love.

—1 Corinthians 13:13

Parker and Suzie were in their late twenties and neither was interested in an extended engagement. Mr. Olson and Mary had the same mindset. The two lovebirds were intent on marrying sooner, rather than later.

By heavenly coincidence, both couples paid an unscheduled visit to Reverend Higgins the last Saturday in August. Pulling into the church parking lot simultaneously, all four got out of their cars with cheerful greetings.

"Jack, Mary! What a nice surprise," Parker called out.

"What brings you here on a Saturday morning?" asked Suzie.

"Mary and I were thinking we'd like to tie the knot as soon as possible," announced Mr. Olson, looking very pleased with himself. "So we're here to discuss arrangements."

"Plus, the Mets are mathematically eliminated, so there's no sense in waiting until after the postseason," quipped Mary, locking her arm in his.

"We're here for the exact same reason," Parker happily responded.

"I want to get this guy to the altar before he changes his mind." Suzie laughed, pretending to reel him in with a fishing pole.

"Ha! Maybe we can all go on the newlywed game together," joked Mr. Olson.

The happy couples walked across the street and up the church steps to the minister's study. Reverend Higgins was puffing away on his pipe while putting the finishing touches on his sermon for the next morning.

"Well, now, what brings four of my favorite people here on this fine day?"

Suzie spoke up before anyone could answer. "As you know, Mary and I are newly engaged," she said, holding out her hand, flashing the diamond ring Parker had given to her. "And we wanted to begin to make wedding plans."

"Well then. We're open for business," boomed Reverend Higgins, reaching for his calendar. "What did you have in mind for timing?"

"How about…yesterday?" said Mr. Olson, which earned him a warm kiss on the cheek from Mary.

"As soon as possible," said Parker.

"I see, well, did you have a fall wedding in mind? Maybe something around the Christmas holiday?"

Mary leaned forward, cleared her throat, and spoke for the group. "Actually, we were thinking of a summer wedding."

"Splendid. That will give us a full year to plan," answered Reverend Higgins.

Suzie interrupted, "Right, yes, and speaking for Parker and me, we were initially thinking of a nice, comfortable engagement. But we're not getting any younger you know, plus my biological time clock is ticking." She mimed a bomb going off, as Parker blushed. "So actually, we were thinking of this summer. From the looks of it, Mary and Jack were thinking the same thing."

Reverend Higgins was taken aback. "Well, holy of holies, I'll be jitterbugged. Nothing like plenty of advanced notice!"

He restuffed his pipe and struck a match. After a brief moment of contemplation, he launched out of his chair, pacing back and forth and thinking out loud in a swirl of sweat smelling pipe smoke.

"Hmm, this does present a bit of a challenge. We only have one sanctuary, one minister, and one weekend before Labor Day." Folding his arms, he leaned against a bookshelf. "I've got it. Why don't we go for a doubleheader?"

Jack looked at Mary and Parker looked at Suzie. Then both couples looked at each other. Huge smiles broke out with enthusiastic nods all around.

"Based on the reaction I just saw, I believe we have a winner," surmised the reverend.

Suzie and Mary hugged tightly, then sat together holding hands as they talked about exchanging vows all together at the same time. Parker and Mr. Olson stood, saluted each other, and warmly shook hands. The two couples quickly decided they would serve as each other's maid of honor and best man.

"Hold on a moment. I better check my calendar for next weekend," said the reverend. "Oh dear, I was planning on attending the Scottish Highlander's bagpipe festival at Bear Mountain Park."

Four slightly panicked looks broke out.

"But I think I have something slightly more important now," he bellowed. "Okay then, it's on the calendar for one week hence."

"Good one, Reverend. You had me there for a minute," said Parker, leaning back in his chair.

"Now that we have a date, there's some planning to do. What kind of ceremony do you want? Are there any special readings or music you have in mind?"

"Gosh, we haven't thought about that yet. Can you give us twenty-four hours?" asked Mr. Olson hopefully.

"Jack, I've been doing this for so long that you can tell me next Saturday morning when you arrive. Say, it's almost lunchtime. Why don't the five of us head over to Squires for a bite to eat so we can discuss things in detail."

"Great idea! My treat," announced Mr. Olson.

"I was hoping he'd say that," muttered Reverend Higgins out of the side of his mouth, making a big show of escorting everyone out of the building.

Squires was an institution in Briarcliff. A cozy pub with cheery red-checked tablecloths, it was the kind of place that made everyone feel comfortable.

The circular table in the back corner was available so they snagged it. None of them needed a menu. They all ordered Squires burgers before they even sat down.

Reverend Higgins brought his Bible and a hymnal to help with selecting verses and music. All four insisted on writing out their own vows. Parker and Mr. Olson also agreed to wear their army dress blues for the occasion.

"It's not as easy to fit into that uniform as it used to be," commented Parker.

"Son, I've had to take mine to the tailor five times over the years," answered Mr. Olson. "But I'm still having the french fries!"

Mary and Suzie decided to keep things simple with white summer shifts for their wedding dresses. "Whiggs has some pretty eyelet ones," Suzie told her. They both agreed to shop there after lunch.

Waving a french fry at the group, Reverend Higgins offered up a suggestion. "Assuming you might need a venue for the reception, I'd highly recommend that you consider our Parish Hall. It's dog-friendly and comes at a great price." He grinned widely. "Free."

Once again, all four were in complete agreement.

"What a great idea. How can we thank you, Reverend?" asked Mr. Olson.

"Nonsense. Of all the things our Parish Hall has been used for in the past, this will be one of the best events yet."

"I remember when they used to have Briarcliff High School canteen dances there back in the '60s," recalled Parker.

"Those were so much fun! What was the name of the local band that always played?"

"The Country Casuals?" suggested Suzie.

"Right! I think you're the smartest woman in the world," said Parker, leaning in for a quick peck on the lips.

Suzie agreed to take the lead on arranging a caterer. Mary would oversee decorations and flowers. Parker and Mr. Olson were in charge of getting the word out to invited guests. They chose a 6:00 p.m. ceremony so that the west-leaning sun would have maximum effect on the stained-glass Tiffany windows throughout the sanctuary.

"Do I get to provide a brief homily?" asked the reverend.

Mr. Olson couldn't resist. "Have you ever provided a brief homily?"

"Ha! You've got me there."

"Well then, we'll leave everything in your hands, Reverend." Mr. Olsen patted him on the back.

"Bully!" shouted Reverend Higgins in response.

"Dearest, what about our wedding song for the reception?" asked Mary, looking at her Jack.

"Oh yes, another detail we'll have to look after," he answered. "Was there anything you had in mind?"

"Now that you ask, I've always loved Louis Armstrong and his signature recording."

"What a Wonderful World?" Mr. Olson smiled. "Bully!"

"I'll take that as a yes," interjected the reverend.

Turning to his bride-to-be, Parker asked, "What about you, Suzie? Any thoughts? I'll let you decide."

"Me? Make an important decision like that all by myself? Why, there's dozens of options to choose from," said Suzie, feigning exasperation.

"It's okay, honey. You can think about it."

"No, wait." She ran her hands through her blond locks, concentrating for a moment, then blurted, "'You are so Beautiful' by Joe Cocker." Parker just smiled back at her. He knew her all too well. *Anything she wants*, he thought.

"I have to confess, it's not hard for me to see God's hand in all this. Four people coming together the way you all did doesn't just happen by accident," declared the reverend.

"I openly confess that I felt led to this point," said Mr. Olson.

"Same here," said Parker. "Unmistakable."

Both men wondered if the other had heard the same voice leading them along.

"Well, I'd say that we've got everything we need," said Reverend Higgins, slapping his hand on the table. "A venue, four people who were meant to be with each other, and the very presence of God among us."

"Plus our favorite pastor," added Mr. Olson.

"If nothing else, your hungriest pastor." The reverend looked at Mary, then down at her plate. "By the way, Mary, are you planning to finish those fries?"

Without hesitating, he picked one up and dipped it in ketchup.

"Don't mind if I do."

33
CHAPTER

SO LONG, SUMMER

He changes times and seasons, he removes kings and sets up kings; he gives wisdom to the wise and knowledge to those who have understanding.

—Daniel 2:21

A fresh supply of crisp autumn air arrived early that providential Labor Day Weekend of '75. Sugar maples were starting to show splashes of color and the days were getting noticeably shorter.

Football practice was about to begin and the guys were doing their best to get ready. One necessity was football cleats so Charlie's mom drove them to Bob's Army-Navy in Ossining.

"For once I'm happy not to have an older brother," said BB. "I know guys who are getting hand-me-down cleats this season."

"Same here. That has to be one of the worst kind of hand-me-downs," declared George.

As always, Bob's had a great selection to choose from. Charlie, BB, and George each got black Adidas cleats with white stripes. DMarks, however, lit up when he got a glimpse of white Puma's on display.

"You think those are gonna help you run faster or something?" joked BB.

"Man, the varsity players are going to be all over you when you show up wearing those babies," warned George.

"Everyone knows white cleats are for show boaters," cautioned Charlie.

"It's a calculated risk," DMarks replied. "I figure no one will mess with me since Will and I are bros now."

The guys looked at each other with raised eyebrows.

"He's in for it on Rookie Day," said BB.

On the way back from Ossining, Mrs. Riverton dropped them off at the ballfield behind the middle school. They wanted to put on their new cleats to break them in.

As they sat on the steps outside the Boys Locker Room lacing them up, there was a sense that a transition was underway. They were turning a page in their young lives and each double knot they tied seemed to add more closure on their middle school years.

They warmed up by jogging the perimeter of the field a few times. After that, they started in with line drills and wind sprints.

Charlie brought a football so he could work on his passing game. The guys were in seventh heaven running post patterns, down-and-outs and buttonhooks. After a solid hour's worth of practice, they took a break.

Sitting around up in the shady hills of Law Park, they kicked off their cleats and gulped Gatorades.

"I think I'm done for the day," declared DMarks, brushing blades of grass off his new Pumas.

"Yeah, let's not overdo anything. We're going to need everything we've got for double sessions," Charlie added.

There wasn't much talk as a few new realities began to set in. Briarcliff High School was on the other side of town, which meant they wouldn't be making their daily walk to school through Law Park anymore. For that matter, they wouldn't be able to walk up town to Weldon's after school either. Life as they knew it was changing, and they were conflicted.

They moved along a little slower than normal as they made their way home to the Tree Streets. Then, one by one they to slapped fives before parting ways to walk to their individual houses.

"Get a good night's sleep tonight guys," urged Charlie.

"Yeah, everyone in bed early," added DMarks. "Got to look our best tomorrow."

"Steak and eggs for breakfast!" shouted BB.

"I'll be sleeping with my football tonight," George called over his shoulder.

Their outward confidence belied uneasy feelings, and they all knew it. To be sure, they were excited about the season ahead. Their shared dream, going all the way back to flag football, was to put on a Briarcliff Bears jersey and play other schools in full pads. But they were heading into unknown territory and it rattled them.

After dinner that night, they each dialed one another on the phone to talk things over. Ready or not, their time had come. The individual phone conversations helped take the edge off the looming reality of 9:00 a.m. conditioning and drills with the varsity team.

They each spent a little extra time in prayer at their bedsides that night. Still none of them slept soundly.

The next morning, Mrs. Riverton dropped everyone at Briarcliff High School at 8:30 a.m. She put the car in park, then dashed around in front to snap a photo of them as they got out of the car. But they put their hands up to cover their faces, shooing her away.

"Just give it your best, boys," she said, sensing their nervousness. "I remember when I tried out for field hockey and—"

Charlie interrupted her gently, "Ah, thanks, Mom," giving her a shy smile and a wave.

Grabbing their gym bags, the other boys muttered their thanks too.

As they walked tentatively down the sidewalk to the gymnasium entrance, a group of varsity players walked by.

"Out of the way rookies," said one, elbowing George right off the sidewalk, confirming for the guys they were indeed low men on the totem pole.

Coach Hoffman was standing outside the gym entrance with a clipboard in his hand and a whistle around his neck. Old school and organized, he greeted Charlie and the guys and assigned them each a half locker so they could store their gear. He was a nice man, but all business when it came to the football program.

"Welcome to the big leagues, gentleman," he said, handing each of them a navy-blue practice jersey with Bears Football silk-screened on the front and Rookie on the back.

Their steps grew more hesitant as they walked through the rear entrance of the boy's locker room, poking their heads around the corner to get a partial view inside. Then, one jittery step after another, they moved along, looking for their assigned lockers.

Thankfully, their lockers were in the way back, comfortably away from the varsity crowd. As they got changed for practice, Charlie reminded them of the special lifelong bond they shared. "All for each and each for all," he said, nudging them.

On the other end of the locker room, some of the varsity players were jacking up the intensity level. Husky voices and backslapping bear hugs were everywhere as teammates greeted each other. A pair of stereo speakers set on top of a row of lockers was blasting "Frankenstein" by Edgar Winter over and over.

Charlie and the guys exchanged tense glances. It was time to make their way to the practice field. In order to get there, they had to walk through the gauntlet of seniors and their ear-splitting psych music.

"Remember. We get each other's backs from here on out," reminded DMarks.

They looked each other in a solemn way, nodded in solidarity, and began their walk, heads down, hoping not to be noticed. Less than a minute later, they stepped outside to a sun-drenched utility area with huge sighs of relief.

"That wasn't so bad," said BB as they walked toward the practice fields. Then, they were spotted by a pair of captains.

"Hey, rookies! Where do you think you're going?"

Charlie spoke up first, "H-H-Heading to practice."

The captains stood there with hands on their hips, looking down and shaking their heads.

One spit, then spoke up. "What kind of upbringing did you neophytes have? Seriously, you can't be from Briarcliff."

The other chimed in. "You don't show up to a party empty-handed. Now get back in there and grab those tackling dummies. C'mon, hustle!"

The guys practically sprinted to the equipment room, beyond intimidated. Their minds were scrambled as they fumbled around, grabbing as much as they could.

The two captains stood with arms folded looking on impatiently.

"Dang rookies have no manners. We're going to have to work with them on that," said one.

"Nothing a few extra line drills won't cure," smirked the other.

As the guys were hauling gear out of the equipment room, Will Morris came trotting by.

"Excellent move, guys. It's kind of expected that rookies will take care of getting stuff to and from the practice field. Good job! The other captains will be impressed," he said as he jogged away.

The guys stopped and looked on. He totally stood out among all the other players. Just the way he moved was so impressive. It was like watching an NFL player which, to them, was art in motion.

"Now he tells us," groaned DMarks.

"Lesson learned," said Charlie.

"One of many to come," added BB slapping his friend on his shoulder pads.

As they hustled down the hill their cleats made a click-clack crunching sound on the gravel pathway. Their minds exploded and they were on autopilot.

At 9:00 a.m. sharp, the players gathered around and took a knee. Coach Hoffman stepped forward to welcome everyone while laying down some ground rules.

"Gentleman. I'm glad to see such a strong turnout. There are a lot of familiar faces and a few new ones too. Whether you're a returning player or a first-timer, everyone is on equal ground as of right now." He paused and scanned the gathering to make sure his point registered with everyone present.

Charlie and the guys looked at each other. So far so good. They mimed back and forth.

"Allow me to lay out a few policies everyone will be expected to abide by. Number 1, helmets will be worn at all times. Number 2, mouthguards will be used on every play. Number 3, chinstraps will be snapped in place from the time you step on the field until you hit the showers after practice. And number 4, play until the whistle is blown. Any questions?" He glanced over the top of his half-rim eyeglasses.

"Dang, I'm already sweating like a dog with this helmet," DMarks complained."

Don't be such a creampuff," whispered BB.

"One more thing. We have a saying around here. It's always okay to try your best and fail, but it's never okay to fail at trying your best." Coach Hoffman paused to let his words sink in. "It's never okay to fail at trying your best," he said again for emphasis, which resulted in a few "booyahs" from the captains.

"What, no Vince Lombardi quote about winning?" murmured DMarks, which earned you're-an-idiot glances from the guys.

"Okay, captains, line 'em up," instructed Coach Hoffman blowing his whistle, signifying that the first practice was officially underway.

The players jogged onto the practice field as the four captains spaced themselves about ten yards apart. All the players fell into single-file lines in front of them. Will and the other captains then walked silently in between the lines and players. The solitary hush stoked a sense of anticipation throughout the team. Then, on cue, the captains shouted at the top of their lungs.

"*What game is this?*"

"*Football!*" everyone hollered back.

"*Who plays football?*" the captains screamed.

"*Bears play football!*" came the response.

"*Who are we?*" the captains roared.

"*Briarcliff Bears!*" everyone bellowed.

"*I can't hear you!*" yelled the captains, cupping their ears.

"*Briarcliff Bears!*" the team echoed back.

From there, the entire team crouched, running-in-place, repeatedly smacking their hands on the sides of their helmets, then their thigh pads, following Will's lead. After about a minute, the team broke into a series of calisthenics including jumping jacks, pushups, squat thrusts, and leg lifts.

Wow! Welcome to high school football, Charlie thought.

It's way too soon for me to feel like I have to throw up, thought DMarks as he fought the urge.

After about ten minutes, the coaches instructed everyone to break into groups based on which position they wanted to play. There was one station for offensive backs, another for linemen, a third for linebackers, and a fourth for defensive backs. Different drills were conducted at each station, which allowed the coaches to assess everyone's skill level.

Will Morris was the star quarterback and linebacker. In his leadership role, he ran a tight ship along with the other captains. The morning drills and workouts pushed everyone to their limit. Most guys were completely winded, some were even a little dizzy, and there were those unfortunate ones who had to dash into the woods to throw up.

At noon, Coach Hoffman mercifully blew his whistle, signaling that morning practice was over. The guys half-walked, half-limped back up the hill to the locker room.

"I'm starving," moaned DMarks. "But I might actually be too tired to eat."

"You'll feel better once we get out of the sun," assured Charlie.

"This is at least as tough as they said it would be," grunted George, as they all sat by their lockers, yanking off their sweat-soaked jerseys.

"I think I lost five pounds out there," DMarks grumbled.

"Well, we've got three hours to recover before the afternoon session begins," said BB.

"I'll take it," said George.

Charlie's mom was waiting outside the high school to pick them up.

"Wow, you guys look beat. I can't tell if you need a hug, an extra-large coffee or two weeks of sleep," she said.

"Actually, Mom, what we need is to fuel up. Can you take us to Weldon's?"

"Can do," she replied, stepping on the clutch and putting her VW Bug in first gear.

They all gave Law Park a wistful glance as they passed by. After pulling into a space outside Weldon's, the guys stiffly climbed out of the car. Even Mrs. Riverton winced at the audible groans.

"Enjoy your break you guys. I'll pick you up in two and a half hours to bring you back to practice." Then, she sped off to Todd School to get her classroom ready for the first graders.

The guys got roast beef wedges and Cokes, then hobbled down to Law Park, collapsing on a couple of park benches. As they gobbled away, DMarks looked down at the pool.

"What wouldn't you do to dive in right now?" he asked.

"Oh, man, that water would feel so good. I got aches in places I didn't even know existed," echoed George.

"Why'd we have to get kicked out of the pool? Why couldn't we have been kicked out of the library or something?" asked BB.

As DMarks reached for his Coke, he felt the cross with a crown of thorns pendant shift beneath his shirt, followed by that now familiar flowery breeze. In that moment, he happened to glance up, noticing James Dennis down on the pool deck looking directly at him. He was twirling his whistle around his index finger, standing at ease.

DMarks reflected, then signaled to him with a peace sign.

James Dennis took off his Ray-Bans and nodded in response.

Charlie happened to notice the nonverbal exchange. He was glad to see his friend settling another score.

They finished their lunches and stayed put, resting on the shady hillside. The full body weariness they were experiencing was not like anything they had ever known. At one point, George even nodded off.

All too soon, Charlie's mom pulled into the parking lot near the library. The realization that it was time for the afternoon practice session was a painful thought. The guys slowly got onto their feet and hobbled over to the car.

On the way to the high school, Mrs. Riverton mentioned that the New York Giants were going to scrimmage on the Bears' football field that week. Apparently, their facility at Pace University was under repair, and they needed a place to run game-simulated practices.

"So beware of Giants out there," she kidded.

That news made the guys perk up a bit. "Seriously, Mom?" asked Charlie.

"Yep, heard it directly from the district superintendent."

"How great is that?" BB chimed in. He was a huge Brad Van Pelt fan.

At 3:00 p.m. sharp, everyone was back on the practice field and lined up for calisthenics. Afterward, they separated out to the various practice stations the same as they had done that morning.

DMarks was holding his own with the other linemen, but after hitting the blocking sled for the tenth time, he went to the back of the line and took his helmet off for some quick relief. Unfortunately, one of the captains happened to see him.

Running up from behind, he snatched DMarks's helmet.

"Hey, Goldilocks. Drop and give me twenty."

Surprised, dejected, and more than a little bit angry, DMarks complied, hitting the ground and pumping out pushups.

At the same time, the Giants had begun to make the short walk through the woods separating the Briarcliff High School and Pace University campuses. It was a surreal site to see the likes of Lester Simpson, Bobby Hyland, Ron Johnson Craig Morton, Spider Lockhart, Dan Fowler, and John Mendenhall appearing out of the woods.

Lester noticed DMarks was getting worked over and decided to see what was going on.

"Derrick! Haven't seen you in a few weeks. How you doing, bro?" asked the giant-sized Giant.

DMarks was completely winded, so he just gave a thumbs-up.

Lester glanced at the flabbergasted captain, then down at his young friend. "You okay, man?"

The old DMarks might have used the opportunity to strike back. But instead, he kept his cool.

"I'm good, Lester." He exhaled, hands on his hips for support. "My captain here is just trying to make me a better player."

The Giants' offensive lineman gave the captain an intimidating glance, nodding his head.

"Right on, my man. Work hard. It will pay off in the fourth quarter," advised the Giants veteran as he turned to walk with the rest of the squad.

The antagonistic captain was impressed.

"You're all right, Marks," he said with an approving nod. "White cleats and all. Here's your helmet back. Now keep it on until practice is over, okay?"

After practice, in the locker room, Charlie spoke up as they put their gear away.

"I love you, guys, but I don't have the energy to do anything after dinner tonight. In fact, I'm not sure I have enough energy to even eat dinner."

"I hear ya, man. Over and out for me, too," added BB, shutting his locker.

"I'd say something, but I'm too wiped out," added George.

"Will's being so cool to us," said DMarks. "Too bad we didn't save his life earlier in the summer."

"Best athlete in town, and he can't swim. Who knew?" added BB, shaking his head.

"Briarcliff College has an indoor pool that's open to the public on weekends this fall. Maybe we can take him there and give him some swimming lessons," suggested DMarks.

"What's going on with you?" asked George. "It's not like you to be so considerate of others."

I know what's going on with him, thought Charlie.

"Dude," DMarks said, stretching out his arms, "I'm really just thinking of the cute Briarcliff College lifeguards that will be there. Maybe I'll swim over to the deep end and call for some help myself."

The boys were glad that DMarks helped to lighten the mood, but it hurt to laugh. Slinging their gym bags over their aching shoulders, they shuffled out to the parking lot, happy to have survived the first day of JV Football.

34

CHAPTER

I'M A BELIEVER

Now faith is the assurance of things hoped for,
the conviction of things not seen.

—Hebrews 11:1

It had been a good first week of practice, so Coach Hoffman gave everyone Saturday afternoon off. Even the most dedicated players were glad for the opportunity to rest.

After lunch, Charlie turned on the TV and crumpled into this beanbag chair to watch *Wide World of Sports*. Barnes and Noble made themselves comfortable on either side of him.

"Just give me a half hour, guys. Then we'll go on a nice walk."

A little later, DMarks stopped by. He rapped twice on the screen door, slung it open, and walked straight to the kitchen for a tall glass of Mrs. Riverton's homemade iced tea.

Charlie got up to greet his friend.

"Thirsty?"

"Ahh. That hit the spot."

"Well, enjoy it while you can. That might be the last batch until next summer."

"I'm telling ya, your mom should bottle this. Someday, someone's going to make a lot of money on flavored iced tea."

"Yeah, yeah. Like the next Pet Rock, eh? Hey, I was just going to take the dogs out. You down?"

"Sure, as long as it'll be a slow walk."

"For sure."

Charlie reached for the dog leashes as DMarks downed another glass of iced tea. With Barnes and Noble leading the way, the two incoming freshmen limped and shambled over to Law Park.

They were glad for an empty bench in a shady area near Gooseneck Pond. The fresh September air felt revitalizing and restorative. They sat for a while, not saying much of anything. For the first time maybe ever, they were happy that there was nothing to do.

"I hurt all over." DMarks sighed as he shifted around, trying to find a comfortable position to sit in.

"Yeah, but it's a good hurt," Charlie acknowledged, tossing an acorn to a squirrel.

"They warned us JV football was going to be a tough step forward."

"And they weren't kidding," said Charlie as he tentatively flexed his right shoulder. "I think I threw a hundred passes this morning."

"Ha! That's Mickey Mouse stuff compared to all the dirt I ate with the other linemen."

"I noticed. Hats off to all you guys in the trenches."

"Thanks, but trust me, I'm only there because I can't throw or run like you."

"It isn't all fun and games for us, either. Ever get hit from your blindside?"

"To be clear, Charles, I do the hitting." DMarks hunched his shoulders with a menacing grimace. Charlie just smiled at his friend's limitless overconfidence.

They both had a lot of thoughts running through their minds as they looked out across the pond and all the way to the pool area. But talking about it took too much energy.

As they sat taking it easy, they noticed an unfamiliar noise coming from the other side of the park.

"What is that ruckus? asked DMarks.

"Beats me. It's not like anything we've heard here all summer. Sounds like someone's beating a drum or something," Charlie answered.

"You'd think by now that we'd know all the different sounds in this park."

"Right? For all the time we spent here morning, noon, and night."

They shifted around to see what the racket was, then looked at each other with "do you believe this?" looks.

The drumbeat sound was a basketball bouncing on the newly paved court in Law Park. There, on the other side of Gooseneck Pond was a full-court game of five-on-five.

"Did they just reopen the basketball court?" asked DMarks in disbelief.

"I'd say you're looking at the answer, right there," said Charlie, grinning and shaking his head.

"Can you believe this? After all we went through this summer," said DMarks, raising his fists to the sky.

Neither could ignore the irony. The first day of summer break the court had been padlocked. Now, on the last day, it was open for play.

DMarks drew a deep breath and was about to rant about it when Charlie cut him off.

"Don't say it," he urged. "That's life, man."

The longer they sat, the more they reflected on the layers of memories from the summer that was. Eventually, Charlie spoke up.

"One heck of a summer."

DMarks tilted his head, pausing to reflect. "Ya know, it got a bit crazy, but all in, it was the best summer of my life."

"I hear ya. We made friends with some of the New York Giants, golfed with Willie Mays, went to Playland, and Cape Cod."

"And saved Willie's life."

"Right, yes. That was huge."

"Actually, the highlight for me was getting to know your friend Sky. Although, I'd love to be able to ask him a few questions in person," added DMarks, folding his arms across his chest.

"Talk to me," said Charlie.

"Like why is it so hard to live in a way that's in step with what's in the Bible?"

Charlie laughed. "Welcome to the club."

"I mean, I go to church and that feels right on Sunday mornings. But it ain't easy to keep that going all week long."

"Buddy, that's an age-old challenge that's gotten the best of, well, the best of 'em."

"You sure seem to make it look easy."

"I guess I've got you fooled."

"You know what Tom, the youth director, told me at church? That there's a difference between being a churchgoer and being a Christian."

They both paused to let that sink in.

"I guess it's a growth process. Just compare where we are now to when we first started Sunday School," Charlie pointed out.

"Getting back to Sky. It's like he was sent to help us deal with Will this summer."

"Well, if you look at what the Bible says about angels, that fits within their job description."

"Yeah, but why would God bother with a jerk like me?"

"God loves jerks like you," Charlie said, shoving his friend in a good-natured way.

"What was up with the fresh breezes and the smell of altar flowers all the time?"

"Well, two Christmases ago, I'd feel wrapped up in these super warm and comforting feelings. For you, he seemed to make his presence felt a little differently."

"If it wasn't me talking, I'd be skeptical. But I know it was real."

"Well, keep an open heart to it."

"Now don't go getting all touchy-feely with me. Just because I'm down with your man Sky and all this God stuff doesn't mean I'm about to turn into some kind of choirboy."

Charlie smiled. *A big tree just fell*, he thought.

They hung out a bit more and eventually limped back to the Tree Streets, grateful that Barnes and Noble could tow them up any hills they encountered.

Stopping by Jackson Road Park, they slapped fives. Charlie headed home with the dogs while DMarks walked back into Woyden's Swamp and over to School's Out. He wanted to snag his transistor radio.

Climbing up to the treehouse one painful step at a time, he hoisted himself inside. It was quiet and peaceful as he looked out over the landscape. Almost predictably, an especially refreshing breeze kicked up along with the keenest scent of alter flowers yet.

DMarks lingered in the moment, eyes closed, inhaling fully and taking in the wonderful comfort it gave him.

"That you, Sky?" he asked out loud in an allegorical way.

"Who did you expect?" answered a familiar, audible voice.

DMarks was stunned. Opening his eyes wide, he spun around with a racing heart.

There, right in front of him was Skylar Northbridge, all six-foot-five of him, in the flesh. Same piercing blue eyes, same thick mane of brownish blond hair, same cool beard.

Sky just beamed back with his trademark, megawatt smile. He looked laidback and content in his faded blue jeans and leather sandals. The sleeves of his white untucked button-down shirt were rolled up to his muscular forearms.

It didn't happen often, but DMarks was speechless.

Sky looked warmly at his young friend.

"You gave me a run for my money this summer."

"Seems like I did a lot of running this summer," DMarks replied after gathering his wits.

"Glad you had ears to hear."

A sly grin spread across DMarks's face. "I was listening the whole time."

"You could have fooled me," said Sky with a deep, rich belly laugh.

"Sorry I was such a slow learner."

"Actually, compared to some of the assignments I've had, you were pretty good."

"So where you been over the last two years? Are ya going to stick around this time?"

"I wish I could, but I have a lot of travelling to do."

DMarks tried not to show his disappointment. "Well, when's the next time you'll be back in Briarcliff?"

"One never knows. My boss has been keeping me extra busy, but I'll be in touch from time to time."

"Well, how can we reach you if we need something?"

"Just pray. Word will get to me."

DMarks squinted his eyes and half tilted his head. "It's that simple?"

"It's that simple. God always hears our prayers."

After a healthy pause, Sky peered deeply into DMarks's eyes.

"Remember, buddy. Always be willing to take one for the greater good. This life is not all about this life and your life is not all about you."

"I kind of like that. Mind if I quote you?"

Sky smiled back approvingly.

"You've come a long way this summer. I'm proud of you."

"Kind of proud of myself now that you mention it."

"Just remember where your blessings come from big guy," cautioned Sky.

"I say my prayers at night."

"Maybe you should start praying throughout your day."

"Hey. I got stuff to do, places to go, people to see," DMarks responded, stretching his arms out wide.

"And if you want to end up in the right place with the right people, doing the right thing, it would be a good idea to talk it over with God."

"Yeah, yeah. I know. But I got two feet I can stand on pretty well."

Once again, Sky looked on with a patient, sunny smile.

"Peace is the heritage of a humble soul. Remember that, my young friend. It will come in handy."

DMarks turned and looked out across Woyden's Swamp as he pondered Sky's suggestion. In that moment, a formidable gust of wind blew through the treehouse. DMarks twisted back around to respond to Sky, but he was gone. A hollow feeling came over him as he stayed put trying to absorb the consecrated encounter.

He thought through all that had happened over the last two months, reliving it all, lost in his thoughts. Then, he noticed a singular snow-white feather in the spot where Sky had been standing. Stepping over to it, he leaned down, picked it up, and studied it at close range, running his fingertips along the edges.

After a few minutes of reflection, he exhaled in a fulfilled way, then clambered down the treehouse steps with the transistor radio and feather tucked under his arm like a football. As he descended, he felt the cross with a crown of thorns pendant trundling around underneath his T-shirt.

"You're the man, Sky," he said out loud.

Leaping off the last step, he felt energized, refreshed, and focused as he began to walk home. The wheels were turning in his mind when he noticed that the aches and pains had faded away.

He locked in on the future as a single thought emerged. *With Sky in my corner, I'll be unstoppable in high school!*

EPILOGUE

It had been an eventful summer, and the guys knew that they'd never forget it for as long as they lived.

But time waits for no one, and ready or not, it was time for them to take a big step forward. Although the guys had mixed feelings, they were ready to turn a page.

The amount of homework in ninth grade was an eye-opener. The hour-long classes and marathon study halls also took some getting used to. But they were good students, so everyone managed fine.

With the high school being way over on the other side of the village, they couldn't walk up town after school each day. However, they were sometimes able to hitch a ride with older kids to Friendly's or McDonald's, just a stone's throw away in Pleasantville.

The bond shared by Michelle and Charlie continued to prosper. While most incoming freshmen had their girlfriends stolen away by upperclassmen, Michelle never took the bait. She had her guy and wasn't interested in testing the dating waters.

DMarks, BB, and George immersed themselves in sports, academics, and their pursuit of girls. While DMarks got involved with student government, BB was brought up to varsity, which was a rare thing for a freshman. Meanwhile, George surprised everyone by joining the Briarcliff High School Chorus and taking on small parts in choral productions.

Mary Dalton put her house in Ossining on the market, took her new last name, and moved in with Mr. Olson. Together, they began a complete redo of the interior of the house with fresh coats of paint, wallpaper, and brand-new furniture throughout. Mary also put her green thumb to use refurbishing flowerbeds, trimming shrubs, and edging the expansive backyard lawn. Mr. Olson stayed right by her side, happily following the lead of his beautiful bride on all her various projects.

Annabelle and Taylor seemed amused by all the bustle, but mostly, they were content to just be all together under the same roof. They also clearly loved their volunteer work comforting patients over at Phelps Hospital.

Parker and Suzie honeymooned in Disneyworld. When they arrived back home, he carried her across the threshold, and they settled into marital bliss. She loved having a man in the house, and he was happy to have someone who wanted to take care of him. Both got involved with civic activities around town and even began to talk about having children.

Will Morris developed into one of the most well-liked older kids in town. He was caring, patient, humble, and always put himself second in any given situation. All the younger kids looked up to him, and he enjoyed interacting with them. His athletic abilities continued to lead the way for Bears varsity sports while attracting scholarship attention from numerous colleges. Ultimately, he settled on the University of Florida Gators where he was recruited to play middle linebacker.

The new basketball court at Law Park became particularly popular thanks to the fact that it was outfitted with lights on huge stanchions, which allowed for pickup games until ten at night. It was still ruled by the older guys, but somehow, a more inclusive spirit prevailed. Never again were younger kids run off the court.

Jackson Road Park also returned to status quo. Charlie and the guys passed stewardship of School's Out to the next group of middle-schoolers in the neighborhood. It was theirs to make all their own.

Charlie, DMarks, BB, and George were growing up quickly, but they were handling the challenges and adapting to life's changes and trials. None of them knew what the next four years had in store, but there was one thing they did know for sure. Whatever came their way, they'd get through it together.

Sky stayed busy as ever. He regretted that his other projects prevented him from spending the summer of '75 in Briarcliff. But while his work took him all around the world, he knew the small village on the banks of the Hudson would always have a special place in his heart.

Trust in the Lord with all your heart and lean not
on your own understanding; in all your ways submit
to him and he will make straight your paths.

—Proverbs 3:5–6

To laugh often and much; to win the respect of intelligent
people and the affection of children…to leave the world
a better place…to know even one life has breathed easier
because you have lived. This is to have succeeded.

—Ralph Waldo Emerson

The End

ABOUT THE AUTHOR

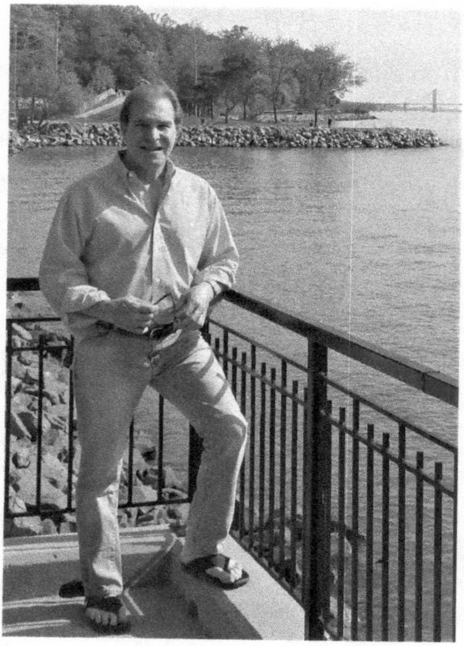

Tom Leihbacher resides in his hometown of Briarcliff Manor, New York. He and his wife are active in community and church activities. In addition to membership at Sleepy Hollow Country Club, he enjoys dining at the local restaurants, spending time at his family home on Cape Cod, and taking long, daily walks with his rescue dog, The Gipper. His first novel *A Gift Most Rare* was published in October of 2020. *Summer Up!* is the sequel. There are two more books under development in this four-part series. Please visit www.tomleihbacher.com for more information.